a Queen among Alphas

A.D. BURNELL

To the brave women and men who dare to speak out and stand up. To every person who pushes back against adversity in hopes of making this world a better place. I see and admire all of you and you each inspire me. Thank you.

A Queen Among Alphas is the first book in the Queen Among series and is a work of fiction.

Any similarities to persons living or dead is coincidental.

The Queen Among series looks to create empowering characters, broach taboo subjects, and represent minorities who are often neglected. It also seeks to take mythological beings we have come to know and give them a new twist. The first book acts as an introduction to the universe, so as we move forward you will find the universe and its creatures expanding and stepping further out of the realm of familiarity.

These books will depict coarse language, graphic violence, sex and triggering subjects such as sexual assault, abuse, and suicide. It is NOT suited for persons under 18 years of age. If any of these are sensitive to you or go against your moral sensibility then these are not the books for you. If you wish to continue reading, please tread with caution.

Chapter One
Amelia

I'm awoken to the dreadful sound of my alarm. Well, technically it's my phone playing 'Kokomo' by The Beach Boys, but since I've selected it as my alarm I've begun to hate the song with a passion. I used to love that song, but if I keep using it to wake me up in the morning, I may never want to hear it ever again.

I reach over to turn off my alarm and roll onto my back, taking a moment to relax and enjoy the peaceful silence and darkness of my room. This is the only time of the day when I can feel calm before I step out into the chaos that is my life.

"So, what's on the schedule today?" Asks Zara in my head. Zara is my wolf spirit. Now before you go jumping to conclusions and calling me a 'werewolf', allow me to explain some things.

By a human's definition I *am* a werewolf, but please don't ever call us that. We really hate it. What I, and the rest of my kind, am actually called is mutolupus, but we're happy to just call ourselves wolves. It's kind of shocking how much myths and stories got right about our kind, but there's also plenty they get wrong.

"Hello! Earth to Amelia, I know you can hear me," huffs Zara.

"Sorry Zara, I guess I spaced out; what's up?"

"Let's go for a run. I want to get my paws dirty," she says excitedly. I chuckle

I love how full of life she is.

"*You want to go for a run before training? Won't you be too tired?*" I ask and she growls at me.

"*I could run around the whole pack and still take on every warrior on the field, don't insult me, woman,*" she says smugly, sticking her snout up at me and making me laugh. It probably sounds weird to think that I can see a wolf in my head, but this is normal for us and has been normal since I was born.

For the most part, I look human. The only differences are I'm stronger, faster and have superior senses to that of a human and I can heal faster, as well as a couple of other things.

Oh and the whole shifting into a wolf thing.

Zara is my best friend; I don't think anyone is as in sync as we are. We never fight or argue – unless playfully. We are the dynamic duo. Like most wolves, she has been with me since birth, but I didn't shift into my wolf form until I was sixteen, as most wolves shift at sunrise on their sixteenth birthday. The worst way to wake let me tell you that.

I don't know what I'd do without my wolf, she's as vital to me as breathing. Zara and I aren't your average wolf though: we are of Alpha blood and are soon going to be the Alpha of our pack. But today, I'm just Amelia.

Getting up I stretch out my limbs and walk across the room to open my thick purple curtains. It's 5 am so there's no sun out yet, which is a relief for my eyes. I strip down and make my way to my walk-in closet and change into a black sports bra, black shorts, put on socks and sneakers then quickly tie my shoulder-length blonde hair up in a high ponytail.

Time to get my training on.

I make my way out of my room and down the three flights of stairs of the packhouse. It's basically a big mansion and is where the ranked wolves of the pack live. Alpha and Beta suites and offices are on the fourth floor, and Gamma and Delta suites and offices are on the third floor. The second floor is exclusively for pack guests, so this is where people from neighbouring packs stay when they visit. Then you have the first floor which has the dining hall, conference room, gym, pool, entertainment room, living areas and kitchen.

Pack members are always in and out of here for various reasons and the warriors always have breakfast here after training. Actually, a lot of pack members like to have their meals here because it's where everyone can come and congregate. The packhouse staff also live here, but they have their own wing on the first floor. The staff are a mixture of non-ranked wolves and Omega wolves.

Omega wolves are wolves who are – for whatever reason – unable to shift. They have heightened senses and can even speak to their wolf spirit, but because they can't shift a lot of packs mistreat Omegas or treat them as less than everyone else, but we don't believe in that. We don't enslave anyone and being staff here is a paid job like any other. It's offered to anyone who wants it, and we offer them free room and board if they wish.

Rank is important, as it keeps order, but ultimately we believe respect is something you earn. At least that's what my father taught me and how he runs this pack. We even have some Omega warriors. We don't focus on what they lack, we look at what they have and how they can better the pack.

I have one foot out the back door when the scent of oranges and pine hits my nose. I quickly duck just as a body comes flying over my head and tumbles along the ground before jumping to his feet.

"One of these days I'm going to get you; mark my words," he says wagging a finger at me.

I grin, "You've been saying that for years and I'm still waiting." He smiles back and wraps his arm around my shoulders.

Vitali Hughes is one of my best friends; we've been thick as thieves our whole lives, and we train together all the time. I know, no matter what, he has my back.

He's 6'1" and ripped all over with sun-kissed skin, shaggy chin-length brown hair and hazel eyes. He's twenty-two and, he doesn't know it yet, but I'm going to make him my Beta. Traditionally the Beta title is passed down to the next family member, same with Gammas and Deltas – sorry I should clarify, next MALE family member – but ultimately it's a position bestowed upon you by the Alpha, and I need people around me I can trust.

I'm about to become the first female Alpha, or at least the first in North

America. Let's just say people didn't take it too well when my father declared that when the time came, he'd pass the title to me. Some pack members were excited. Others, not so much.

Vitali was happy for me and I always knew I'd make him my Beta. I sure as hell wasn't going to appoint the current Beta's son, Ryker Mathers. The moron barely has two brain cells to rub together and doesn't give a crap about the pack or training. He thinks he's Goddess's gift to women and, somehow, thinks he's going to be a Beta just because his daddy was.

Over my furry butt, he will.

Vitali and I walk down to the training field, which is only a five-minute walk from the packhouse. The field is surrounded by a dense forest of trees and consists of a running track, a combat area in the centre of the track and an obstacle course with bleachers around the perimeter of the track.

"How are you feeling? Just one more week and not only will you be twenty-one, but you'll officially be our Alpha," Vitali says excitedly.

"I couldn't be more excited. I've been preparing for this for as long as I can remember. I can't believe it's finally here," I tell him enthusiastically.

"I've heard people talking about challenging you on the night of your elevation," he grits angrily.

"Let them," I shrug. "I'll take on every last one of them. The last thing I want is to kill my own pack members, but if they're not willing to submit and accept me as their Alpha, even though it is my blood rite, then they have to accept the consequences," I say flatly.

The Invictus Pack is the second largest pack in the United States and is based in Oregon with around two thousand pack members. My pack is my family and I'd do anything for them, but if they're not willing to show me respect just because I'm a woman then screw 'em. Neither I nor my wolf is going to just roll over and take it. So if they want to challenge me, they better have dug their graves already.

Vitali lets out a groan. "Woman, you're killing me. You know it gets me going when you're in badass mode," he teases.

"Don't go blaming me for your high libido," I laugh.

We make it to the training field and slowly more pack members start making their appearance. Pack members eighteen and over begin training at 5:30 am for two hours five days a week. Warriors train for an additional two hours after that, perfecting more advanced techniques. Pack members aged between ten and eighteen train at 7:30 am and only train three times a week. We want them to stay sharp and be prepared and know how to defend themselves, but we also have to think of their schooling. This is why the pack schools don't start till 10 am. Education is still important, but Pythagoras Theorem won't save you if the pack is under attack.

"Everyone line up!" Yells Gamma James.

Gamma James Grey – or uncle as I often call him – is my father's third in command. He's forty-four and is responsible for training the pack and our warriors. He has skin that reminds me of dark chocolate, pale blue eyes, and black hair in a marine's buzz cut. He's 6'5" and built like a heavyweight champion. As usual, he is wearing nothing but workout shorts and sneakers. He loves showing off his muscles, mostly because they are pretty imposing. I've been body-slammed by this guy and I'm here to tell you that it is not a fun experience. He also loves showing off his tribal tattoos that cover his chest and arms.

Tattoos aren't fun at the best of times, but they're more painful for us wolves. We heal too fast and don't scar easily enough to use the traditional method. The only way to get a tattoo is to use a tattoo gun made with pure silver. Any injury caused us by silver, once healed, leaves a scar. Gamma James' tattoos are basically a giant warning sign screaming, 'I'm dangerous and pain means nothing to me.'

"Just once I wish my old man would wear a shirt," whispers a voice beside me. I have to stifle a chuckle. Gamma James is now shooting daggers with his eyes at his son, Tyson. Whispering doesn't do much good around wolves

Tyson is the spitting image of his father, just a couple inches shorter, no tattoos and not as bulky. But he's working on it. Tyson is twenty and one of my other besties and for that reason, he'll be taking on the Gamma position after his father.

I think you just like annoying your dad," I say to Tyson through the pack-link.

"Not my fault he makes it so easy. But seriously, he really needs to learn to wear a shirt. I mean, why have them, if you refuse to wear them?" Tyson replies. He's got a fair point.

"This morning we will begin with fifty laps, followed by a blind obstacle course I have prepared in the woods followed by sparring," Gamma James announces, making several people groan.

Vitali, Tyson, and I put our game faces on.

We love training. To keep ourselves in the zone and make sure we're always doing our best, we make every training session a contest.. Though it's mostly a competition between the two of them since they have yet to beat me in anything.

"What did I miss?" Comes the voice of Evalyn, one of my other best friends.

I love her to death, but the woman is late to everything. She never had an interest in training, but after she was badly injured in a cur attack two years ago, she's since started taking training more seriously.

Curs are packless wolves. Commonly, they've been exiled from their pack for committing a crime. Or, on the rare occasion, they renounce their pack. Not all curs are bad, some even try to find new packs, but most packs turn them away, sadly. The ones exiled for serious crimes, however, tend to take exile as an opportunity to be as feral as they please, and they are the ones that pose a threat.

I'd honestly hoped to name Evalyn as my Delta, but she's nowhere near where she needs to be for me to give her that kind of title, and I can't just pick people because they're my best friend. I need people who are strong and smart and are good choices for the pack. People I can trust who will also challenge me and give me different perspectives on a situation so we can come to the best solution. This is why the position will go to her brother, Chris. Their dad is Delta Xander and Chris has worked hard to earn the position of Delta. It would be foolhardy for me not to choose him. Though looking around I notice he's not at training this morning, but I have a feeling I know why.

"You're late, Miss Melgren," says Gamma James tersely.

"I'm sorry, Gamma James, I slept through my alarm," she explains sheepishly. I feel bad for my girl because I know she's in for a brutal training session now.

Evalyn is twenty years old, 5'5", just a little shorter than my 5'8". She has wavy light brown hair down to her waist – which is currently up in a ponytail – and sky-blue eyes with ivory skin, and not a muscle on her. She's pretty slender, but she's still beautiful and has one of the most infectious smiles on the planet.

I notice Tyson has a guilty look on his face as he looks at Evalyn and I realise why she was late. Tyson must have kept her up all night and that's why she overslept.

"That's your problem, not mine. A hundred push-ups," Gamma James orders, making me cringe.

For a wolf, a hundred push-ups are easy, but Evalyn isn't very strong and her lack of training for most of her life hasn't helped. She'll be lucky if she can manage fifty. You'd think since she's his daughter-in-law he'd go easy on her, but he's not one for nepotism.

"Yes sir," she gulps, dropping to the ground and starting her push-ups. One thing I respect about her; she doesn't whine. She sucks it up and will complete any challenge even if it kills her.

"The rest of you! Fifty laps, now!" Gamma James yells and we all take off and start racing around the track.

Vitali and Tyson are ahead of me trying to outdo each other, but I'm keeping a steady pace. It's a marathon, not a sprint. There's no prize for first place, but I still save my energy for the final lap, unlike these two. Running isn't just about staying fit; it's about understanding and increasing our stamina; learning how to preserve our energy and when to tap into it. Every exercise we do has a purpose, but most don't seem to get that.

"Good morning, sweetheart," comes my father's voice through the pack-link.

"Good morning, dad," I say cheerfully.

"How's training this morning?"

"So far so good, I'm on my tenth lap," I tell him.

"Keep it up. After training, come to my office, we need to talk about your Alpha ceremony," he tells me, and I detect an edge to his voice.

"Is everything okay?"

"Just some matters we need to be prepared for. Also, your mother wants to go over some party details with you."

"Don't you want to help her with that?" I ask slyly.

"That's not funny, Amelia. I still haven't recovered from her Luna ceremony where I suggested the wrong type of flowers." I can hear him cringe and it makes me laugh out loud.

"Bad Alpha, picking the wrong flowers," I tease. Dad can strategize a battle plan with his eyes closed but ask him to plan a mutolupus ball and he looks like a headless chicken.

"How will I ever live with the shame? Anyway, shall I see you after training?"

"With bells on!" I say and then close the link.

I'm coming up on my final lap, so I tap into my reserve energy and start sprinting at full speed. I take over Vitali and Tyson in seconds and leave them in the dust while I hear them shout behind me and just like that I'm passing the finish line.

I walk over and grab a water bottle and take a few sips as I catch my breath.

"Are you trying to beat your personal record, Amelia?" Asks Gamma James.

"Not this week. But maybe next week," I grin, him giving me a smile in return.

"Are you nervous?" He asks.

"People keep asking me that. I'm not nervous, I'm excited."

"I can honestly say it's been an honour to train the first female Alpha. You've always pushed yourself to train better than anyone else and I've found myself having to push myself harder just so I could do justice to your training. A good Alpha pushes their pack to always strive to be better, that's how I know you will make a terrific Alpha." His words are full of sincerity and my heart swells.

"Thank you, Gamma James, that means everything to me," I say, my voice thick with emotions.

"*Damn, Gamma gonna make this wolf cry,*" says Zara.

We're all relaxing as we wait for the last few people to finish their laps, then we move onto the obstacle course. I love obstacle courses; I think they're so much fun and this one has been set up further in the woods, so I know there's something extra fun in store for us.

"Today you will be blindfolded," Gamma James announces. "The object of this exercise is to rely on your other senses. Specifically hearing and smell. In battle the enemy may blind you or distract you, so you don't see an attack coming. Honing your other senses is your best chance at survival. Amelia, you're up first."

I get up, walk over, grab a thick black piece of fabric, and step up on a large log stretching across a small lake that cuts through the woods. I tie the fabric around my eyes tight and take in a deep breath. I can hear the animals all around the forest, I can hear the breathing and heartbeats of my pack members and I can smell... well, everything. There's something in the air that my nose doesn't like, I'm not sure what it is though.

"Begin!" Yells Gamma James.

I take a careful step forward and hear a cracking sound from up in the trees. Multiple cracks - along with the sound of something moving with momentum. Just as I go to take another step, I can hear and feel something coming fast from my right, so I quickly drop my body down onto the log just in time to sense something whoosh over me. I suddenly notice lots of things whooshing over me back and forth. I turn my face to the side and inhale through my nose when I feel the object whiz past me again.

Quercus garryana, also known as Oregon white oak.

Logs. I have to dodge freakin' logs. Is this an obstacle course or an Indiana Jones booby trap?

If I stand up, I'm going to get knocked into the lake by one of these swinging logs, so I decide to combat crawl across the log.

As I move along the length of the log, the scent of paint wafts into my nose. It's close, like really close, but there's another scent the paint is masking. I take a long whiff and recoil as the smell burns my nostrils.

Silver.

I didn't see any silver on the log... the paint. Sneaky bastard. He put silver on the log and painted over it to disguise it. Damn, he's good.

Okay, so if I keep crawling, I'm going to burn myself with silver. If I stand up, I'm going to get hit by a flying log. I have no option but to stand and try to dodge the logs... blindfolded.

I shift to my hands and knees and tune everything out except the sounds of the swinging logs. I count how many seconds pass before the log passes over me.

Seven seconds.

I come up with a plan of attack. As I hear the log above me pass, I stand and step forward; I can feel the silver plate under my shoe; I try to keep my balance and not slip on it. I freeze as I hear the next log coming and feel as it just barely brushes by me. I take another step, freeze, and wait for the next log. I repeat this three more times, then finally sense I'm out of the path of danger. I go to jump off the log when another scent hits me... lupine. Lots of it.

Lupine is a beautiful flower that looks like a much larger version of lavender.

If I jump off this log, I'll land in a lupine patch. Uncle J is not playing around. Silver and lupine are toxic and lethal to a mutolupus, but as long as nothing gets in the bloodstream I should be okay, so while this would be unpleasant we're not in mortal danger. Uncle J wouldn't endanger our lives for the sake of training. My best chance is jumping as far as I can and hoping I'm out of the danger zone.

I crouch down and coil my muscles ready to leap, forcing all my strength into my legs and push off the log hard to the point I feel the log splinter under me. I propel myself through the air and hopefully a safe distance over the lupine, landing on my hands and feet.

Everything sounds and smells clear, and I know I'm in the clear when I hear the sounds of cheering. I stand straight and take off my blindfold, turning around to see the rest of the group – well most of them – cheering excitedly. Vitali, Tyson, and Evalyn are going nuts, and I can't help but smile and laugh. Uncle J claps his approval and gives me a proud nod. Warriors in the trees reset the logs and I join the rest of the group.

How did I miss them?

"That was badass, Amelia!" Tyson says pulling me into a tight hug as I hug him back.

"I was nearly having a heart attack," says Evalyn clutching her heart.

"I wasn't worried," Vitali shrugs.

"Liar. You were gripping my arm so tight I thought it would break off," scoffs Evalyn.

He rolls his eyes. "Oh please. It only felt tight because your arms are so scrawny," Vitali says mockingly. Evalyn narrows her eyes and stomps on his foot with all her strength; Tyson and I start laughing while Vitali tends to his foot.

"How's that for scrawny?" She says as she crosses her arms and juts out her hip. Tyson wraps his arms around her and pulls her close, making her instantly relax.

"Calm down, my Little Firecracker, he was just joking," he says softly as he kisses her temple making her eyes close contentedly. I love how happy they are, but I can't help but feel envious.

After we finish the obstacle course – with half the group not successfully completing it – we head back to the field to begin sparring. Just as we get to the sparring area I hear the most obnoxious sound hit my ears.

"I see I'm just in time for the best part," says Ryker.

Damn, and my morning was going so well.

I'd say he was good looking, but I'm so repulsed by his personality that I find him physically unattractive. He's 6'1", black hair that's ear length in the middle but he keeps it slicked back with the sides of his head shaved. He has dark brown eyes, pale skin and is moderately toned. He has a few tattoos on his left arm, but even his tattoos seem obnoxious.

"Ugh, I hate that guy," says Zara.

"Me too girl, me too."

"Even his wolf isn't a fan of him," she says, nearly making me crack up

laughing.

"You're kidding!"

"I'm serious, his wolf Kit argues with him all the time; wonders how he got saddled with such a sucky human. I feel bad for him."

One thing I find cool is that wolves within a pack can communicate with each other, and we – their human counterparts – are completely oblivious to it. They just have their own little social circles, but Zara keeps me filled in most of the time. It's pretty fascinating. Though they can't say anything that betrays their human, even if they want to.

"Mr. Mathers, you're over an hour late. Explain yourself," says Gamma James in a menacing tone.

"I'm the Beta's son, I don't see why I have to do this," he says flippantly. Several people roll their eyes. I told you he's obnoxious.

"Amelia is the Alpha's daughter and yet she manages to be here on time, so there's no excuse for you." The veins in Uncle J's head are pulsating and I can tell he's pissed. He hates Ryker too. Ryker turns his attention to me and sneers, though I remain unfazed.

"She's a girl, she needs all the help she can get," he spits.

I snort. Though honestly, I hate when men call me a 'girl,' it's so condescending.

"I have a question for you, Ryker. Next time we're under attack, what will you do? Walk up to them; puff out your chest and say, 'I'm the Beta's son, don't attack me'? Impressive strategy, I'm sure every supernatural being will flee with their tails between their legs when they hear that," I say sarcastically while several pack members laugh, further pissing him off. Even Uncle J chuckles.

"Fucking bitch," he grits as he takes a step towards me, but I remain rooted where I am. I could take him with both hands tied behind my back.

"MATHERS!" Gamma James shouts. "I won't have you disrespecting me, this pack, or your future Alpha. Since you can't show up on time like everyone else, you can do two hundred push-ups followed by two hundred laps of the track. Now go, and I can assure you I'll be reporting this incident to your father and the Alpha," he promises.

"You can't be serious!" Ryker gasps in shock.

"Move! Now!" James orders with a growl. With that, Ryker angrily skulks off and starts doing push-ups.

And this, ladies, and gentlemen, is precisely why I will never pick him as my Beta.

If you're wondering why he hates me so much, it's because the idiot had it in his head that since my parents never had a son, the next viable option for Alpha was the Beta's son, Ryker. My parents never hinted at such a thing. They had decided the moment I was born that I would be Alpha. But when they made it abundantly clear to a fourteen-year-old Ryker, he went absolutely ape shit. Even tried to pick a fight with me to "prove" I was too weak. All it proved was how easily I could break his face. I suspect Beta Declan put the idea in his son's head, but I have no proof. Declan has always been loyal to my father, but he's standoffish with me, and it only got worse when it was clear I would be made Alpha.

At just a week shy of twenty-one, I'm accustomed to people challenging my position. I've heard the rainbow of insults. 'An Alpha is a man's position', 'a woman can't be an Alpha', 'women are weak', 'she'll weaken the pack', yadda, yadda, yadda. I won't lie and say it doesn't suck or hurt, because it does. Especially when it comes from your own pack, but I won't ever let them beat me down. I was born for this; I know I can be a great Alpha and I won't let anyone stop me. Whatever it takes, I'm going to be the best Alpha the Invictus Pack has ever seen.

Chapter Two
Amelia

After training I run to the dining hall, fill up a plate with as much food from the buffet as I can, grab a bottle of apple juice and race to my father's office. We wolves burn off calories super-fast thanks to fast metabolisms, so we need to eat a lot for energy and right now I'm desperate to get some food in me, but I need to talk to my dad. So, I decide I can snack on this while we have our meeting and then I'll go back down for more later.

I reach dad's office and I hit the buzzer next to the door. The majority of the rooms in the packhouse are soundproof. It's hard to have private meetings or be intimate when people with super hearing are all over the place, so soundproofing is pretty necessary, but that also means me knocking is pointless and him yelling 'come in' is equally pointless. You have two options: use the pack-link for entry or use the buzzer that is installed in every room. The buzzer makes a knocking sound, so it at least has the illusion of someone knocking.

Cool right? I know, I'm the one who came up with it when I was sixteen.

After a few seconds, my dad's office door clicks and automatically opens, allowing me to step in. I close it behind me and my dad releases the button under his desk that opens the door. Gotta love technology. I walk over and put my plate and juice on his desk, walk around and kiss his cheek.

"Morning daddy," I say cheerily.

He beams up at me and kisses my cheek in return. "Good morning, sweetheart. James told me how fantastic you were during the obstacle course this morning. Not that I'm surprised," he says proudly, making me grin.

"Not what I was expecting, but I had a lot of fun," I tell him as I sit down and start eating. "I was thinking Tyson should incorporate more courses like that during future training sessions. Courses that force us to focus on specific senses," I add. Dad smiles at me with a thoughtful look on his face.

Alpha Elias Dolivo is not just my dad and the Alpha of the Invictus Pack, he's my idol and he's been my greatest cheerleader since before I was even born. Dad is forty-eight years old, has blonde hair styled with a buzz cut, is 6'5" with chestnut eyes and off-white skin. Dad still works out like crazy, so he's just solid muscle from head to toe, which is pretty common for Alphas. I got my hair colour and my personality from my dad, the rest I got from my mum.

"It's good to hear you thinking about how you want to handle the pack once you take over from me. I take it you've decided who to name as your council then," he inquires, and I nod as I swallow some sausage.

"Vitali will be named as my Beta, Tyson as my Gamma and Chris as my Delta," I say confidently.

"Excellent choices. And thank you for not selecting Ryker as your Beta," he says with relief.

"I'd rather suck on lupine, thanks," I say while wrinkling my nose. My dad laughs then sighs shaking his head.

"I don't know what is with that boy. He's nothing like his father, not that he has to be, but he reminds me so much of his grandmother," he shudders.

"Maybe if Beta Declan hadn't spoiled him he'd have turned out different," I say belligerently. Honestly, Beta Declan isn't that great either, he just hides it better.

"Now, about your elevation," he says rubbing his face, and I can see how tense he is.

"You're not getting cold feet, are you?" I ask nervously.

"Absolutely not," he scoffs, "I've already booked my first vacation with your mother." He winks.

"Oh I see, promote me then ditch me. Thanks a lot," I chuckle.

"Precisely," he grins. "But in all seriousness, you know I'll be forced to ask if anyone chooses to challenge you for the position of Alpha," he says carefully, and I nod.

While becoming Alpha is in your blood, the system does have to have a modicum of fairness to it. During the ceremony, anyone can challenge me for the Alpha position, and we must fight to the death – though many civilised wolves just allow the opponent to tap out. Whoever wins will get the job. Sounds harsh but we're wolves; this is just how it works.

Besides, do you want someone around who ultimately wants to get rid of you? Cause I don't.

"I fear we may have a few challenges," he sighs.

"A few? As in more than one?" I ask in surprise. He nods with disgust; he's not happy about this. Again, all because I'm a woman.

My parents are strong believers in our creator Morrtemis, our sovereignty-goddess. We even have a temple on our pack lands dedicated to her. Having such strong beliefs in our great Goddess is why they've been preparing me to be Alpha since I was born. They believe the Goddess doesn't make mistakes and if she blessed them with a daughter, it was for a reason; for me to lead the pack in a new era. Not so I can be dealt off and become some Alpha's Luna. Which is grossly common among other packs. The point is, my parents believe that things happen for a reason, and so they never questioned for a second that I should be Alpha. Sadly, not everyone thinks that way.

Just think over the logic of my species for a moment.

We worship a female deity, the mother of our species. There are many Gods and Goddesses, but she was known for being a fierce warrior who took no prisoners on the battlefield. She showed little mercy to her enemies but would move heaven and hell for those she loved. We honour her, we celebrate her, we exalt her name and yet my species still refuses to acknowledge that a woman can be Alpha. Hypocritical much?

"Amelia, I've seen you fight. I know what a strong fighter you are, and

I believe you can take on anyone who challenges you. Even those who have trained alongside you underestimate you. I think that once you take out your first challenger the others – assuming they aren't over-confident – will back off," he hypothesises.

"We can only hope," I say with a gentle smile as I take another bite of food. "It'll be okay, dad, I'm not scared. I've got this," I reassure him as I reach out and squeeze his hand. He squeezes mine back.

I'm digging into my food when dad goes still, indicating he's getting a link from someone. When his face breaks out into a goofy grin, I know what that means, and I can't help but smile. Dad, at wolf speed – which is pretty damn fast, bolts to the door, swings it open and pulls my mother into his office. He kicks the door shut as he dips her, giving her a long kiss. She giggles and returns the kiss, holding his face.

My parents have been together since she was eighteen and he was twenty, but, even now, they still act like lovesick teenagers. I couldn't be happier for them. I hope I have that one day.

Wolves age a lot slower than humans, so both my parents still look in their twenties. My mother is a beauty. She's 5'8" like me, with waist-length auburn hair and these amazing turquoise eyes that she so kindly gave to me. She's naturally very pale but she spends a lot of time in the sun, so she has more of a natural tan now.

She always dresses elegantly; today, she's wearing a maroon chiffon wrap-around dress with sleeves and a V-neck that shows a tasteful amount of cleavage – probably for dad's benefit – paired with black leather pointed knee-high boots. My dad wears a mix of casual and formal, he always pairs slacks with a stretch t-shirt and dress shoes. Quite the hunky look.

I realize his brown pants and maroon shirt coordinate with mum's outfit, and I wonder if it's intentional or if that's just how in-sync they are, after all these years.

They're still kissing and now I'm just feeling awkward, so I clear my throat. Slowly dad breaks their kiss and pulls them both up, staring at her like she's the only woman in the world.

"Keep that up, Elias, and I'll forget why I came here," my mum chastises.

"I thought you came to see me," he pouts, and I roll my eyes.

"You're a bonus, my love," she says kissing his pout and walking over to give me a big hug.

"Oh good, you noticed me," I tease as I smile and hug her back. She softly smacks my arm.

"Your father has already gushed to me about your performance on the course today; I wish I had seen it."

"I'll buzz you for the next one," I promise. She nods and sits down next to me in front of dad's desk.

I love dad's office, so much I don't plan to change anything about it. It's all wood and deep browns with cream accents. Dad's large mahogany desk is opposite the door with a large white plush desk chair behind it. There is a large window behind him with wooden shutters. Along the left wall, there's a lovely nook that is flanked by bookshelves on either side. The nook is surrounded by five glass panels that form a sort of semi-dodecagon shape, also with wooden shutters. In that nook, against the window, are two white-cushioned armchairs sitting side by side a small circular table between them with a small lamp.

Two white cushioned armchairs sit in front of my father's desk, and along the right wall is a long four-person white sofa flanked by two bookshelves, with a light brown wooden coffee table in front of the sofa. The entire floor is covered in a white rug with gold and brown accents.

The room is cosy and sophisticated and in just a week it's going to be mine.

My mother reaches out, taking my hand and giving me a soft look. "Just one more week. How are you feeling? Nervous?" She asks softly while patting my hand.

"If I had a dollar for every time someone asked me that, I'd have the pack financially set for life," I say rolling my eyes. Dad sniggers as he takes his seat.

"I shall stop asking then." She smiles. "Now we have everything arranged for your birthday party. The training ground is being completely converted and the staff are making the final decisions on the menu, which you will need to give final approval on, and the whole pack knows to set their calendars. Also, Torie has graciously offered to DJ for your party," she announces enthusiastically and my face splits into a grin.

"No way, that's fantastic! Thank you so much," I exclaim.

Torie is an Omega, a warrior and our pack's best tracker. Seriously her nose has us all beat, but on top of all that Torie is the best DJ around. She makes most of her money working at a human club in the city, but she's often requested by other packs for parties since she's that talented and doesn't charge insane fees. So having her DJ my party is fantastic news.

"Don't thank me, as I said, she offered. Now since we're having your Alpha ceremony the day after your birthday instead of on your birthday, we will have the training field cleared in time in case..." she trails off glancing uncomfortably towards my dad. I sigh and give her hand a reassuring squeeze.

"In case of challenges. I know, dad told me. It's going to be okay; don't stress." This makes her frown.

"You can ask me to not stress about a lot of things, but don't ever expect me not to stress and worry about the safety of my only pup," she scowls, and I give her a sympathetic smile.

"I know, I'm sorry," I say kissing her cheek.

"Are you sure you don't want a formal ceremony?" She sighs. "An Alpha ceremony has always been a formal event." She tries once again to persuade me to change my mind.

"Mum, we've talked about this. The ceremony will be traditional but in a casual setting. Me being challenged is inevitable whether we like it or not and I'm not going through all the effort of doing hair and make-up and squeezing into a dress just to have to ruin it all by stripping down and shifting. It's just easier if everyone can dress casually, it'll make shifting easier too," I explain.

"She's right, Fleur. I think the pack will appreciate it and it doesn't hurt to win some brownie points with them early on," he says winking at me. I giggle.

"I suppose you're right. A cookout was a good idea, besides there's always the Vernal Ball next month," she smiles cheekily.

"Oh, I have made some notes regarding the ball. I have them in my binder in my room. I'll get them after this and then we can go over them," I say. Mum claps her hands excitedly.

The Vernal Ball is a mutolupus ball held during the Vernal Equinox every year. Packs alternate every year on who will host it and this year it's Invictus' turn. It's a time for packs to come together in hopes of finding their animai.

You see, an animai is someone who has been created and chosen by the Goddess Zarseti to be your soulmate. When the Gods began creating different beings, wars started to break out, so to establish peace and bring species together, Zarseti created animais. You can find them once you come of age – which is eighteen – and when you do, an otherworldly bond is formed. You could be fated to anyone; your own species or another. Either way, they are the perfect person to complete you, they become your world; the very air you need to breathe.

So, these balls are a good chance to see if people can find their soulmate. You're not guaranteed to find them, since there is a chance they may not be a member of your species, but statistically, chances are they will be. My mum and dad are each other's animai, so are Tyson and Evalyn.

The balls also boost morale and encourage inter-pack relations. The Vernal Equinox is when the sun is exactly above the equator and day and night are of equal length. Sun and moon, day and night in complete harmony, the perfect time to bring packs and souls together.

"Maybe you'll finally meet your animai this year," my mum says, her voice dripping with glee. Mum's a big romantic and loves to gush about soulmates, not just her own but soulmates in general. She's been excited about me finding mine since I turned eighteen, but a quick glance at my dad tells me he, and I, are still apprehensive.

Don't misunderstand, dad wants me to find my animai, and so do I. Finding your animai is the greatest thing that can happen to us and some spend their lives searching for theirs.

My pack views the bond between animais as sacred and take them very seriously. To disrespect it in any way is a crime in most packs, ours included. That may sound harsh, but if you knew the damage it can do to someone, having the bond broken or abused, you'd understand. That being said, dad and I are both concerned as to how my animai might react when he finds out I'm an Alpha.

"Don't think like that. He will love us; we are made for each other. No one will be better for him than us and vice versa," Zara whines in my head, but I can still hear the nerves underneath. I send her some extra comfort through our bond. I don't want her worrying.

We're casually discussing more details regarding my birthday, my Alpha ceremony, and the Vernal Ball when I'm interrupted by a link.

"Hey Amelia, where are you?" Asks Chris.

"In a meeting with mum and dad. Is everything alright? You weren't at training this morning," I say with concern.

"I couldn't leave Mei," he sighs. *"Think you can stop by our suite after your meeting?"* He asks gently, but there's a tone of pleading. I internally scoff. As if I'd say no.

"I'm going to grab a shower after the meeting and then I'll come to your suite. I don't want to stink up your room," I tease to lighten the mood.

"Much appreciated," he chuckles. *"See you soon."* And with that, he closes the link, allowing me to focus back on what mum and dad are saying.

We cross a few more T's, dot a few I's, and I rush out of the office, taking my empty plate with me. I run the plate to the kitchen – vowing to return for more food soon – run all the way to my suite, dash into my room, and jump in the shower.

Once I'm clean, I run into my closet and get dressed, opting for black skinny jeans, Vans, and a white turtleneck. I leave my hair down to dry and race down to the Delta suite on the third floor. Days like today, I am grateful for wolf speed, although you really can't rush a shower. Well, maybe if you're Superman or the Flash.

I ring the buzzer and wait. A moment later Chris is answering the door with a relieved look on his face. "That was quick," he smiles.

"You know I hate to keep people waiting," I say stepping in. He nods in agreement, shutting the door behind me.

The suites are all relatively the same with the main entrance of the suites being communal areas. In this one, the door is on the far-right side and stepping in, the first thing you see is the kitchen area on the right-hand side of the room. It's all dark wood with black appliances and a long brown marble island with 4 barstools. Next to the kitchen is a large black glass circular dining table that seats six and then the living area makes up the rest of the room.

The living area has a large cream L shaped sectional on top of a large cream rug with a low black glass coffee table in front of it facing a large 56" plasma TV along the wall to the left of the door. There are also shelves on the wall that go around the TV filled with books and movies. There are two doors along the back wall, one leading into the Delta couple's bedroom and the other door is a small storage room. The door to the left of the room was Evalyn's until she moved into the Gamma suite with Tyson, but she still uses this room sometimes. The door to the right of the kitchen is Chris's room.

"How is she?" I ask Chris as I turn to face him.

He sighs and rubs his face. "It was pretty bad; she was screaming so loud I thought she'd rip her vocal cords apart." There's so much pain in his voice and on his face. "What do I do Amelia? My animai is in pain and I can't stop it," he says with tears filling his eyes and my heart breaks for him. "She's a beautiful person inside and out, she didn't deserve any of this. I want to hunt down every last person who hurt her and make them suffer for the rest of their miserable lives," he growls, the irises of his hazel-green eyes glowing as his wolf Axel pushes through.

They want to make the people who hurt Mei pay and I don't blame them.

I step forward and calmly squeeze his shoulders. "Take slow breaths, Chris, you and Axel need to breathe," I try to soothe him. "*Zara, can you help Axel calm down?*" She leaps to attention in my head.

"*On it, I'll take care of him,*" she says confidently.

I lead Chris over to the sofa and sit with him. "Chris, you need to listen to me. You are doing everything you need to be doing for Mei. You are giving her sanctuary, comfort, patience and, most importantly, your love. She needs time to heal, but she's strong. I felt it the day you brought her to the pack. She'll come around when she's ready. In the meantime, just be there for her like you are," I reassure him as I rub his back. He takes slow breaths and nods his head.

"I love her so much, Amelia. I don't care if I never get to mark her. I just want her to be okay," he says sorrowfully. It kills me to see one of my best friends like this. Seeing your animai in pain is some of the worst torture. "You know she smiled for me yesterday. A real full-on smile," he says with an excited twinkle in his eyes. I can't help but grin for him.

"Really? That's great! It means she's making progress." He nods in agreement.

"Her smile is so beautiful I think my heart stopped beating." His words make me chuckle. The man's in love.

"You two are going to have some knock out looking kids, I'm calling it now."

He grins at the mention of children. "If they look anything like their mother, they'll stop traffic," he says proudly.

I notice Chris is dressed down today in just some black shorts and a grey tank top. Chris and Evalyn don't look very much alike outside of hair colour. He's two years older than Evalyn at twenty-two and has long brown hair that he keeps up in a bun and a short bushy beard. He's 6'1" with olive skin, muscles galore and he's solid as a rock. He has his mother's hazel-green eyes, whereas Evalyn has sky blue eyes a shade lighter than her father's. Their father has dark olive skin and their mother has ivory skin. Evalyn got her mum's ivory skin and Chris got a nice blend of the two. Genetics is a crazy thing, but mix Chris's genes with Mei's and damn, no one stands a chance against that genetic combo.

Just as I'm picturing what their kids would look like, Mei tentatively steps out of her and Chris's room. Chris is instantly out of his seat and over to her before I can blink, taking her hands in his in a comforting gesture.

"Are you hungry? Thirsty? Can I get you anything?" He asks in a gentle tone. She shrugs and then spots me, so I give her a gentle wave.

"Good morning, Mei, it's nice to see you up and about," I say warmly. She gives me a polite nod and latches onto Chris's arm. The man is grinning like a dork, and I just know his wolf is preening in his head.

"Can I have something to eat?" She quietly asks him.

"Of course, anything you want," he says nodding eagerly; love poured into every word. She bites her lip nervously.

"You can ask for anything, Mei, I'll make sure the chefs whip it up," I encourage her with a smile. I want her to feel safe and welcome in our pack, but I know we need to take baby steps.

"Even congee?" She asks nervously.

Chris and I grin, it's the first time she's suggested something specific that sounds more in keeping with what she likes versus what's convenient for us. I quickly link the chefs to whip up three servings of congee. I have no idea what that is, but the chefs seem thrilled at the idea of making it and I'm still hungry, so, may as well give it a try.

"I think you've just made our chefs' day. They're excited that they get to make something new," I tell her. This makes her frown.

"I don't want to put anyone out," she says getting anxious and it makes me sad. Chris doesn't hesitate to calm her, damn he's a good partner.

"Mei, please don't worry yourself. She's being honest. If she says the chefs are excited it's because they are. They love getting to try new recipes," he says wrapping his arms around her and kissing the top of her head while breathing in her scent. She slightly relaxes and closes her eyes, nodding against his chest.

They are such a cute couple.

Mei is a stunning young woman. She has dark, wavey brown hair down to her waist, cream skin, chocolate brown monolid shaped eyes – very soft feminine features. She kind of looks like Constance Wu, not going to lie. She's 5'1, so a whole foot shorter than Chris. He looks like a giant swallowing her up when they are side by side; it's rather funny.

She's wearing black sweatpants and a white cotton t-shirt and socks. She's not ready to go shopping for clothes so she's been borrowing clothes from Evalyn. They're pretty much the same size so that's worked out. Other pack members her size were more than happy to offer clothes if she needed it. I felt so proud the day they did that.

"Would you like to come sit?" I ask gently as I pat the spot next to me. Mei looks at me and then looks up at Chris.

He nods. "Go on," he encourages gently. She takes his hand, and they walk over and sit on the couch which makes me smile warmly at her progress.

"Chris told me you are going to be the Alpha," she says quietly. Chris looks stunned to see her starting a conversation. I'm equally stunned but I try not to show it. I want her to have a sense of normalcy, so I nod affirmatively.

"Yes, my ceremony is next week. The day after my birthday. I would love for you to attend. I completely understand if the party is too much, but the Alpha ceremony will be more low-key, so maybe if you feel up to it you can stop by for a bit. But there's absolutely no pressure. You don't have to come down or meet anyone until you're ready," I reassure her. She takes a breath and nods while Chris keeps her hand in his, gently running his thumb over the back of her hand, letting their bond soothe her.

"Thank you for letting me come here. Thank you for welcoming me into your pack," she says with a small nod of her head. I slowly reach out and touch her other hand and wait till she lifts her head so I can look in her eyes.

"You are family, and we are beyond honoured to have you. I mean that," I tell her with the utmost sincerity as tears fill her eyes.

Animai of the year Chris is quick on the ball again as he tucks her into his side. He mouths a 'thank you' to me while he comforts her and I give him a smile.

Mei has been here for the past month, and we've been focusing on helping her with her trauma before initiating her into the pack. Mei has been through absolute hell and it's hard to not believe that fate brought Chris and Mei together.

Mei was born in a pack in China called the Tian Pack, which I think she said means heaven. Ironic considering there was nothing heavenly about it. See, Mei isn't a mutolupus, she's an entirely different creature and a very rare one at that.

In a lot of Asian countries, her kind was once revered as deities by humans. While like us, they were made by the Gods, they are not Gods themselves. They don't have packs and tend to keep to themselves as those who used to worship them now fear them – or so I've read.

Her father was a mutolupus, but his pack killed her mother when Mei was five after they found out what she was. They were the kind of pack that don't tolerate other species or mixing of the species. Everything they stand for spits in the eyes of the Gods.

Mei's father fled here to the United States hoping to find a pack to take them in, since China was no longer safe. But the first pack they encountered thought her father was a cur and chased them into the woods. He was mauled to death in front of her eyes. The pack members had no idea what she was and so they took her in and decided to make her a slave.

For years they beat and tortured her, until the day Chris went to the Albus Mons Pack shadowing his father. They were there on behalf of our pack to get their RSVP to the Vernal Ball since they weren't taking our calls. As soon as they entered the packhouse, Chris was instantly hit with Mei's scent – which is how we first identify our animais – and when he found her, he and his wolf nearly tore the place apart in retaliation for what was done to her.

His father had to calm things down to prevent a pack war. Ultimately, they agreed to release her to us saying – and I quote – "She wasn't fun to play with anymore." Chris didn't hesitate to get her the hell out of there and, safe to say, we rescinded our invitation. We don't want people like that on our lands and we don't want Mei's abusers anywhere near her. The necessary people were contacted to handle the Albus Mons Pack.

We were so happy Chris found his animai, but we were heartbroken when we saw the state of her. Her physical wounds have since healed; some bones unfortunately had to be reset. Chris was losing his mind when that happened, and I don't blame him. But it helped with her healing. The wounds in her mind and heart will take longer to heal – if they ever will – but we're all here for her.

We had no idea what she was, we couldn't even tell from the scent. It wasn't until a week ago she trusted Chris enough to tell him what she was and with her permission, he told me. I was beyond shocked. I'm thrilled to have someone like her in our pack though.

Once we get her on her feet she'll be the greatest asset this pack has ever had, if she wants to be that is, I'd never force her. As long as she feels happy and safe, that's good enough for me and I know it's good enough for Chris. I will do everything I can to ensure she feels welcomed into our pack. Anyone messes with her, and they'll be answering to me. Assuming Chris doesn't rip their heads off first.

Chapter Three
Amelia

I t's 8 am when my eyes finally open, since I felt I deserved a little sleep-in. Look, I know 8 am doesn't *sound* like a sleep in but compared to my usual schedule it is. I can see Zara is still softly sleeping away and I smile. Perfect; I can execute my plan. I can't risk her waking up or knowing what I'm doing, so I put a barrier up between us in my mind.

I rarely ever do this; a lot of people – especially those at odds with their wolf spirit – tend to keep them silenced fairly often. I think it's quite cruel and stupid. I could never keep Zara locked away like that, I love her too much. That may sound vain since I'm talking about a personality in my head, but Zara is her own entity – we just share a vessel.

Getting out of bed, I do some stretches and twists before I leave my room and the Alpha suite. On my way downstairs, several pack members stop me to kindly wish me a happy birthday and I thank each of them. I then make it outside and begin my trek into the woods.

We wolves are very durable so the rocks and twigs under my feet don't bother me in the least. As I walk deeper into the woods – staying on pack territory – I keep my nose to the wind and my ears open.

I'm on the hunt.

I can hear and smell some small animals nearby but I'm hoping to find something a little bigger, maybe a stag. I decide to try a different direction when a scent makes its way to me on the wind; a grin splits across my face. This is perfect!

I strip out of my pyjama shorts, top and underwear then place them over a tree branch. We are more than accustomed to nudity, it's not that big a deal. Depending on the day, if a human entered the territory, they might mistake us for a nudist colony.

Once I'm in my birthday suit – HA! Birthday suit, get it? Because today's my... oh never mind.

I drop the barrier in my mind and am met by a very displeased Zara.

"*What the hell, Amelia? Why did I wake up to a barrier?*" She sneers. I giggle at my grumpy wolf.

"*HAPPY BIRTHDAY!*" I shout in my mind. Her sneer vanishes and she's immediately yipping and wagging her tail with glee.

"*Happy Birthday Amelia,*" she giggles shaking her head. "*How do I fall for that every year?*" She asks in amusement.

"*Good to know I can still surprise you,*" I say cheerfully.

Technically speaking, wolf spirits don't have birthdays, or at least no one I know gives their wolf a birthday, but I do. Zara has been with me since birth; in my eyes that was the day she was born, so I happily share my birthday with her. Each year, I put up a barrier just long enough to put a surprise together and drop it for the reveal, she's so unaccustomed to the barrier that she never realises what I'm doing. Works every time.

"*Time to shift, Zara.*" This makes her ears perk up.

After a moment of searing heat, I'm quickly on all fours shaking out my fur. Immediately everything around me becomes amplified. The colours around me are more vibrant, the smells more prominent and the sounds more amplified.

The first shift is the worst. Mine took four hours and twenty-three minutes and was absolute hell. All I did was scream and writhe in pain while every bone in my body broke and rearranged. The second shift was a significant improvement, and by the third shift, there was no pain. Now it takes me a couple of seconds to shift and instead of pain, all I feel is a burst of searing heat spread through my body and then it's gone.

Zara is a stunning wolf; I was in awe the first time I saw her form. She's black and white with black on the top half of her coat going from the tip of her nose down to the tip of her tail and white on the bottom half from the tip of her jaw again to the tip of her tail. She looks like she walked through white paint and ended up dip dyed. She's also a good 6'5" tall, which is pretty normal for Alphas.

Alphas are commonly around the 6 feet mark as are other ranked wolves. Other wolves are usually around 4-5 feet, but the Alpha is always the biggest in the pack. Dad is two inches taller than me in wolf form.

"So, what's my surprise?" Zara asks excitedly.

"You tell me," I reply coyly.

I give Zara full control and feel as her ears are perked up listening to her surroundings and I watch as she points her snout up and sniffs the air. A gentle breeze moves past, and I know she caught the scent.

"No way!" She exclaims, making me chuckle.

"I was surprised too, but it's just perfect. It's all yours, girl."

"Oh, thank you, Amelia, this is going to be awesome!" She exclaims again, and she takes off into the woods at top speed; the trees around us becoming a blur.

Zara and I have had an understanding since we first shifted: when in wolf form I would give her complete control because technically speaking this is her body. I would just be the passenger giving guidance. When in human form, I would be in control and she would be the passenger. The only time we would relinquish these roles is if we felt the other was in danger. We are a team. We have mutual respect and understanding and that's what makes us so unbeatable. I chill in the back of her mind while I watch her do her thing.

She is an exceptional hunter. Zara approached her prey at lightning speed but began slowing down the closer she got. Once she was close enough she began taking tentative steps as she crouched down and her eyes locked on their prize.

Damn, it was huge!

Standing near a stream, lapping at the water was a moose that had to be at least 6 and a half feet tall at the shoulder and if I had to estimate, weighed around one thousand pounds. I couldn't believe the luck when I caught its scent on the wind, and the breeze is working to her advantage. She's currently crouched downwind, so the wind is blowing her scent away from the moose, making it easier to take her prey by surprise.

While I'm content with cake and music for my birthday, Zara is a wolf and deserves to have moments where she can be herself, and hunting for food in her own body is what she loves to do. For an Alpha wolf to bag such a large kill like this, well, that'll boost her ego for ages.

I watch as Zara slowly edges closer to the unsuspecting animal, her body coiling, ready to strike. At breakneck speed she lunges at the moose, tackling it to the ground, landing a shallow swipe of her claws to its side. She leaps off, giving it a chance to get back up.

I can see the fear in the wounded animal's eyes, but also its determination to survive. It gets up and charges at Zara, aiming its antlers right for her, but she's quick to dodge them, manoeuvring to the back of the moose. She quickly attacks, biting into its hind leg and tugging it back, causing it to drop to the ground as it lets out a cry of pain. She lets it go and moves back. I roll my eyes. Zara could have killed it in the first strike, but she's the play with her food type. Thank the Goddess she doesn't do this during real fights.

Zara gives the poor moose one more chance to fight back before she sinks her teeth into its throat. She clamps her jaw down hard, and I feel its neck snap between her teeth. Just like that, the animal is finally dead and Zara dives into her kill, enjoying her oversized breakfast.

After gorging on moose, Zara heads back to where I left my clothes, collecting them in her mouth and making her way back to the packhouse. I can tell her muzzle is covered in blood and no doubt the white in her fur is now a garish crimson red, which is now getting on my clothes that are in her mouth. I don't mind - we wolves are used to getting blood on our clothes.

"Thank you for the birthday surprise. I feel so lucky to have been paired with you," she says, and I can feel through our connection how sincere she is; it warms my heart.

"My pleasure Zara, same time next year?" I chirp.

"It's a date," she chuckles.

Returning to the packhouse, Zara's appearance gets a lot of notice. People nod in respect; some look concerned while others are smirking. Vitali bounds over to us with a big smile on his face.

"Good morning, birthday ladies. Want me to hose you down?" He asks jovially. Zara just snorts, though I can tell she is very tempted by the offer of playing with a hose. Sometimes she's like a giant puppy dog.

"I heard that! How very dare you?!" She exclaims, once again making me chuckle. Zara pulls herself back and pushes me forward, and with a quick burst of heat, I'm back on two legs and throwing my clothes back on.

"So, what did you find for her this time?" He asks curiously.

"A moose. A huge one," I grin proudly as his eyes widen.

"Not that I'm surprised, but way to go, Zara," he applauds making Zara preen. The moment is interrupted by a scoff nearby and of course, it's Ryker.

"As if you brought down a moose. I can picture a lot of wolves doing it, but not you," he says snidely. Vitali and I roll our eyes. This guy is an absolute moron. My wolf is larger than his in every way and an Alpha; taking down a moose is child's play for us.

"Ryker, I think you need to make a visit to Dr Richard's office," I say while walking towards the packhouse with Vitali in tow.

"Why would I need to do that?" He asks in confusion.

"Because something is clearly wrong with your sense of smell, otherwise you would have smelt that the blood I am currently covered in was moose blood," I tell him impassively and hear Vitali snigger while Zara is in hysterics

Ryker stands there; his face blank with surprise before it morphs into anger. I can tell he wants to hit me, but I ignore him. Idiots like him are not worth my time. Though I did always wonder... since he's so convinced he's going to be the next Beta, you'd think he'd be kissing up to me as his future Alpha.

The Alpha and Beta have to be in sync and act like a well-oiled machine, which is one of the many reasons I'm giving the role to Vitali.

"Is that dickhead ever going to grow up?" Vitali asks as we walk through the packhouse.

"I am pretty sure that ship sailed long ago."

Passing through the house, I get more nods and birthday wishes and it makes me feel great. Vitali is telling me how excited he is for the party tonight when our conversation is interrupted by Beta Declan.

"Happy Birthday Amelia," he says flatly.

"Thank you so much," I say, throwing on my best smile and making him scowl. I don't know what this guy's problem is, but he's always so sour around me. I know it pisses him off when I don't retaliate, so instead, I kill him with kindness. He's looking at the blood all over me, but his face looks almost calculating, which is not the reaction you'd expect from someone in this situation.

"I hope you saved some of your energy, you're going to need it for the ceremony," he says smugly, but there's a sinister look on his face. Zara starts growling. "Enjoy your day, Amelia," he says as he walks off.

"*Well that wasn't ominous at all,*" Vitali says through the pack-link. I nod in agreement as we head upstairs.

"*That guy has always hated me. I'm starting to wonder if Ryker is going to be one of the people to challenge me tomorrow,*" I speculate, much to Vitali's surprise.

"*That pipsqueak?! He doesn't stand a chance against you. Challenging you would be suicide.*"

"*Not disagreeing with you, but think about it. He refuses to acknowledge me as his future Alpha and if he – at the very least – thought he'd be getting the Beta position, he should be trying to get on my good side. But he's not. And then there's the comment his dad made. All signs would suggest Ryker plans to challenge me tomorrow,*" I say calmly.

After a moment of silence, Vitali doubles over in a fit of laughter.

"*I'll go get the shovels now shall I?*" He asks and I laugh.

I promise this isn't ego talking. I know how strong and capable both Zara and I are. Not only do we outrank Ryker, but he barely ever trains, so performance-wise he's weaker than the average wolf. Even Torie can kick his ass; that says a lot about her skills and his lack of skills.

We get to the Alpha suite, and I step in to...

"SURPRISE! HAPPY BIRTHDAY!" Is shouted from my parents, Gamma James and Lacey, Tyson, Delta Xander and Kennedy, Evalyn, Chris and... Mei?!

Shit.

I quickly duck behind Vitali. This is the first time she's come out of the Delta suit and she's seeing me covered in blood. Just great.

"I've got her, Amelia, she's not looking," says Chris through the pack-link. I'm glad he figured out I wasn't just scared of a surprise; that would be embarrassing.

"Thank you so much for the surprise, everyone. I'm just going to go shower and then I'll join you all."

I speed off to my room, which is through the door on the left. Once I'm in, I rush to the bathroom, throw my clothes in the hamper, step into the shower, and work to scrub all the blood off me. I really hope I haven't just contributed to Mei's trauma. I'm starting to think I should have let Vitali hose me down outside.

After a very thorough shower, I complete my usual morning routine and then head into my closet to pick something to wear. It's my birthday so I want to look nice. I pick out a lovely white maxi dress with blue floral prints on it, bishop sleeves and a low sweetheart neckline. Very feminine. I put on a pair of white strappy wedges with cork bottoms and then put my hair up in a large hair clip since it's still wet.

I make my way out to the communal area, my eyes searching for Mei.

The Alpha suite is almost identical to the Delta suite, the only difference is our suite is decorated in black and white. The kitchen is all black fixtures and cabinets, with a black island and white marble countertop. The room is covered with a black carpet because white would be a bitch to clean. The living area has a large half circular white sofa, around a white coffee table that faces a large electric fireplace. This is bordered by black shelves with a large plasma screen TV on the wall above the fireplace. Behind the couch, is the dining table, which is a large rectangular glass table with eight white upholstered dining chairs. The walls are painted a soft grey.

If you're wondering how large the sofa is, it can comfortably fit nine people, but if you squish everyone together then you can squeeze in thirteen. This means everyone here can fit on the couch, but I notice my parents, Uncle James and Aunt Lacey have pulled over some dining chairs instead.

Mei is tucked under Chris's arm, sitting on the edge of the sofa furthest away from me. I slowly make my way over and kneel in front of her.

"Mei?" I say softly to get her attention. She looks down at me and I can see she's nervous but I'm not sure if it's me or being out of her room. "I am so very sorry you saw me like that. If I upset you or made you uncomfortable in any way, I truly apologise," I say gently.

"Chris said it wasn't because of an attack," she says quietly. I notice he keeps gently rubbing her back.

"No attacks, I promise," I say giving her a warm smile. "It was a birthday surprise for my wolf, Zara," I tell her, and she looks at me confused. "I see today as our birthday, not just mine. So, I like to treat her with something good to hunt. She loves it, though now I'm feeling a bit bloated," I chuckle patting my belly. Mei gives me a genuinely warm smile and Chris looks a mix of surprised and elated. I can hear his heart pounding fast while he kisses her temple. She directs her smile at him and now I think he's going to pass out.

"You have a special relationship with your wolf," she comments sweetly.

"I sure do," I grin. "She'd love to meet you eventually; when you're ready of course."

"I would like that," she says smiling and nodding, and now Chris has tears in his eyes. I think their bond as animais is going to kill him. "Maybe… I can shift, and you can see what I look like too," she says while wringing her fingers in her lap. There are a couple of gasps while the rest of the room goes silent, and I can tell it's making Mei even more nervous. So can Chris and he pulls her closer.

"Are you sure you're ready for that?" He asks gently.

She looks up at him, taking a breath. "Not today, but maybe soon. I think I can trust everyone here."

He hugs her tightly and smiles. "I promise we are all here for you and we all want to see your shifted form, especially me and Axel. We won't let anything happen to you. Not ever," he vows. She smiles and kisses his cheek. Chris blushes through his beard.

Too cute!

I look around and see all the happy faces. I'm proud to call these people my family. I see Tyson on the other side of the couch trying to hide the tears in his eyes. He may look all macho on the outside, but he is someone who wears his heart on his sleeve. Evalyn is cuddling him and looking at him sweetly.

Which reminds me...

"No grandpa and grandma?" I ask sadly.

Dad gives me a gentle smile. "Sorry sweetheart, their flight got delayed so they won't make it on time. But they'll be here for the Alpha ceremony tomorrow," he promises. Sucks I won't see my dad's parents until tomorrow but that's better than nothing.

Vitali walks over and hands me a small white box with a blue ribbon around it, with a card tied to the ribbon. "This is from my mum and dad. They're still visiting my Aunt's pack in Hawaii, so they can't be here. But they sent this and wish you a very happy birthday. They said – and I quote – 'be sure to give hell to anyone who challenges your title.' They also told me to record the whole thing," he grins and I chuckle.

"Great. You can be the camera crew for tomorrow," I joke and open the box. Inside is a stunning blue topaz hairclip that's been shaped to look like a blue hibiscus. It's so gorgeous, I can't help running my fingers over it. I take it out and immediately clip it into my hair.

"How do I look?" I ask as I model the jewel in my hair. I get many smiles and nods.

"It suits you perfectly, and it goes lovely with your dress today," my mother praises. I glance down at my dress and chuckle. She's right; it matches perfectly.

"My present is next!" Chimes Evalyn.

I spend the rest of the afternoon opening presents and enjoying a delicious lunch prepared by the packhouse staff. I know I said I was bloated from the moose, but like I said, we wolves have a fast metabolism. I was ready for more food by the time lunch came around.

My day could not have been more perfect – surrounded by the people I love. The Beta family wasn't here, not that I'm surprised. I overheard my father venting about it to my mother during lunch. He was pissed off and felt disrespected. It's not that they are required to be here for my birthday – I sure as hell don't want Ryker near me, or any of them for that matter. But they were personally invited by their Alpha, and rejecting the invitation for no good reason is extremely disrespectful. While I didn't personally feel slighted – because I genuinely just don't care – it did make me more apprehensive about tomorrow.

This just further leads me to believe Ryker is going to challenge me, and, while I don't feel the least bit bad for what will inevitably happen to him, I do feel sad for his parents. Unless Ryker taps out, they'll end up grieving the death of their only son and I'm certain it'll shatter my father's friendship with Declan. Though, I have noticed their friendship hasn't been so great over the last few years. I think if dad didn't know I was taking over, he would have replaced Declan as Beta ages ago. But that's just speculation.

The highlight of my day so far was seeing Mei interact with everyone. She's really starting to come out of her shell, and it was great getting to know her as a person. She fits right in and everyone loves her. I can't wait to officially make her a member of this pack. This is her home and where she belongs.

Eventually, everyone went their own ways to start getting ready for the larger party. Mum headed off to check on the setup, dad went off with his Gamma and Delta to make sure the patrols are tight this evening, handle some other pack business, and maybe even scold his Beta. I didn't ask.

I've decided to stay in what I'm wearing; I see no reason to change. I can still dance the night away in this outfit, so instead, I decide to go lay down in my room and take some time to reflect.

"You're worried about tomorrow, aren't you?" Zara asks gently.

"No, not worried," I shake my head.

"Then what? You can tell me," she encourages.

"I wonder how many there will be. Dad hinted that there may be more than one," I answer.

"So? We'll take on every single one and make them regret it. We were meant for this; I know you know this. No one is going to stand in our way," she says confidently. I smile at her optimism.

"What if it's too many? The more fights we have to participate in the weaker we'll get. The last challenger might win by default just because I was exhausted from the other fights," I say, voicing my concerns. I know I can tell Zara anything and she'll never judge me for it.

"Hmm. That's a valid concern. Though we've taken on dozens of curs at a time and come out unscathed. But then again, they haven't had the training your challengers have. Not counting Ryker of course." That makes me laugh.

"So, let's go in with a game plan," I tell her and she nods in agreement.

"I like a good plan. What do you have in mind?"

"I think I should fight in my human form for as long as I can, only letting you take over when I feel my strength waning. This would give me time to get my strength back while you're fighting. If we're still fighting by the time my strength comes back and you feel you're getting weak, then we'll come together and show them just how united we are," I explain. I watch as she paces back and forth, full of anticipation, like she's already pumping herself up for the fight.

See, while we'd share injuries, we've learned to use our individual spirits to reserve energy. We can use it and lend it to our other half to aid in combating fatigue or even speed up healing. Like I said, we're the ultimate team.

"This is an excellent idea and a perfect strategy, though I expect no less from you. It'll also mean potential opponents won't be able to predict our moves as the fights go along since they won't know what form we'll be taking or when. This will give us an element of surprise," she agrees. *"We're going to make a terrific Alpha, Amelia. I'm proud of you already."* Feeling and hearing Zara's pride for me makes me very emotional. I wipe away tears as they form in my eyes.

"I'm proud of you too, Zara."

Before I knew it, it was quarter to six and the party was about to start.

I get up and slip my shoes back on and take my hair down which now has a natural wave in it from drying while up in my hair clip. I once again make the journey downstairs to the back of the packhouse and down to the training grounds, and holy crap! It looks like an outdoor club.

I'll say this for my mother, she knows how to throw a party.

The smell of different types of foods is permeating the air, making me salivate. My stomach is instantly ready to pig out again. If I weren't a wolf, I'd be the size of an elephant, I swear.

The training ground is almost unrecognisable, except for the bleachers. The track and sparring field have been covered by a massive light-up dancefloor that can fit the whole pack. Tall speakers surround the dancefloor and down on the far end, a DJ booth has been set up. Closer to the packhouse are tables with all assortments of foods. I notice there are strobe lights mounted into the trees pointed towards the training ground.

This has to be the coolest 21st birthday in the history of 21st birthdays.

As soon as I get towards the dancefloor, I spot Torie down at the DJ booth. She gives me a smile, a nod and starts the music. She's awesome.

She's twenty-six and has brown hair down to her bustline that is combed over to the right side while the left side of her head is shaved clean. She also has this tribal design of a wolf tattooed onto her scalp where her hair is shaved off. She's wearing her usual black tank top, black skinny jeans, and probably black leather boots. She's 5'3", has pale skin with a peachy hue to it and she is built like a linebacker. Broad shoulders, thick thighs, head to toe muscle. She has forest green eyes and an armband tattoo around her right bicep. She looks like a stereotypical badass, and honestly, she is.

People often don't believe she's an Omega and maybe that's why she worked so hard to bulk up, but that's not my business.

She picks up the microphone and holds it close to her mouth. "Come on Invictus Pack, time to get on the dancefloor and wish the birthday girl a happy twenty-first birthday!" She shouts, pumping everyone up. The grounds erupt into cheers and I watch my pack members merge in from all directions and start occupying the dancefloor.

I'm immediately swarmed by my best friends, but I notice no Mei. That's okay; her coming to lunch was a big step and I was very grateful for it. I know a party like this would have been too much. I dance my way over to Chris.

"You don't have to stay here. Don't feel like you have to choose between us and Mei," I tell him.

He smiles at me. "She and I talked about it. I want to be here, and she encouraged me to have some fun. She felt proud that she took steps forward today, but it was still overwhelming for her. She wants some time alone and partying with my favourite people will help me not to stress about being away from her," he explains and I nod in understanding.

"Then party it up and return when you're ready," I tell him, but he blindsides me and pulls me into a hug. I rub his back, taken aback by the gesture. "Are you okay?" I ask him, feeling concerned. He nods and briefly presses his forehead to mine. This may seem overly intimate, but this is how wolves show affection. It's not inappropriate for us.

"Thank you, Amelia. For how supportive and welcoming you have been to her. She warms up around you and it means everything to me. I'll be very proud to call you my Alpha tomorrow." Each word is more heartfelt than the last and I can't help but well up with tears.

"See, this is why I didn't wear make-up," I joke while wiping my eyes as he laughs. "I promise we will keep her safe. Anyone messes with her; they answer to me. That's assuming I survive tomorrow," I say with a playful wink, but he immediately stiffens and obviously the others were listening because they surround me instantly.

"What do you mean if you survive tomorrow?" Evalyn asks worriedly. I sigh. Well, that joke backfired.

"The Alpha told her to expect multiple challenges at the ceremony tomorrow," Vitali answers for me, eliciting growls from Chris, Tyson, and Evalyn.

"Dicks!" Tyson exclaims. "I know it's tradition and keeps us fair but it's disrespectful as hell. Name another pack that has had multiple challenges during a single ceremony," he spits in indignation.

"Alpha Bruce of the Messis Luna Pack had two challenges in a single night. Lost to the second challenger, which led to Alpha Edwin taking over the pack," I say casually.

Tyson rolls his eyes. "Alpha Bruce was an asshole, half the Alphas in the country wanted to challenge him. But that was for the betterment of his pack. This is different," he says sardonically.

"They're only doing this because you're a woman," huffs Evalyn.

And there it is.

Yes, I am very well aware of their reasons, but it doesn't matter and I'm choosing not to care because it changes nothing.

"So what? Guys, a challenge is a rite of passage, whatever their reasons it doesn't matter. A challenge must be upheld, and I say bring it on. Unless you four think I can't handle it." I raise my eyebrow in question at them. They each scoff.

"Don't be ridiculous," Tyson says.

"Of course, we think you can win; we just don't appreciate a bunch of morons disrespecting our Alpha," Chris says scornfully.

The moment he says that I watch as each of their eyes begin to glow, like neon orbs shining in the dark. This happens when their wolves show their presence. I can see it in their faces, their respect for me, their future Alpha. I swallow the lump in my throat at the sight of the people I cherish most accepting and acknowledging me as their Alpha.

"*We have amazing friends,*" Zara tells me, equally choked up.

"*We sure do, Zara. We sure do,*" I reply pulling my friends into a big group hug. "Having the support of you guys gives me more strength than you will ever know."

"Trust us, we know. But we promise you will always have our support," Evalyn tells me. I beam at each of them. It's also good to see they've relaxed, and their eyes have returned to normal. But I have to admit, seeing four wolf spirits push forward in solidarity with you feels amazing.

"What's with the group hug?" Asks a tinkly voice behind me. I smile as I turn and see Jennifer. Instantly everyone's mood improves. I walk over and pull her into a hug.

"Oh, they were just being all sooky. Don't worry about it," I tell her with a wink as she returns my hug while giggling up at me.

"Happy Birthday Alpha," she says gleefully, making me chuckle.

"I'm not Alpha yet, Jen, but thank you all the same," I tell her.

Jennifer is an absolute treasure of a person, not just to me, but to our pack. She's an Omega and, sadly, much weaker than the average one. In some packs, she would be considered a runt, but everyone adores her. She was the pack's miracle pup.

She's 4'8" – which for a wolf is extremely short. She's got short, curly, light brown hair with blonde highlights that reach her chin, piercing blue eyes, cute chubby cheeks, and pouty lips. She has cream skin and a narrow waist but is surprisingly busty and she looks beautiful in a soft pink blouse and black leggings.

"Are you excited for the Vernal Ball?" I ask her. Her face breaks into the most radiant smile as she nods excitedly. The others behind me chuckle.

"You're eighteen now, Jen, time to find your animai and break the heart of every other man out there," Vitali tells her with a wink, making her look down and blush. "That blush could stop hearts you know," he says flirtatiously and she blushes even more. Evalyn elbows him in the ribs, making him wince.

"Don't mind Vitali," I tell her. "But he's not wrong, whoever he is he'll be lucky to have you."

"You really think so?" She asks, her eyes alight with excitement.

I nod, unable to stop smiling. "Absolutely. But if he ever gives you grief he'll answer to me," I tell her seriously, but that makes her smile more.

"You're the best, Alpha." I smile shaking my head. She gives me a tight hug and then runs off when some friends call her. I smile, watching her skip away.

"Aww the little runt found herself some friends," says a shrill voice to my left. Growls resound from all around, and I turn to face the culprit.

"Jealousy looks about as good on you as that makeup, Jane," I comment brightly.

Jane Lahde. A proverbial pain in my ass. She's like the female version of Ryker. Thinks she's the Gods' gift to men and that she's the most special person in this pack. She's not even good enough to lick my boots. Jane could be beautiful if she wasn't such a raging bitch. Plus, she's wearing enough makeup to make a clown blush.

"What's wrong with my makeup?" She hisses. My friends are instantly pissed off because she's openly talking back and disrespecting her – and their – future Alpha. It's a big no, no when it comes to pack etiquette and is a punishable offence. Ryker gets away with it because he's too pathetic for me to acknowledge. And the whole, his dad is the Beta, thing.

The pack members around us are a mix of pissed off and excited. They're listening in, probably looking for a fight to entertain them.

"Where do I even begin?" I say rolling my eyes. I can't wait for the day she gives me a reason to kick her out of the pack.

"I think the reason you're friends with that runt is because you can relate to her. Face it, Amelia, you're a wannabe Alpha that nobody wants. I'd say you should stick to being a Luna, but I don't even think you'd be good at that either," she sneers and there are several gasps around us. Despite the music, this is all easy to hear thanks to our advanced hearing.

Zara is growling like crazy at the disrespect and tries to push forward, but I remain calm as I take slow steps towards her. I project my Alpha Spirit onto her.

An Alpha Spirit is an energy that an Alpha can exude that can intimidate lower wolves, bring wolves to heel, or even make them follow commands. I may not be Alpha yet, but because I'm of Alpha blood, I'm able to do this.

Jane immediately whimpers and her head drops in submission.

"Say that again. I'm not sure everyone heard you," I say in an amused voice, as I continue to project my spirit onto her. I can feel her and her wolf cowering under its force. She says nothing. "What happened, Jane? You were more than happy to openly disrespect your future Alpha in front of your entire pack, surely you can do it again. Perhaps you'd even like to challenge me at the ceremony tomorrow." My voice continues to sound amused, but there's a sadistic smile on my face.

Her eyes nearly bug out of her skull and even under all that makeup, I can tell the blood has drained from her face. She reeks of fear.

"No?" I ask her. She rapidly shakes her head. I step up to her, getting into her personal space and now she's full-on trembling, which Zara and I take great satisfaction in. "Disrespect me or a member of this pack again and see what happens," I whisper calmly in her ear. She shivers and audibly gulps. "Say 'yes, Alpha'," I tell her.

"Yes, Alpha," she says through gritted teeth.

"Louder," I command.

"Yes, Alpha!" She says loud and clear.

"Good. Now run along," I say, like a parent to a child. She quickly rushes off.

"I can't tell if she's crazy or has gigantic balls," says Tyson.

"Or maybe she has a death wish," says Vitali.

These two.

"She's not worth the headache. Let's just enjoy the rest of the evening," I encourage.

The drinks are flowing, the food is disappearing, and I am dancing up a storm on the dancefloor. A couple of hiccups here and there and the occasional fight needing to be broken up but overall I'm having an absolute blast.

I'm just finishing my umpteenth drink when the music comes to an abrupt stop. People start to whine but then I see the crowd part as my parents carry out a massive six-tier birthday cake with sparklers on it.

I smile wide as everyone starts singing me happy birthday. The cake is absolutely stunning, too pretty to even eat. It's white with gold swirls and each tier base is surrounded by roses. I get close to it, and it smells... oh my Goddess it smells divine. There's a white buttercream frosting, but on the inside, I can smell chocolate and... caramel. Oh yes! Caramel is my absolute favourite.

I hug and kiss my parents thank you as they set the cake down and hand me a knife. Taking it, I make my way over to Torie and borrow the mic from her and she throws me a wink.

I turn and address the pack. "I just want to say thank you to every single one of you for the birthday wishes, the gifts and for celebrating with me tonight. This birthday wouldn't be the same without all of you to share it with," I declare, and am met with cheers and howls of joy. "Before I cut this cake could Leo Meyer, Daniel Owens and Joanna Johnson please join me up here," I request.

Slowly the people I called make their way over to me with big smiles. I smile back at them as I lead the pack in another round of 'happy birthday,' but this time directed at Leo, Daniel, and Joanna. Joanna looks embarrassed, Leo looks relaxed, and Daniel looks proud. I hand the mic back to Torie and walk over to the cake. I motion for the other three to join me. I have them place their hand on the knife along with mine and the four of us cut the cake together as the pack cheers.

"Happy Birthday, you guys," I tell them with a wide smile they return.

"Happy Birthday Alpha," they say in unison.

Obviously, I was not the only person in this pack born on February 21st. Having big parties in your honour is a pretty cool perk of being the Alpha's daughter, but it's just not in me to ignore my pack members who share my birthday. I mean they're here, why not celebrate it together? It's not like I have a monopoly on birthdays.

"Have I told you how proud I am to have been paired with you?" Zara asks me.

"Once or twice," I say cheekily.

Torie starts the music back up and I help my parents distribute cake amongst everyone, setting aside an extra slice for Chris to take to Mei. Once everyone who wants one gets a piece, I go and take a seat on the bleachers with my friends. We smile, crack jokes, and enjoy each other's company.

I bask in the moment, taking in all the happiness around me because as of tomorrow, a lot is going to change. I'm ready for all the challenges that await me, literal and metaphorical. I don't expect the road ahead to be an easy one, but it's the one I'm proudly taking. I just hope I can do my pack the justice it deserves and bring us into a new era. If I can't, I'll at least die trying.

Chapter Four
Amelia

You ever have those moments in life that feel like the calm before the storm? That's what I'm realising yesterday was. Yesterday was filled with joy and celebration, but ever since I woke up this morning, I've felt the clouds of impending doom lingering over me. Bad things are coming. Call it wolf senses, women's intuition or whatever you like, but I can feel in my very bones that trouble is waiting for me just around the corner.

The day has been another round of festivities. The outdoor rave was dismantled in record time and replaced by a good old-fashioned barbeque. Picnic tables with the classic red and white checked cloths have been set up around the back of the packhouse and a small stage has been erected.

I'm dressed in a simple white satin blouse and a full length, ruffled, white skirt with white sandals. Casual but classy. This should be a positive setting, but unlike the excited energy I felt yesterday, today everyone feels apprehensive and it has me on edge.

I'm sitting at one of the picnic tables with Vitali, Tyson, Evalyn, Chris, and Mei – yes Mei decided to join us – trying to listen to what Evalyn is saying but my brain keeps focusing on the whispers around me and the looks thrown my way.

If you're wondering if this sort of behaviour is normal among pack members during an Alpha ceremony, the answer is no. I don't like this and neither does Zara, but I continue to appear unbothered as always.

"There's my little Cupcake!" Comes a voice I haven't heard in months. I jump out of my chair and throw myself at my grandfather who catches me without hesitation.

"Grandpa! You made it!" I exclaim and he chuckles, hugging me tight and nuzzling me.

"Of course, we made it. We're so sorry we missed your birthday yesterday," he says guiltily.

"Planes being delayed on my grandpups birthday? It's just not on," comes my grandmother as she walks up behind my grandfather. I chuckle, let grandpa go and hug my grandma who envelops me in a hug only grandma can give. I lean back and smile at them.

"You guys have nothing to be sorry for. You're here now and that's all that matters," I tell them brightly.

Grandpa Alden and Grandma Sorrell are the former Alpha and Luna of this pack. They've been spending their retirement years travelling the world and even visiting packs in other countries. They're still called on sometimes for their council, after all, you never really stop being an Alpha or a Luna.

They have the kind of relationship I hope to have one day. So in love all these years later with an amazing zest for life and they are a total riot. Especially grandma. Thanks to their wolf blood, they don't look their age at all. They're in their late sixties but you wouldn't guess from looking at them.

My dad takes after Grandma Sorrell. She has blonde hair styled in a bob and has chestnut eyes. Dad and grandma both have a very pointed nose which I did not inherit. Dad got his height from grandpa since grandma is only 5'1".

Grandpa, however, is 6'5", has dark black hair with a hint of grey hair forming in his sideburns. He has soft greyish brown eyes and is still built like a tank. They look so cute, with grandpa in black slacks and a navy-blue button-down shirt and grandma in a soft yellow sundress, with a white wide-brim hat.

"Luna Sorrell, it's good to have you back home. Still not looking a day over thirty," Vitali says with a wink. Grandma playfully swats his shoulder, but grandpa lets out a displeased growl and smacks him up the back of his head.

"Don't go getting any ideas, pup," says grandpa. I chuckle while Tyson, Evalyn, and Chris snigger.

"Wouldn't dream of it, Alpha," Vitali says with a cheeky smile.

"For a moment I wasn't sure I was at an Alpha ceremony, it's so… informal," Grandpa says, his nose scrunching up in disapproval.

I sigh. "I know a cookout isn't traditional or maybe even appropriate for today, but it felt like the best option. Things are going to get messy, and it just didn't make sense to go to the effort of making everything look elegant just for it to get ruined," I explain. Grandma nods in understanding.

"I think it's lovely. A formal gathering would have been nice, but a cookout certainly does bring a pack together. The end result is still the same," she says with a smile.

"My granddaughter can't even have the ceremony she deserves because of a bunch of ingrates," mutters my grandpa angrily. My grandma holds his hand to calm him, and he does immediately, giving her a loving smile. "Don't mind me, Cupcake, I'm just a grumpy old man," he says to me.

I shake my head and kiss his cheek. "You're neither grumpy nor old, you just love me," I tell him with a reassuring smile.

"Darn right I do," he says proudly, beaming back at me.

"If only more men were like you, Alpha," says Evalyn. "You bagged a good one, Luna Sorrell," she comments, causing grandma to smile proudly at my grandpa.

"Don't I know it," she says winking at Evalyn.

Grandma quickly spots Mei sitting next to Chris. She's been sitting at our table the whole time, Chris playing bodyguard. A few pack members have come over to say hello and those interactions seemed to go well. "Who is this darling young lady?" My grandma asks walking over to Mei. Mei instantly blushes and tries to hide in Chris's arms, but he's beaming with pride.

"This is Mei Liu, my animai," he says proudly and Mei blushes further.

"Congratulations, my boy!" Cheers my grandpa, giving Chris a big pat on the back.

"It is a delight to meet you and have you in our pack, dear," grandma says warmly to Mei.

"It's very nice to meet you, Alpha and Luna," Mei says softly with a small nod. Grandma nearly falls over from glee.

Calm down, woman.

"Oh Alden, isn't she just darling?!" Grandma exclaims, and grandpa gives her an amused look.

"We're not having any more pups. That son of ours was enough," he says in mock exhaustion. Grandma swats his chest. We all just chuckle at their antics. I'm so glad they're here, this wouldn't have been the same without them.

We're all sitting around enjoying grandpa and grandma telling us stories about their travels when my dad comes up and squeezes my shoulders. "It's time," he says softly, and I instantly tense. I'm excited to become Alpha, I'm just concerned about what comes after. I nod my head as I get up and face him. My father is looking down at me with so many emotions, pride being the most prominent, but I see the underlying fear. I think he'd feel this way regardless. After all, I'm his only pup.

I notice the table has gone quiet, so I glance back at everyone. My friends all have broad smiles. Grandma has tears in her eyes and grandpa has the same look on his face as dad. I smile at them as dad leads me up to the small stage in front of everyone. Mum's already standing to the side trying to hold back her tears of joy.

"EVERYONE!" He exclaims, getting the pack's attention. Everyone instantly falls quiet and turns to face us. "Today is a blessed day for this pack and a proud one for me and my Luna. Today you witness history in the making. Today our..." I look up at my dad to see tears in his eyes as he chokes on his words. Seeing my strong father so openly emotional in front of his pack has tears filling my own eyes. "Our beautiful daughter takes her oath and becomes not only your new Alpha but the first female Alpha!" He announces proudly.

Well, first female Alpha in North America, like I've said, I'm not sure about the rest of the world. But had he said that in his speech I doubt it would have sounded as impactful.

There are cheers from the pack, but I notice not everyone is cheering; some are even faking it. Even though I expected it, I can't help feeling somewhat rejected.

Mum comes over and hands my father a small dagger with a black and red hilt and a very reflective gold blade. My father takes the dagger and we face each other.

"Amelia Dolivo, do you swear fealty to the Invictus Pack and each of its members, current and future?" He asks me, his voice full of authority as his Alpha Spirit radiates from him.

"I do," I say with conviction.

"Do you swear to always serve your pack and its needs to the best of your abilities?"

"I do," I answer, my conviction never wavering.

"And do you swear to always fight for your pack, striking down any enemy who may wish us harm?"

"I do," I say fiercely.

"Do you swear to always love your pack?" He asks me, his face softening. I smile at him. I know the words I must say but even if they were written for me, these words are in my heart. I mean them with every fibre of my being.

"I swear to love and honour the Invictus Pack, as my ancestors before me once did and will continue to do so until I take my last breath," I announce with no pretence or façade, just pure emotion. I look at my pack and smirk. "But even then, I'll probably still love you guys," I say winking at them.

Okay, that last line was all me. This earns me chuckles from the pack and a few hoots. I'll take that. I look at dad to see him grinning at me. He places the blade of the dagger against his left palm and slices his hand as he speaks.

"I, Alpha Elias Dolivo, in the eyes of Goddess Morrtemis, relinquish my title and power as Alpha of the Invictus Pack to my daughter, Amelia Dolivo," he declares. He hands the dagger to me; I take it and slice it across my left palm as I speak.

"I, Amelia Dolivo, in the eyes of Goddess Morrtemis, accept the title and power of Alpha of the Invictus Pack from my father, Alpha Elias Dolivo," I say, clasping my left hand with his.

The response is instantaneous. A white glow radiates from my father, moving away from his body down his arm and into mine, then spreads throughout my body and it feels… intense. I gasp at the overwhelming sensation. I feel stronger, more confident, my senses – though already sharp – feel even sharper and my connection to my pack strengthens.

What used to be a gentle hum in the back of my mind that made up the link with the pack, has now become noticeable threads. I feel bonded to every member of this pack. We are tied to each other now.

Then comes the burning pain on my chest, it's unpleasant but bearable. I look down and watch as the Mark of the Alpha appears on my chest directly over my heart. I smile in awe at the mark that once resided on my father's chest. It's a wolf's paw print and looks like I've been branded with iron. But as the redness dissipates it's replaced with an iridescent sheen. This mark is binding and cannot be forged.

I smile up at my father, pride, and power coursing through my veins. The cut on my hand has healed and I feel like I could lift a tank right now. My father beams at me, but then his features turn hard, and I know what's coming.

Damn, I was hoping to bask in the good vibes a little longer.

"Before I can officially declare Amelia your Alpha, per law I must ask, is there anyone here who wishes to challenge my daughter for the title of Alpha?" His face is calm, but his voice is like a stone. He knows he has to do this, but he's not happy. I take a slow breath and brace myself.

"I, Beta Declan Mathers of the Invictus Pack, challenge Amelia Dolivo for the title of Alpha!" Comes a voice from the crowd and my head snaps to it.

I'm utterly shocked, but I keep my face neutral. No emotion, I show nothing. But inside, I'm losing my freakin' mind. I glance over and see Ryker looking at me with a smirk on his face like the cat that got the cream.

That's why he's been such a smug little shit. Why he was happy to openly disrespect his future Alpha. I thought he was going to challenge me, but he knew it would be his father.

What in the actual fuck?

"Declan!" My father growls in anger and disbelief. "You are the Beta of this pack; how dare you challenge my daughter?! Have you lost your damn mind?!"

My father's hands are in fists and he's shaking with rage. His chestnut eyes are glowing bright, his wolf Greer coming forward; they're both furious. Their Beta didn't just challenge me, he disrespected and betrayed them. Damn, even mum's turquoise eyes are glowing, she and her wolf Paityn are pissed off too.

Me? Well, I'm seventy percent shocked by the turn of events, but I'm thirty percent not shocked. Look, I knew the guy had an issue with me, so this honestly checks out.

"I'm doing this for the pack, Elias! She is too weak to be an Alpha. No woman can be Alpha. You will damn this pack. I warned you years ago, but you refused to listen and now you've left me no choice," he declares.

Pack members are watching in stunned silence, though there are some growls from some members who are in support of me as Alpha, I think you can name a few of them. Before my dad can respond, my grandpa shoots out of his seat.

"Outrageous! What kind of Alpha could you make? A Beta who betrayed his Alpha, challenged his new Alpha, and declared to all the women in the pack that he finds them inferior," he scoffs. "You're just proving how unfit you are. My son never should have made you a Beta."

"You always hated me, old man," Declan spits back scornfully.

"Thank you for proving my instincts correct," grandpa says smugly, though he's still furious. Even grandma is livid; if looks could kill, Declan would be six feet under right now.

Am I the only person not looking like they are about to rip someone's head off?

"You know what we need to do. We've got this," Zara tells me. She's pumped

and ready for action, the new power in our veins fuelling our adrenaline. We're ready for blood.

I may be friendly, and I love my pack, but don't go thinking I'm a pacifist. I'm a wolf to my core and there's a part of me that is consumed by blood lust; a part of me that thrives on it. I just control it better than most Alphas, or wolves in general.

Declan is about to spew some more toxic bullshit and I'm done.

"I, Amelia Dolivo, accept the challenge of Beta Declan for the title of Alpha," I announce calmly. Instantly all eyes are back on me and none of them are glowing. Declan is smirking like some movie villain, mum looks terrified, and dad is... expressionless. He stares at me, so I give him my best smile. He relaxes and nods his head.

"The challenge will begin on the training field in fifteen minutes!" He announces. He quickly pulls me into a tight hug, which I return eagerly. I breathe in his familiar scent of apple and cinnamon which always calms me.

"*I have every faith that you can do this. You're the best fighter in this whole pack. Show them why they should never mess with you,*" comes my dad's voice in my mind. I smile up at him, but he just holds me tighter and nuzzles me. I nuzzle him back.

"I have to go change," I tell him and he unwillingly lets me go. But before I can make a move, I'm pulled into my mum's arms.

"Don't you dare die," she says in a warning tone.

"Noted," I chuckle, but hug her tight all the same. I pull out of her arms and make my way through the tables to the packhouse.

I glance over at my friends who have the worst poker faces ever. They're worried for me and aren't bothering to hide it; they're also pissed off. They want to come and comfort me, but I don't have time. I shake my head for them to let me be. I need to focus on the task at hand.

Killing Beta Declan.

The pack is making their way to the training field as I get to the backdoor, my mind replaying all the fights and training I've seen Declan in over the years and trying to come up with a strategy. I'm deep in thought when Ryker steps in my path, blocking the doorway.

"I can't wait to see my father sink his teeth into your pretty neck. But honestly, I hope he shows you mercy because I'd just love to have my fun with you when this is over," he says sickeningly. I suppress the shudder of disgust that wants to roll over me. I want to hurl; Declan and Ryker have some serious screws loose in their heads. I look up at him, my eyes and face devoid of any emotion. He blinks in surprise.

"Watch your back, Ryker. Because after I kill your father today, my eyes will be on you," I say impassively and I watch him gulp, shock evident on his face.

He quickly replaces the shock with a snare, "Enjoy death, bitch," he hisses before storming off.

I smirk and head up to my room, changing into a sports bra, short workout shorts and sneakers, then tying my hair up. I take a breath, looking in the full-length mirror in my closet, my fingers tracing over the Mark of the Alpha. This is what I was meant for; I'm not letting anyone take it from me. Especially not some sexist prick. I don't even want to think what would become of the pack if he took over.

"He'll never take over because we're going to kill him," Zara says nonchalantly.

"Time to teach that Beta who's Alpha," I reply as I make my way down to the training ground.

When I return, the whole pack is sitting in the bleachers, ready to watch and find out who will be their new Alpha. Declan is off to the right side of the field whispering with his animai, Saree, and Ryker. Meanwhile, my dad is standing to the left of the field with my mum, grandpa, Uncle James, and Uncle Xander. I see grandma – with a murderous look on her face – sitting in the front row behind them with Vitali, Tyson, Evalyn, Chris, and... Mei again? I look at Chris with surprise and concern. This is going to get violent; she shouldn't see this. As if reading my mind, he links me.

"She insisted on being here. She wants to show her support for you," he tells me, his voice full of pride.

His words touch me. With all she's going through, she braved it just to support me, her potential Alpha. That just gives me more fuel to unleash hell on this dickhead. I give Mei a bright smile as I make my way over. She gives me a thumbs up and I chuckle softly as I stand beside my dad.

"I still can't believe he's doing this. I knew he was against you being Alpha, Amelia, but I never thought he'd take it this far," says Xander solemnly. His face is frozen in a scowl, so I clap him on the back.

"Don't look so glum, guys. If it wasn't him, it would have been someone else. He has every right to challenge me and now he'll find out why it was the dumbest decision he ever made," I tell them, letting some of my Alpha Spirit radiate off me. It makes each of them stand a little straighter and I can see them feeding off my confidence.

Grandpa steps closer and pulls me into a hug. "Kick his ass," he tells me as I hug him back.

Uncle James is standing there as stoic as ever.

"No final words for me, Uncle J?" I say cocking an eyebrow at him.

He shrugs. "Anything I say would not be final words. I've trained you since you were a pup, I know what you can do. Declan is a dead man; he will die as a traitor to this pack," he says that last part with a snarl.

These people know how to boost me up. I nod to my dad. He takes a breath and kisses my mum's temple then walks onto the field, me trailing behind him. We get to the centre of the field and Declan makes his way to us. We face each other as dad stands in the middle.

"Beta Declan Mathers of the Invictus Pack has challenged potential Alpha, Amelia Dolivo for the Alpha title. This is a fight to the death. Whoever wins will be declared your new Alpha," he announces to the pack who has gone deadly silent. "When you are ready, begin!" He exclaims and then runs back to his place by my mum.

Declan gets in a fighting stance and smirks. "I promise to kill you quick," he says with a smirk. I simply stand there looking impassive. I don't move, I don't react. Still as a statue. He quirks his eyebrow at me. "Giving up already? I knew you were too weak for this," he spits.

At that moment he lunges at me, his hand going for my throat. I remembered this is his favourite move, so I set him up for it easily and he gladly took the opportunity. I let his hand wrap around my throat and he grips it tightly, making my head spin. I still don't flinch. The pack is going nuts, but I can't make out what they're saying.

My expressionless face quickly forms a smirk as I wrap my left hand around his wrist and snap it, taking full advantage of the new strength coursing through my body. The bone comes out at a nasty angle as he lets out an agonised groan.

With my hand still gripped onto his wrist, I kick my foot into his sternum at full force. I can hear the sound of his bones cracking as my foot makes contact. If he was a weaker wolf, that kick probably would have killed him. I let his wrist go as he goes flying back across the field, landing in a crumpled heap on the grass.

He clutches his chest with his good hand, and I can hear his laboured breathing. I stand still watching impassively. His injuries will start to heal immediately, but a broken bone takes at least a full hour to heal. The pain will become tolerable but it's now his weak spot. His right hand, however, is now useless. Only way that's healing properly is if he can get to the pack hospital and have the bone reset. He's now one hand down.

Declan is furious. He just got his ass handed to him by a woman – a woman half his size. But we're not done; this is to the death. I don't hesitate or give him time to recover. I run at him at full speed, but he manages to roll away just in time and get to his feet, doing his best to ignore the pain he feels.

I start throwing punches, managing to land two to his face, but he dodges the others. He fakes a punch with his left, and as I go to dodge it, he swings a kick from his right directly into my ribs and I hear and feel one of them crack. As my body recoils from the attack on my left my face collides with his left fist. I hear and feel the crunch of my nose as it breaks. I can feel the warm blood pouring down my face and into my mouth. There goes my sense of smell.

I spit the blood from my mouth and put all my focus on the fight. This pain is temporary, the bleeding will stop in a few seconds, and I can get it set later. I have one goal, to kill him, and until I meet that goal, any pain I feel is meaningless to me.

In life, I'm friendly and compassionate. But what he doesn't realise, is that in a fight I'm a ruthless, calculating, killing machine and he just messed with the wrong wolf.

He charges at me, thinking I'm distracted, but I throw my forearms out in front of me to push him back and collide with his still mending broken sternum. He buckles from the pain as the air leaves his lungs. But he's not giving up yet. I wouldn't expect him to, he's the Beta. He's meant to be strong enough to go toe to toe with an Alpha, but he'll never be as strong as one. His mistake was going into this assuming I'm weak just because I'm a woman.

As he drops to the ground, he kicks my legs out from under me. As I start to fall, I shift my weight, landing on my front with my arms supporting my weight and preventing my ribs from taking on the impact. I go to throw a kick in his direction but when I glance back, he's moved away.

His breathing is more laboured, and his green irises are glowing. Within seconds he's shifted into his wolf Braxton, but Declan is very much in control. He crouches down snarling at me, but he can't put full weight on his right paw. In fact, I bet shifting with that break hurt like a bitch. I smile knowing that.

I quickly get up and take a defensive stance as his wolf stalks towards me. His wolf is 5'8" with grey and brown fur, white legs and looks ready to take my head off. He charges at me – poorly due to his bad paw. I start charging towards the angry animal, the shouts of the crowd completely drowned out by the blood pumping in my ears. Declan lunges at me and as he lunges, I drop and slide leg first underneath him like I'm sliding onto home plate. As I pass under his belly, I land a punch to his damaged ribcage and hear another satisfying crack. This causes him to lose momentum and crash land into the grass. While he's down, I speed over and tackle the wolf, wrapping my arms around his neck and yanking backwards. He starts to struggle, snarl and yelp.

His struggling is causing my ribs to protest but I ignore it. He's kicking his legs around trying to get me off, while also trying to turn and snap at my face, but I only tighten my hold. I tighten and yank until finally I hear his neck snap. He goes limp and lifeless in my arms. I slowly let him go and get up on my feet, catching my breath.

I stand and look at the dead wolf at my feet as it shifts back into its human form. A naked, dead Declan lays there; his eyes open wide; the bone in his neck protruding. I feel no guilt, no remorse. In fact, I feel powerful. The blood pumping in my ears starts to clear, and now I'm hyper-aware of screams and howls. They sound agonised and angry all at the same time.

I look over to find the source and see Saree Mathers, Declan's animai and the female Beta of our pack, on her knees screaming hysterically. The sight of it hurts my heart. She didn't just see her soulmate die, she felt it. All of it. My heart goes out to her, but this is what he chose. Ryker is standing next to her, not even attempting to comfort her. He's just staring at his father's lifeless body, his eyes wide with shock. I look to my right and see my parents looking proud and relieved.

Suddenly their eyes widen in alarm.

"YOU MURDERING BITCH!" I turn just as I get tackled to the ground by Saree, the impact causing pain to radiate through the rib fracture Declan gave me. Her brown hair is sprawled around her, her blue eyes glowing as she tries to claw at my face. She looks deranged. "I'LL FUCKING KILL YOU!" She screams in my face. I'm barely trying to fight her off because I know she's acting out of grief. When someone loses their animai, many are known to go insane or die. I see she's the former. "We should have killed you years ago, like we planned!" She spits venomously at me, shocking me.

They had planned to kill me? What the fuck?

Fuck the grief, it's clear she and Declan had it out for me for years. Both her hands grip my throat, taking my shock from her words as an opening. I quickly snap out of it and I use the opportunity to plunge my fists into her chest.

"You're right. You should have killed me," I tell her in a calm tone.

Her movements stop, her hands loosen from around my neck and her eyes are wide as saucers. I push past the resistance in her chest until my fist comes out the other side. I listen to the sounds of her bones breaking and the squelch of her organs against my flesh. She coughs, and blood splatters onto my face. I feel the warmth of her blood pour down my arm. It's surely a gruesome sight.

I watch as her eyes become lifeless and her body goes limp on top of me. I shove her off me and pull my fist from her chest as my dad rushes to my side.

"Amelia! Amelia are you okay?" He asks in a worried tone as he cups my cheeks.

"She said–"

"I heard," he interjects with a furious glint in his eyes. He helps me to my feet – not that I need it – and takes a breath. "Is there anyone else who wishes to challenge my daughter for the Alpha title?!" He asks the crowd. We wait but hear nothing. I glance over to Ryker who is… looking cool as a cucumber. He must be in shock.

"I don't trust him. He's planning something," Zara sneers in my mind.

"Maybe. We'll keep an eye on him, just in case," I tell her.

After another minute, no one says anything. My father sighs with relief and proudly raises my non-bloody hand in the air.

"I proudly declare Amelia Dolivo the new Alpha of the Invictus Pack!" He shouts and lets out a celebratory howl, which I quickly follow and then the pack follows until the air is filled with proud howls.

Well, mostly.

I grin at my father and step forward, looking around at the pack as I speak. "My first act as your Alpha is to name your new Beta, Gamma, and Delta who we will swear in tomorrow. I name Chris Melgren your new Delta," I declare.

Everyone cheers as he stands proudly, smiling at me, giving me a small bow, Mei beaming up at him with so much pride it makes him blush when he sees it.

"I name Tyson Grey your new Gamma," I declare.

Tyson stands and claps his hands together and shakes them above his head in victory before giving me a small bow.

"And I name Vitali Hughes as your new Beta," I declare smirking at Vitali.

He looks at me in complete shock as Tyson, Evalyn, and Chris leap at him and congratulate him. He slowly stands up, smiling in a bit of a daze and looks around at the pack before giving me a small bow.

"*When the hell did you decide this?*" Vitali asks.

"*I've always known you'd be my Beta, there was no one else,*" I tell him honestly watching his face soften as he sits down, still looking shocked.

I glance over at Ryker who has gone from cool as a cucumber to looking murderous at me. But he says and does nothing. Considering I just killed both his parents, at least he has some brains left in his head not to pick a fight with me right now. But something is cooking in his head, I can see it in his eyes. I don't know what it is, but it's not going to be good.

"Let's get you to Doctor Richard and get that nose fixed, then you can lead the pack run. How are the ribs?" My dad asks with concern as he wraps his arm around me.

"Fine, if I don't think about them, they should be healed fully soon," I tell him.

He nods and kisses my forehead. "I'm so proud of you Amelia. My Little Alpha," he whispers against my forehead.

Alpha.

I'm finally Alpha.

The wave of excitement and relief crashing over me is indescribable. I can't believe it finally happened.

"*We're finally the Alpha, girl! Time to get this pack into tip-top shape and then find our animai,*" Zara announces.

"*One thing at a time. We'll find him eventually, but first, we have to settle in as Alpha and have a memorial for Declan and Saree.*"

Zara sneers. "*They were traitors, Amelia. They were going to kill you. They don't deserve a proper burial,*" she says bitterly. I understand her feelings, but we can't act personally on this.

"*I know and believe me I want to look into this more. I want to find out if Ryker knew about any of this. They were still the Betas of this pack and served it for many years. And, the challenge was legal. So, we will bury them as we would any other pack member. With dignity and respect,*" I tell her calmly. I refuse to start my reign as Alpha by dishonouring the dead.

"You're right," Zara sighs, *"It's the right thing to do."*

"Is everything alright with Zara?" Asks my dad. He can always tell when she and I are talking.

I smile and nod. "Just preparing our first Alpha duties," I tell him.

He smiles and leads me off the field to the pack hospital. I can't help stealing a glance back at the two bodies on the field. People I knew my entire life wanted me dead, all because I was to be a female Alpha. What a waste of life. But at least they will be reunited in the next one.

Chapter Five
Amelia

This past week has been hectic as hell. After getting challenged, killing two people I was practically raised by and getting my nose fixed, I got started on my Alpha duties. The following day, we had a ceremony officially making Vitali, Tyson and Chris my Beta, Gamma, and Delta. It went off without a hitch and the transition process, for the most part, has been pretty smooth.

We then had a small funeral for Beta Declan and Saree, to which very few showed up. Since then, we've been in meetings each day going over pack paperwork, evaluating the current state of the pack and discussing what changes – If any – we'd like to make.

Tyson has begun implementing his new training regime, which everyone seems to be loving so far. As the Gamma, his job is to oversee the training of pack members, warriors and also handle overall pack security. His father wasn't thrilled about him making changes to the training routine of the pack, but once he saw it in action, the pride was written all over his face.

Chris dove into the pack finances, finding where changes are needed that will benefit the pack. Chris has a knack for numbers and has degrees in business and finance. As the pack's Delta he handles our money. My dad – now me – owns several businesses which are very lucrative and help us financially support the pack, but the bulk of our financial success is actually thanks to my mum.

My mother is a brainiac with a talent for handling the Stock Market. The money we have made since she started doing this fifteen years ago has made us a very wealthy pack. We don't flaunt it, but we are more than financially stable. Mum had been sharing her Stock Market prowess with Chris and he's taken to it like a duck to water.

Vitali, as my Beta, is my right-hand man. He has to be able to do a bit of everything, but his primary job is pack politics. Yes, we may be wolves, but we have our own politics to deal with, whether it be inside the pack or in dealing with other packs. A Beta often acts as a representative of the pack on behalf of the Alpha when the Alpha cannot be present. Vitali is a natural mediator, and despite all his joking, he's a very level-headed person. He instantly took to the role, delving into pack reports and meeting with members to discuss disputes and then settle them. He's also looking into any upcoming trips he may have to take on behalf of the pack.

Safe to say, I've chosen my council well.

Then of course, there's me. I am in charge of everything. Ultimately everything has to go through me, all of it needing my final approval. It's a lot of work and it can get exhausting sometimes, but it's worth it. Just over two thousand people are my sole responsibility, so that means working hard to take care of them. There's no room for slacking off.

Chris and I are currently sitting in my office… wow, that still feels weird to say. This has been my dad's office since I was a baby, calling it mine now hasn't quite sunk in yet. We're going over the expenditure for the Vernal Ball.

"Honestly, Amelia, you've actually spent less on this event than the last three pack events combined," Chris tells me while he sits in the armchair opposite my desk.

Chris is the most presentable guy among my friends. Hence why he's wearing a navy-blue pinstripe button-down shirt – a couple of the top buttons undone – a black vest, and black slacks with black loafers. Of course, his long hair is up in its usual bun. It's sophisticated but approachable. I bet Mei drools over it.

As for me, it depends on the day. Today I'm in black slacks, a collared, long-sleeved white chiffon blouse, cinched at the waist with a chiffon ribbon. I've also paired the outfit with blue pumps for a pop of colour. No makeup as usual. I really don't think I need it, nor do I have the time.

"How is that possible?" I ask in confusion as I flip through my binder regarding the ball. In it I have detailed and labelled everything we have purchased and everything we had yet to purchase. I'm very meticulous. "We have purchased a lot so far. I mean, as the first ball I'm hosting I do want it to make a statement. Have I gone too simple?" I ask with a frown.

"Amelia, relax," Chris chuckles. "The ball will look grander than grand. No disrespect to Luna Fleur, the woman is incredible when it comes to numbers and money, but it seems that kind of goes out the window when she's organising events and parties. She goes a little… okay, she goes very overboard, damning the expenses. Fortunately, we are more than capable of affording these things. You on the other hand are your usual methodical self. Always looking for the best deals or cheaper rates for the things you want," he states nonchalantly.

"Why does that sound like a polite way of calling me frugal?" I ask narrowing my eyes at the not-so-great comparison to my mother.

"I don't think being financially conscious is frugal, Amelia," he snorts. "You're not cheap – trying to save a buck because you can't part with a dime. You're smart and not willing to spend the pack's money frivolously. If this was about upgrades to the pack hospital I doubt you'd even care about the amount, you'd sign the check with your eyes closed," he says with a goofy smile.

I nod in agreement. "Well, I'd make sure the money was being put to good use first of course. But yes, I think funding our medical facility is something that should not involve bargain hunting. Table linens that may never be used again, that's a whole other matter," I say drily.

"Exactly my point," he shrugs. "So trust me, this ball isn't close to breaking the budget and I know it'll be magical. Has to be if our Alpha is going to meet her man," he says wiggling his eyebrows and making me roll my eyes.

"I swear, it's like you and my wolf are in cahoots. We'll find him when we find him. If it's at the ball, great. If not, oh well," I shrug.

Before Chris can respond, the knock tone for the door buzzer sounds and I get up to answer it. I'm greeted by one of the packhouse staff members, Kylie.

"Afternoon, Kylie. What can I do for you?" I ask her, smiling warmly. She returns my warm smile with one of her own.

"Just bringing you today's mail, Alpha," she chirps as she passes me a stack of envelopes.

I take them off her hands. "Thank you very much. Was there anything else?" I ask. She looks down and wrings her fingers nervously. I'll take that as a yes. "Kylie, whatever it is please don't be nervous to tell me," I gently encourage. I can sense Chris stiffening in his seat behind me, awaiting what she has to say.

"I, um, well… could I have next week off? It's just, my animai, Izac he–"

I hold up my hand cutting her off before she can say more. I hear Chris quickly muffle a laugh and I shoot him a glare.

Butthead.

I smile at Kylie. "You don't need to tell me why. Of course, you can have next week off. Just make sure you run it by Maggie first, so she can fill your shifts if she needs to and to see if you have any annual leave you can take advantage of."

"Thank you, Alpha!" She exclaims, smiling brightly before running off. I smile and shake my head as I close the door and walk back to my seat.

Chris chuckles and teases, "Oh, you evil dictator. Got the pack staff nervous to ask you for time off."

I roll my eyes, "I know the transition can take getting used to but come on. These people should know I'm not going to become like that just because I'm Alpha."

"Well, they didn't think their Beta would betray their Alpha either," he mutters disdainfully.

I let that one go. He's right. Beta Declan's actions – and Saree's – shook the pack. They were people the pack trusted, and for them to do what they did – It has many of them rattled. So, I guess Chris has a good point.

While Chris is going through texts on his phone and smiling like an idiot – which clues me in on who he is texting – I go through the mail. I stop on a plain white envelope with my name scrawled on the front in very neat handwriting. Picking up the gold letter opener from my desk I cut into the envelope and pull out the white paper inside and read it.

My body goes stiff.

> Congratulations on the new position. Enjoy your time as Alpha while you can, Amelia. Your pack will be mine soon.

I read the words over and over again.

Someone is threatening me and my pack. Zara is snarling, ready to take on whoever this person is. I can feel Chris's eyes on me. I tear my eyes away from the note to see his brows furrowed.

"What's wrong?" He asks with concern. "I know you, Amelia. You've got that impassive face. You only do that when something is wrong or you're upset," he explains.

He's right, when something happens or someone comes for me, I turn my emotions off. It's become a reflex at this point. Now I even apply it to my fighting style. I put the paper down and turn it to face him. He looks down at the paper and begins reading, his expression darkening.

"Fuck," he breathes.

I decide to link Tyson and Vitali. *"My office. Now,"* I say flatly.

"On my way!" Says Tyson.

"Will be right there. What's happened?" Asks Vitali. I don't reply, I'll show them when they get here. I get up and open the door for them. Stepping back behind my desk, I pick up the envelope and note, sniffing them both. I can smell my scent and Kylie's on the envelope but nothing on the note itself. I frown, not liking this one bit, even Chris has gone terribly quiet. Within a couple of minutes, Tyson and Vitali are in my office. Tyson closes the door behind him.

"Now will you tell us what's happened?" Vitali asks impatiently. I hand him the note and he reads it while Tyson reads over his shoulder. They both go rigid.

"Who the fuck sent this?" Tyson demands through gritted teeth.

"It's anonymous."

"Maybe it's just a prank," Vitali offers.

I shake my head. "Whoever sent it was smart enough to wear gloves. They didn't leave a scent on the note or the envelope," I explain. This makes them frown.

"Whoever this fucker is, he clearly has a death wish. They just openly threatened our Alpha," Tyson says as he starts pacing my office.

"It's not that open of a threat. They sent it to Amelia specifically and didn't say who they are. Why the mystery?" Asks Chris.

"Because they want to play mind games with me. Get in my head before they attack to try and weaken my defences," I surmise casually.

"They messed with the wrong Alpha. Clearly, they know nothing about you if they thought this would rattle you," scoffs Vitali tossing the note on my desk.

"Any thoughts on who it might be?" Asks Tyson, causing me to laugh sarcastically.

"How about anyone against the idea of a female Alpha?" I say pointedly. They each cringe.

"Fair point. Your position pisses a lot of people off," Tyson nods thoughtfully.

Everyone is silent for a few minutes as we think. Then an idea finally comes to me.

"Chris, go get the papers you prepared for Ryker Mathers' inheritance," I instruct. He doesn't question me; he simply nods and zips out of the room in a flash.

"You think it's Ryker?" Vitali questions.

"No idea," I shrug. "But he's certainly a possibility, and one I can look into first."

Chris comes back a few minutes later and hands me the paperwork. I thank him and scan through them to make sure everything is in order. I nod once I see everything is good.

"*Ryker, can you please come to my office,*" I say to Ryker through the pack-link.

"*Fine,*" he says curtly. He's still a prick, but I can't really get too mad at him right now. I did just kill his parents. Though he has yet to seem at all bothered by it, which is another reason for me to suspect him.

"Tyson, open the door please," I instruct, and he does so immediately.

After eleven tedious minutes, Ryker finally graces us with his presence. He walks in and looks around at everyone, confused.

"What's all this?" He asks suspiciously.

"We were just in the middle of a meeting and finishing up a few things," I answer as I hand the papers over to him. "These are regarding your inheritance. We've made sure everything is as it should be, it just requires our signatures and then everything will be in your name moving forward."

"Cool," he says casually and shrugs as he flips through the papers. I don't miss the looks Chris, Tyson, and Vitali give each other. Ryker is scanning the papers at a fast pace, and I know he's not actually reading them. He's quick to grab a pen and sign his name in all the appropriate sections before sliding the paper back to me. "Is that all?" He asks in a laid-back tone.

I nod calmly. "That's everything. I'll sign these and have them filed. The rest is up to you. I'm sorry that this happened, Ryker," I say sympathetically.

"No, you're not," he snorts, getting up.

"I'm not sorry for defending myself and I'm not sorry for preserving my title, but I am sorry that it cost you both your parents," I clarify. It's true, I'm not sorry for killing them. The bastards wanted me dead first. It was a challenge to the death, someone had to die and like hell was it going to be me. Doesn't mean I feel good about making someone an orphan, even a jerk like Ryker.

"Whatever, Amelia. Can I go now?" He asks with a bored huff. Chris glares at him, Tyson growls and Vitali takes a threatening step forward.

"That's 'Alpha' to you. Show some respect," Vitali seethes. Ryker just smirks at him, but you can still see intimidation in his eyes. Betas, Gammas, and Deltas as ranked members hold authority, their wolves are stronger, and their words carry weight. Just not the same level as an Alpha.

"That's all, Ryker. You may leave," I say before he says something that sets these guys off. Ryker waves a hand dismissively and struts out closing the door behind him.

"I fucking hate that twerp," Tyson spits.

"What was that all about?" Vitali asks, while calming himself down. I take the documents and flip to Ryker's signature placing the note down beside it. I examine them side by side.

"Nothing remotely similar in the handwriting," I sigh. Their shoulders slump.

"One suspect down, an unknown amount to go," Chris sighs.

"So, basically we're looking for a needle in a stack of needles. Fantastic," Tyson huffs.

"There's no postal address on this," Vitali points out.

"That means someone hand-delivered it to our PO Box. Tyson, get C.J. to hack their CCTV and see if he can find the person who delivered the letter. Maybe we'll get lucky and have a face to identify," I instruct.

"On it," he nods and runs off to follow my orders.

"For now, we continue as normal, but we keep our eyes and ears open for anything suspicious. I know this could still be a prank, but I don't for one second believe it is and I'd rather not take chances. Also, with the ball three weeks away, I do not need us on the brink of an attack when we have visitors from other packs coming," I tell them as I sit back in my chair.

"We'll handle this, Amelia. No one is messing with our Alpha or our pack," Vitali declares sternly. I smile at him and Chris as he nods in agreement. I'm beyond lucky to have them.

"You're both excused. I have to speak to my dad," I say, rubbing my face. They nod and leave.

You might be thinking I feel angry or upset or scared. I honestly feel none of those things. I knew challenges lay ahead of me. I even expected attacks, which is why we changed the training routine and have an entirely new and improved patrol system in place. People will come to threaten my position and I won't sit idly by while it happens. I will protect my pack, protect myself and show everyone out there just what happens when you fuck with this Alpha.

***

We're one week away from the Vernal Ball and there has already been another threat mailed to me since then. A generous offer of, 'Give up now and I'll let you live.' It made me feel all warm and fuzzy inside.

As wolves, we're no strangers to violence. When someone wants to pick a fight, we fight. But this person wants to toy with me first, try and get in my head, make me paranoid. Can't say it's working. I'm not scared and I'm definitely not paranoid. In fact, I'm grateful for the letters and I look forward to the next one.

Each letter I receive tells me a bit more about my invisible enemy. In the first letter, they made sure to refer to me by my name, but never call me Alpha directly. This is a blatant form of disrespect among wolves and is enough to start a feud, so this tells me they do not see me as a real Alpha. They want my pack, so that means they're power-hungry. The fact they offered to spare me if I hand over my pack denotes arrogance; they think they're doing me a favour by making this offer. While none of this tells me who the enemy is, it's helping me get into their head far more than they are getting into mine.

I've spent the last hour in the packhouse gym working out while taking work calls and talking to Evalyn, who is doing a more moderate workout alongside me. She's been dealing with a bit of separation anxiety the past couple weeks. For the past two years, she and Tyson have been practically attached at the hip, now with all his new responsibilities as Gamma, they don't have 24/7 time together and she's finding the change difficult.

"I know this is an adjustment for you. You and Tyson have been inseparable. Regardless of his new responsibilities, you will always be his animai and will always be his priority. He'd never let anything come between you guys. Just because you're not around each other all the time doesn't mean you can't be there for Tyson. Show him you're here for him, and then in time maybe start helping him with his Gamma responsibilities,"

I suggest, doing pull-ups while she runs on the treadmill facing the full-length mirror along the back wall.

"How can I possibly help him? You know I'm a crappy fighter," she argues.

"No one is asking you to be a fighter, you don't need to fight to help him. You are strong and smart, talk to each other and I'm sure you can find a way to contribute. It would make you both feel better, I'm sure," I suggest.

"But what would I even do?" She queries.

"Help with pack security? You've got a good head on your shoulders, put it to use. Just talk it over with him and brainstorm ideas," I encourage. Once we're finished in the gym, we make our way towards the dining hall.

"How is ball prep going?" She asks me.

"Really good, it's all coming together perfectly," I say brightly

"I can't wait to see the end result," she chirps as we enter the dining hall.

The dining hall is large enough to fit the entire pack. It has a stained-glass ceiling, tanned hardwood floors and three glass walls with evenly distributed glass doors. Four rows of light brown wooden tables extend down the length of the room, where everyone sits along benches on either side of the tables. Think of the dining hall in Harry Potter, only brighter and no magical ceiling. There are the main entry doors attached to the packhouse along the non-glass wall and, further down to the right, is another set of doors that lead to the kitchen. Along the windows on the left-hand side is a large table with a buffet-style spread where everyone can come and help themselves. It's always an open and friendly atmosphere.

Evalyn and I make our way to the buffet, grab a couple plates, and start serving ourselves up some grub, then find a place to sit. We're in the middle of chatting and eating when I spot Mei nervously entering the dining hall. We quickly get her attention and wave her over, much to her relief. She sits in front of us, throwing her legs over the bench.

"I'm so glad I found you," she says with relief. She's really been coming out of her shell lately, which is great.

"Is something wrong?" I ask in concern, Evalyn looking equally concerned beside me. Evalyn loves Mei and is thrilled to have a sister. They'll officially be sister-in-laws when Mei and Chris mark and mate each other.

"No, nothing is wrong," she smiles softly shaking her head. "I wanted... I know I'm not officially part of your pack yet, but I was hoping I could join training sessions." She pauses to take a deep breath and continues meekly, "Chris is always trying to tell me how strong I am, and I know that's technically true, but I don't *feel* strong, and I definitely don't feel brave. But I want to. I was hoping joining training would help."

I beam at her, this is fantastic! I'm so proud of her. "Of course, you can, I think that would be fantastic for you. You can start off with one-on-one sessions first and ease into training with the pack if you prefer."

"Who would be my trainer?" She asks nervously.

"Tyson or Chris. I could even train you if you want," I tell her. Her eyes light up when I offer myself.

"You would train me? But you're the Alpha now. You're so busy," she frowns.

"It would be my pleasure," I say as I reach out and squeeze her hand. "Besides, given how strong you are, or can be, you may as well go against the strongest person in the pack." I wink at her and she giggles.

"Amelia is a really good trainer. She gave me one-on-one lessons when I was recovering from that cur attack. It made me feel more confident to train around the pack again," Evalyn says encouragingly.

"Okay, let's do it," Mei says with determination, making Evalyn and I grin at each other.

"As for being a pack member, Mei, you know we can do that anytime you want," I tell her.

She goes quiet and picks at her cuticles. "Could we... could we do it now?" She asks quietly stunning me for a second, while Evalyn squeals in delight. I elbow her in the ribs; she winces, shooting me a glare.

"Are you sure?" I ask gently. Mei simply nods. "Let's head to my office then," I say getting up and looking down at Evalyn. "Not a word out of you to anyone. Let Mei be the one to share the good news," I tell her sternly.

She pokes her tongue at me. "I'm not a total idiot," she huffs, rolling her eyes.

Mei gets up and we both make our way to my office. When we get there, I'm stunned to find a bouquet of pink roses nestled into the door handle of my office door. What the hell? I reach forward and take the flowers admiring them. While I hate the colour pink, I have to admit these flowers look and smell lovely.

"Who sent them?" Mei asks. I look for a card but don't find one. I'm trying to pick up a scent, but the smell of the flowers is throwing me off.

"No idea," I shrug.

"Maybe you have a secret admirer," she says happily. I unlock my office using my thumbprint and step in with her. I close the door and place the flowers on my desk.

"As flattering as that is, I'm not interested. I'm happy waiting for my animai." Mei nods in understanding.

"*Damn right we're waiting for our animai. Whoever this mystery jerk is, tell him to take a hike,*" says Zara belligerently.

"*Calm down, you don't even know it's an admirer. They could be thank you flowers. No need to get testy,*" I tell her. This pacifies her as she flops down in my head.

"Will I have to make a speech like you did at your ceremony?" Mei asks me.

I smile, shaking my head. "No, no speech. But you are going to have to drink my blood, I'm afraid," I admit sheepishly.

"Ew," she sneers making me chuckle.

"You just drink a little of my blood and then you'll just feel the connection to the pack snap into place. I know you're not a wolf, but I believe the same rules apply. It may give you a bit of a headache or be overwhelming, but I promise you'll be okay," I explain as delicately as I can.

She nods and pushes her shoulders back. "Let's do this." I smile proudly at her.

I walk over and grab a tumbler off the shelf, let my canines distend, then bite into the flesh of my wrist, drawing blood. I hold my wrist over the glass and let the blood drip in. A few drops land in the glass before my bite heals itself and I let my canines retract. I walk over and hand the glass to Mei.

She takes a breath wrinkling her face in disgust, pinches her nose and downs the drops of blood from the glass while I try not to laugh. Within a moment I feel her thread to me and the pack tie into place, just as she lets out a gasp and her knees buckle slightly. I'm quick to catch her. Her thread feels much stronger than any of the others for some reason.

"I got you. Slow breaths," I instruct while I rub her back. Her face is crumpled up, but she listens and takes slow breaths and within another moment her features relax. She smiles up at me. I blink in stunned surprise at the eyes that are greeting me.

Gone are her chocolate brown eyes, instead replaced by pools of gold with a vertical black slit for a pupil. Takes me a moment to compose myself as I wasn't expecting it, but I manage a welcoming smile.

"Welcome to the Invictus Pack, Mei," I say proudly. Tears form in Mei's reptilian eyes, as she embraces becoming part of the pack. She throws her arms around my neck and hugs me tightly. Too tightly, in fact, her grip is near crushing my bones. She clearly isn't aware of her own strength, but I say nothing as not to dissuade her.

"Thank you so much," she whispers emotionally into my neck. I smile and give her a tight hug in return, though nowhere near as tight as hers.

"Chris will be thrilled when you tell him," I say and I feel her tense in my arms before she lets me go.

What a relief!

I pull back to look at her, noting her eyes return to their human chocolate brown. "What's wrong?" I ask with concern.

She sits in one of the chairs in front of my desk and lowers her head. "I don't deserve him," she says dejectedly, her words surprising me.

I sit in the chair next to hers. "Why do you think that?" I ask gently.

She lets out a deep sigh, her eyes focused on the carpet. "He's so… perfect. He's kind and loving and understanding. He takes such good care of me and never asks for anything in return. Hasn't even once pushed me to mark or mate with him and I'm sure that's very hard for him and Axel. He could have any woman he wants. Why is he wasting his time on someone damaged like me?" She says in a quiet voice full of sadness. I watch her in sympathy. Her insecurities are completely valid, but she's way off about Chris.

"You're wrong, Mei," I say while I take her hand. She slowly looks up at me with unshed tears in her eyes. "Chris is definitely what you say he is. But he and Axel don't want any other woman. You're it for them. You've been it for them before they even met you," I tell her. But she just looks at me in confusion. "Look, this is not my business or my place to say, but I'll take the risk. Mei, Chris is a virgin," I tell her casually. Her eyes widen in shock and her mouth drops open.

"But… he's…" she says trying to form words but is unable to – much to my amusement.

"Handsome? Great catch? So what if he is? That doesn't mean he throws himself at women or takes the offers of women who throw themselves at him. For as long as I've known him, he has always said he only ever wanted to be intimate with the person the Goddess chose for him and no one else. That he would wait for her. He didn't know who she was, who *you* were, but he was willing to wait for you and I know he'll keep waiting until you're ready," I say with a reassuring smile.

Tears fall from her eyes, but there's a loving smile on her face. "How could I be so lucky to find someone like him?" She asks in disbelief.

"He says the same thing about you, and if you ask me, with the shit you've lived through, the universe owed you at least one good thing in your life," I tell her. Mei wipes away her tears and gives me a bright smile while shaking her head.

"I got more than one good thing. I found my soulmate who I adore, his parents treat me like their own daughter and his sister treats me like I'm her sister. Then there are the friends I've been gifted. Friends like you, Amelia," she says with the utmost sincerity making tears well up in my eyes. Taking in the emotional moment we embrace in another hug.

Getting to witness her progress is inspiring and becoming worthy of her friendship touches my heart. Stories have been written about her kind – dramatized of course – they were seen as blessings and protectors. Worshipped as benevolent beings. She feels blessed to have been welcomed into our pack, but I feel like we have been blessed to have her.

I can't help feeling the timing is perfect. Threats are looming on the horizon and the universe just dropped a powerful being into our lap. But first, she needs to get strong; not for me, not for Chris and not for the pack, but for herself. She needs to embrace what she is, and when she does, may the Gods show mercy to anyone who gets in her way.

Chapter Six
Amelia

Standing in front of the full-length mirror in my closet, I look over every inch of myself.. I can't remember the last time I was this nervous. Right now, the urge to throw up is extremely high.

Tonight is the night of the Vernal Ball and I have been working tirelessly to make sure everything is perfect. Mum and Evalyn took over for a bit so I could come upstairs and get ready, and now I'm just trying to steel myself to go back down.

For tonight, I wanted to look my best, so I've gone for a natural look, applying very light makeup. My blonde hair has been styled in curls and pinned into an elegant up-do with opalescent moonstone clips. My dress is probably the most beautiful thing I've ever put on my body. It has a sheer black, high neck at the front with a V-cut in the back and is adorned with black sequined patterns scattered over the sheer fabric. It moves down into a sweetheart bust with a dark green bodice that is also adorned with black sequined patterns. The bodice stops mid-thigh and then flares out in dark green chiffon. I've finished it off with emerald satin open-toe heels that are encrusted with diamonds on the back. I feel so elegant in this dress.

"Our animai is going to love you in that dress. You look stunning!" Zara gushes.

"Thank you for the compliment," I say graciously, while ignoring the first

part of her comment. I don't want to think about it. I just want to focus on being the host.

With that said, I step out of my bedroom and am met with a gasp from my mum. I look up to see her in a stunning burgundy velvet off-the-shoulder gown, and her hair straight-as-a-pin. She's looking at me with tears in her eyes. Dad is next to her in a black tux, a burgundy dress shirt and matching tie. Maybe they do coordinate their outfits. I notice dad has tears in his eyes too.

Oh boy.

"Amelia, sweetheart you look absolutely gorgeous. Beyond words," says my mum in adulation, coming over to kiss my cheeks.

"Thank you, mum, so do you," I say with a smile, taking her hands and squeezing them. I look over at dad who is drying his eyes. "Dad, are you okay?" I ask softly.

He clears his throat and walks to me in two long strides pulling me into a big hug. I relax into his embrace hugging him back. "I can't believe how grown-up you are. What happened to my little pup who was always clinging to my leg?" He asks, his voice thick with emotions.

I try to hold my own emotions back; I'm not redoing this makeup. "I'm still your pup, dad. Just no more leg clinging." My parents chuckle.

He pulls back to look at me while cupping my cheeks. "You're beautiful," he says softly and gently kisses my forehead.

I take a deep breath. "Look, no more making the Alpha cry. You two go down to the ball, I have to go and greet the guests," I instruct.

They smile and walk out arm in arm. I take another deep breath and then finally make my way to the dining hall. I am so proud of how everything has come together. Everything looks just how I envisioned.

The usual full-length tables and benches have been moved to the back of the packhouse and replaced with circular tables. Our pack's colours are green and black, and I've implemented that into tonight's décor and my outfit. The tables are covered in emerald-green tablecloths, with black plates and black cutlery. The chairs are covered in black satin fabric with emerald-green sashes tied around the back. The centrepieces consist of a single emerald candle surrounded by black roses. I know, black roses are a death omen, but I don't believe in flower symbology.

All of the glass doors are open making the space feel more open and inviting. Fairy lights elegantly surround the room and lead to outside where a dancefloor has been set up, with the open doors opening right onto the dancefloor. The music is set up at the right end of the room and speakers are placed both inside and outside. Gentle music is playing to start the evening.

Guests will be entering from a lit path that leads them directly to the open doors on the left and the buffet has been lined up along the main pack entrance wall, so that the glass walls remain unobscured. The bar is just outside next to the dancefloor. Everything is spread out to ensure people move around. Pack members of age are floating in, taking in the atmosphere and getting themselves situated. I do a final check of everything, make my way to the open doors and stand ready to greet our guests.

A low whistle to my left distracts me from my nerves. I turn to see Vitali saddling up to me in a maroon tux with a black dress shirt, black loafers, and maroon tie, his shaggy brown hair still looking very shaggy.

"Damn, Amelia, you look incredible," he says as he stands beside me. As my Beta, he's expected to greet the guests with me.

I give him a wide smile. "And you are looking very dashing. Some of our own she-wolves are already eye-fucking you."

He snorts with laughter, "I guess they have good taste then." He winks and I shake my head. He gives my shoulder a tight squeeze making me look up at him. "This place looks incredible. I'm really proud of you," he tells me softly.

"Thank you, Vitali," I tell him as I pull him into a tight hug. He returns my hug and then lets me go.

"*Tyson, how are the patrols going?*" I link.

"*So far so great. The first few cars are making it through the territory now,*" he tells me.

I take a breath and look up at Vitali, "It's showtime."

One by one, I greet the Alphas of numerous packs. Some have brought their Lunas and Betas and, of course, they have brought many of their single pack members. Some Alphas and their packs give me less than warm greetings, but they're, at least, being civil. I'll take that as a small win.

As I'm greeting guests, I'm aware of the occasional declaration of the word 'mine,' as people find their animais, so I'd say the night is off to a good start. The next group of guests to arrive are from the Dies Lupus Pack, this includes Alpha Drew and Luna Siobhan, their Beta Jacob and many of their pack members.

"Alpha Drew, Luna Siobhan, Beta Jacob," I say as I extend my hand in greeting. "It is a pleasure to have you as our guests. This is my Beta Vitali," I say introducing Vitali who greets and shakes their hands.

"Everything looks exquisite, Alpha Amelia, I'm sure many memorable moments will be made tonight," says Luna Siobhan enthusiastically.

"Congratulations on becoming Alpha, though I heard it was a rocky start," says Alpha Drew with concern.

"Thank you, Alpha Drew. But it was nothing I couldn't handle," I say nonchalantly.

"I couldn't believe it when I heard it. I never thought the former Beta was capable of such betrayal. He's learned his lesson now, though," he says smugly.

"Hopefully everyone else will take the hint," says Vitali.

"Yes indeed. But do know you have an ally in me, Alpha Amelia," Alpha Drew says warmly.

I smile in gratitude, "I greatly appreciate the support."

Just then I notice Vitali go stiff as a board beside me. I look up to see his nostrils flared, and his hazel eyes glowing. One of the Dies Lupus pack members steps forward and shouts that famous word 'mine' directly at Vitali. For a split second, I see elation and love shine in Vitali's eyes before it quickly morphs into confusion and anger. His eyes dull down and, in a flash, he is bolting in the other direction out the door at the opposite end of the room.

Shit.

Standing next to Luna Siobhan, looking utterly devastated, is a young man who apparently is Vitali's animai. I was not expecting that and based on Vitali's reaction he wasn't either. He's a very attractive young man, short, cropped brown hair, beautiful blue eyes, sharp nose, sharp, pointed jaw with a hint of stubble. White skin with a natural glow, looking very handsome in a grey tux, a white dress shirt and black tie. Come to think of it, he reminds me of Taron Egerton.

Luna Siobhan wraps a comforting arm around the young man who looks so lost and hurt, I want to hug him.

"Eric, it'll be okay," says Alpha Drew, patting him on the shoulder, nothing but sympathy in his eyes. The man named Eric just nods, unable to lift his head.

Damn, damn, damn.

"Chris, I need you to come to the entrance and take over greeting guests, I have to go find Vitali. Don't ask, just get here," I order him. Within a flash, Chris is at my side looking concerned.

"Where's–" I start to ask where Mei is, but Chris anticipates my question.

"With my sister. I wouldn't leave her alone," he says. Of course, I shouldn't have even asked.

I reach out and squeeze Eric's shoulder. "Eric, is it? Please go inside with your pack. I'll bring him to you, I promise," I say softly.

He looks at me with heartbreak in his eyes. "He doesn't want me," he says in a broken voice.

I shake my head. "He's just confused. I'll talk to him," I reassure him and nod at Alpha Drew.

Alpha Drew nods back and escorts his pack members into the hall. I take a deep breath and head out the other side of the hall. I follow Vitali's scent until I find him in the bushes pacing like a maniac and kicking up the dirt.

I sigh. "Vitali…" I call his name gently. He freezes and snaps his head towards me.

"I'm not gay, Amelia," he defensively.

"No one is saying that," I tell him, as I slowly walk closer to him.

"Really? That damn Goddess seems to be saying it. She fated me to a guy! A guy! What the fuck?!" He shouts gripping his hair.

I move closer pulling him into a hug and holding him tight. "Breathe. I want you to breathe," I coach him with a soothing tone. His body weight slumps into me as he buries his face in my neck. I feel a teardrop hit my neck as he clings to me like I'm a life raft. "She fated you to someone who will make you happy and love you. Isn't it at all possible that you're bi, or pan or omni or any other sexuality other than straight?" I ask him delicately. "Are you saying you've never thought of another man that way?" I press, still trying to be cautious. He immediately looks away from me, not able to look me in the eyes. I sigh. "Vitali, I'm your best friend. Why didn't you ever tell me?" I ask cupping his face.

He lets out a haggard breath as he slowly looks down at me. Tears in his eyes as his chin quivers. "We're wolves, Amelia. Everything about us is meant to be about survival of the fittest, carrying on the species. If people knew the truth, they'd think I was a weak wolf. We're not supposed to… I mean, it makes no sense." he says quietly.

"Don't you dare start giving me that shit," I scoff. "I'm not supposed to be a female Alpha, but here I am. And who was there by my side every step of the way despite all the odds, despite all the cruel things people said? You were. Do you really think I would ever turn you away for something like this? Reject you for just being yourself?"

I don't know why I'm shouting. Maybe I'm a little hurt, or maybe I'm just angry that someone I care about has been denying themselves all these years while supporting me the whole time. I feel like a fucking failure as a friend. He takes a deep breath, tears slipping down his cheeks.

"So, you like men and women, what's the big fucking deal? You're still my best friend and still my Beta; still someone I'd trust with my life," I tell him firmly.

His arms engulf me in a bear hug as he nuzzles into my neck. "Thank you," he whispers with so many emotions in his voice. I squeeze him tight. "I really fucked up in there, didn't I? Goddess, he must hate me," he gulps looking scared.

I rub his back and smile. "He doesn't hate you. He thinks you hate him," I say, and Vitali's face crumples in guilt. I take his hands in mine. "How does Blaise feel?" I ask.

He takes a breath before answering. "He's happy. Well, he's furious with me, but he just wants his animai," he tells me sadly, but I smile and nod. It's always the human side that has issues, not the wolf side. I mean, if the Goddess has no issue pairing two men together, I don't see why it should be the concern of lower beings.

"And ignoring what everyone else thinks, what did you feel when you saw him?" I ask him as a warm smile creeps up on his face.

"I was really happy. I just wanted to pull him into my arms and not let go," he admits.

"There you have it then!" I exclaim, slapping him on the back. "Now let's go in there and find your soulmate, who is very handsome, by the way. I'm surprised Goddess Zarseti felt you were worthy of such a looker," I tease.

"Bitch," he says through narrowed eyes and I laugh.

Wrapping my arm around him, I guide him back into the hall. The nerves roll off him in waves as I lead him to the table where Eric is sitting. Before we reach the table, Eric is out of his seat, watching us apprehensively.

Poor guy.

"Eric, this is my Beta Vitali. Vitali, this is Eric," I introduce them, giving Vitali a gentle push forward. Their eyes lock on each other, their heartbeats competing for first place in a sprint.

"Eric..." Vitali whispers reverently. Instantly Eric pulls him into a bone-crushing embrace and slowly Vitali relaxes, giving himself over to the other half of his soul and wrapping his arms around him.

The beautiful sight brings tears to my eyes. Crisis averted. Thank the Gods! Well, thank *me*, technically.

As I'm stepping back to give the new couple some space, Zara starts pacing anxiously in my head. Before I have the chance to ask her what's wrong, I'm hit by the most incredible scent of Caramel, my favourite flavour in all things.

The intoxicating scent is flooding my senses and I can barely focus. My feet start moving of their own accord in search of the source. I move past a few people and that's when I see him – time stops. All sights and sounds funnel out and all I can see is him.

"ANIMAI! HE'S OUR ANIMAI!" Zara starts screaming like a foghorn.

She didn't have to say it. I knew it as soon as I smelt him. He looks…
there are no words to describe him. He is positively the most gorgeous man
to ever walk the face of this earth.

He's 6'5", with luscious shoulder-length black hair that I desperately
want to run my fingers through. He has deeply tanned skin and his green
eyes with brown flecks – that remind me of the forest in spring – are glowing
brightly as he stares at me. I think I've stopped breathing. He's inhumanly
gorgeous. He has a wide jaw, a full, but pointed, nose and plump lips that
I want to devour, nestled among a neat, short black beard. He's wearing a
navy-blue tux with a black lapel, black shiny loafers, and white dress shirt
that is slightly unbuttoned at the top, exposing a hint of his extremely
muscular and smooth pectoral muscles. The tux hugs him so snugly that I
can tell underneath, he is an absolute beast.

And he's all mine.

As if reading each other's minds we walk to each other, our eyes never
leaving each other. His minty fresh breath with a hint of bourbon, hits my
face and my knees nearly give out. His hand reaches up and the back of
his fingers graze ever so lightly against my cheek. My eyes roll back in my
head as a soft gasp leaves my lips. His touch is electrifying. It's sending an
addictive current through every inch of my body, making the muscles at
the apex of my thighs clench in need. He's barely even touched me and I'm
already a mess.

"Mine," he whispers in a deep, husky voice and I gulp and shiver at the
sound of it.

Holy crap!

"Right backatcha," I manage to say in a breathy voice. I watch as his
Adam's apple bobs before he gives me a literally heart-stopping smile.

Oh fuck.

His hand drops down and he intertwines his fingers with mine and that
addictive electricity spreads through me once again. He starts guiding me
past the tables and out the door I just came through to a stone bench nearby.

I'm too absorbed in the feel of my hand in his to even question what's going on. He sits down and tugs me down next to him, not letting go of my hand, which works for me.

"You're so beautiful," he tells me, his eyes no longer glowing. My cheeks, however, heat up a few degrees. I'd say 'you too' but beautiful doesn't cover the god-like specimen before me.

"*You can say that again. Our animai is yummy as hell!*" Zara swoons in my head.

"What's your name?" I ask him, slowly regaining my composure.

"Marcus," he says grinning. Oh, that smile should be illegal! "And what is your name?" He asks as he plants a kiss on the back of my hand, causing a shiver to ripple through me and my breath to hitch.

"Amelia," I answered smiling at him. He nods as if he's contemplating my name. "I've never seen you at one of these before," I say. He runs his fingers through his hair making me envious that his fingers get to do that and mine don't.

"I'm starting to regret that now. I might have met you sooner," he chuckles. "I'm the Beta of my pack and I usually stay behind to take care of things. My Alpha only found his Luna not that long ago," he explains. That's pretty fair.

"Who is your Alpha?"

"Alpha Jasper," he answers proudly.

"Oh! You're from the Aurum Obscuro Pack," I say enthusiastically. They are a really nice pack, they're also the largest pack in North America with just over 3000 pack members. "I'm very familiar with Alpha Jasper, he's a good man," I say with a smile, which he returns.

Alpha Jasper is my favourite Alpha, after my dad and grandpa.

"Yeah, he is. He's my best friend too; more like my brother. I actually wasn't going to come tonight, but he ordered me to," he says shaking his head, his beautiful hair moving majestically around his face.

"Remind me to send him a thank you card," I say, taking his hands in mine. He glances at our hands and then looks up at me. No one has ever looked at me with so much adoration before. It's overwhelming. He takes a moment to look me over slowly, taking me in like I'm a drink of water and he's been deprived for weeks. His teeth sink into his lower lip and I'm mesmerised by the action. My brain instantly pictures him sinking those teeth into my flesh. Gods, he's perfect.

Thank you, Goddess Morrtemis for creating this man and thank you Goddess Zarseti for giving him to me.

"You look absolutely breathtaking," he breathes, as he cups my cheek in his palm. My eyes close as his touch again ignites my body, yet somehow relaxing it at the same time. I find myself leaning into his touch. "Can I kiss you?" He asks softly. My eyes fly open to meet his and all I can do is nod. I want nothing more than for him to kiss me. Thankfully he doesn't make me wait.

With his hand still cupping my cheek, he leans in toward me, slowly, his eyes assessing me. I lean in, closing the space between us and he places his lips on mine. There's an explosion of electricity. Warm, wet pillows move against my lips at a soft and tantalising rhythm, which I happily return. Our lips move against each other, our breath mingling; the smell of his minty breath and the bourbon still lingering on his tongue. His caramel scent combines to send me into sensory overload.

My fingers make their way into his luxurious hair, feeling perfectly at home nestled among his black locks as our lips continue to move in sync. An involuntary moan escapes my lips and at the sound of it he deepens our kiss and again I match him eagerly. His tongue brushes against my lips sending delightful shivers through my body. My core tightens and clenches as his lips send my hormones into a frenzy. A deep erotic growl rises from his throat as soon as my arousal hits his senses, and it makes me gulp.

Our lips break apart as we gasp for air, our foreheads pressing against each other. In this moment everything is perfect, perfect in ways I never thought existed.

"So, um… which pack are you from?" He asks sheepishly, and I can't help the laugh that bursts out of me. He smiles at me, his eyes twinkling with delight, "What's so funny?"

"You just kissed the life out of me and the first thing you ask me is what pack I'm from?" I snort with laughter, and he quickly joins me.

"Okay, that was pretty lame of me. I just really want to get to know you," he says sincerely. I smile at him and let my fingers stroke his jawline as his eyes close and he leans into my touch.

"This is my pack," I tell him.

Wait, does he not know who I am? A wave of apprehension hits.

"Stop being so negative. After that kiss, no way is he letting us get away," Zara says confidently, though for some reason, I don't share her confidence.

Animais are supposed to love you unconditionally. Our worlds start and end with each other. But... I quickly push down the negative thoughts flooding my brain before they get out of hand. His hands cup my face, calming my nerves instantly, and I can't help but sigh in content.

"Are you okay? You seemed a bit panicked there for a moment," he asks me with concern.

"I'm fine," I say shaking my head. Zara is right, I need to stop being so negative. "Tell me more about you," I encourage him.

Time slips away from us as we go back and forth talking about anything and everything. While everything I'm learning about him is new, I feel like I've known all of this all my life. It's a crazy feeling, but it is equally incredible.

"I don't know anyone who rock climbs as a hobby," I comment with interest.

"It's amazing. The adrenaline, the workout. The view once you make it to the top. It's like being on top of the world," he says serenely and I smile.

How did I get so lucky?

"Maybe you can take me some time," I suggest.

His eyebrows rise in surprise. "You'd want to? It can get pretty rough," he says in warning.

I snort and wave a hand dismissively. "I think I can handle it. Plus having you as an instructor is quite the incentive," I smirk.

He grins at me pulling me close, my body automatically moulding into his. "It would be my pleasure," he whispers as he leans in closer to me.

Just before our lips can touch an ear-piercing scream filled with pain comes from inside the hall and I am instantly on my feet.

What the fuck just happened?

Vitali is at the doorway in a flash, his worried eyes meeting mine. "Amelia hurry! It's Jennifer!" He shouts.

Oh no.

I look up at Marcus who is now standing and looks both worried and confused. "I'm sorry, I have to handle this." While my very soul wants to stay with him, my pack needs me.

At mutolupus speed, I race into the hall with Vitali hot on my heels. I see a crowd gathered around something… no, someone, on the floor. I push everyone aside to find a pale Jennifer collapsed on the floor. I drop to my knees and hold her face looking her over. There's no colour in her cheeks and her heartbeat has dropped significantly, filling me with dread.

"*Doctor Richard, I need you at the dining hall immediately!*" I shout through the pack-link.

"*On my way, Alpha,*" he replies. I brush her hair out of her face then look around at everyone watching with either concern or curiosity.

"Someone want to tell me what the hell just happened?" I demand.

"Ask him," spits Vitali venomously. I look up and follow his eye line to find a young man staring down at Jennifer with shock and horror all over his face and sweat on his brow. He looks eighteen or nineteen. I look between them… dear Goddess, please tell me he didn't.

"What happened?" I ask hesitantly, fearing the answer I'll receive. I'm aware of Marcus approaching from behind me. I can feel his presence and smell his scent around me, but I don't focus on it.

"I… I rejected her…" he says in a shameful whisper. Gasps escape from people around the room and growls resound from my pack members. Jennifer is a treasure to us all, we adore her. To know someone did this to her has everyone out for blood. I have to swallow the bile rising up my throat.

"Silence!" I order my pack members with my Alpha Spirit. I need everyone calm; I do not want this turning into a bloodbath. I turn my attention back to the young man. "Why?" I ask through gritted teeth. He says nothing, though I have a suspicion. "If you have the guts to reject her, then you have the guts to say why. Spit it out!" I demand, my Alpha Spirit pushing forward making him whimper. I may not be his Alpha, but I'm still an Alpha and therefore his wolf can't help but be submissive to me.

"She... she's an..."

"Spit. It. Out," I seethe, making him gulp.

"She's an Omega," he finally admits. I fucking knew it. I scoff in disgust.

In that moment Doctor Richard shows up. Alpha Lucas of the Alpine Pack stands behind him, looking at Jennifer with concern and shooting daggers at the young man. Doctor Richard begins examining her, a frown growing on his brow, and I know it's not good. But still, I hope for good news.

"Has she accepted his rejection?" Richard asks me.

I glance over at the young man, "Based on the lack of pain on his face, I'd say no."

Richard sighs. *"Jennifer is already much weaker than other Omegas. Even a strong Omega at the best of times has lost their life to a rejection, their wolf unable to survive the pain. Half the rejection has nearly killed her. Finishing it will indeed take her life,"* he tells me privately, his words full of sorrow.

I shake my head adamantly. "She's not dying," I vow.

I pull Jennifer's limp body into my arms and hold my hand against her cheek.

"Zara, I need your help. We need to focus on healing her," I tell her.

"Ready when you are," Zara tells me.

I close my eyes and together Zara and I focus on the pack-link, specifically looking for the thread that ties us to Jennifer. Once we find it, we project our healing through the pack-link and directly into Jennifer.

This is something Zara and I learned we could do a couple years ago. We'd never heard of another wolf doing it, but we somehow knew to try. We're able to share any of our wolf abilities with a member of our pack and right now I'm hoping I can use it to save Jennifer. Slowly her eyes flutter open and meet mine.

"A-Alpha Amelia? What... what's happening?" She asks weakly, her eyes barely staying open. Goddess forgive me and be with me.

"Jennifer, sweetie. I need you to look at me. I am so, so sorry, but I have to ask you. Do you accept your animai's rejection?" I ask her gently. As soon as the words are out, tears spill from her eyes and a look of undiluted heartbreak spreads over her features and my heart clenches at the sight. "I know it hurts, but I need to know," I press.

She tries to breathe through her sobs, managing a stiff nod. That's all I needed. I pull her up and rest her back against me, wrapping my arms around her shoulders, securing her in place. Richard is watching in fear. But he makes no move to stop me. He trusts me and for that, I'm grateful.

"Whenever you're ready, say the words," I gently encourage her. I take a breath and, with Zara push every ounce of our strength through the link and into Jennifer. I feel my Alpha Spirit radiating off me, but I keep my focus on Jennifer.

"I… Jennifer Ryder, against the will of Goddess Zarseti, accept your rejection, Landry Green," she sobs as another scream tears through her, though it's nothing like the first one. Her scream, however, is overshadowed by the scream coming from her animai. Landry drops to the ground clutching his chest as he writhes in agony, tears pouring down his face.

Good, I hope it hurts. His pack members surround him and try to help him. It all becomes too much for Jennifer and she falls unconscious in my arms. Her pulse sounds steady at least. I take a deep breath, grateful she survived, though I barely call this surviving.

"Doctor Richard, please take her home. I want her sedated and I want two nurses watching over her, alternating shifts. Monitor her condition and continue to sedate her if you feel she needs it. I'm sure you agree, her body needs time to heal," I order him gently.

He nods, a look of sympathy on his face, as he looks over Jennifer. "I'll make sure she's okay," he sighs. "I helped bring her into this world. I didn't lose her then and I won't lose her now. Though I never could have expected this for her," he says, crestfallen. He takes Jennifer into his arms and carries her through the crowd.

As I get to my feet, I encourage the crowd to disperse and return to what they were doing. The atmosphere around me is so thick, not even a knife could cut through it and I'm finally aware of a particular set of eyes burning into me. I turn around and see the eyes that remind me of the forest in spring are looking at me, but that adoration I saw in them earlier is gone.

My stomach drops and those nerves are back in full force. Marcus is looking down at me with a mixture of shock and confusion. I want to be wrong but, honestly, he looks a little appalled. My palms are sweating and Zara is whimpering. This is very bad. Despite alarm bells ringing, I stand tall and don't let it bother me as I step towards him.

"You're the Alpha?" He asks disdainfully, and I feel the wind get knocked out of me.

Here we go again.

Chapter Seven
Marcus

I've never wanted to go to these events. I've always been more than happy to stay at the packhouse and tend to business. Anything that gets me out of going to one of these stupid balls. It's like the mutolupus version of speed-dating if you ask me. A bunch of singles coming together, moving around a big room hoping to find a partner. And if you don't find them, you leave feeling like shit. Not my idea of a fun time.

I'd love to find my animai. I'm twenty-four now and, while I enjoy casual hook-ups, they don't satisfy that empty feeling that can only be filled by your soulmate. Yet, I still don't like going to these events. Call me stubborn.

We're sitting in the Peugeot Traveller on our way to the Invictus Pack for the yearly Vernal Ball. It's their turn to host this year. In our car are two warriors riding up front, then me, my Alpha Jasper, and my Luna Isabelle in the back. It's an eight-seater, two seats up front, six in the back: two rows of three facing each other, foldable tables in the middle. We travel and live very comfortably.

I'm sitting facing Jasper and Isabelle, sipping my bourbon on ice, and dreading each passing second as we make our approach. There better be an open bar at this thing.

"Are you okay, my love?" Jasper asks Isabelle while he rubs her hand comfortingly.

She gives him a small smile. "I'm fine. It's just hard being away from Blake. But I will be okay. I know I need to get used to it," she says calmly and Jasper kisses her cheek reassuringly.

The two are in matching formal attire, Isabelle in a baby-pink flowing dress with capped sleeves, a V-neck and a slit down the side. It compliments her shape and the colour suits her fair skin and blonde hair. Jasper went for a simple charcoal suit with white shirt and a baby pink tie to match Isabelle. The pink really pops against his ebony skin.

Jasper isn't just my Alpha; we've been best friends since birth. He's more like an annoying older brother even though he's only older by two months. He finally found his animai and Luna – Isabelle – last year and they were pregnant with their first pup almost immediately. They wasted no time. Isabelle gave birth last month and this is her first time going somewhere without him. They're great friends of mine and I'm honoured to serve as their Beta. I'll even admit their son is pretty cute, too. But, as much as I love them, I'm still annoyed I got dragged into going to this. Can't believe Jasper pulled rank on me for this shit.

"Are you going to be brooding all night?" Jasper smirks at me.

I glare at him. "I should be back at the packhouse making sure things are handled in your absence."

"That's what I have a Gamma and Delta for. It's important for you to attend these, too. Not just in hopes of finding your animai, but because it is important for inter-pack relations," he says as if explaining it to a child.

"Yes dad, I'm well aware," I say bitterly. He chuckles and shakes his head.

"Besides, we all know you wouldn't have been spending your time combing through paperwork. You'd have probably called Davina to keep you company," Isabelle says snidely.

Here it comes.

Davina is my ex, we dated for a couple months a couple years ago and that's time I'll never get back. The sex was great, but she was a bit too obsessed with wanting us to mark each other even though we aren't fated. My wolf Ace was vehemently against the idea and so was I, so I ended things. But we do still hook up occasionally – or used to.

"And the problem with that is…? I'm a man with needs, Isabelle," I shrug.

"You want to hook up with people, that's fine, but you need to stay away from Davina. She's obsessed with you and every time you call her up, it just encourages her," she scolds. I know that she's right, which is why I haven't bothered with Davina. I just hate being lectured.

"She's right, Marcus. Davina's already banned from the packhouse for breaking Quinn's nose after you gave her a hug," he says with disgust. We were all pissed off that day.

Quinn is a sweet Omega who works in the kitchen at the packhouse. I saw her crying one day – turned out her human mum was pretty sick – and she was naturally upset. I tried to comfort her and gave her a hug to make her feel better. Just so happened, at that moment Davina showed up and felt the need to lay some stupid claim on me. She yanked Quinn out of my arms and decked her. Broke her fucking nose.

I was livid, so were Jasper and Isabelle, so they banned Davina from the packhouse and forbid her from shifting for a month. She spent a week texting and calling, apologising and telling me she loved me. I got so sick of it; I blocked her number. I haven't gone near her since the Quinn incident.

I finish my drink and put the glass back into the bar area.

"Are you two done lecturing me? I'm here with you, aren't I? And I fully supported you banning Davina, Quinn didn't deserve that shit. Can we talk about something else for the rest of the drive?" I ask sitting back rubbing my temples. This night sucks already.

We finally arrive and are welcomed into the territory by the patrols. We drive up to the packhouse and everyone starts unloading from the cars. We have three other cars with us filled with single wolves hoping to find their soulmates. The whole thing is just weird.

Jasper helps Isabelle out of the car and keeps her tucked under his arm, the two of them still as lovesick as the day they met. I'm extremely happy for them; they are a great couple, but I can't help being a little envious. I know I play the field, but I really do want what they have. I want someone I can come home to.

Once we're out of the cars and everyone is organised, we follow a trail lined by fairy lights that leads to an open set of glass double doors. I see this is where the ball is being held. Fairy lights are everywhere, giving the night an enchanting glow. The hall is surrounded on three sides by walls of glass and a gorgeous stained-glass ceiling. The wall along the right-hand side adjoins the packhouse. The place looks… magical.

It's decked out in a green and black theme, which I rather like. There's a dancefloor outside, a DJ and, to my relief, an open bar. The sounds of music and mingling fill the air, but there's something else that has the hair on the back of my neck standing on end. Ace is pacing in my head getting antsy all of a sudden.

"What's with you?" I ask him, but he just huffs and says nothing. Fine, be that way.

Our group finally gets to the front, and we're greeted by a guy in a dark green tux with a white shirt and black tie, his hair up in a bun.

"Alpha Jasper, Luna Isabelle, it is an honour to have you and your pack members join us tonight. I'm Delta Chris," he greets us in a friendly manner.

Jasper reaches out to shake his hand. "Pleasure to meet you Delta, the gentleman behind us is my Beta, Marcus." I give the Delta a stiff nod. "Where is your Alpha this evening? Is everything alright?" Jasper asks, with genuine concern.

Why is he so concerned about their Alpha?

"Everything is fine, Alpha Jasper; our Beta just found his animai and it took him by surprise. Alpha just went to make sure everything is fine and left me in charge of the meet and greets for a bit," he explains cheerfully.

"Oh, congratulations to your Beta! That's wonderful news!" Exclaims Isabelle. She's a tough Luna, but she's a romantic at heart.

I step closer, hoping to urge everyone to step inside when I catch a whiff of a scent lingering in the doorway. It's a little faint, so whoever it belongs to was here a few moments ago. I can't focus on anything around me. All I can focus on is the intoxicating scent of mangos and pineapples. Goddess, it's driving me crazy.

"It's our animai's scent! Go find her!" Ace yells.

"You don't have to tell me twice," I answer. I completely ignore the Delta and my pack and storm into the hall. I'm on a mission. My soulmate is here, and I need to find her.

The scent is consuming my every thought, this tropical aroma has already captivated me. I haven't even seen her yet and I know she's perfect. I'm following the scent through the crowd when I see her and for a moment my heart stops. She's the most exquisite thing I've ever seen in my whole entire life.

Glowing turquoise eyes stare at me like two bright fireflies, guiding me to her. She's about 5'8 with the perfect hourglass shape that I desperately want to outline with my hands. Her body looks toned, no defined musculature, but I can tell she works out. Her white skin looks radiant in a green and black gown that hugs her body perfectly. I'm a little jealous of her gown, to be honest. I want to cling to her body like that.

She has blonde hair that reminds me of sunshine, but it's curled and put in an up-do with jewels scattered through her hair. A perfect button nose, delicate little lips that I want to feast on, and a cute round chin I want to caress. There's something strong about her that's not registering in my head right now. Goddess, everything about her is like she's my own personal tropical vacation. The scent, the sunshine hair, the eyes the colour of clear beach waters. She's my paradise.

Like magnets pulled together, we start walking towards each other. We're close enough for me to feel the heat radiating off her body. Her scent hits me in full force and I just want to bask in it forever. I'm desperate to touch her, taste her, hold her. I need this woman like I need air. I reach up and gently brush the back of my hand against her cheek. She gasps at my touch; her eyes rolling back, and the most satisfying and erotic burst of electricity explodes up my fingers and through my body before making a b-line right for my groin.

Fucking hell! This woman might be the death of me, but what a way to go.

"Mine," I whisper, the need evident in my voice. I hear her gulp and watch a small shiver roll through her. The sight of it makes my dick twitch. Just the sound of my voice gets a reaction out of her.

"Right backatcha," she says in a breathy voice full of the same need as me.

Fuck me dead, she has the sexiest voice I've ever heard. Hearing it now makes me gulp. I can't help the smile that splits across my face hearing her acknowledge me as hers too. I need to be alone with her. I don't want to have this moment around all these people. I reach down and take her hand, intertwining our fingers and relishing how perfectly her hand fits in mine. Electricity rushes through me. I tug and guide her out the back and look for somewhere to sit. I see a stone bench a few steps away and take a seat on it, pulling her down beside me, not once letting her hand go.

I can't take my eyes off her. Can someone be this perfect? I'm convinced she's a goddess instead of a wolf. That would make more sense.

"You're so beautiful," I tell her, though the word hardly does her justice. Her cheeks turn a beautiful shade of pink and I badly want to kiss them.

"Yes, kiss her! Then mark and mate with her!" Ace cheers in my head.

"As tempting as that is, I want to get to know her first," I say, much to his displeasure.

"What's your name?" She asks me, her eyes are back to normal, and she looks like she's getting in control of herself. Makes me wonder what she'd be like out of control.

"Marcus," I tell her. "And what is your name?" I ask her while I gently kiss her hand. Fuck, her skin feels so soft and the contact is making my lips tingle. I just want to kiss every last inch of her. She shivers again and again, it excites me.

"Amelia," she breathes, a beautiful smile on her face. Amelia. Her name is as beautiful as she is. Sounds familiar, though. "I've never seen you at one of these before," she comments. Damn it. I'm going to get such a big 'I told you so' from Jasper now.

How many of these has she attended?

How many times have I missed the chance to have her?

Fuck, I'm an idiot.

"I'm starting to regret that now. I might have met you sooner," I chuckle, laughing at my own stupidity. "I'm the Beta of my pack and I usually stay behind to take care of things since my Alpha only recently found his Luna," I try to explain, feeling guilty for making her wait for me. I leave out the part about my stubborn ass hating balls. She nods as if my answer is acceptable.

"Who is your Alpha?" She asks casually.

"Alpha Jasper," I say, puffing out my chest a little. We're the biggest and best pack in the country. Being the Beta and having him as my Alpha and best friend is an honour.

"Oh! You're from the Aurum Obscuro Pack," she smiles enthusiastically. Of course she's heard of us, everyone has. "I'm familiar with Alpha Jasper, he's a good man," she says sincerely. She must be the daughter of a ranked wolf, so it's not too surprising she's met Jasper. He's very friendly and likes to meet everyone.

"Yeah, he is. He's my best friend too; more like my brother. I actually wasn't going to come tonight but he ordered me to," I say shaking my head at the fact that I, once again, almost missed the chance to meet my animai because I'm an idiot. I owe Jasper a thank you, but he'd be too smug about it.

"Remind me to send him a thank you card," she says softly while taking my hands in hers. Her touch is the most incredible thing I've ever felt. I don't ever want her to stop touching me.

I once again find myself lost in her eyes; her eyes that remind me of a tropical beach. My tropical goddess. How have I lived so long without her in my life? It's like I was sleepwalking through life before I met her. Even though we just met, I feel like I've known her all my life.

"You look absolutely breathtaking," I tell her because it's the truth. Her cheeks flush that beautiful pink again and I can't resist the urge to take her face in my hands. Her eyes close at my touch and she lets out a soft sigh that warms my heart. Her face fits in my hands so perfectly, like this is where they were meant to be. "Can I kiss you?" I ask softly. I've never asked before, but she's the most precious thing in my world. I want to know she wants me to kiss her.

Her eyes fly open, and she gives me a gentle nod. Thank Goddess! I lean in towards her but hold back a little, giving her one final chance to change her mind because there's no going back after this. She closes the gap between us, and I take the chance to place my lips on hers. The moment our lips touch it's like every cell in my body comes alive. Kissing has never felt this good. I caress her delicate lips with my own, enjoying every stroke our lips make. She weaves her fingers into my hair and the contact sends another jolt to my dick.

Fucking hell, it's like I've never been touched before now.

Our kiss continues – much to my pleasure – and just when I think it can't get better a soft, sexy moan comes from her mouth. The sound of it has me hard, instantly. Fuck, she has the sexiest moan ever. I want to hear it again. I deepen our kiss, now kissing her with more urgency and she keeps up with the pace I set, kissing me with just as much urgency. I brush my tongue against her lips to tease her and I'm rewarded with another shiver from her gorgeous body and then…

Holy. Fuck.

The scent of her arousal hits me like a fucking wrecking ball, the smell of it invading my senses and eliciting a growl from deep in my chest. I want to claim her so fucking bad. She gulps and the sound of it is so sexy, I'm now painfully hard.

As much as I want to claim her, I don't want to rush this. She's too precious and I want everything to be perfect. So, with great difficulty, I let us break apart and take in air. But I'm not ready to let her go, so I rest my forehead against hers and breathe in her tropical scent.

Shit, I was about to claim her, and I know nothing about her. I'm such an ass.

"So, um… which pack are you from?" I ask, feeling like a moron. To my surprise, she bursts out laughing and it's the most beautiful thing I've ever heard. Her laugh is infectious, I can't help smiling at the sound of it. "What's so funny?"

"You just kissed the life out of me and the first thing you ask me is what pack I'm from?" She says, still laughing and now I'm laughing too because she has a point. Why was that my first question? When did I become such a novice?

"Around the time you met our amazing soulmate," Ace teases, and I ignore him. He's such a jerk.

"Okay, that was pretty lame of me. I just really want to get to know you," I tell her honestly. She smiles and runs her fingers along my jaw, and the feel of her fingers instantly soothes me.

"This is my pack," she answers, but a second later I feel her body tense.

I open my eyes to look at her and she looks panicked, her heart has started to thump faster in her chest and this time it's not from arousal.

Did I say something?

Do something?

Has the pack hurt her?

I know there are some fucked up packs out there, if this is one of them and they have hurt my animai, I'll fucking kill every last wolf here. I cup her face in my hands hoping to calm her down.

"Are you okay? You seemed a bit panicked there for a moment," I point out, still feeling a little worried. She manages to compose herself, her heartbeat slowing down. I'm impressed how easily she's able to regulate her heartrate.

She shakes her head. "I'm fine. Tell me more about you." She appears more relaxed, which relaxes me.

We fall into the best conversation I have ever had. We talk about everything. I learn her favourite colour is green and she hates pink. Though I'm starting to love the colour, at least the shade of pink her cheeks turn when she blushes. She loves horror movies – which I was not expecting. I tell her how I like to fix cars and that my favourite hobby is rock climbing. She even suggests tagging along next time – which again surprises me. I get a bit nervous, I wouldn't want her to get hurt and you need to be pretty strong for it. However, she just waves me off saying she can handle it. She jokes about having me as an instructor being an incentive and I have to admit, I love the idea too.

Talking is so effortless with her and so is the flirting. I pull her into me ready for another round of kissing when a scream cuts through the air and puts me immediately on edge. Amelia is on her feet before I can even register what's going on. Just then a guy in a maroon tux appears in the doorway.

"Amelia hurry! It's Jennifer!" He shouts, his features a mix of anger and fear. I immediately stand up. Has something happened to one of Amelia's friends?

"I'm sorry, I have to handle this," she tells me and before I can even blink, she's gone back into the hall. I wish she had waited for me, but I can tell this is an emergency.

I follow her scent and find her on the floor tending to a young woman while guests surround them. The poor girl looks sickly pale and her heartbeat is dangerously slow.

"What happened?" Amelia asks looking at a young man who looks scared shitless.

"I… I rejected her…" he says quietly, looking down in shame. Several people around him gasp, but I'm surprised when a number of them growl furiously in his direction. I mean, rejection is a dick thing to do, but it's his choice.

"Silence!" She orders, with so much authority in her voice, my jaw drops. The wave of energy that spreads out from her hits me hard. The growling immediately stops, and several people lower their heads.

She… she used the Alpha Spirit. But, only an Alpha can do that…

I watch the scene unfold while my brain still tries to put two and two together. I keep ending up with five.

"Why?" She asks the man through her gritted teeth. She's furious. The guy remains mute, like a dumbass. "If you have the guts to reject her, then you have the guts to say why. Spit it out!" She demands, authority and dominance dripping off every word. I shake my head not wanting to believe what's happening. The guy stutters and Amelia is getting fed up. "Spit. It. Out." she seethes. A part of me – against my better judgement – is getting turned on seeing her ferocious side, but I quickly ignore it.

"She's an Omega," the kid admits.

Wow, the dirtbag rejected his animai because she's an Omega? How fucking shitty. Doesn't he realise he could have killed her? Though by the sound of it, she's not going to last much longer. I feel sad for the young girl, who I can tell Amelia cares about a great deal. I can see the disgusted faces around the room. It's not a law, but among people who have a heart, it's a kind of an unwritten rule that rejection of an Omega has to be handled with care, since it can often result in the Omega dying.

A man who looks to be in his fifties – though it's hard to tell with wolves – with brown hair with a sprinkling of grey, a thick brown beard kneels down and starts examining the unconscious girl. I take it he's the pack doctor.

He and Amelia converse about the matter of rejection and it seems this girl collapsed before she could accept. I assume they're speaking through the pack-link and I doubt it's a good conversation. Acceptance will no doubt kill the young she-wolf.

"She's not dying," Amelia says adamantly.

She picks the girl up and holds her in her arms and holds a hand to her cheek. The energy that can only come from an Alpha Spirit starts rolling out of her, but the sensation isn't one of dominance it feels… healing, which makes me more confused. A moment later the young girl's eyes flutter open and meet Amelia's.

"A-Alpha Amelia? What… what's happening?" She asks weakly.

Everything becomes a jumble after that. I can't hear or think properly.

Did she just call Amelia 'Alpha'?

But… that's not possible. She's a woman. She can't be an Alpha.

"How are you this stupid? How did you not notice her Alpha Spirit the moment we were near her? It's stronger than Alpha Jasper's," Ace says in a duh tone. I knew I felt something, but I didn't think… it couldn't be. How can she be an Alpha? *"What's the big deal? Why are you so upset about our animai being an Alpha?"* He asks in annoyance.

"How the hell are you so okay with it?! We're a Beta, we're naturally submissive to an Alpha. If she's an Alpha, then are we supposed to be submissive to her? My soulmate will be my superior or some shit," I spit angrily.

"Fuck, you are such an idiot and a hypocrite," he says, shocking me.

"Excuse me?"

"You were just thinking how much of a jerk that kid was for rejecting his animai because she's an Omega and here you are throwing a hissy fit because ours is an Alpha," he says in aggravation.

"It's not the same thing and I haven't rejected her."

"You better fucking not. You even think of rejecting her and I will lock myself into the very depths of your mind and make sure you can never shift again. I will never speak to you again. I love her, Marcus," he whimpers. Fuck, he loves her and her wolf already. I can't really blame him, it's in his nature. But it's also in his nature to be dominant, we're wolves. Women are meant to be the submissive ones.

Not liking where my own thoughts are going, I tune back into what's going on and find Amelia holding the girl, cradling her in such a protective way that for a moment, my heart swells with pride. She cares for her pack very much.

Amelia's eyes open and I'm surprised to see her turquoise eyes glowing. A wave of her Alpha Spirit hits everyone in full force, and I notice everyone standing straighter at the feel of it. Again, it's not dominating, but it's not healing either. This time I feel strength. Strength is radiating off her and even though it's not directed at me, it makes me feel stronger just being in its presence.

What the fuck is she doing?

"I… Jennifer Ryder, against the will of Goddess Zarseti, accept your rejection, Landry Green," the girl sobs as she lets out another scream.

The guy who rejected her lets out his own scream, collapsing into a painful heap on the ground. I notice a glimmer of satisfaction cross Amelia's features before it disappears. The girl collapses again and Amelia's eyes stop glowing. She looks at the girl with so much compassion and sadness, before handing her over to the doctor with orders on how to take care of her.

My eyes never leave her as she gets to her feet. I scan her chest looking for… fuck, there it is. The Mark of the Alpha. I didn't notice it before because the sequins on her dress hid it, but now that I'm looking for it, it's easy to find.

I'm waging a war with myself, and I don't know what to do. I've been fated to an Alpha. A female fucking Alpha.

How did I not notice?

What does this mean for us?

What does this mean for me?

A million questions are swirling in my head and the more I come up with, the angrier I become. A few minutes ago, everything was so perfect. I found my soulmate, and she was everything I wanted and more. And now… now I don't know what to think. I'm aware of Amelia slowly stepping towards me. Her face is unreadable, unlike before, when we were alone together.

"You're the Alpha?" I spit, far more harshly than I intended. My emotions are getting the better of me. She flinches at my tone and I instantly feel like shit.

But does that stop me? No.

Why? Because I'm an asshole.

She's quick to compose herself. "Is that a problem?" She asks calmly. Too calmly, actually.

"Why didn't you tell me?" I ask through gritted teeth.

She rolls her eyes. "How did you not notice?"

I'm not sure how to respond. "How are you an Alpha? You're a woman," I say and, for a second, anger flashes in her eyes.

"Stop upsetting our animai, you jackass!" Hisses Ace.

"Nothing gets by you, does it? I'm the Alpha the same way your Alpha became one; I was born one," she says matter-of-factly.

"So, is this like, a temporary position?" I ask, still trying to understand.

"Temporary?" She asks calmly.

"As in, you hold the position until you find your animai and then he becomes Alpha, and you take over as Luna," I explain. She looks as if I just slapped her.

"Are you actually suggesting that I should hand over my birthright to my animai?" She asks in a tone that makes me shiver with dread. There's no emotion in her face or voice and now I'm worried. I reach out placing my hands on her shoulders hoping my touch will calm her. She doesn't move or react and now I'm scared.

"Amelia, you don't know what it takes to be an Alpha. There's a reason males are always Alphas. I'm not trying to disrespect you; I just don't think you understand what you're doing," I say gently as I cup a hand to her cheek.

"For Goddess sake, stop talking! Are you trying to get us killed?! I don't want to die with you!" Ace screams at me.

"Would you calm down; she's not going to hurt us," I scoff.

"YOU JUST OPENLY CHALLENGED AN ALPHA, DICKHEAD!" He screams in a panic. She's my animai, she wouldn't see this as a challenge. Would she? I'm just trying to help, she'll understand.

I look into her eyes as she takes a step back away from my touch. The action makes me want to hurl. I can't read her right now, but I can tell she's furious. At that moment, Jasper and Isabelle walk over.

Fuck, this isn't good.

"Amelia! It's so good to see you!" Exclaims Jasper, pulling her into a big hug. I can't stop the growl that comes out of me. I don't like him touching her. He's got his own woman. What's worse is now she's smiling. She looks happy to see him and it hurts because I want her smiling at me. "What's with you?" Jasper asks me with a raised eyebrow.

"Your Beta seems to be territorial when it comes to his animai," she says casually. My head snaps towards her. She just said we're soulmates like it was nothing. Just how bad did I fuck up? Jasper and Isabelle are looking between us wide-eyed.

"Holy shit, man. Congratulations!" He exclaims pulling me into a big hug, which I return, though my eyes don't leave Amelia. "So that's where you ran off to."

"We're so happy for you both, this is wonderful news!" Isabelle says cheerfully while hugging Amelia.

"Well, it was wonderful news. I'm not so sure anymore," she says, still keeping her emotions in check.

Fuck. Fuck. Fuck.

I suck in a breath.

"I don't get it, what's going on?" Jasper asks confused.

"Your Beta seems quite upset with the fact I'm an Alpha."

Damn, she is throwing me under the bus. Jasper and Isabelle look at me in shock.

"I'm sure there's been a misunderstanding," Isabelle says trying to be rational.

"Oh, I didn't misunderstand anything Luna Isabelle. I think Marcus here was quite clear when he told me women can't be Alphas and that I'm simply a placeholder for my animai."

"I did not say you were a placeholder. Don't twist my words," I say in annoyance.

"Did you, or did you not ask me if my position was temporary? That I would hand it over to my animai and step aside as Luna?" She asks calmly, her hands clasped in front of her. The pose reminds me of a principal reprimanding a child.

"What the fuck, Marcus? Did you really say that?" Jasper asks angrily. Isabelle looks at me with disgust.

"It was an innocent question," I say defensively. Before Jasper can start in on his lecture, Alpha Lucas of the Alpine Pack walks over.

"Alpha Amelia, might I have a word?" He asks politely.

Amelia looks behind her and nods, "Yes, Alpha Lucas. Just one moment," she turns her attention to me. "If you wish to reject me then I kindly ask you wait until tomorrow. I still have an event to host," she says in a business-like manner, and I gulp. Shock catapults through me, making my heart sink and drop out of my ass.

Reject her?

What? I don't want to reject her. Is that what she thinks?

"What the hell do you expect?" Ace snarls.

"Oh, and congratulations again on your pup," she says warmly to Jasper and Isabelle, "I hope you got my gift." She sent them a baby gift? I didn't know that.

"You don't know a lot of things," scoffs Ace.

"Would you shut up?!" I shout at him. Damn wolf is getting on my nerves.

"Yes, we got your gift, it was so beautiful. Thank you so much," Isabelle says graciously, but I see sympathy in her eyes. I'm in for it, I can tell.

"Blake hasn't stopped playing with it," Jasper tells her proudly. Amelia gives him her beautiful smile and I feel a pang in my chest because I fear she may never smile at me again.

"I'm very glad. Please excuse me," she says and then walks off with Alpha Lucas. I don't like it. I don't want her around other men.

I look to see Jasper and Isabelle looking at me murderously.

Shit.

Before I can say anything, Jasper grabs me by the scruff of my neck and drags me into the packhouse, away from the party. I manage to shake him off and follow him to the second floor, where he leads us to a guest room. I guess he and Isabelle got settled already.

"Where the fuck do I even start?!" He shouts.

Here it comes.

"Dude, let me explain. I don't plan to reject her," I tell him. He relaxes a little at this.

"Good. Okay, that's good news. But why the hell would you say something so fucked up to your own soulmate? I don't know what's worse, you openly disrespecting an Alpha which could cause us problems, or you being an absolute asshole to the woman the Goddess made just for you," he says in frustration.

"I was shocked. How was I supposed to react? There's no such thing as female Alphas," I say in justification. He just scoffs at me.

"There is now. I've known Amelia for years; everyone knew she was going to be an Alpha. Her father announced it years ago and she's been training her whole life for it. I was thrilled when I found out Alpha Elias finally passed the torch to her; she's not just an ally, she's a friend. She's dealt with enough sexist shit in her life, she doesn't need it from her own fucking animai, Marcus," he says bitterly. He always said he was close friends with the future Alpha of the Invictus Pack, but I just assumed it was a guy. He never said their name.

"I'm not being sexist, It's just not normal. There are no female Alphas for a reason. Women aren't built for that kind of role. She-wolves are naturally submissive," I say dismissively.

He cocks his eyebrow at me, "I dare you to say that to Izzy because I would love to watch her punch your damn lights out. You're being a fucking asshole. We haven't had any female Alphas because those before us were old fashioned morons who made that stupid decision. There's nothing that suggests the daughter of an Alpha can't be an Alpha. She was born with Alpha blood for fuck's sake."

"She'll be vulnerable. She's not safe. As soon as more people learn that this pack is run by a woman, the wolves will be at her door. Literally," I say with genuine worry. People will come for her and her pack. I can't let that happen. He laughs mockingly. "What's so fucking funny?" I ask crossing my arms. He's starting to piss me off

"Just how little you know Amelia. She's stronger than you have made her out to be." I don't like how familiar Jasper is with my soulmate, even if he is my Alpha.

"We just fucking met!" I shout, exasperated.

"Exactly! You just met her and you're already assuming she's weak because she's a woman. If she was so weak, she wouldn't have been able to kill the former Beta couple when they challenged her at her Alpha ceremony," he tells me. This news makes me freeze in my tracks.

"Wait, what?"

"Do you know anything? A month ago, at her Alpha ceremony, her title was challenged by the former Beta and she killed him. After that, his animai tried to kill her. As I heard it, she punched her fist through the woman's traitorous chest," he says with a sneer.

I don't know what to say. The former Beta did that? That's so fucked up. She won against two challengers? I have to admit I'm impressed.

"How do you know all this?" I ask him. He rolls his eyes.

"We're friends, we stay in touch. The same reason she knew about Blake. That toy wolf he's always cuddling? Amelia had that made for him," he explains tenderly.

His voice always softens when he talks about his son. I've seen that toy wolf; it's pretty cute. It looks like a mix of Jasper's wolf and Isabelle's. Blake screams the roof down if it's not near him. I had no idea that was a gift from my Amelia.

I rub my face in exhaustion. This night has been insane, a rollercoaster for sure. I'm still happy I met my soulmate, I just don't know how to handle knowing she's an Alpha. I don't know what this means for our relationship.

I mean, if we have pups, who will look after them?

Will she expect me to be a househusband?

Will she want me to be a fucking male Luna or some shit?

No. No fucking way. I'm a Beta; I'm a warrior. I'm not going to be my animai's bitch.

"I don't know what is going on in your head, Marcus, but you need to sort your shit out. Sleep on it and then talk to Amelia in the morning. You're my brother and I love you, man, but if you hurt Amelia, I'll break your fucking jaw," he warns me, exiting the room and leaving me to my overwhelming, destructive thoughts.

Chapter Eight
Amelia

Last night was the worst night sleep I have ever had. Well, I guess I can only say that if I actually slept, which I didn't. How did the best night of my life turn into the worst so quickly?

Over the years, I've heard all the derogatory and condescending comments about me being an Alpha and I've taken them all in stride. But having to hear them come from my own soulmate – the person made for me, the person who was meant to love and support me unconditionally – was like being cut open with a silver blade. Every word he spoke cut deeper and deeper.

When he disrespected me so blatantly in front of, not just my pack, but several other packs as well, it took all my self-control not to put him in his place. But I didn't want people to see me being so affected by his words. Zara was devastated. Watching and hearing her whimper while our own soulmate degraded us broke my heart.

I have no idea what today will bring. I know I have a lot of things I need to handle, so I'll focus on those and not the matter of my animai. This is surely purgatory. Every fibre of my being is begging and needing to be with him, but I guess that's the bond at work. It's somewhat easy to ignore when I remember his cruel words and the harsh tone of his voice. I can't be surprised. I always feared this would happen and here we are.

Pushing unpleasant thoughts aside I get up and get ready. I shower, do my morning routine and then get dressed. I avoided washing my hair so the curls from last night would stay intact. I think they put a bit more life into my face today. I dress in an emerald satin button down blouse, black slacks, and white open toed pumps, wearing no makeup as usual. I think I look great and ready to embrace the day.

Stepping out of my room I see my mum and dad in the kitchen area with my mum making breakfast.

"Oh good, you're up! Come eat, I made your favourite," my mum says cheerfully.

"Thank you, mum, but I'm not hungry. I won't be having breakfast today," I announce.

My parents heads snap in my direction. "Amelia, what's wrong? You have the biggest appetite of anyone I know," my dad asks in a worried tone.

"I'm just not hungry and I have a lot on my plate today," I say casually.

"Any update on Jennifer?" Mum inquires nervously.

"I'll be checking in on her after my meeting, to see how she's doing."

"That poor child. She did not deserve such a cruel thing to be done to her. Thank goodness you were able to help her," says mum with relief. I nod in agreement.

Never have I been so grateful to be able to do what I can do, or today I'd be planning Jennifer's funeral. The thought makes me shudder. Rejection is one of the worst pains you can endure. I've heard it described as the pain of a thousand deaths and, based on the screams last night, I'm thinking maybe that is too simple of a description.

"Speaking of animals, rumour is you met yours last night," dad says with a raised brow. My heart sinks. I was hoping they hadn't found out about that, but I'm not that lucky. Damn packs spreads more gossip than TMZ.

"I'd rather we not talk about it," I say as I head to the door.

"So it's true?! You found your animai?! Oh, Amelia this is wonderful. We should celebrate," mum cheers and I lose the hold on my control.

"There is nothing to celebrate!" I snap. I take a breath to calm myself when I register their surprise – I am not the type who snaps. "I'm certain he is going to reject me," I tell them dismissively.

I'm trying to act like this doesn't bother me when the very thought of my soulmate rejecting me causes my heart to fracture into pieces. While Goddess Zarseti created soulmates as a way to maintain peace and harmony between the species, the Gods have always been big supporters of free will. So, she also stipulated that an animai can reject their other half if they choose, but it comes with a price.

"Reject you? Why?" Dad asks in a low, threatening voice.

"He didn't take me being an Alpha well. In fact, he was angry and condescending," I shrug. My dad lets out a menacing growl and the knife he was holding snaps in his hand. My mum has gone from cheerful to looking like she's ready to bathe in blood.

"Where is he?! I'll knock his block off!" Dad snarls.

I roll my eyes. "You will do no such thing. I appreciate you wanting to protect me, but this is my life, and I can handle it myself. Please, for me, stay out of it," I say calmly but firmly.

Dad huffs in disapproval, "Fine."

Dad is very protective, and I love him for it, but he also knows when to let me fight my own battles and considering this is my soulmate, he knows he has to stay out of it.

"I have to go. I'll speak to you both later," I say kindly, leaving the suite.

As I enter the hallway, I collide with a hard chest, the scent of liquorice invading me and I resist the urge to gag. I don't have to look up to know who it is.

"Careful there, wouldn't want to hurt your pretty face," comes the verbal equivalent of nails on a chalkboard. I take a step back and look up at Ryker's smug face.

"Is there a reason you're lurking outside my suite?" I ask him pointedly.

"I guess I was feeling a little homesick. It's strange not living here anymore," he shrugs.

With his parents gone, and him not a ranked wolf, he was forced to move out of the packhouse. Vitali, being my Beta, now occupies the Beta suite. Ryker and homesick do not belong in the same sentence. He has no reason to be up here.

"As sympathetic as I am, you should not be up here and you know that," I say as I step around him to head downstairs.

"I hear your animai rejected you last night," he says in an almost sympathetic tone, which I'm sure is as fake as press-on nails.

I turn to look back at him. "Do I look like someone who was rejected last night?" I say in a bored tone.

He shakes his head and steps closer. "Amelia why are we playing this game?" He says in a soft whisper. What is happening right now? "Don't you know that I want you? I've always wanted you. Goddess, I was so angry when I learned you found your animai. But then I was so happy to hear maybe you had rejected each other because you should be with me. We should be together Amelia. I know you know that," he says, holding my shoulders, giving me a gentle look. His touch is like bugs crawling under my skin. I'm frozen for a moment as I process his words before I burst out in a fit of laughter.

"*Is he expecting us to believe this crap?*" Zara asks in disbelief.

"*Oh I'm sure he is,*" I say in amusement. Ryker has officially lost his marbles.

"Why are you laughing? I'm serious," he says with a hint of frustration.

I move his hands off me. "If I recall you were gloating and taunting me about my impending death when your father challenged me," I point out.

His eyes narrow, but then he composes himself, "My father was in earshot, I had to play it up. It's why I've been a jerk to you all these years. I knew how my father would react if he knew I liked you."

"*And the award for best male performance in a drama goes to...*" Zara announces, nearly making me snort with laughter.

"Ryker, I wasn't born yesterday, but nice try. Also, if you touch me like that again I'm going to rip off your fingers and shove them in your ears," I say with a bright smile. Anger flashes across his features before he reins it in.

What the hell kind of game is he playing? Couldn't get the Alpha title with his dad's challenge so chosen one is the next best option? What is wrong with his family?

"Did you like the flowers I sent you?" He suddenly asks.

That was him?

"I hate the colour pink," I say bluntly. They were lovely but I'm not entertaining this bullshit.

"No you don't. Every girl likes pink," he says arrogantly.

What kind of dumb stereotype is that?

Suddenly the intoxicating scent of caramel hits me and it's like my body has become a livewire. Damn, I don't need this right now.

"Actually, her favourite colour is green and she's not a girl, she's a woman," comes Marcus' deep and very pissed off voice. I'm feeling very conflicted right now. On one hand, it warms my heart to have him know this fact about me already and want to step in and protect me. But, on the other hand, I am very certain it has a lot to do with him thinking I actually need protecting in the first place because I'm a weak woman, and that makes me feel a bit sour.

"Who the fuck are you?" Ryker spits venomously.

"I'm her animai," Marcus says as he places a possessive arm around my waist.

Gosh, it feels so warm and comforting being in his arm like this. Even through my clothes, his touch is sending electricity through my body. And, he smells good enough to eat.

"Who the fuck are you?" Marcus bites back.

"I heard you were going to reject her," Ryker says smugly.

"You heard wrong," Marcus says menacingly as the two stare each other down.

Wait, he's not going to reject me? That should be good news, but I have a bad feeling. It doesn't matter right now; I am so not in the mood for this testosterone driven bullshit.

"Ryker, it's best you leave now. I don't want to see you on this floor again," I say using my Alpha Spirit. He grits his teeth and tries to resist, but his head eventually lowers in submission.

"Fine," he says curtly as he storms off. I take a breath and turn my attention to Marcus. Gods he looks good. He's in simple dark-denim jeans and a black t-shirt that is so tight, it is causing some very dirty thoughts to appear in my head.

"*Our animai is dreamy! He's a jerk, but he's a dreamy jerk,*" says Zara.

"My eyes are up here," says Marcus with a smirk on his face. Make that a smug jerk.

"What are you doing here, Marcus?" I ask him calmly.

"I was hoping we could talk. I don't like how we parted ways last night, I couldn't sleep a wink. Things were said and I'd like us to sort it out," he says sincerely. Well, I'm glad he's mature enough to want to have a conversation.

"I didn't like how things turned out either. I don't like feeling like my soulmate hates me," I say honestly.

His eyes widen with guilt and hurt as he cups my cheeks, his touch soothing me with that indescribable electricity. I want so badly to wrap myself around him and feel every inch of him, but I'm holding onto my sanity and dignity.

"Amelia, you're my soulmate, you were made for me. I don't hate you; I could never hate you," he says strongly, as if trying to drill the words into me. I relax a little. He sighs, pressing his forehead against mine and I relish the feeling of being this close to him, his warm breath fanning my face. "I just hate that you're an Alpha," he says dejectedly. My need and desire for him evaporates and I instantly recoil out of his touch, wanting to put as much space between us.

"*Zara, I apologise in advance, but I may end up punching our animai today,*" I warn.

"*Girl, if you don't, I will. How dare he say that to us?!*" She says angrily.

"Do you actually hear the words that leave your mouth, or do you find a way to tune them out?" I ask in irritation. He blinks in surprise. "You don't hate me; you just hate that I'm an Alpha. It's the same damn thing," I spit.

"It's not the same thing at all," he argues, clenching his jaw.

"I am an Alpha by blood. It is who I am, so to hate what I am, is to hate me," I retort.

"No, you chose to be this. There's a difference," he says through gritted teeth and I feel like I've been sucker punched in the gut.

"You would never even dare say that to another Alpha and the only reason you dare say that to me is because I'm a woman. This tells me not only do you have no respect for women, but you also have no respect for me as your own soulmate. Because if you did, you wouldn't be saying such hurtful things," I say indignantly..

He flinches back at my words "I do respect you, Amelia..." he trails off.

"Do not even bother. I have neither the time or patience to hear what excuse you have or what ridiculous arbitrary reason you'll come up with to insult my position in my own pack. So, if you'll excuse me, Beta Marcus, I have business to attend to," I say curtly and calmly walk off, leaving him there with his mouth hanging open.

"How come you didn't punch him?" Zara asks.

"I don't want to hurt him, but honestly that kind of thinking isn't even worth the exertion," I explain and then sigh, *"We may have to reject him; you know that right?"*

Zara whimpers. *"I know, I don't hold it against you. I support whatever you decide. We deserve a strong soulmate who can stand beside us and if he can't be that, then we have no choice,"* she says confidently. I'm proud of her, I know it's so much harder for the wolf side to reject the very person the Goddess made for them, it goes against their entire instincts, but I'm glad she has my back on this. *"But... can we give him a little time first? To maybe change his mind?"* She gently requests.

"That's a fair request. After all, I haven't even known him for twelve hours. But what made you ask?" I ask curiously.

"His wolf Ace doesn't share his views. Ace loves us, he's happy and proud to be fated to an Alpha," she says happily. This makes me smile. Like I said, it's always the human who is the asshole. Maybe Ace can help change Marcus' mind.

"I'm glad to hear that. I will give it some time. But understand, Zara, I'm not going to dedicate my time to trying to convince Marcus to respect us. I already have to prove it daily to everyone else; I'm not going to degrade myself like that to my own soulmate," I say fiercely.

She nods quickly, *"I absolutely agree. He needs to sort his own shit out first."*

Again, I am so grateful to have a wolf like Zara. No matter what, we will always be a team.

As I walk down the hall to my office, I see Alpha Lucas waiting outside and I can tell from the look on his face he heard the entire interaction. Just great, like I really need more things for people to use against me.

"Alpha Lucas, so sorry to keep you waiting," I say politely.

"Not a problem, Alpha Amelia, thank you for making time to speak with me this morning," he says warmly. I unlock my office door and step in with him, closing the door behind me. He takes a seat in one of the armchairs in front of my desk. "First, I want to deeply apologise for what my pack member did to that young woman. She did not deserve that; I am appalled and ashamed. Has there been an update on her condition?" He asks with genuine concern.

"Not yet," I sigh, taking a seat behind my desk. "I plan on checking in on her shortly." He nods in understanding. "Alpha Lucas, I hope the young man's views on Omegas are not ones that are held by you and your pack," I say reticently.

He lets out a deep sigh, "I can assure you they are not ideals I personally hold, but they were held by my father, and so there are many within my pack who still view Omegas as inferior members of our species. I've been doing my best to improve this, but it's a bit hard when the older generation are whispering this crap into the ears of the current generation."

I nod. "So is it safe to say the young man has a parent who has been instilling these views upon him?"

Alpha Lucas nods in return, "His father. His father is a warrior in my pack, and he has a special disgust for Omegas. I try to be a good influence, but I'm not there in their homes. There's only so much influence I can have." He lowers his head in shame.

"Alpha Lucas, naturally I can't punish your pack member or request a punishment on the grounds of a rejection. While I don't agree with it, it is his Goddess given right to reject his animai, even if it makes him a world class idiot." Alpha Lucas snorts in agreement. I continue, "However, his ignorance and carelessness did almost cost me the life of a very valued member of my pack, and I don't take that lightly."

"What do you propose?"

"A punishment of one month's community service to be served here, at my pack. For a month, he would be expected to live as an Omega. This would mean no shifting," I say going into business mode.

Alpha Lucas blinks in surprise. "Not what I was expecting, but I have to admit I do love this idea," he smiles broadly. "Can I ask why you wish for his punishment to be served here and not in his own pack?"

I sit back in my chair, "Unlike Lady Macbeth, I believe what's done *can* be undone. I saw the shock and horror written all over his face when he watched the life draining from Jennifer. There was shame in his voice when he admitted his reason for rejecting her. I don't think he's a bad kid, I think he's just had a negative influence and maybe some time away from that influence and a chance to get to know the woman the Goddess chose for him might do him some good."

Lucas smiles warmly, "Most Alphas wouldn't bother with matters concerning an Omega, or even the matter of rejection, but you are. I keep finding more reasons to respect you."

"Jennifer means a lot to me and this pack, I only want the best for her. Zarseti chose them for a reason, I believe that. One of them just has to believe it, too."

"Then why have her accept the rejection? And how did you manage to stop it from killing her? I've never seen anything like that before," he asks in wonder and curiosity.

"A trick I've learned. I'm unsure if it's a trick specific to Alphas or just me, but I'd be happy to go over it with you in hopes it is something Alphas can use to help their pack," I explain.

He nods eagerly. "I would appreciate that a great deal. But you didn't answer my first question."

"Sometimes we have to lose something to appreciate it," I say softly. He gives me a knowing smile.

After I finish my meeting with Alpha Lucas, I leave the packhouse and drive to Jennifer's house to check in with the nurse on duty. I feet some relief when I see colour in her cheeks and hear a steady heartbeat. The nurse informs me Jennifer had woken up a couple hours ago but became distressed and was in physical pain, so was sedated again. The nurses alternating shifts may have to continue to do this over the next few days. I know when she comes to, she and her wolf spirit will have to process this, but hopefully, by then, my plans to repair the situation will be in effect.

Once that's done, I check in on a few of the local businesses to see how things are doing around town. Most packs really are just their own isolated town or village unless you're the kind of pack that is more rustic and lives off the land. So, think of an Alpha as the mayor – It comes with a lot of responsibilities.

I'm so proud of our pack, we are a thriving little metropolis, always buzzing with activity. There are cafés, restaurants, parks, salons, hardware stores, grocery stores, a library, a day care/pre-school, elementary school, and a high school. We even have a small cinema. It doesn't play new releases, but everyone loves going there and watching the large variety of movies they offer.

After a couple hours, I return to the packhouse to check on our guests. The visiting ranked wolves stay in the packhouse while their fellow pack members reside in the guest house next door.

The guest house is like a mini-hotel, reserved for occasions like this. The packhouse is massive, but we don't have beds for everyone who is visiting. Of course, those who found their animais go home with them. Stepping into the packhouse, I'm immediately greeted by a very peppy Kylie.

"Good morning, Alpha! I have your mail for you," she says cheerfully, more so than usual.

I smile and take the mail from her. "Thank you, Kylie," I say appreciatively. She looks like she very badly wants to ask or tell me something, but before she can she's being engulfed by muscular arms.

"Gotcha!" The man cries, nuzzling her neck and making her giggle.

"I wasn't lost, Izac, you know exactly how to find me," she says poking her tongue at him, but she is still all smiles.

"I do and I did," he agrees looking up to me. "Morning, Alpha," he says with a smile.

"Good morning, Izac. Ditching training to whisk your animai away?" I ask, raising an amused eyebrow.

"Guilty as charged," he confesses, without a hint of remorse.

"Well, you have wasted your time, I have work to do," Kylie shuts him down. Poor Izac is pouting like a wounded pup.

"Work? I don't know of any work you have to do. Schedule seems clear to me," I shrug, feigning ignorance. Kylie's eyes blow wide and Izac's face breaks out into grin.

"Thanks, Alpha, you're the best!" He cheers as he throws Kylie over his shoulder and races off with her to the sounds of her giggled protests. Those two are positively adorable. I'm sure to link Maggie to let her know Kylie will be off for the rest of the day.

I make my way through the packhouse heading in the direction of the dining hall. Most of the party setup is still there, the staff not having had time to clear it. But they have managed to pack up the table centrepieces and the fairy lights, so now the dining hall just looks like a fancy restaurant.

I'm flipping through the mail when a shrill voice makes its way into my eardrums, and I immediately cringe at the sound. Sometimes I think that, if I ever need to interrogate someone who invades our lands, I should just have them sit in a room with Jane for a while. That would make them spill their secrets, for sure.

"Of course, her animai would reject her," she laughs, or at least I think it's a laugh – either that or someone is strangling a dolphin. "No man wants a woman who thinks she's better than them and acts tougher than them. I mean did you girls *see* that tall piece of man candy? How could the Goddess pair someone as gorgeous as that to someone as fugly as Amelia?" She asks spitefully.

Honestly, I'm not mad Jane is calling me names behind my pack. It's laughable, actually. However, she is talking about my fucking animai and that fact has me seeing red. A wave of possessive anger rolls through me like a tidal wave, and it's picking up momentum the more the bitch speaks. Zara is snarling ferociously in my head; she wants to come out and sink her teeth into Jane. Hell, she's not just talking about any animai, she's talking about the animai of her fucking Alpha. Does this bitch want to die today? I'm not exactly happy with the situation between me and Marcus right now, but that doesn't change the fact he's mine and I've warned this bitch before.

Slowly I follow the sound of her torturous voice and find her sitting in one of the lounge seats that are in the sitting room just outside the doors of the dining hall. She's such a cliché, she's the pack slut *and* the pack gossip. She's sitting with four of her little minions, and I notice Jane's eyes on something in the dining hall. I follow her eyeline and see none other than my animai, who is eating with Chris, of all people. I'll unpack that later, after I teach this bitch a lesson.

I walk up behind her and the four women with her instantly pale at the sight of me. Jane is oblivious until I let me Alpha Spirit start projecting off me. The moment it hits her, her body starts to quiver and she starts whimpering, which gives both myself and Zara great satisfaction.

"Did I, or did I not, warn you against disrespecting me again?" I say icily and watch as her quivering intensifies. She slowly turns to look up at me, a mix of anger and fear in her caked-up features. "You just don't listen, do you?" I tut.

"She was just jo– " I silence her minion's feeble attempts to defend the bitch with a glance that instantly has her and her wolf cowering.

"I don't give second warnings, Jane. You've disrespected your Alpha and worse," I lean toward her ear and smell the fear cascading off her. "You were looking at and talking about my animai. A future leader of this pack; something I will not tolerate," I say in a deadly voice.

I'm not delusional, I have no idea what future there is for me and Marcus, especially in terms of titles and pack roles, but this mutt doesn't need to know that. I'm still her Alpha and you don't disrespect an Alpha and you don't fuck with an Alpha's soulmate unless you want to die.

Wolves are very territorial creatures; Alphas are one hundred times worse. It's forbidden to mess with anyone fated to an Alpha because it's a quick way to start a war. Honestly, I'd love nothing more than to rip her throat out and bathe in her blood right now as I watch the life leave her eyes – but I'm a rational person and she hasn't broken any pack laws. Sadly, she gets to live.

"Please, A-Alpha, I di-didn't mean to," she stutters, not that I care.

"*Uncle J, how do you feel about coming out of retirement to dish out some punishment?*" I say through the pack-link.

"*Count me in, Alpha. Who am I punishing?*" He asks eagerly.

"*Jane Lahde.*"

I can hear him groaning through the link. "*I'm not surprised. What she do this time?*"

"*Gossip about me and my animai while eye fucking him,*" I say angrily.

"*Say no mo… wait what?! You found your animai?! Why am I just finding out now? Why haven't you announced it to the pack yet?*" He fires off.

I sigh. "*It's complicated. Please just meet her at the training grounds. Oh, and make it hurt,*" I instruct him.

I hear him laugh maliciously. "*For you, Alpha, it would be a pleasure,*" he says, cutting the link.

"Congratulations Jane, you have a training date with Gamma James. Best you run along," I say cheerfully.

She looks confused. "What? I don't have training and he's not Gamma anymore," she says in irritation.

"He's coming out of retirement just for you. Enjoy," I say with a sadistic smirk on my face.

Fear fills her eyes when she sees the look on my face. She slowly gets to her feet and walks off. I shoot another hard glare at the other women, and they quickly scatter. Sad excuses for wolves if you ask me. I know Tyson would have loved to make Jane suffer, but he's busy with pack training and I want Jane's treatment to be very special. Uncle J will have her in tears within ten minutes.

"*You should have him take pictures so we can look at it later. Personally, I'd love to watch the bitch fall apart and cry like the pathetic creature she is, but I know we are busy bees,*" says Zara with a wistful sigh and I chuckle.

"*There are security cameras that faces that direction, we can look at the recordings later over some popcorn, maybe invite the gang and make a night of it,*"

I suggest.

"*Now that's my idea of a movie night!*" She says gleefully.

I'm still smiling and shaking my head as I resume going through the mail, stopping on a white envelope with my name scrawled on the front. Just what I need today, another letter from my invisible enemy. Before I open it, I link Chris and Vitali to come to my office. I tell Tyson there's another letter and that I'll fill him in later.

Looking over I see Chris excuse himself from Marcus and quickly shoot out of his chair, rushing rush over to me. I nod for him to go on ahead while my eyes linger on the eyes of my animai. Those beautiful eyes that I got lost in last night, eyes that, for a short time, held so much adoration for me. How quickly they had turned into something harsh and hurtful. Now their forest depths look at me with confusion and a great deal of concern. It makes my heart skip a beat. He stands up as if to come over, but I shake my head. I mouth 'later', and he looks torn and frustrated, but ultimately he nods in agreement. I have to handle this matter first before dealing with him. One problem at a time. I turn and head upstairs to my office.

"*At least we know he cares about us, that's something at least,*" Zara says optimistically.

"*As nice as that is, what are the chances that if I told him about the threats, he would use that as proof against me being an Alpha?*" I point out. She sighs and slumps down, knowing I'm right. Not that I want to be. I'd rather be wrong on this.

Once upstairs I see Vitali and Chris patiently waiting, so I let them in and close the door behind me.

"Something has happened," Chris deduces.

I step around my desk and hold up the envelope. They each suck in a breath.

"Another one?" Vitali grits.

I nod and rip the letter open. "Get ready, Amelia. I'm coming for you," I say, reading the note inside. They each stiffen.

"Fuck. So, there's going to be an attack on the pack," Vitali fumes.

I nod placing the note down, "We already assumed this would happen, which is why we've taken pre-emptive measures. Tyson has upped our defences. Patrols are on alert; new triage protocols are in place and the pack has been reminded of safety and evacuation procedures. If and when an attack occurs, we will be ready. All we can do now is wait."

"How are you so calm? Some asshole out there wants you dead, Amelia," Chris says angrily.

I sigh. "What do you expect me to do? Throw a fit and start tearing up the packhouse? We're wolves, this shit was bound to happen. The odds were inevitably worse when I took over. I'm not going to cry or whine; I'm going to do what I can to protect this pack and kill whoever is after me," I tell him firmly. "Also, what were you and Marcus talking about?"

"Nothing," he says with a shrug.

"Please tell me you weren't pulling the big brother routine on him," I say rolling my eyes.

"If he didn't, I will. Each of us want to take turns knocking his damn teeth out. He had no right treating you the way he did last night," spits Vitali.

Pain lances through me as I remember Marcus's harsh words. "Marcus is my animai; you will stay out of it. Do I make myself clear?" I say firmly, letting my Alpha Spirit push forward.

They lower their heads. "Yes, Alpha," they say in unison.

"We just care about you; you can't blame us for worrying about you. Plus, you're our Alpha, it's not easy for us to watch some asshole treat our Alpha like that," Chris says gently.

I sigh. "I love and appreciate the concern and I'm grateful I have your support. Just don't go making things more complicated, okay?" I ask pleadingly. At the end of the day, they're my friends and I love them, and I know they just want to look out for me. I'd do the same for them.

"We'll try to behave. But if he steps out of line, no promises," says Vitali assertively. I chuckle and hold my hands up in surrender.

"That's more than fair. Speaking of animai, how are things going with Eric?" I ask kindly. Vitali's face breaks into the brightest smile I've ever seen, and it makes me smile and relax. It also makes me feel a pang of envy, but

I push it away.

"Things are amazing. He's... he's perfect in every way imaginable. I apologised and explained why I ran off and he was completely understanding. We had the most incredible night together. We stayed up and talked. It was the most intimate experience of my life," he says, looking all dreamy eyed.

Chris is grinning at him. "He seems like a great guy, man. Finally, someone who can tame you," he teases, throwing an arm around Vitali. I chuckle; Vitali has always been the wild one.

"Ha, ha, very funny," he gripes, but the smile doesn't leave his face. "Thank you, Amelia. For knocking some sense into me and being there for me," he says with sincerity.

I wave my hand dismissively. "You'd have come around eventually, I just sped it up. I wish you felt like you could have come to one of us and told us this ages ago," I say, feeling guilt that my best friend had to hide half of who he is.

"Yeah, me too, Vit. We would have never made you feel different or shunned you. We accept you as you are; an obnoxious loudmouth that we can't live without," Chris says casually, and we all laugh.

"I can't believe we've all found our animais," Vitali says in disbelief. Just like that, my good mood deflates. I'm good at keeping up pretences around the pack, but I have no reason to with my friends. They're my family and I trust them with my life. If I can't be me around them, then who can I be me with?

"I don't think you should place me in that category just yet," I say solemnly. They both look at me with such sympathy, immediately walking over and wrapping their arms around me. I welcome it. I really needed some comforting right now.

"That Beta is an idiot. He'll come around when he gets to know you. You're too amazing to ignore." Vitali kisses my cheek.

"I hope you're right," I say half-heartedly.

"The guy has some warped views, that's for sure. But finding your animai changes you. He'll realise he's wrong and that he's lucky to have been fated to an Alpha," Chris says comfortingly.

"In the meantime, don't be afraid to let him see what a badass Alpha you are. In fact, I'll stop speaking to you if you do," Vitali threatens making me laugh.

"I'm always me. I couldn't be anyone else if I tried," I tell them.

"That's our girl," Chris says proudly as they smile at me.

I pull them into a tight hug and enjoy the moment. No matter how hard things get, no matter how many times I get knocked down, having their support always keeps me going.

"You guys better not be having a group hug without me or I'm going to be super pissed," Tyson grumbles to us through the pack-link, and we break away, laughing. Yeah, these guys are truly the best medicine out there.

Chapter Nine
Marcus

Last night was by far the worst fucking night of my life. I couldn't rest, I couldn't sleep, I just wanted to run and find Amelia, taste her delicate lips, feel her curvy body under me and make sure she didn't hate me. I know we have some issues to handle and some strong differences in opinion, but I still fucking want her. She's mine. She was meant for me.

Instead of calmly talking to her, I insulted her and the guilt is eating away at me. It also doesn't help that Ace spent all night calling me names, some of which were very creative. Didn't know my wolf had such an extensive vocabulary – I'd be impressed if it wasn't directed at me.

First thing in the morning I had Jasper tell me where to find the Alpha suite. I ran to talk to Amelia and try and sort this out, but I nearly lost my shit when I found some mangy little shit stain making a move on my woman. Ace wanted to rip his throat out and I was all for it, but I don't think that would have gone over well, so I reined it in.

Amelia didn't seem interested in him, in fact, she seemed annoyed by him, which helped calm me down. We had a tender moment; she let me touch her which made me feel on top of the world but hearing her say she felt like I hated her fucking broke me. She's my soulmate, my everything, I'm supposed to love and protect her and instead, I made her feel like I hate her. I'm such a fucking asshole.

And then, because apparently I can't help myself, I put my foot in my mouth *again* and ruined everything. I told her I hated that she's an Alpha and the look on her face made my blood run cold. I knew I'd fucked up, but I couldn't shut up. Words kept pouring out of me. Ace kept screaming for me to shut up, but did I listen? No. She shut me down and walked off without even a glance back at me and it hurt. It fucking hurt. That's the second time I've watched her walk away after I made her feel like shit and, at this point, I wouldn't be surprised if she rejects me.

"Your parents must have dropped you on your head as a child. How can you be this stupid?" Ace asks angrily. Yeah, he's still furious with me.

"I don't know, okay? I want her, I want her more than anything. But then I get near her and the second I'm reminded she's an Alpha it's like a switch flips in my head," I explain pathetically.

"If you lose us our soulmate, I will make your life a living hell, I promise you that. We've been given someone amazing and special and you're treating her like dirt," he snarls.

I groan and rub my face in frustration.

Why did she have to be a fucking Alpha?

What the fuck are the chances of that?

I had to be fated to the first, why me?

"Oh, so you're saying you wish we'd been fated to someone else?" He asks menacingly. If Ace didn't live in my head, he'd have killed me by now.

"I'm not saying that at all, Ace."

"Then what are you saying?!"

"I DON'T FUCKING KNOW!" I scream at him. Maybe this is karma for not being better towards the opposite sex.

Deciding I need a distraction and something to eat, I head downstairs and am instructed that breakfast is served in the hall where the party was held. I go in and it looks mostly the same, but I can tell they're gradually packing up. I make my way to the buffet and stack a plate with eggs, bacon, toast, and pancakes. I sit at one of the circular tables and start eating.

Wow, I don't know what their chef does to these eggs, but they're phenomenal! I'm digging into my food when someone takes a seat at my table. I realise it's the guy who greeted us last night; Delta Chris, I think his name was.

"If it isn't the guy who openly disrespected my Alpha," he says in a clipped tone. I narrow my eyes at him.

"Can I help you with something?" I ask curtly.

"You can tell me what your problem with your animai is," he says snidely. I sigh. I don't want to talk about it with this guy.

"That's none of your business," I say flatly.

"She's my Alpha, my best friend and practically my little sister. I don't care if you're her animai or not, I won't sit back and let you treat her like shit," he says menacingly. I can't help but smirk a little, Amelia definitely made a good call picking this one as her Delta. He's fiercely loyal.

"So, it doesn't bother you that your Alpha is a female?"

He rolls his eyes. "Why the hell should it? I've known Amelia would be Alpha since the day she came out of the womb. She's what this pack needs. She's an amazing person and an amazing Alpha. We're lucky to have her. *You* are lucky to have her," he says that last part a little softer and it makes guilt run through me.

"You wouldn't understand. I don't know what any of this means for us and our future. I don't have it in me to be subservient to a woman," I say bitterly.

Chris scoffs. "Who asked you to be? Because I know it wasn't Amelia. Have you even stopped to talk about your future with her, or did you just go around and make assumptions within an hour of meeting her?" He asks bitterly. I look down because he's not wrong. We haven't talked about it, the last two times I've tried to talk to her have blown up in my face. "That's what I thought." He smugly bites into a breakfast sandwich.

"How would you feel if you found out your animai was stronger than you?" I ask pointedly. But he just starts laughing, shaking his head.

"Beta Marcus, my animai *is* stronger than me. She's even stronger than my Alpha. Hell, she's stronger than every Alpha. But unlike you, my dick doesn't shrivel up at the thought of it. It makes me proud, proud that a

Goddess thought me worthy enough to be her soulmate. I love everything about her, and her strength is just one of the things I love," he sighs, and I see pain and sadness on his face. "She's not as strong as she should be. Not yet anyway. A lot of people hurt her and it weakened her. But I will spend the rest of my life making sure I am there to help her be the strong woman she's meant to be. Because that's what you do for someone you love," he says with conviction.

I sit back somewhat dumbfounded. His animai is stronger than an Alpha? What kind of wolf is she? I glance and spot a mating mark on his neck, but I furrow my brows in confusion. It looks very different.

When a mutolupus marks their animai you bite them in the junction between their neck and shoulder, which is an erogenous zone for our kind. It links you both emotionally and physically, it's more binding and lasting than humans putting wedding rings on each other. Marking is the supernatural version of marriage, only it's more significant. We wolves don't do weddings. Well, some do. Usually the ones fated to a human or the ones who just like the novelty of weddings. But it's not a common practice for anyone in the supernatural community.

I can't help but wonder, is that something Amelia would want? I shake the thought away and focus again on Chris' neck. It's not like any mating mark I've ever seen. For us, when you mark your animai, the bitemark morphs into a small silver paw print, specifically the paw of the wolf who marked you. Paw prints, like fingerprints, are unique. Chris doesn't have a small paw print, he has… okay, this sounds crazy, but it looks like two puncture marks. But, the marks are covered by two small scales, like a reptile's. They have this black and gold shift to it. What the fuck is that?

"Is that your mating mark?" I gesture to his neck.

"Sure is," he says grinning proudly and puffing out his chest.

"I've never seen a wolf's mark look like that before," I say curiously.

"Who said my animai was a wolf?" He smirks. That gets my attention. What is she? There are a lot of supernatural creatures all over the world, but I can't think of any that make a mark like that. Before I can ask him more about it, his body stiffens, and he zones out. I can tell someone is linking him.

"I have to go," he says in a hurry as he gets up. "Talk to Amelia," he encourages, before rushing off.

As he rushes through the doors into the packhouse, I see Amelia standing in the sitting area. The two exchange a look and instantly I can tell something is wrong. I get to my feet and our eyes lock. The beautiful eyes of my paradise – she truly looks like a goddess. Her hair is down and the curls from last night are framing her gorgeous face. Her black slacks showcase an ass that I desperately want to feel in my hands and hear her sweet moans like I heard last night. She's wearing a blouse in her favourite colour and it's low-cut, teasing me with her delicious cleavage. Green really looks amazing on her.

I want so badly to run over, kiss her and hold her, but the blank expression on her face makes me think better of it. Something is wrong, I can feel it. I start to take a step, but she shakes her head in a sign to stay put. See? She's already telling me what to do. But I've caused enough issues, so I decide to stay where I am. She mouths 'later' to me, and I relax a little. I can wait. I'll ask her what's going on later. With that she turns and walks away, my eyes glued to her ass. Fuck this is frustrating!

I slump into my chair with my head in my hands. Meeting your animai isn't supposed to be this much work. Everyone I know who's mated with theirs did not have to go through this shit. I feel like the Gods are punishing me.

"So, have you apologised to your animai yet?" I hear Jasper's voice to my left. I groan and rest my forehead on the table. "What did you say to her this time?" He asks, and I can hear the irritation in his voice.

"She thinks I hate her, but I told her I don't," I mumble into the table.

"I detect a 'but'."

"I… told her I hate that she's an Alpha," I say flinching, waiting for him to blow up at me, not that it's any of his business. I hear his slow hard breath through his nose. He's mad.

"What in the name of the Goddess compelled you to say that to her? Are you intentionally being a fucking asshole? At this point if she rejects you, or even kills you, I'm going to pardon it. I'll call it justifiable homicide," he says fervently.

Why does it sound like he enjoys the idea of me getting murdered by my soulmate?

"I get it, okay? I shouldn't have said that."

"You shouldn't even be thinking it, for fuck sake," he retorts. "Now join me in our room, I need to make a Zoom call and check in on the pack." He gets up and walks away. I follow him up to our guest room. It's a small suite with a simple lounge area and two bedrooms, decked out in soft creams and browns. Pretty neutral.

"Where's Izzy?" I ask him.

"Checking in on the people who found their animais last night and mingling with some Lunas. She'll be heading home with everyone first thing tomorrow morning. You and I are staying an extra day or two."

"Since when?" I ask in surprise.

"Since I said so," he says with finality.

Once in our suite, we sit on the couch and he starts up the laptop on the coffee table to begin the Zoom call. Once the call connects, we're greeted with the faces of my other two knucklehead best friends, Jasper's Gamma, Calix, and Delta, Aiden. Calix is actually the oldest of us. He's twenty-five, Jasper and I are twenty-four and Aiden is twenty. I was the last to find my animai.

"Hey, guys! How was the ball?" Asks Aiden cheerfully.

"There was some drama, but overall, it was a really great occasion. A lot of people found their animai last night," says Jasper.

"So Alpha Amelia handled her first big event well then?" Asks Calix while he digs into a bag of potato chips.

My head snaps to him. "You knew the Alpha was a woman?" I ask in shock. They exchange a look with each other.

"How did you *not* know?" Questions Calix.

"Yeah dude, all the packs are talking about the new female Alpha on the block," confirms Aiden. What the fuck?! How did I not know any of this? I notice Jasper suppressing a smirk and I want to punch it off his face.

"Did you go and piss off the Alpha, Marcus?" Calix sighs.

Jasper snorts. "Oh, he did a lot more than that," he says drily. "She's his animai."

Calix chokes on his chips and Aiden just looks at me with his jaw hanging open. I, however, glare at Jasper, who ignores me.

Asshole.

"You're fated to the Alpha? I... wow, I mean, congratulations on finding your soulmate, man," Aiden says once he finds his voice.

"Thanks," I say tersely.

"Gee, don't sound so happy about it," Calix mocks. "You look like someone dented your car."

I run my fingers through my hair in frustration. This is why Jasper brought it up. What is this, some kind of soulmate intervention? "It's just been a shock to the system is all," I say defensively. I don't want to talk about this.

"He's been acting like a sexist twat. He hasn't just insulted his animai; he's degraded an Alpha and that shit reflects badly on me as his Alpha," Jasper huffs in indignation.

Okay, that last part fucking stung. I work my ass off to be a good Beta and hearing my Alpha basically say I'm bringing him shame is a hard hit to my pride.

"Wow. You really are a moron. Don't you care about her at all?" Aiden asks, his eyes full of disappointment.

"Of course, I fucking care! Everything was perfect until I found out who she was. Fuck, I mean, I was catching feelings for her instantly," I tell them.

Calix snorts, "Catching feelings? You make love sound like the fucking flu."

"Help... I'm... catching... feelings," Aiden teases between fake coughs, making Jasper and Calix snigger.

Fucking pricks.

"Seriously dude, that's one of the dumbest things I've ever heard. You don't catch feelings, it's not a contagious virus," Calix rolls his eyes.

"Are you assholes done?" I ask in a scathing tone.

"Far from it. Anyway, how are things at the pack and how is my son?" asks Jasper leaning in.

"Everything is great, Alpha, promise. Muse and Darla have been showering Blake with attention and Kiara has pretty much claimed him. She throws a fit when someone takes him away from her," Aiden says with amusement.

Darla is Calix's animai and Muse is Aiden's, Kiara is Aiden and Muse's one-year-old. As the first kid born among our group, she's grown up with a lot of attention. That girl has us all wrapped around her little finger. It's scary sometimes. She may be one, but she's super manipulative.

"Maybe Kiara and Blake are fated," Jasper coos. Jasper is a badass Alpha, I mean he is a monster on the battlefield, but when it comes to his pup and his Luna, he's as innocent as a kitten.

"I hope Blake can handle an older woman," Aiden teases with a wink.

"Hey, that's my son you're talkin' about. He can handle anything. Unlike some people," Jasper says, cutting me a look. He just had to sneak that in, huh? Calix and Aiden just laugh. Remind me to punch these guys in the face when I see them. "Izzy is returning with our pack members tomorrow morning. She can't handle being away from Blake much longer. But Marcus and I are going to stay an extra day or two," he informs them.

"Any particular reason?" Calix inquires.

"Now that Amelia is Alpha we want to go over our allyship. We'd talked about it in the past, but I said I would only commit to it once she took over as Alpha," he says, shocking me to the core.

When the hell did this happen?

Why does no one tell me anything?

"Maybe if you weren't so busy screwing she-wolves like that bitch Davina you could have focused more on your job as Beta and then you would be more in the know," Ace says wryly.

"Don't you have a bone to chew or something?" I snap.

"Sure. Let's shift and I'll go find one and munch away," he says arrogantly.

"That sounds like a great idea. We look forward to hearing how it went," says Calix.

"Also, I feel like I have to stay close to Marcus before he says one more stupid thing and gets himself killed."

"I do not need a wingman when it comes to my Goddess-damn animai, you jackass," I snap at him.

"Really? Coz you've bombed twice now," he points out.

"Ouch. Oh, by the way, Davina has been calling asking for you," says Aiden slyly.

"Tell her to fuck off then," I spit.

"She hasn't come to the packhouse has she?" Asks Jasper in a low voice.

"No, and we wouldn't let her in if she did. Don't worry, Alpha," reassures Aiden.

"We'll just tell her you have found your animai if she calls again. Well, that's assuming you still have an animai by the time you get back," says Calix casually.

"The fuck did you just say?" I ask icily and I know my eyes are glowing, but they don't look fazed, in fact, they look smug. I'm really going to beat their asses. "I'm not rejecting my animai and if she tries to reject me, I'm not fucking accepting it," I growl.

"Does that mean you can accept her being an Alpha?" Asks Jasper with a raised brow.

"I... I don't know. Maybe we can find a compromise. Maybe she doesn't really want to be an Alpha, but only did it because her father had no other heir," I suggest. This makes everyone roll their eyes and groan.

"Just let her kill him, the man is a lost cause," says Calix.

"How about you try to get to know her before you make assumptions about her and start deciding her life for her?" Snaps Jasper.

"Why are you so fucking protective of *my* animai? She's mine, not yours!" I shout as another growl breaks from me. Jasper's eyes glow for a split second and I can see he's furious. His wolf could technically view this as a challenge and kill me, but I don't fucking care. Why is he always acting and talking so sweetly about my damn soulmate?

Fuck... did they used to... I think I'm going to throw up.

"We'll speak later," he says as he closes the laptop.

"You going to answer me or fucking what?" I spit. He gets up and starts to walk away. But I'm too riled up. He seems closer to Amelia than I am. I want to be close to her like that, it should be me. I get up and spin him around grabbing him by his shirt and slam him into the wall. "Fucking answer me!" I yell. His eyes glow and he grabs my wrists, twisting me into a headlock.

"Calm down, Marcus!" He orders releasing his Alpha Spirit. I fight against it – giving myself a headache – but eventually, my wolf and I submit to the force of it. "As your Alpha, I don't owe you a fucking explanation, but as your friend, I'll answer you," he says calmly as he lets me go. I stand to face him rubbing my neck. "Over the years I'd see Amelia at various pack meetings shadowing her dad, just like how I shadowed mine, even when she was just a little girl. She wowed me from such a young age, and we instantly became friends. I didn't see anything wrong with her being an Alpha, it felt right. She had such a strong Alpha Spirit even as a kid and she was friendly to everyone," he says, and I can hear the warm affection in his voice. It makes jealousy boil in my veins. "But then I started to notice it," his voice dropping an octave. My body goes rigid, and I just know I am not going to like this next part. "At every meeting, she was bullied by the other kids, future Alphas, Betas, or even non-ranked wolves. Even Omegas would get in on the action just to fit in. They were merciless, always telling her what a freak she was, how a girl can't be an Alpha. I hated seeing it and I always tried to defend her. I even saw the adults doing it. Grown fucking men picking on a child. All because they were scared. And you know how she reacted to all of it?"

"She broke down," I surmise painfully, my heart constricting just thinking of my beautiful animai as a little girl, huddled up crying because of everyone's cruelty.

"No dumbass, she never cried once. She handled it with grace and dignity, even when she was just eight-years-old. She never let their words get to her. She handled their abuse far better than even grown Alphas. If they tried to cut her down with words, she put them in their place. When they got physical with her and tried to assert their dominance over her, she kicked their asses. They always underestimated her, and it always cost them some broken bones." My little animai did all that? Pride swells inside me now picturing her standing up for herself and putting those wolves in their place. I'd like to wring the neck of anyone who dare lay a fucking hand on her, but I mean, I guess it makes sense. If she is an Alpha, then an Alpha bends to no one. "That's why I'm protective of her and why I'm so fucking mad at you, Marcus. You're treating her the same way everyone else has her whole life. The things you said to her she has had to hear her whole life. You're her soulmate, you're the one person who she's meant to be able to rely on. She needs your support and instead, you act like everyone else," he says bitterly.

His words hit me like a wrecking ball. I find myself slumping against the wall and sliding down onto the floor. What have I done? I knew my words hurt her, but this... this hurts so much worse. My beautiful animai, the one I'm meant to protect and devote my life to, I've been treating her like all those assholes did. Fuck, how does she not hate me? She'll reject me for sure. We haven't even known each other a whole day and I've already proven myself to be a terrible soulmate. There's no way she'll want me after this. Fear clutches my heart and spreads through me like sharp icicles. I feel like I can't breathe. Tears prick my eyes. The thought of losing her makes me feel like I could die.

I'm vaguely aware of Jasper sitting down next to me ad wrapping an arm around me.

"What have I done, Jazz?" I whisper, the weight of the situation crushing me.

"Talk to her. Give her a chance and show her you're not like them," he encourages and then sighs, "I know the idea of having a female Alpha for an animai is still hard for you, but maybe, for now, don't focus on that. Just focus on getting to know her as Amelia, not as an Alpha."

I nod weakly. I can do that. It's a good place to start. I take in a deep, shaky breath and, as I do, I hear a buzzer at the door. Yeah, turns out all the rooms in this place have buzzers since all the rooms are soundproof. Smart idea, actually. Jasper squeezes my arm and gets up to answer the door.

"Oh, hey Amelia," he chirps, and my head snaps up to the doorway. My eyes instantly connect with those stunning turquoise orbs.

Chapter Ten
Amelia

Forest eyes look up at me and the first thing I notice is the glassy sheen to them. Was Marcus crying? He doesn't look like the type who cries. He seems more the type to mock a man for crying, telling them to 'stop acting like a girl.'

"Is everything okay in here?" I ask softly.

"Yeah, everything is fine," Marcus says, quickly getting to his feet.

My eyes have a mind of their own and quickly rake themselves over his body and I know they can hear the way my heart picked up a little because Marcus is smirking and Jasper looks smug. I calm myself and get my heart back into a steady rhythm noting Marcus's surprise.

"I said we'd talk later and now it's later. So, I was wondering if you'd like to join me for a walk?"

Marcus opens his mouth to speak but Jasper beats him to it. "Marcus would love to go for a walk with you," he says cheerfully.

I chuckle. "Surely your Beta can speak for himself, Jazz," I tease, again noting Marcus' surprised face.

Jasper snorts. "I don't particularly trust my Beta's judgement right now," he says shooting Marcus a look, to which Marcus just glares back at him. I nod in understanding.

"Shall we?" I gesture to Marcus, and he nods, stepping out of the guest suite.

Together, we make our way downstairs, out of the packhouse and begin slowly walking nowhere in particular. It's both comforting and tense. It's comforting because being this close to my animai is soothing my soul, but I'm tense because I'm waiting for him to make another jerk comment.

"Can I ask you something?" He says hesitantly. I nod for him to continue. "Just something I've been wondering. Last night when that girl got rejected, what did you do exactly?" He asks curiously.

"I shared my healing and strength with her," I tell him.

He looks confused. "You have abilities?" He quizzes.

"No more than any other wolf or Alpha."

"Then how do you explain what you did? How did you even do it?" He asks, his brows furrowed.

"A couple years ago there was a cur attack. One of my best friends, Evalyn, was hurt really badly. She was losing blood faster than she was able to heal. I knew that even at full speed she'd bleed out before we got her medical assistance. In that moment I just wanted so badly to help her. I wanted to give her my strength just so she could hold on long enough. I could feel a part of me reach out to her through our pack-link. I didn't know what I was doing or if I could, I just knew I had to try. Zara and I latched onto our link with her and projected our healing and strength to her and, by some miracle, it worked. The bleeding started to slow down just enough for us to get her to the hospital where they took care of the rest," I explain to him. He stares at me in silence, his eyes whirlpools of emotion.

"I've never heard of anyone else doing something like that before," he says almost suspiciously.

"Neither had I. I suspected it was because I'm an Alpha, so after telling my father, he decided to test the theory. It was hard and took him a lot of time, but he was able to do the same thing. He's only been able to do it twice. He finds it very difficult and draining," I tell him.

"And you don't?" He asks with a raised eyebrow.

"I can't explain it. I've done it many times and each time it got easier. I've never felt drained afterwards. Helping Jen was the first time I've done it since I took over as Alpha, and now it's even more effortless than before," I say with a shrug, but now his frown is deeper. After that, we slip into more silence and continue walking aimlessly.

"I heard about what happened with the previous Beta." His fists clench and his jaw sets.

"I gather Jasper told you," I guess.

"Were you hurt?" He asks, and I look up to see so much concern on his face. Warmth spreads through me.

"Not much," I shrug, "I was all better in under an hour."

He relaxes a little. We slip back into silence again, which I'm okay with.

Marcus is like an oasis in the desert when you've been travelling alone for miles. You see the lush greenery and delicious water in the distance and hope blooms in your chest, so you start racing towards it. But no matter how far you run, the oasis continues to seem out of reach. That's when you realise the oasis was just a mirage.

"Amelia..." he trails off as he comes to a stop. I turn to face him and wait to hear what he has to say. "I care about you a lot. This is supposed to be easy and effortless; we were made for each other. I don't mean to keep coming off like an asshole, it's not fair to you and I know I'm just sending mixed signals," he sighs, running his fingers through his luscious black hair, making me fight the urge to do the same. I like the way his biceps flex as he does it, it reminds me of how it felt to be pulled into his arms and how badly I want to feel that again. I quickly clear away my thoughts before they go too far. "I don't want to hurt you, but I'm confused. I don't know how this is supposed to work," he admits, sounding dejected.

"You never even asked," I point out. He nods shamefully. "So, ask now," I prompt.

He takes a deep breath. "If we mate and mark each other, where would we live? Am I expected to move to your pack? What happens when we have pups? Do you expect me to become some househusband while you're off playing Alpha?" His tone is starting to turn bitter, and I don't like it. "If I'm here with you, what would I be to the pack? Do you expect me to be their... their Luna?" He says 'Luna' through gritted teeth, like the title is an insult. Of course, because anything traditionally associated with women is insulting, I guess. Never mind the fact that a Luna is a higher rank than a Beta.

"I understand you're a Beta to your pack, but I'm an Alpha so I can't just up and leave my pack, nor do I want to. If we have pups, I'd expect us to raise them equally, like proper parents, regardless of my *playing* Alpha. As for becoming Luna, why not?" I shrug. I know this is likely to set him off, but I want to see how he reacts. As predicted, he looks disgusted.

"You can't be serious. I'm a man, you can't fucking expect me to be some prissy Luna," he says in disgust.

"Prissy? Is that what you think of your Luna?" I ask with a raised eyebrow. For a second he balks, realising he just insulted his Luna.

He takes a breath to compose himself. "That's how most Luna's are," he points out.

I roll my eyes. "It's a title Marcus, how one treats it is up to them. There are plenty of sadistic, violent Alphas, but that doesn't mean that's what defines an Alpha. My father's Beta betrayed his pack and tried to kill me, does that mean you're a traitor too?" I ask him calmly.

That one shocks him. "I would *never* betray my Alpha or my pack," he says with powerful conviction, his eyes glowing, and I can feel his wolf's spirit radiating off him. It doesn't affect me, but for a weaker wolf, it definitely would. His spirit feels stronger than most Betas.

"Seems to me that's because he was always meant to be ours. He had to be strong enough to stand beside us. He needs to get out of the whole forced gender roles stuff. We're not even human, why should we care about that crap?" Zara scoffs in irritation.

"That's my point, Marcus," I say softly.

"So where does that leave us?" He asks tiredly.

"I don't know. I'm not the one with the issues," I point out.

A flash of annoyance comes over his features as he steps close to me, his scent overpowering me and for a second all I can focus on is him and how delicious he smells. I want to lean into his scent, into his warmth and just bask in it. The damn magic that binds animais' together is an overpowering force and in these moments, the pull of it is hard to ignore.

"Do you even care? You act so aloof, so unbothered, that I'm starting to wonder if you even care that I'm your animai," he says sardonically.

I snap out of my haze and glare up at him. "Oh, I'm sorry. Would you rather I broke down and cried? I'm not going to be jumping up and down in excitement or pacing around worrying if you like me or not, especially since you've been very vocal about your thoughts and feelings, each one more hurtful than the last. You care for me, you want me – you just want me to be something and someone else. You just wish I weren't who I am. You want me because I'm yours but you're hoping to change me so you can be more comfortable. How do you think I feel listening to my own soulmate look at me and speak to me like I'm some kind of abomination?" I spit. He flinches back at my words and actually looks hurt and ashamed. "Not once have I made any comments about changing anything about you, I've not put any expectations on you because I don't care about that stuff. I just wanted my animai. Unfortunately, he wants me to be someone I'm not," I tell him.

We're looking at each other, a silent stare down full of emotions. Neither moving. Neither speaking. Tension just swirling around us. Zara has gone so quiet; I'm actually starting to worry. Even if she's not speaking she's always active in some way or another, I always feel her presence, but right now it's like she's shutting down. The silence is broken by Tyson running over to us, slowing down as he gets closer.

"Um… is everything okay over here?" He asks tentatively.

I compose myself and turn my attention to him. "Everything is fine. How was training?" I inquire.

Tyson glares at Marcus for a moment before turning his attention back to me. "Good, everyone did great. You'll be joining in tomorrow, right?"

"Of course, I'm excited to see what your surprise is," I smile at him.

He grins mischievously and rubs his hands together. "Oh, it's going to be great; I promise," he tells me. "I'm just going to go do a sweep of the border and then–"

I hold my hand up interrupting him, "No, you are going to shower and then go and spend some quality time with Eva."

"Amelia, after today's revelation, I need to make sure everything is fine," he says with determination.

"Tyson, you're overworking yourself. I love and appreciate you working so hard for me and the pack, but you need to pace yourself. You're going to burn out and then you'll be no good to anyone," I explain.

He rubs his face in frustration, "This is my job, Amelia."

"I wasn't asking you to take a break, Tyson, that's an order from your Alpha. Go upstairs, go shower, and be with Evalyn. Everything will be fine, you've done a terrific job, now go and relax," I say pushing my Alpha Spirit forward.

He takes a breath and sighs in defeat. "Yes, Alpha," he says and runs off to the packhouse.

"You'll thank me later!" I yell after him with a smile. I love his dedication, but man needs to slow down.

"Didn't think of introducing me?" Marcus says sounding a little hurt. His emotions are like a freakin' yoyo.

"And who would I introduce you as, exactly? You may not have noticed, but my friends don't like you much right now, and I'm the only thing keeping them from punching you in the face," I tell him proudly. I'm not proud my friends want to hurt my animai, but I am proud of how protective they are of me.

"I bet I could take them," he says arrogantly.

"Perhaps you and Jasper should join us for training tomorrow. Get out some of that aggression," I suggest.

He quirks an eyebrow at me. "I'd rather get my aggression out another way," he says suggestively in a low voice with a smirk.

I can't help but gulp at his words as the muscles between my thighs clench with need. It's not fair how much power his voice has over my body.

"I hope you don't think I'm just going to jump into bed with you," I say, trying to stay composed, but I know my beating heart is giving me away.

He sighs looking down, "No, I don't expect that. I'd be concerned if you were so willing to sleep with me considering how much of an asshole I've been."

"So then stop being an asshole," I say, like it's the most obvious conclusion. It's really not that hard.

"Believe me, I'm trying. It may not seem it, but I am trying," he says with a sarcastic laugh. He sighs and reaches his hand up, gently brushing the back of his hand against my cheek. I close my eyes and, for a moment, let myself enjoy the electricity his touch sends through my body. I wish his thoughts and words could be as gentle as his touch. "I don't know what's wrong with me," he whispers sadly.

My eyes snap open and look into his. His eyes are full of pain and confusion. He's torn between wanting to be with me and accepting a lifestyle he doesn't agree with. I can't change his views for him, but I hope he comes around. I hope he can accept and support me as I am. I would do the same for him.

Chapter Eleven
Amelia

The rest of yesterday went surprisingly well. Marcus and I didn't spend too much time together – mostly because I was busy – but the time we did spend together was decent. We kept the Alpha topic off the table for the time being. A silent decision made in order to keep the peace. It didn't stop things from being awkward, but it at least prevented another fight. Arguing, fighting; these things have never bothered me. But doing them with the person made for you by the Gods themselves is not just painful, it's draining. It's like having your very soul tied to a stake and whipped over and over again until it just ceases to exist.

I wonder what the Goddess Zarseti was thinking when she created the magic behind animais. To make their bodies, minds and souls be so dependent on each other. To make them so vital to each other. Did she think people would be less likely to fight their crueller instincts and prejudices if the bond tying them to another was all-consuming? If so, that does make some sense, but then I wonder… how cruel or damaged does a person's soul have to be for them to hurt or reject their animai? I mean, this is some powerful magic – how do you fight against it?

It's 7:30 am and I've just made it to the training field. I haven't been able to attend a single training session because of the prep work for the Vernal Ball this last week and had to settle for the occasional gym visit. I need a proper session. I need to push myself, and Zara wants to come out and tussle. I put my nice, chilled metal water bottle on the bench and walk over to Tyson.

"Anything you need from me today?" I ask him.

"Since Mei is joining us, I think she should be your sparring partner. You've been training with her one-on-one, so you know what her limits are and you're also the only one likely to not get killed by her."

"Works for me. We're still starting off slow, but those instincts of hers are coming to the surface. I debated finding a way to trigger her aggression, but I think that would just get me killed. I think the best approach for her is allowing her to adjust a bit at a time, that way she maintains control," I explain to him, and he nods in agreement.

"Have either of you sparred in shifted forms yet?" He inquires.

I shake my head, "She's too nervous. She understands how much stronger she is in that form and is worried she'll hurt me." I smile softly. It's amazing how someone blessed with so much strength and power is so sweet and gentle. Makes for a silent assassin, I suppose.

"I'm sure you'll work on that," he says just as Evalyn jumps onto his back. She's looking happier than I've seen her in weeks. Tyson looks back at her, just as happy and their lips lock on each other.

"I take it you two had a good night," I tease. Evalyn throws me a big grin while nodding her head enthusiastically making me chuckle. "Anything you want to say to me?" I ask Tyson, smiling.

He rolls his eyes, "Thank you, Amelia, for sending my ass home to my girl."

"You're very welcome," I grin at him. Gradually we're joined by the rest of the group, including Chris, Mei, Vitali, and even Vitali's animai, Eric. Wasn't expecting that. I'm thrilled to have him join, but I admit I have to squash down the feeling of being a seventh wheel.

"I hope it's okay that I join in," Eric says hesitantly.

"Babe, I told you it's fine," says Vitali softly, giving Eric's hand a reassuring squeeze.

"He's right. The more the merrier," I say brightly allowing Eric to relax.

I throw Vitali a wink that he happily returns it. They really are a cute couple.

"Listen up!" Tyson says getting everyone's attention. "We're going to start with– "

"Sorry we're late. Hope we haven't interrupted," Jasper says apologetically, rushing over, Marcus at his side.

I glance at Marcus, momentarily distracted by his workout shorts and grey tank top, the kind that dip really low at the sides showing off every delicious muscle Goddess Morrtemis blessed him with. I fight the urge to gulp and think over what I'm wearing. Got my hair in a ponytail, am wearing a black sports bra and blue, white, and black cheetah-print leggings.

Do I look okay?

Wait, why should I care?

"It's not wrong to want to look good for our animai, Amelia. It's only natural. Trust me, you look great and I'm sure showing this much skin is going to make him suffer," Zara sniggers. Her words give me some satisfaction.

"You're right on time, we were just getting started," I tell him and then address my pack members, "Everyone this is Alpha Jasper and Beta Marcus; they will be joining our training session today so please show them respect."

"Yes, Alpha," they all say in unison. I nod for Tyson to continue.

"As I was saying, today I want everyone to start with fifty burpees followed by one hundred laps on the track with weights. After that, we'll move on to today's obstacle course and then we'll finish off with sparring. Let's go!" He shouts, clapping his hands together.

Evalyn pouts at Tyson like a wounded puppy. "Burpees? I'm terrible at those," she says disgruntled.

Tyson walks over and kisses her forehead. "The Eva I know never backs down from a challenge. Come on, I'll do them beside you." She beams up at him and the two begin their burpees together.

Everyone spreads out and starts their workout. I don't know how, but Marcus and I have ended up working out facing each other. Thank the Gods, Zara is keeping count, otherwise I'd have completely lost track. I'm exercising on autopilot because my eyes are completely focused on every move Marcus' muscles make. His sweat is intensifying his caramel scent and

I find myself fighting the urge to jump on him and lick him. Damn bond. However, I do notice Marcus' eyes glued to my chest every time I jump, so maybe he's fighting the same urges as me right now. I suppress a smirk.

As soon as Zara calls out fifty burpees in my head, I stop, shake my arms out and walk over to the track. I strap the weights to my wrists and ankles and start running. As I do, I notice Mei is already on the track. I pick up the pace just until I get to her side and then I start running at her speed.

"How does it feel training with the pack?" I ask her.

"Part of me is nervous, mostly about how they'll react to me. But the other part of me finds this exhilarating," she tells me.

"Your nerves are completely understandable but try to remember you're stronger than them and you're a ranked member of this pack. Them saying shit to you is them asking to get their asses kicked," I tell her cheekily.

"I'm ranked?" She asks in shock. I chuckle.

"Of course, ever since you and Chris became animais. You two mating and marking each other sealed the deal. You share his Delta title," I explain to her.

She thinks over that for a moment. "What do I have to do?" She asks nervously, but I detect interest, which I like.

"Entirely up to you. Honestly, most women fated to a ranked member other than an Alpha don't really do anything with the title, which is stupid. I mean, it's there, you have it, put it to use," I say with mild annoyance.

These women would do anything to snag a ranked wolf, but then do nothing once they get one besides boss people around and go on shopping sprees. Well, not counting the previous Gamma and Delta females, they were dedicated to pack and family, supporting their animais and helping their Luna, so they were very active. Beta Saree, however, definitely milked that rank for all it was worth. Kinda glad I punched my fist through her chest.

"How about for now you work close with Chris and see how you feel and if it's not really for you, but you still want to be involved I can find something for you, how does that sound?" I offer.

She smiles and nods enthusiastically, "That sounds wonderful, thank you, Al... I mean, Amelia," she says bashfully.

"You're welcome," I chuckle. After a couple minutes, Jasper and Marcus catch up to us. I'm actually surprised how easily Marcus is keeping up.

"Hope you don't mind if we run alongside you ladies," Jasper says in his usual cheerful manner.

"Plenty of room, so I don't see why not. Jasper, this is Delta Mei, Chris' animai. Mei, this is Alpha Jasper of the Aurum Obscuro Pack and his Beta, Marcus," I introduce them. I see a flash of hurt in Marcus' eyes because I again didn't introduce him as my animai. You really can't blame me given how he has repeatedly treated me. I don't see him publicly declaring me either, except when he got all territorial with Ryker. Probably too ashamed.

"It is a pleasure to meet you, miss," says Jasper.

"Likewise," she says nervously. She's still not comfortable around new people, which I understand. Trauma doesn't disappear that quickly.

"Care to race?" Marcus asks me, smirking.

"Not particularly."

"Afraid you'll lose?" He taunts.

Jasper throws him a disapproving look. I'm sure goading works on other Alphas but I'm not like other Alphas. I've always had good control over my emotions, and I'm not easily riled up. Considering people have tried to goad me into proving myself my whole life, I learned quickly never to give them what they want unless I was just really in the mood to put some jerks in their place that day.

"Nope. Just content to stick to my usual routine," I say, casually. He huffs a little.

"Your Alpha is right there, race him if you're looking for a challenge," I suggest. If I race Marcus and win, his ego will take another hit. If I race him and lose, he'll feel validated in his feelings about a female Alpha. Either way, I lose, so no way in hell am I racing him.

"Come on Marcus, last one to reach a hundred is on diaper duty for a week," Jasper taunts and then picks up his speed.

"Oh, fuck no, you are not leaving me to handle that shit factory!" Marcus yells and starts racing Jasper.

I sigh with relief, grateful Jasper stepped in. He's done that since I was a kid; finding diplomatic ways to step in and protect me from whatever was going on. I was grateful for it then and I'm grateful for it now.

"Why is your animai so determined to challenge you?" Mei asks but her tone is offended. Aww, she's offended on my behalf, I'm touched!

"I really don't know, Mei," I sigh.

Jasper was the first to complete one hundred laps with Marcus close behind him, so I guess he's on diaper duty. Now that I'd love to see. Mei and I sped up on the final lap and she beat me easily, which didn't bother me. It was good seeing her let loose.

Once everyone had finished their laps and removed their weights, we all gathered at the obstacle course. On the way, I pick up my water canister and take a long sip of the cooling water, which tastes bitter for some reason. Did I not wash the canister? I put the bottle down and join everyone, eager to see what Tyson has set up. He has something hidden under a cloth, but I can't make out what it is.

"So, how does this work?" Jasper asks, coming up beside me.

"A year back Tyson's father, Gamma James, began implementing obstacle courses to better test and push our reflexes. The results proved beneficial, so it became a regular part of training. Recently James began introducing courses that tested and trained our senses. Tyson and I loved this, so we decided to mix it into regular training," I explain to him.

He smiles, "That's absolutely brilliant. Wish I'd thought of that. No hard feelings if I steal your ideas."

I chuckle, shaking my head. "If it helps your pack, by all means, steal it."

"Selfless as ever. You're going to be one hell of an Alpha, Amelia," he says sincerely.

"Aren't you tired of saying that?" I ask playfully.

He shrugs. "Nuh-uh. Plus, I'm only speaking the truth," he nudges me. I hear a displeased growl from behind me and instinctively it makes me shiver pleasurably, but at the same time, roll my eyes. "Touchy isn't he?" Jasper teases and I can't help but chuckle.

We all step up and fall silent, waiting for Tyson to give us our instructions.

Excitement is rushing through my veins; I love a challenge.

"Today's sensory course is inspired by our Alpha's Alpha challenge," he says surprising me.

"Alpha, can you tell everyone why Beta Saree was able to get the jump on you so easily?" He asks, in full instructor mode.

"The sound of her approach was muffled by the noises of the pack, and I was unable to pick up her scent moving towards me because my nose was broken," I casually answer. I have no hesitations in answering this, everything can be used as a learning opportunity for myself and the pack. I'm impressed with Tyson for using my fight as a learning opportunity.

"Another example of how crucial our senses are to survival. It is imperative that we hone each of them so that, should one be rendered useless, the others are quickly able to pick up the slack," he explains. He pulls away the sheet to reveal one of those machines that spits out tennis balls. Now, this should be interesting. "Meet the Spinshot Player. It has a capacity of a hundred and twenty balls and feeds the balls from nineteen to sixty-eight miles per hour with a feed frequency of two to ten seconds. Today you will be blindfolded and given nose plugs and have to rely on your hearing only to dodge the balls," he announces with a grin. Everyone is murmuring. Vitali, Chris, and I are grinning at each other, and Evalyn has gone pale. Poor thing. "Oh and another thing. I'll be using baseballs instead of tennis balls. Baseballs are going to hurt a lot more, so take that as an added incentive to dodge them," he smirks.

I glance over and see that Jasper and Marcus look both surprised and impressed. I swell with pride for Tyson and my pack. We take training seriously.

"Alpha, care to go first?" He says wiggling his eyebrows.

Normally, I would happily go first. It's important for pack members to see their leader take on the same challenges with no hesitation. It encourages them. "I would love to. But I think someone else should go first this time." I smile and Tyson cocks his head to the side curiously. "Mei, you're up."

Mei's eyes go wide and Chris snaps his attention to me, visibly agitated. "Amelia, are you crazy? No way. She's not ready for this."

"Chris, she won't get stronger if you're always treating her like a soap bubble. Have a little faith," I say encouragingly, looking at Mei. "Mei, this is about sound and speed. I've seen how fast you are when your natural reflexes kick in. You can do this. Besides, gives me something to try and beat," I wink at her. She looks at the machine deep in thought.

Chris squeezes her shoulders. "Xingan baobei, you don't have to do this. She won't make you," he tells her, which is true. If she says no, that's fine. But there's a fighter lurking underneath the trauma. She wants to be stronger, even if it's just so no one hurts her again.

She adamantly shakes her head, looking determined, "I want to do this."

I grin proudly. Chris and Mei stare at each other for a moment before he sighs and steps aside. Mei takes a deep breath and steps forward. She takes the blindfold and nose plug from Tyson and puts them on, standing in front of the wooden wall that is normally used for climbing exercises. She stands still, taking slow breaths to calm down her racing heart, just like I taught her. Evalyn walks over to hold her brother's hand tight for support and Chris gladly takes it. I give Tyson the go and he turns on the machine.

Once the machine starts up, a baseball comes flying out at top speed, aiming directly for Mei's face. At a speed much faster than that of a mutolupus, her hand snaps up and catches the ball. A proud smirk stretches across my face while everyone else gasps in surprise. Chris looks like he's going to pass out.

Balls start flying out one by one at different intervals, some closer together than others, never in the same place twice, but all aiming directly for Mei. She either catches or dodges every single ball with a speed that is incredible to watch. After a few minutes, Tyson turns off the machine and the pack cheers for Mei. She removes the blindfold and nose plug, a bashful smile on her face. Before she can step away from the wall, Chris has raced over, scooped her up and is swinging her around, burying his face in her neck.

"You were so unbelievably amazing. I mean, I was having a heart attack the whole time, but you were incredible!" He claims her lips in a loving kiss that she returns, her cheeks heating up in the process. They are so freakin' cute!

"Think you can beat that, Alpha?" Tyson taunts.

I chuckle. "No idea. Let's find out, shall we?"

I walk over and take the blindfold and nose plug from Mei as she and Chris re-join the group. Once they are on, I immediately feel unsettled. Not being able to hear or see is one thing but, as a wolf, not being able to smell is probably the hardest to adjust to. It instantly makes me feel off balance and I have to push the feelings away. I move my focus to what I have and not what's lacking. On what I can hear. I can hear hearts pumping, one beating faster than all the others and somehow, I know that heartbeat belongs to Marcus. Wow. Is that part of the animai bond too? I can pick up his heartbeat in a crowd… there's something so intimate and intense about this.

Focusing back on my surroundings, I can hear how each blade of grass moves against the other in the breeze. I can hear the animals moving in the forest. Now I focus a little harder, tuning out everything around me and listening to the sounds in front of me. I can hear the machine starting up, the vibrations of it, the motor and even the sound of the balls being fed through and then I can hear the sound of a projectile cutting through the air. I can sense it coming towards my right shoulder, so I quickly twist my body out of its path. I feel the ball whizz past me and hit the wall behind me with a loud crack.

For a few minutes I continue to dodge and catch balls, and I would love to gloat and say I had a perfect score, but no. A few managed to hit me and man, did they hurt. I quickly examine myself and can see a couple ball-sized bruises on my torso. I'm sure there are a couple on my legs and one particularly nasty one that hit me right in the head. Fortunately, with fast healing, I'll be fine in minutes.

"Looks like Mei is holding the record so far, Alpha coming in at a respectable second place. Who wants to go next?" Tyson asks.

"I will," Marcus says. My head snaps up and our eyes lock. There's determination in his eyes and something else. I'm not sure what and I'm not sure if I want to know.

Marcus walks over to me, and I hand him the blindfold and nose plug.

For a brief moment, our fingers touch and my entire body goes nuts from the contact. My breath hitches, heart rate spikes and my desire and overall need for him floods my system. I can tell he's having the same reaction. I compose myself and walk back to the group as Jasper comes to stand beside me, a displeased look on his face.

Why do I feel like my animai drama is causing a rift in their friendship?

"Don't blame... for... Marcus'... okay?" Comes Zara's voice making me frown. Why does she sound like a radio station where the signal keeps dropping out?

"What did you say?" I ask her.

"What do you mean... say... like you can't... so rude..." comes her voice.

Again, I am only picking up every other word. The others keep dropping out. What is going on? In twenty-one years I have never, ever had issues communicating with Zara. For the first time I feel rattled. I don't like this at all. But I don't let it show on my face. Maybe I'm just tired...

I focus back on what's happening in front of me in time to see Marcus dodging and catching baseballs at a very impressive speed, even for a Beta. Gradually the frequency gets the best of him, and he starts missing a few, with the ones he misses making contact with his body and I cringe each time he's hit. Seeing him get hurt, even just minor injuries, is making me uncomfortable. My entire being is protesting, unable to stomach the sight of my animai in pain, no matter how tolerable that pain may be for him. The next ball to fly out at him hits him square in the collarbone and a painful cry comes out of his mouth, as the ball breaks his collarbone with a sickening crack. I watch as the bone breaks through his skin.

Fuck!

"MARCUS!" I shout and before I have time to think, I am over at his side. He's hunched on the ground, clutching his collarbone. Jasper is at Marcus' side not a second later. Tyson has thankfully turned off the machine.

"Fuck, man, that looks nasty," says Jasper as he examines the wound.

"That's going to need resetting. Come on, I'll take you to the pack hospital," I say softly as I fight down the urge to hurl at the sight of Marcus' injury. I don't have a weak stomach. We're just not programmed to be okay with our other half being injured. I start to put my arm around him, but before I can touch him, he pulls away from me. Anger and pain are written all over his face.

"I don't need your fucking help!" He spits through gritted teeth.

I wince as the tone of his voice and the look in his eyes have shards of ice piercing my heart. I can't handle it, but I compose myself. Now he's got a problem with me helping him? Why? Because I didn't break a bone? This is getting ridiculous.

"I can get myself to the pack hospital, I don't need you," he says in a low venomous voice, but this time I don't react at all.

"Marcus!" Jasper growls, projecting his Alpha Spirit. "Watch your fucking tone."

I wave him off, "It's fine." I stand up and take a step back. "Don't let me get in your way," I say calmly.

Marcus gets to his feet, his face contorted in a grimace as he tries not to move the arm with his broken collarbone – an injury which is particularly painful. Even though I'm mad that once again he's letting his ego get between us, I still care about him, and it hurts to see him in pain. I want so badly to help him. I know the touch of your animai can soothe your pain, but he doesn't want that. Rejection hits me full force again. Hurts far worse than those baseballs did.

Marcus starts walking off but after a few steps, he comes to a stop. I stand there and cross my arms over my chest observing him, "Let me guess. You just realised you don't know where the pack hospital is." His body tenses up and I shake my head, looking at Jasper, "If you remember where the pack hospital is, could you please escort him?"

Jasper nods. "Not a problem, I remember the way," he says getting up and walking over to Marcus.

"Oh. Before you go." I walk over to them and stand in front of Marcus. "Let me impart some wisdom my father once shared with me. Suffering through pain when you don't have to doesn't make you strong. It makes you an idiot." His eyes widen in shock as I step away and return to the group. "Tyson, please continue the session," I instruct.

I quickly pick up my water bottle and take a few sips; the bitter taste still present. I hear Jasper and Marcus leaving the training field, but I don't spare them another glance. I can tell pack members are linking each other to gossip about what just happened, but I don't give them the satisfaction of a reaction.

I'm half tempted to bail on the rest of training, but honestly, I need sparring more than ever. When the sensory course was over we got right into sparring. Mei and I fought hand to hand and then Vitali and I sparred in wolf form. Vitali's wolf Blaise is grey all over with his tail being a shade darker than the rest of him.

For some reason Zara let me be in control of the shift, not that I mind. Honestly, I'm grateful to be able to use this form to get out my frustration, but it feels weird for some reason and Zara isn't speaking to me. I don't know why. Surely, I haven't done anything to piss her off. That being said, fighting with Vitali went great. He's a good fighter and can hold his own against me. He got in a few good swipes and bites but wasn't able to take me down. But he never went easy on me, and I appreciate him for that.

Throughout training, I couldn't shake the feeling that everyone was talking about me, and it was putting me on edge. Once the training is all over I get dressed and sit down, finishing off my yucky tasting water. It's not like mould or bacteria will kill or hurt me. The immune system of a mutolupus is too strong for that. I sit on the bench and rest my head in my hands, feeling fuzzy.

"Amelia, are you okay?" Vitali asks gently as he rubs my back.

I nod slowly. "I'm fine. I guess I'm just feeling thrown off a little," I say with a weak smile. Is this what rejection feels like? Cause it sucks.

"I think maybe you should see Doctor Richard; you're not looking so good," he says with concern, but I wave him off.

"Vit, I said I'm fine," I say more forcefully now. "Thank you for caring, but I'm good. I just need a shower and some food." I get up and start making my way to the packhouse, my vision becoming blurry with each step I take.

As I make my way into the packhouse all the voices sound muddled together and there's an unpleasant buzzing in my ears. I rub them to get rid of it, but it doesn't do anything. As I pass through the sitting areas my vision blurs more and now I can hear whispering.

"Some Alpha, not even her soulmate wants her. Maybe the Gods hate her," I hear one voice whisper.

"Of course, they hate her. She's going against the natural order. Beta Declan should have killed her," whispers the other voice. Anger flares through my body, heating me up from the inside like a furnace.

"I'm so fucking over this disrespectful bullshit!" I snarl. Before I know it Vitali is in front of me, his face full of worry.

"Amelia, what happened?" He asks calmly.

"The fucking whispering! I won't put up with it anymore! I'm their Alpha!" I roar.

Instantly Vitali jumps back in fear, but he tries to maintain his composure, "What whispering? Amelia, no one is whispering I swear." He sounds like he's trying to tame a wild beast.

I just glare at him, the anger inside me is burning hotter by the second. I can hardly think straight and now I'm seeing double. Suddenly Vitali's face twists into a snare and he starts laughing. Like full-blown cackling.

"Gods, you are so pathetic, Amelia. You really will be the end of this pack. Most of us just have to pretend to tolerate you. No one actually wants you." These words should hurt, they should break my heart, but they don't. Instead, a red haze flashes over my eyes as the rage takes over and before I know it, I'm shifting.

Chapter Twelve
Vitali

Training today went great until it wasn't great anymore. I was trying to have fun getting to have Eric beside me for training, but it wasn't easy. We've been talking about him moving to this pack since I'm the Beta here. I wanted him to get a feel for our training routine. I could see he was having fun and that made me happy.

At first, I was beyond shocked to get fated to a man, even though I've always known I was bisexual. I just never wanted to tell anyone. Stupid of me. I should have known my friends would have had my back. Still, I hadn't known what to make of Eric, but as soon as we were together, everything clicked. He's perfect for me in every way and I've never been happier. That being said, it's hard to bask in happiness when my best friend is in pain.

Once again Amelia's animai has publicly disrespected her. He treats her like crap, and it makes me want to rip his Gods-damn head off. Amelia is the sweetest, most thoughtful, smartest, and strongest person I've ever known, and it hurts to see her being treated like this. She acts okay – like always – putting on a front like nothing is bothering her, but I know on the inside, she's hurting. I think this is all really starting to affect her. I noticed during training she kept frowning like something was wrong and during sparring, her moves seemed off. By the end of training, she was starting to look a little grey. She said she was fine and wouldn't go see the doctor, but I know Amelia, something isn't right.

"Anyone else think something is wrong with Amelia?" Chris walks over with his arm around Mei. I nod.

"Is it possible to suffer the effects of rejection without being properly rejected?" Tyson asks, looking just as worried as the rest of us. Eric comes over and wraps his arm around my waist and I calm down a little. I breathe in his sweet scent of pomegranates and let it soothe me as I pull him closer. Letting our bond work like a cooling salve. I kiss his temple and enjoy the tingles that dance on my lips. I smile hearing his contented sigh.

"You think she's going through rejection?" Evalyn asks with concern.

"He hasn't rejected her. I had the same concern, but I think Amelia is sick or something. She wasn't looking well when we finished training," I tell them.

"Mutolupus' don't get sick, Vitali," Chris says with a frown, pulling Mei into him.

"That's why I'm worried," I say. I suddenly have a strong urge to go and check on Amelia. It's not just an urge, it's like a voice inside me is screaming to go to my Alpha, and the voice isn't coming from Blaise. We make our way to the packhouse and as soon as we walk in my eyes land on Amelia. She's sweating, more than she was before, her skin is greyer, and her head is snapping around frantically, a sneer etched onto her face.

"I'm so fucking over this disrespectful bullshit!" She snarls, the sound of it making me shudder. Something is very wrong; this isn't like Amelia.

I carefully approach her. "Amelia, what happened?" I try to ask calmly. Her head is still whipping around furiously, her body in an attack pose. The others are standing back watching with worried faces.

"The fucking whispering! I won't put up with it anymore! I'm their Alpha!" She roars, the force of it so strong the ground begins to shake, and I immediately jump back. I try to stay calm and do my best to appear non-threatening.

"What whispering? Amelia, no one is whispering, I swear," I say softly. There's no one even around, except for staff and a few people who went straight from training to eating in the dining hall, but no one is saying anything about her. Suddenly her eyes lock on me and fear rolls through my body. I watch as her beautiful turquoise eyes turn pitch black. Now I know for a fact something is wrong. She looks fucking possessed and her whole body is shaking.

Fuck, is she about to shift?

"Eric, Eva, Mei, get upstairs now!" I order with my Beta Spirit. It's nothing compared to an Alpha, but it'll make them listen, except for Eric – dominating spirits don't work on animals. They run upstairs just as Amelia shifts into her wolf. She's snarling and snapping her jaws at me; her eyes still pitch black. It's like she doesn't even recognise me. "Amelia, this isn't you, okay? I need you to calm down," I say, but it doesn't work and next thing I know she's lunging at my throat.

Tyson and Chris waste no time and jump on her back. She's inches from my face and she's gone completely feral. Amelia quickly shakes Chris off like he's nothing and he slams into the wall. Tyson holds on until she sinks her teeth into his arm, and he screams in pain. She then quickly throws him off and sets her sights back on me. Just as she lunges, I manage to slide under her and get a tight grip around her neck. I wrap my legs around her torso like some reverse mechanical bull.

She's growling and thrashing and throwing herself around trying to shake me off, but no matter how much it hurts, I don't let go. Chris gets back up and throws himself on her back and, even though Tyson is injured, he latches onto her too. All three of us are trying to hold her down but she's too fucking strong.

"What the fuck is happening?!" Tyson shouts.

"I don't know, but we need to sedate her!" I shout back just as I feel her canines pierce my back. I bite my lips and fight back a scream of pain as blood trickles down my back and soaks my shirt. *Uncle Elias! Grandpa Alden! We need your help on the first floor now! Something is wrong with Amelia!* I shout through the pack-link. They don't reply, but I can sense their panic. *Doctor Richard, get to the packhouse immediately and bring something strong enough to knock out an Alpha!* I shout through the link and close it before he responds. I have to focus or she's going to bite my head off.

Less than a minute later Uncle Elias and Grandpa Alden are in the room, shock and worry all over their faces. "What the fuck is going on?!" Elias screams.

"Something is wrong with Amelia. You have to help us hold her down so the doc can sedate her," I tell them urgently.

They glance at each other with worried expressions but quickly rush over and latch onto Amelia. Her movements start to slow down as she struggles to fight us all off, but it seems to be making her angrier and another fierce growl rips from her, loud enough to shake the packhouse. People have gathered and are watching on in shock as five ranked wolves, including two former Alpha's, struggle to bring down their current Alpha..

What the hell has our girl been eating lately?

"I don't know how much longer I can hold her!" Exclaims Chris, blood staining his face.

"We just have to hold her until the doc gets here," I reassure him. Seconds later, Doctor Richard shows up with the world's largest syringe.

"Hold her as still as you can," he instructs calmly. Elias clamps his arms around Amelia's muzzle and does his best to hold her head still, a look of pain on his face. He doesn't like doing this to his daughter. Doctor Richard comes over and swiftly injects the syringe into the base of her skull and steps back.

After a moment, her growls turn into whimpers and her body starts to slump until, finally, she collapses on the floor. I pull myself out from under her with a bit of help from Chris and look down at the now unconscious black and white wolf.

Elias is immediately at her side, stroking the fur on her neck looking at her with fear in his eyes. Alden grabs a blanket and throws it over Amelia, kneeling beside her, his features filling with fear. Amelia starts to shift back to her human form, but I notice her heart is pounding like a jackhammer, even though she's sedated. It's beating way too fast.

"What's happening to my daughter?" Elias croaks, tears filling his eyes.

Doctor Richard comes over and starts examining her. Elias and Alden both pale when the doc lifts her eyelids, and her eyes are still pitch black.

"Is my granddaughter going to be alright?" Alden asks in a shaky voice.

"I don't know, Alphas. Right now I'm worried about her heart. If it keeps beating this fast, it may kill her." This causes us all to suck in a breath. "We have to get her to the hospital immediately," he calmly instructs.

Elias doesn't hesitate. He picks Amelia up in his arms and races out of the packhouse to the hospital, the doc and his father hot on his heels.

Tyson, Chris, and I look at each other. Each of us is seriously banged up, but we are more worried about Amelia than our injuries. Fuck the pain, we'll heal just fine.

"She's not really going to die, is she?" Tyson asks quietly.

"How can you even ask that?!" I growl. "It just took five of us to bring her down, she's too strong to die," I say angrily. Truth is, I'm terrified. I'm terrified I'm about to lose my best friend and that our pack will lose its Alpha. Fear and despair are creeping through me and latching onto my bones, moving into my lungs. It's like I can't breathe.

"Guys, let's go to the hospital and wait to hear what the doctor says, okay?" Chris says, calmly placing his hands on our shoulders. He's always the calm one – aside from Amelia. We nod and rush straight to the hospital. Once we get to the pack hospital, we find Alden leaning against the wall in the waiting room while Elias paces furiously. Nurses try to tend to myself, Tyson, and Chris but we wave them off. We'll be fully healed soon anyway.

"Can one of you explain what the hell happened?" Elias asks in a deadly tone.

I gulp, "We don't know. I noticed she was looking off-colour after training, but she said she was fine. Then when we got to the packhouse she was on edge and shouting about people whispering and disrespecting her. She was shaking and then her eyes… they went completely black and then she was shifting and trying to rip us apart."

Tears fill his eyes as he falls into a chair. Alden immediately sits beside him and wraps his arm around him.

"What's happening to my pup?" Elias asks in a pained whisper.

"The doctor will tell us soon. She's a strong wolf. Whatever it is, she'll be fine," Aldan tries to comfort his son, but I can see the worry in his eyes.

We're all scared shitless right now.

After waiting in purgatory for a whole hour, Doctor Richard finally comes to the waiting room. Immediately we are all out of our seats.

"How is my girl? What's wrong with her?" Elias asks in a panic.

"Alpha Amelia is going to be okay. We're treating her now and she should be fine in a few hours," a calm smile spreads over Doctor Richard's face and we all sigh with relief. Every muscle that was locked with tension has now been released. She's going to be okay. Thank the Goddess.

"But what happened to her?" I ask. Doc's smile turns into a frown. Not just a frown – he looks furious. This startles me, he's usually always so composed.

"The Alpha was poisoned," he says in a hard voice. All of us look shocked and growl in anger.

Who the fuck tried to hurt our Alpha? I'll kill them!

"We ran a blood test and found wulfenite in her system," Doctor Richard continues in a serious tone.

I have no idea what wulfenite is. Tyson and Chris look equally confused. Elias even looks confused. Alden, however, has gone white as a ghost.

"How is that possible?" Alden says.

Elias looks between the two, "What the hell is wulfenite?"

"Wulfenite is a rare mineral that is particularly toxic to us wolves. In small doses, it causes hallucinations and psychosis and can eventually lead to death. A large dose is inevitably lethal," he explains..

"How much was in her system?" Tyson asks through gritted teeth.

"A large amount, I'm afraid. But it would have had to have been administered to her within the last six hours for her to have been showing such severe symptoms. We've had to put her on dialysis for now," he explains.

"Dialysis?" Elias whispers.

"Our bodies are unable to heal or flush out wulfenite once it's in our system. The only treatment is to put her on dialysis and clean the toxins from her blood for her. She'll be on it for a couple more hours. We'll do another blood test after and if she's clear of the mineral, her body's natural healing can take over. She'll be a little fatigued over the next twenty-four hours, so you'll need to make sure she gets plenty of rest and drinks plenty of water once she gets home."

"Can I see her?" Elias asks.

"Of course, Alpha. But just one at a time for now," Doctor Richard instructs, leading Elias into Amelia's room.

We stand there shocked for a few minutes. Amelia nearly died. Someone tried to poison her... no, not tried, they *did* poison her. We still have guests from other packs, so our suspect pool is massive. Whoever they are, they're going to die a slow and painful death when I get my hands on them.

"Where was Amelia before this happened?" Alden asks, going into Alpha mode.

"She was on the training field with the rest of us for four hours," answers Tyson.

"And no one saw anything suspicious?" He asks.

We shake our heads.

"Only thing that happened was her animai threw a hissy fit after he broke a collarbone and Amelia tried to help him," Tyson says bitterly. Yeah, we're still not fans of that guy. "Wait, you don't think he..."

Chris scoffs, "He may be a chauvinist, but he actually has feelings for Amelia, I can tell. He was in a panic when those balls were flying at her just like I was with Mei. He's a moron who keeps putting his foot in his mouth, but I don't believe for a second he would ever intentionally hurt Amelia, at least not physically."

"We can go and check the security footage. Track Amelia's movements over the last six hours and see if we find anything. It's better than blindly pointing fingers," I tell them.

Alden nods in agreement. "Good idea. I'll go and update Fleur and Sorrell. They've been stressing over the last hour while also trying to hold down the fort. Pack members are going insane wondering what the hell happened earlier, so they're trying to do damage control. You three boys go get cleaned up and then find out which son of a bitch poisoned my granddaughter," he orders.

"Yes, Alpha," we say in unison and rush off to the packhouse.

We walk through the doors to see the state of the packhouse. The packhouses usual calming and inviting feel is gone. Now it looks like a crime scene. There's blood everywhere, staining the golden hardwood floors and red and gold carpets. There are broken vases and picture frames scattered all over the floor of the main entrance and sitting area and when I turn to the right I see a large dent in the wall above the side of staircase where Amelia threw Chris. The staff has been instructed to leave it for now until we get things sorted out.

We each go to our respective suites to get cleaned up and dressed. Eric, Evalyn, and Mei are in the Alpha suite with Aunt Fleur and Grandma Sorrell. I know I'm not their technical family, but they've been extended aunts, uncles, and grandparents since I was a kid, and they treat me as such. I still respect them as my Alphas and Lunas though.

Once I'm back to looking presentable, I meet the guys on the third floor in Tyson's office. Tyson quickly lets us all in and shuts the door. On pack grounds, we have a security hub that handles our electronic security and it's also supported by an IT team, but all the feeds go directly to Tyson's office since security and training are his main responsibility. He sits at his desk and starts up his computer.

"So, how do you want to do this?" Chris asks.

"I think we should each focus on something different. Vitali, you focus on watching Amelia in the footage, I'll focus on watching the people around her and Chris you focus on the background. This way, we can get through the footage quicker and hopefully won't miss anything," Tyson suggests. Chris and I nod in agreement and pull the chairs from the other side of his desk around to his side.

"Doc said within the last six hours, so start back around 7:00 am this morning," I instruct. Tyson pulls up the security feed from this morning and shortly after he starts playing it the feed drops to nothing but static.

"What's wrong?" Chris asks with a frown.

Tyson types away and closes and reopens the feed but the same thing happens, so it's clearly not a glitch on our end. At around 7:30 am the feed drops out; I don't know whether to be enraged or feel sick to my stomach.

This attack was definitely planned.

"Someone cut the feed to the training ground," Tyson seethes.

"How the fuck did the security hub not notice this?" I spit, shooting out of my seat, "If they turn out to be traitors…" My voice is low and threatening.

"Hey, I know those guys and they are not traitors," Tyson says defensively.

"Oh, like Beta Declan wasn't a traitor?" I say pointedly. This shuts them up. You can think you know someone all you like, but that doesn't mean they aren't capable of bad things.

Tyson goes stiff and I know he's linking someone. I pace around rubbing my temples. I desperately want to be cuddled up with Eric right now and have a mini-breakdown over everything that has happened, but right now I have a job to do. My best friend and Alpha need me; I can break down later.

"Guys…" Chris says quietly. Tyson and I both look in his direction. "I think this is what that letter was about." My blood runs cold and I stop pacing. "Think about it, Amelia gets another letter yesterday telling her an attack is coming and today she gets poisoned. That's not a coincidence."

Shit, he's right. We were all so focused on what happened, we totally forgot about the threats. There's no way this isn't related..

"That still doesn't tell us how or who cut the security feed. But this was clearly premeditated, and they are covering their tracks." Anger continues to build inside me. Blaise is just as furious as I am. He's just as protective of his Alpha. I don't know who this fucker is, but they're dead. They just don't know it yet.

"Did anyone notice a scent they didn't recognise at training today?" Tyson asks.

"We have a bunch of wolves from other packs visiting us, of course, we're bound to pick up scents we don't know," I argue.

"Are you going to offer anything helpful or just shoot down everything we say?" Chris asks, clearly getting annoyed.

"I'm sorry, I just… I hate feeling helpless. We don't know who did this because they're covering their tracks, so we're still at square one," I sigh in frustration.

"No, we're not. Only the feed to the training ground was cut, so we at least know that the poisoning had to have occurred there, otherwise, why cut that specific feed?" Tyson points out.

"That's a good point. So, if the poisoning happened during training, how the hell did they do it without her noticing? It couldn't have been with a needle or anything like that, we would have all seen that happen. So it had to be something subtle," Chris theorises.

We're quiet for a moment while we each brainstorm answers when it hits me.

"Her water canister! Remember, Amelia was complaining after the obstacle course that her water tasted bitter and how she needed to do a better job at cleaning it?"

"Do we know where the canister is now?" Tyson asks urgently.

"She was carrying it with her when she went back into the packhouse," I tell them.

Chris is immediately up out of his seat and out the door, no doubt to look for the canister. If he finds it, we can get it tested and see if that's how she was poisoned. And, if we're lucky, we can pick up some prints off the bottle.

It's only a minute later when the buzzer for Tyson's door goes off. I look at him as he presses the button under his desk. In walks C.J., one of our warriors, head of our IT team and the security hub. He must have been who Tyson was linking before.

"Thank you for coming, C.J.. Do you know why I've called you here?" Tyson asks, rising to his feet.

"I suspect this is about what happened to one of our security cameras today," he says calmly.

"So you knew about it and didn't think to mention it to anyone?" I scoff angrily as I cross my arms over my chest. C.J. seems surprised by my tone, but I don't care. I only care that our Alpha is laying in a fucking hospital bed and the person who did it is still breathing.

"Beta Vitali, I had every intention of informing Gamma Tyson of what happened," he says defensively.

"Just what did happen exactly?" Tyson asks calmly. I don't know how he's so damn calm right now.

"We were monitoring the feeds as normal when, early this morning, the camera overlooking the training ground lost visual. At first, we thought it was a technical glitch and began running diagnostics, but those showed us it wasn't an IT error. I sent Nicki down to check the camera and she reported that the cable was detached. It was just the one camera and there were no attacks, so we assumed maybe a bird had done it. Nicki reattached the cables and we got it up and running again without issue," he reports.

"How long did we lose the feed for?" Tyson asks.

"Fifteen; twenty minutes tops," he says.

"Plenty of time to spike the canister and flee," I say rubbing my face. C.J. watches us with a confused expression.

"Alpha Amelia was poisoned sometime in the last six hours. We believe the camera was tampered with, and the poisoning occurred during the break in the feed," Tyson explains.

C.J.'s face goes pale, and his body becomes rigid. His hands ball up into fists at his side and his honey eyes are glowing. "Is the Alpha okay?" He asks in a strained voice.

Minus a few assholes, mostly everyone in this pack adores Amelia. She loves and cares for everyone and they love and care for her. When they find out what happened, the entire pack will be out for blood.

"Doc figured it out in time. She's in the hospital and they have her on dialysis to get the poison out of her system," I tell him.

"I fucked up," he shakes his head shamefully. "I never should have assumed it was just an accident. If I'd done a better job, we could have caught whoever did this. I've failed our Alpha."

"Stop it. You didn't do anything wrong. You followed protocols, you ran the necessary tests, and you repaired the damage quickly. You were right, at the time there was no reason to suspect foul play. Don't beat yourself up over this, man. Amelia wouldn't want you to," Tyson comes around the desk and pats C.J. on the shoulder. I get how he feels, though. Our Alpha was poisoned right in front of us and none of us noticed. We all failed her.

A minute later Chris finally re-joins us in the office.

"Did you find the canister?" I ask.

"Yeah, it was downstairs among the rest of the mess. I rushed it to the pack hospital for testing and have given instructions to try and get some prints off the canister. It's worth a try, but if whoever did this was smart enough to cut the camera feed, they were probably smart enough to wear gloves," Chris says glumly.

"You're probably right, plus whoever sent the letters managed to do so without leaving their scent. If it's the same person, I doubt they'd leave prints," I tell them through the pack-link. Only myself, Chris, Tyson, Uncle Elias, and Grandpa Alden know about the letters. C.J.'s not permitted to know this information without the Alpha's say so.

"So right now either someone in this pack is a traitor and is behind the letters or is working with the person who is. Or, somehow, this person managed to sneak into the territory and poison Amelia and leave without anyone noticing," says Chris.

"I hate to say it, but I think it's more likely that someone in the pack is working with whoever is behind this..." says Tyson.

That realisation fills us with anger and dread. Someone – or multiple someones – is conspiring against our Alpha. The pack I love and have always felt proud to be a part of has members in it who would dare do something like this. First the Beta couple, now this. The very thought makes me sick to my stomach. But it doesn't matter who this traitor is. They won't get away with this and that's a promise.

Chapter Thirteen
Amelia

As I feel myself waking up – though I don't remember going to sleep – I'm immediately hit with the smell of disinfectant. Beyond that are two familiar scents that always remind me of home. Apple, cinnamon, and lilacs. My dad and mum's scents. The second I move my body the smells are forgotten and instead all I can think about is how horrible I feel. My head is pounding, and my body feels weighed down by rocks.

What the hell happened to me?

"Amelia! Oh, Amelia! Can you hear me?!" Zara's worried voice shouts in my head.

"Loud and clear," I tell her as she whimpers. I feel her nuzzling into my mind, giving me comfort and affection.

"I was so scared. I kept trying to reach you, but you couldn't hear me. I thought I'd lost you," she sobs.

"Hey, don't cry you big, softy. I'm okay, I'm right here, I promise. I'm sorry I scared you," I tell her gently. I have no idea what happened, but I hate knowing she is scared and sad.

"Don't ever leave me again, okay? Promise me," she says sternly.

I smile. *"I promise,"* I tell her as I mentally caress our bond to calm her. I've never seen her like this before. My poor Zara.

"Amelia? Open your eyes, my Little Alpha," I hear my dad say. It's a gentle whisper but I can hear the pleading in his voice. I force away the fog and slowly open my eyes. My eyes slowly adjust, and I look at the two figures sitting in armchairs on either side of me. They look so worried, but also so relieved.

"What am I doing in the hospital?" I croak out. Damn, my throat is drier than beef jerky. Mum quickly reaches over and pours a jug of water into a cup and puts a straw in it. She leans over and helps me take a few sips. "Thank you," I say, still a bit hoarse.

"There was an incident. You've been in the hospital for five hours. We were so scared," mum's voice quivers and tears pool in her eyes.

I reach out squeezing her hand, "What incident?"

"Amelia, sweetheart, what do you remember?" Dad reaches out to stroke my hair. The action is very soothing and is helping me relax, distracting me from the aching in my muscles.

"I remember training. I remember Mei doing terrific and I remember Marcus breaking his collarbone and then…" I frown as I realise everything after that is completely blank. "I don't remember anything after that."

"You were poisoned. Someone slipped wulfenite into your water canister," dad says through gritted teeth.

My eyes widen in surprise, "Wulfenite? Where the hell did someone get wulfenite?"

Wulfenite is this rare mineral that is found in shades of reds, oranges, or yellows. It's usually too thin and sensitive to be cut for jewellery, so faceted pieces end up as collector's items. It's not significant to humans or other supernatural creatures, but to a mutolupus, it's highly toxic. If it doesn't make you insane, it kills you.

My dad's anger is temporarily lost as his eyebrows shoot up in surprise, "How is it you and your grandfather knew what that was, and I didn't?" He asks disgruntled.

I give him an amused smile, "Because I spend more time in the library studying than you did." I wink and he returns the smile. "There's no cure for wulfenite poisoning or exposure. So how am I alive?"

"They put you on dialysis to clean your blood. They were able to get the mineral out of you before it was too late. Doctor Richard said you should be able to finish healing on your own, but you'll need to get plenty of rest for the next twenty-four hours," says mum as she strokes and kisses my hand.

"Sounds like a pretty easy treatment plan. I am all for it, especially since I feel like I've been run over by a train," I tell them.

"Are you in pain?" Dad asks in a concerned voice.

"Not pain per-se, more just really strong and uncomfortable aches. At least I know what was going on with Zara earlier."

They glance at each other, then look at me. "What was going on with Zara?" Mum asks.

"She was trying to talk to me during training, but it was like we had bad reception and she was just telling me she wasn't able to communicate with me this whole time; side effect of the mineral I guess. Any idea who did it?"

My dad shakes his head, "Someone tampered with the camera overlooking the training ground, so there's no footage showing us who did this."

I sigh. *"It's tied to the threats, isn't it?"* I link to my dad; he stiffens and places a soft kiss on the back of my hand.

"The boys seem to think so, and I agree with them," he tells me.

I can't say I'm shocked. Look, if someone tells you they're going to attack you and then they do, being shocked just makes you an idiot. But I never anticipated being poisoned. I miscalculated by only preparing for a full-on attack. This was more detail-oriented and took time and planning. This mystery person may be arrogant, but they're clearly very smart too.

"So, when can I go home?" I ask, relaxing into my pillow.

"We'll have Richard come and check on you and hopefully he'll say you can come home. Think you'd be able to walk?" Dad asks softly.

This reminds me of when I was a little girl. I shake my head.

"Want dad to carry you?" He asks, smiling gently.

I smile and nod tiredly.

"Then dad will carry you and put you to bed," he says as he leans over and kisses my forehead. Mum's watching with a soft smile as dad gets up and goes to talk to Doctor Richard.

Yeah, I'm a twenty-one-year-old Alpha and I still love cuddles and being carried by my dad. I feel no shame in that. Plus, I feel like crap, no way am I going to try and walk if I don't have to. My body needs rest and rest it shall have. The sooner I rest, the sooner I can recover and start handing out some cold hard justice, Amelia style.

"I thought I warned you about not dying," mum scolds me.

I chuckle, "I kept my promise. I'm still alive aren't I?"

"You're going to put me in an early grave if you keep this up," she says wryly.

But I can see the stress all over her face and I squeeze her hand, "I'm sorry I scared you, mum. Really."

She just smiles and kisses my cheek softly before nuzzling me, "It's not your fault. People just can't handle how wonderful you are."

Fear, jealousy, anger, resentment. People will find a reason to hate and come after me. I may not know who is behind this, but I will get to the bottom of this. More is going on than I realised though, that much is clear.

Once I get the all-clear from Doctor Richard, I change into some pyjama pants and tank top that mum brought from my room. Before I can comprehend what's going on, my dad scoops me up into his arms. I immediately nuzzle into him, breathing in his familiar scent and taking in his body heat.

Under better circumstances, my animai would be here and his touch and presence would alleviate the aches and fatigue raging against my body. But I'm not that lucky. This works fine too, and I know my dad needs this as much as I do. I know being able to hold and take care of his pup will make him and his wolf feel better. It's a natural instinct for us and it comforts me to know my parents will always be there for me no matter what. I really got lucky having them as parents.

Dad carries me to the packhouse with mum walking beside us, her eyes always darting to me to make sure I'm okay. As soon as we step into the packhouse, my head snaps up as the smell of blood hits my nose. What's worse is I recognise who the blood belongs to. Vitali, Tyson, and Chris…

dread runs through me. I look around and it looks like a fight broke out. The place looks trashed, there's blood everywhere and there are claw marks in the floorboards.

"What happened?" I ask apprehensively.

"You shifted and went a little wild. Vitali, Tyson, and Chris tried to restrain you, but my Little Alpha was too strong for them," he says proudly. "You did a number on them, but they didn't back down, they were very worried about you. Vitali had to call me and your grandfather to help and even then we still were having a hard time. Thankfully, the good doctor showed up and sedated you."

"So, I was too strong for a Beta, a Gamma, a Delta and two Alphas huh?" I say with a smirk, trying to lighten the mood. I am honestly impressed with myself.

Mum shakes her head and dad chuckles, nuzzling me, "I would expect no less from my Little Alpha."

"Is everyone okay?" I ask nervously.

"They're perfectly fine. They're all healed and anxious to see you," mum says softly.

I relax. I can't believe I attacked them.

They take me upstairs and, once inside our suite, I am greeted by everyone. And I do mean everyone: Grandpa, grandma, Vitali, Eric, Tyson, Evalyn, Chris, Mei, Uncle James, Aunt Lacey, Uncle Xander and Aunt Kennedy. Damn, it's a full house.

Grandma is the first to rush over to me, "Oh, my sweet girl. Are you alright? We were so worried." She starts fretting over me, but dad does not loosen his grip.

"Everyone, I promise, I'm fine. I just feel tired and achy."

I look at my guys who look so relieved. For a moment I notice Marcus isn't here and the empty feeling it causes in my heart hurts worse than the ache my body is dealing with. Maybe he didn't know. But if he did, would he even care? My thoughts make Zara whimper, and it makes me feel bad, so I push the thoughts away.

"I'm sorry I hurt you guys. Are you all okay?" I ask scanning them for any leftover injuries but fortunately, find none.

"Give us some credit Amelia, we're not that weak and it wasn't your fault. We're just glad you're okay," Tyson says warmly.

"Just goes to show these boys need to train harder since you were able to get the best of them so easily," James says with a smug smirk. "Xander and I wouldn't have struggled so much with your father."

This earns a fist bump from Xander. Dad just rolls his eyes.

"Cut it out, you two," Lacey scolds, landing a light smack on James' chest, but he pulls her into a hug.

"We weren't trying to attack or hurt her, Uncle James, just hold her down," Chris says defensively.

"The boys did a fine job, James. Give them some credit," grandpa winks at the guys who puff out their chests, thrilled to have the former Alpha defend them. Wolves are easily pleased and easily riled up. Getting praise from your Alpha or Luna is a great honour.

"Amelia, do you want me to stay over and keep you company?" Evalyn asks.

I smile and shake my head, "I appreciate that, but I'm fine. I'm just going to get some sleep. I am really glad you were all here to check up on me and for worrying about me."

"Of course, we'd be here, silly goose. We're family and you're our Alpha. We were so very worried," Kennedy smiles gently.

I smile back. I really do have an amazing support system.

"Okay, that's enough. I'm putting my little girl to bed. You can speak to her tomorrow," dad says sternly, leaving no room for arguments.

I chuckle at the grumpy faces on everyone... except Mei. She has a guilty look on her face, but before I can try to understand why, dad takes me to my room and tucks me into bed, planting a kiss on my forehead.

"I'm so glad you're okay," he whispers with tears in his eyes before he leans down and gives me a tight hug which I gladly return, kissing his cheek.

"Not going anywhere dad, I promise." He smiles and leaves the room. I then get some hugs and kisses from mum, grandma, and grandpa before I'm left to the peace and quiet of my room. Just as I feel myself about to drift off, my door opens and the scent of apricot wafts into my nose.

"Did I wake you?" Asks a meek voice. I force my eyes open and look over at Mei.

"No, you're fine. Come in," I tell her gently, that guilty expression still on her face. She shuts the door and walks over to my bed but doesn't look up at me. "Mei, is something wrong?"

She sniffs, "I'm so sorry, Amelia."

What on earth is she apologising for?

"Sorry? What do you have to be sorry for?" I ask confused.

"I should have healed you," she whispers sadly, tears trickling down her face. My eyes widen in surprise. She feels guilty for not healing me? Silly woman. I pat the spot next to me for her to sit and she does.

I gently take her hand, "Listen to me; do not feel bad for not healing me. Only Chris and I know you can heal people and I think it should stay that way for now until you're stronger. I don't want you bringing that kind of attention to yourself, especially not on my behalf," I tell her firmly but softly.

"But you're my Alpha and you've done so much for me. I should have helped you. But no one would tell me what was wrong and then when they did I… I froze. I didn't know what to do. You'd be all better by now if it weren't for me," she says remorsefully.

Such a pure-hearted soul. I reach up and wipe away her tears, "Mei, I'm fine and I'll be even better by tomorrow. I promise. There's no reason you should have had to heal me when the doctors and nurses were able to do it just as well. Please don't go worrying and blaming yourself. None of this was your fault. As your Alpha and your friend, I forbid you to go around feeling guilty over someone else's stupid actions."

She chuckles wiping her eyes, "Yes, Alpha." Mei leans down and gives me a tight hug, which I return.

"But promise me if you're ever badly hurt again, you'll let me help you," she gently demands. Her eyes flash reptilian for a second and I smile seeing how fiercely she means this, so I nod and accept her demand.

"I promise," I tell her, and she smiles, sighing with relief.

"Good. I'll leave you to get some rest," she says and then gets up and quietly leaves.

On a selfish level, having her heal me would have been nice. But she's one of my pack members and it's my duty to keep her safe, not the other way around. Until she's strong enough to defend herself, I refuse to let anyone know what she is or just how special she is. In time, sure, but not yet. Her safety is too important to me. With those thoughts in my head, I finally drift off to get some much-needed rest.

After getting thirteen hours of sleep – more sleep than I've ever had in my life – I wake up the next morning feeling much better than I did yesterday. Though I'm still not one-hundred per cent recovered, I've had more than enough time in bed, so I get up and throw on a pair of light blue skinny jeans, tan ankle boots, a sky blue tank top and a white crochet cardigan. I'm feeling a bit more casual today and I plan to take it easy.

Once I'm ready for the day I step out into the living area and see my parents and grandparents having breakfast. Their heads all turn to me instantly.

"Sweetheart, you're supposed to be resting," mum says, getting up to fuss over me.

"And here I thought sleeping for thirteen hours qualified as rest," I tease.

"How are you feeling?" Grandpa asks.

"Better than I did yesterday. I'd say I'm ninety per cent better. I still have some work to do, and I want to talk to the guys about this whole situation, but I promise to take it easy. The guys will take good care of me."

"Tough as nails, our girl is," grandma says proudly and grandpa grins in agreement.

"Are you sure?" Dad asks anxiously.

I walk over grabbing some bacon off his plate, "I am positive. I'll check in later, so you know I'm fine." I kiss his cheek and stuff the bacon in my mouth. I'm only now aware I haven't eaten in twenty-four hours, what the fuck? I've missed so many meals! Instantly my stomach starts snarling like a vicious beast and everyone laughs.

"How about I make you a couple breakfast sandwiches to get you started?" Mum asks and I nod eagerly. Yes, food. Please feed your child!

After I inhale my breakfast sandwiches – much to everyone's amusement – I get up and head to my office, linking the guys to come join me. I stand by my desk waiting for the onslaught and they do not disappoint. In record time all three of them are flying into my office and throwing themselves at me. I smile and laugh at their goofiness.

"According to my dad, this is similar to what you guys did yesterday," I tease.

"You scared us half to death, woman," Vitali scolds.

"And you took a chunk out of my arm. You marred my beautiful ebony skin," Tyson says, disgruntled..

"Aww I'm sorry," I say taking his arm and examining it. "Looks fine now though."

"Yeah, you got lucky," he says, pulling me into another hug.

"Aren't you supposed to be on bed rest?" Chris looks me over with concern. It really feels like having three brothers.

"I've slept for more than half a day and I'm feeling better. But I don't plan to push myself, so don't worry. Thank you guys for taking care of me and stopping me from hurting anyone else."

"That's what we're here for. But seriously, that was terrifying. Your eyes were all black, like some kind of wolf-demon," Vitali shudders.

"That some new kind of hybrid?" I ask.

"Would be pretty badass, not gonna lie," Tyson says.

I smile and shake my head. I step behind my desk, ready to get to work; I have many questions for them.

"So, fill me in on your investigation into the matter from the beginning," I instruct them. But before anyone can answer, Marcus comes storming into my office, his forest eyes glowing and full of determination with a concerned Jasper trailing in behind him.

This is what happens when people forget to close the damn door.

Chapter Fourteen
Marcus

Yup, I went and did it again. Maybe I need a therapist. Training with Amelia's pack was actually fun and enlightening. Jasper and I were linking the whole time, throwing ideas back and forth on how we can implement some of their ideas into our own training regime. Seriously, the whole obstacle course and sensory training is a brilliant idea. Mei, who I now know to be Delta Chris' animai, had us floored. I've never seen anyone move that fast, I'm still not sure what species she is, and the curiosity is killing me. I was thinking sanguidae, but her eyes would have given her away.

Watching Amelia get those balls thrown at her was one of the hardest things I've ever done. Ace and I were on edge the entire time, worried she was going to get hurt. Each time she wasn't, we beamed with pride for our animai. When she did get hit, it took every ounce of willpower not to run up to her, pull her into my arms and kiss every spot where a ball dare mark her beautiful skin.

Then the dominant wolf part of me took the entire thing as a challenge. Wanting to prove that I was stronger and better – that royally bit me in the ass. Not only did I end up with a broken bone, but I, once again, lashed out at Amelia when all she was trying to do was help. Her words to me before I left the field about me being an idiot hit me hard. The way I yelled in her face and snapped at her *was* me being an idiot and I hated myself when I saw the hurt in her eyes.

After I got patched up at the hospital we came back to the packhouse, and Jasper put me on house arrest in our guest suite. I can't believe he grounded me. He's barely said two words to me, he just has been icing me out or shooting glares at me and I hate it. My own Alpha and best friend refuses to talk to me, not just that but it's getting on my fucking nerves. This is so damn childish.

We checked in with the guys back home, had food brought up to our suite, watched TV and of course, Jasper had a video call with Isabelle, so he could make sure she and the baby were okay since she's now back in our territory.

I had yet another night of restless sleep and just as I was actually starting to drift off into a proper sleep Jasper was storming into my room.

"Get up!" He shouts.

"Fuck off, I'm trying to sleep," I groan as I roll over trying to go back to sleep. Next thing, I feel him yanking me out of bed by my ankle. I land on the floor with a hard thud.

"Dude, what the fuck is wrong with you?!" I shout as I sit up and glare at him.

"You're what's wrong with me, now get up and get dressed. We're going to go have breakfast and then you are going to go and apologise to Amelia for being a prick," he says tersely.

"She won't want to see me," I say defeated.

"Can you blame her? I'm surprised she hasn't rejected you and kicked us out by now," he says astounded.

"Why does it feel like you want her to reject me?" I spit as I get to my feet.

"Don't be stupid. Of course, I don't want you rejected, I want you to be happy, but what you're doing and how you're acting is completely fucked up. Man, I've known you since we were pups, this isn't like you," he says in a softer tone.

"I feel like I'm going insane. One part of me wants one thing, the other wants something else. It's like a tug of war in my head," I rub my face in frustration.

Jasper sighs. "Get dressed and come and have breakfast," he says, closing the door behind him.

Deciding I may as well do what he says, I brush my hair and teeth and get dressed in navy blue jeans, black boots, a grey t-shirt and throw on a navy blue button-down over the top. I roll the sleeves up, leave the shirt unbuttoned and head out into the living area. Jasper assesses me, nods in approval and then we head downstairs.

As soon as we get to the landing, we notice a lot of movement down below. We look at each other and then slowly walk down the stairs. One guy is patching up the wall, and various men and women are sweeping and binning broken wood and glass while some others are scrubbing the floors. Under the scent of bleach and cleaning chemicals, I can smell blood. I take another look around and sure enough, there are patches of blood everywhere that they haven't cleaned yet.

What the fuck happened down here?

And just how soundproof are these walls?

"Excuse me, what happened here?" Jasper asks one of the staff. The young lady simply shrugs. I have an uneasy feeling settling in the pit of my stomach.

"Amelia went nuts, that's what happened," says a guy sitting in one of the lounge areas with a group of other guys, all in their early twenties, I'd say. Jasper and I glance at each other before walking over. I realise it's the same shit stain who was making a move on Amelia the other day. I don't know who he is, but he's already on my shit list.

"What do you mean 'Amelia went nuts'?" Jasper asks, folding his arms over his chest; authority and dominance oozing off him without even needing to use his Alpha Spirit.

"I hear Amelia finally cracked under pressure, shifted, and went on a rampage in the packhouse. The Beta, Gamma and Delta had to bring her down," the guy says looking way too smug about this news concerning his Alpha – an Alpha he refuses to even address as Alpha. I growl and take a threatening step forward, but Jasper puts his hand out to stop me from moving closer to the prick.

"*Could you be more of a hypocrite?*" Scoffs Ace. I continue to ignore him.

"I guess Beta Declan was right," one of the other guys mutters.

Jasper lets out a snarl that makes them all cower in fear, "Your former Beta was a traitor. Don't put your faith in the words of someone who would betray his oath and his Alpha."

The smug guy doesn't look smug anymore. Now he looks pissed off for some reason. I can't listen to this anymore. I turn on my heel and start making my way back upstairs to Amelia's office; Jasper quickly chasing after me.

"Marcus don't do anything stupid. Just ask her what happened first. This doesn't sound like Amelia," he cautions.

I scoff at him. "You see her a couple times a year and think you know her so well. Look around Jazz, her own pack doesn't have faith in her and it sounds like she's already cracking under the burden of being Alpha. I can't let this happen. I won't lose my animai because she's too stubborn to let some fantasy drop," I say bitterly.

He grabs my arm and pulls me to a stop. "Think before you act or there may be no coming back from what happens next, Marcus," he warns, his eyes almost pleading. But I don't want to listen. Amelia has to stop this; she has to see reason. We get to her office, and we can hear voices inside. I'm grateful someone left the door open, so without missing a beat I storm into her office. Ready to lay it all out and tell her what she's not ready to hear.

Vitali

We were just about to fill Amelia in on everything that happened yesterday when her asshole of an animai storms in with Alpha Jasper behind him. I swear he's asking to get his ass kicked. Tyson is standing to the left of Amelia's desk with me and Chris on the right and each of us is instantly defensive.

Amelia doesn't need this shit right now. She nearly fucking died and even though she's up and smiling, I can see she's not completely back to normal. Her colour is missing its natural glow and even her eyes look tired despite all the sleep she got. Alpha Jasper must notice because he's scanning Amelia over with his face full of concern.

I like him, he's handsome too. He's 6'5" with a completely shaved head – which suits him – intense dark brown eyes and a sexy goatee. His warm, ebony skin is bulging with muscles, not overly muscular, but enough to make you drool. He's dressed in black jeans, sneakers, and a beige short-sleeve button-down shirt that looks like the buttons are fighting to stay on. He's good looking. Eric is hotter, but I might be biased.

"Marcus. Alpha Jasper. What can I do for you?" Amelia asks casually.

"This has to stop, Amelia. I understand you've set some goal for yourself and I'm sure it sounds good, but enough is enough. You're not..." He sighs. "Amelia, you can't be an Alpha," he says slowly as if talking to a child. Growls immediately erupt from myself, Chris, and Tyson. This asshole needs to back off.

"Marcus, that's enough!" Alpha Jasper growls in warning.

I take a threatening step forward, "You've got a lot of balls to talk to our Alpha like that." He flashes a glance at me and then focuses back on Amelia.

Amelia raises her hand signalling for us to calm down. "Gentlemen, let's be civil. I'm curious to hear what Beta Marcus has to say. Please, continue," she prompts Marcus as she takes a seat.

Chris, Tyson, and I all look at each other with worry as Tyson quickly shuts the door. Shit is about to hit the fan.

See, Amelia isn't like other Alphas. Alphas tend to be stubborn and hot-blooded. They're quick to anger, to violence and are natural dominants who don't tolerate challenges to that dominance. Amelia is an anomaly. I don't know if it's because she's a woman or because she's Amelia, but she has always been in control of her emotions and is never quick to anger. She is always able to step back and assess any situation regardless of her emotions. It's one of the things that makes her a great leader.

Amelia may yell or snap or get mad, but in those moments, you know there's nothing to worry about because it's all half-hearted. It's when she gets calm that you need to run, and right now, she is looking scary calm. Almost serene. It's literally the calm before the storm. When she gets this calm and collected, it means she's going to bring down the hammer. In other words, Marcus just poked a savage beast.

"Thank you. Amelia, I heard what happened; they said you cracked under the pressure of being Alpha and went on a rampage. Your own pack doesn't think you can handle this job. Going on a rampage is not normal, Amelia. You could have hurt or killed innocent people," he says, almost sounding concerned.

My fists ball up in anger. Who the fuck told him that shit? That's not what happened. Course it's not like everyone knows the truth, but it's still a stupid conclusion and, when I find out who said it, they're getting punished. Worse, this asshole actually thinks so lowly of his animai, he ate it up with a spoon.

"We'll find out who is saying this and handle it. Amelia will address the pack when she's ready. She's always transparent with them," Chris says to Tyson and me through the link.

I can see Alpha Jasper wants to say something, but Amelia gives him a look to allow Marcus to continue. Which isn't actually a good thing. She's letting him dig his own grave.

"I admire your ambition, I actually do, but you have to face the truth. I don't want to see anything bad happen to you and it's clear that it will because you're just not built for this. No woman is. I'm sorry," Marcus continues regretfully.

The room becomes so quiet you could hear a cotton ball drop. We watch for Amelia's reaction.

Calmly she stands and neatens up her desk, "Alpha Jasper, did we have any other business to discuss during your visit?"

He furrows his brow and shakes his head, "No, we addressed everything already."

She nods thoughtfully, "Good. Then in that case, it is time that you left and took your Beta with you. Beta Marcus is no longer welcome in my territory. In the future, when it comes to our packs working together, should; you need to send a representative, I request that it be either your Gamma or your Delta." Her tone is airy, as if she was ordering a light lunch.

She's not just pissed off, she is fuming angry and, if I know her, she's crushed too. I can't believe he stood there and said that to her. He didn't even ask what happened, he just made an assumption because it suited him. Can he not see that she doesn't look like herself?

Alpha Jasper looks shocked but then composes himself, going into Alpha mode. "As you wish, Alpha Amelia," he says respectfully.

Beta Marcus looks dumbstruck.

"With your permission, I would like to visit your territory in the next week to go over rejection proceedings with your Beta, as I am unable to go through the process right now," she says resting her hands on the edge of her desk.

She shows not an ounce of pain or anger. Chris, Tyson, and I are glancing at each other, waiting for her to blow like Krakatoa.

Beta Marcus's face is turning red with anger, "You can't be fucking serious. Is this how you respond to constructive criticism? You hear something you don't like or don't agree with, so you're just going to reject me?! This is so fucking typical of you women."

Alpha Jasper closes his eyes like he's given up all hope, while the rest of us are growling, ready to pounce on this sexist asshole.

"Constructive criticism," she whispers, the words are so low it's like she's testing how they sound.

Suddenly, the sound of wood splitting echoes around the room. I look and see Amelia's hands crushing the wood of her desk.

Oh fuck.

Part of me wants to duck for cover, the other wants to run and calm her down because she's supposed to be resting and this definitely isn't resting.

"Constructive criticism? Is that what you call what you've been doing for the last three days?" She says in a biting tone, her eyes glowing as they flare in rage. "No. Constructive criticism involves giving me feedback that can help me improve on something, all you've done is degrade me, insult me, and challenge my position as a fucking Alpha." Marcus' eyes widen in shock as she steps around the desk moving towards him. "My whole life, I've listened to people spew the same crap at me – It didn't dissuade me then and it won't dissuade me now." Her features suddenly switch to mock amusement. It's kind of scary. "Ya know, in the span of a month, three people have tried to kill me, while another threatens the safety of my pack. If I didn't back down from that, why in the hell would I back down or throw away my position because of some Beta with masculinity issues?" She's in his face now while we stand back smirking. That's our girl. "I need someone who is strong and secure. Who can stand at my side as my equal. Not someone who takes his very animai's existence as an insult to his fragile ego. I am an Alpha, not some weak little girl who needs a man to dictate her life. If you're not man enough to stand by me, then you don't deserve me. So pack your bags and leave my pack and don't ever return. I'll be seeing you in a week and I hope that when I do, you'll do the smart thing and accept my rejection," she finishes, fury burning in her eyes so hot I'm surprised Marcus' face hasn't melted off. "Now leave my office. I have work to do."

Marcus stares at Amelia as she takes a seat at her desk. He looks broken and horrified. Alpha Jasper is looking a mix of sad and angry. He wraps his arm around Marcus and pulls him out of the door.

"Thank you for the hospitality, Alpha Amelia," Jasper says with a nod before dragging a very out of it looking Marcus with him.

Amelia simply nods and says nothing. As soon as they're out the door, Amelia's knees buckle. Chris and Tyson rush to her side to catch and comfort her, making sure she's okay. After a quick look at her, I storm out behind the Alpha and Beta.

"Hey!" I shout as I catch up to them, "Are you happy now? Did it feel good to kick her while she's down like that?" Marcus looks too weak to fight back. "You're supposed to be her soulmate. How can you justify being so heartless? As for what you heard, next time use your brain, and don't believe stupid rumours." I turn around to march back to Amelia's office.

"What that guy said, it wasn't true, was it?" Alpha Jasper says solemnly. I turn back to face him, and I can see how concerned he is for Amelia. "Please, she's my friend. I know her and that did not sound like Amelia at all. She's too strong for that."

I was right to like this guy. "Amelia was poisoned with wulfenite yesterday. It's true that she did shift and attack me, and it took five of us to restrain her, but it wasn't her fault," I explain as both Alpha Jasper and Beta Marcus' faces morph into expressions of horror. So I guess they've heard of wulfenite.

"Sh-She... no. That can't be. She'd be dead by now. Or completely insane," Marcus says, shaking his head in denial.

"We got her to the hospital in time and she was put on dialysis. They managed to get it out of her system. She's mostly recovered but still a bit weak. She was supposed to be resting, but that plan was shot to hell when her animai stormed in and decided to treat her like shit after she nearly fucking died," I say in disgust.

"I... I didn't know. I swear I didn't know," Marcus' voice breaks, tears filling his eyes.

"Who cares if you knew? Doesn't change the fact you judged her unfairly. You insulted and humiliated her and now you have to suffer the consequences. You deserve worse than rejection."

"That's why she said she'd reject him in a week. Because she's weak and knows rejection will weaken her even more," Alpha Jasper says sadly.

"I imagine that was her reason, but I'd have to ask. Best pack up fast. It's the least you can do for her," I say as I walk off and leave the two to handle their own mess. As I walk away I hear someone behind me drop to the floor and start sobbing, and I want to smirk in satisfaction, but I can't. This whole situation is just too depressing.

Amelia

I'm vaguely aware of Chris and Tyson trying to comfort me, but I feel like I'm not even here right now. How did this happen? I nearly died and instead of my soulmate comforting me, he came in here and started belittling me. I've never felt so low and unwanted in my life.

Worst part is I could hear in his voice and see in his eyes that he actually felt he was helping me. But how is it helping if you don't even stop to get all the facts? Zara is howling in my head, her heartbreak only compounding on my own. My body is both numb and raging with anger, too confused to figure out which to go with.

I look up as Vitali comes back in, anger all over his face. I can guess where he went, but I choose not to ask.

"Amelia…" Chris says slowly as he gently rubs my back. The sadness in his voice just makes the pain in my heart hurt worse.

"You were going to fill me in on everything that happened yesterday," I say quietly. I can feel them looking at each other, not knowing what to do with me. Honestly, I don't know what to do with me either right now.

"Maybe you should go get some more rest," Tyson suggests as he strokes my hair. My three best friends are trying their best to comfort me, but it's not working.

"Please, tell me everything. I need to know." I feel tears start to fill my eyes. I want to be strong and push forward, but I don't have it in me. I never knew heartbreak could hurt this much. "I need to focus on this, just for the moment," I plead. Am I pleading? As their Alpha, I could just command them, but my heart just wouldn't be in it. They look at me with sad, sympathetic eyes. It makes me want to hide.

"We'll tell you everything, we promise," says Vitali.

I slowly sit down and listen as they tell me everything they learned and what their theories are. I try my hardest to focus on what they are saying, but every now and then my mind wanders back to Marcus; the words he said, the look in his forest eyes.

I'm not the type to wallow, but right now, I wish whoever wanted me dead had succeeded, because this is worse than anything I could imagine, and I know rejection is going to feel a million times worse. I feel cold and empty. Every breath constricts my heart. I just wanted to be happy. I wanted to be with Marcus. But I guess it just wasn't meant to be.

Chapter Fifteen
Amelia

The last few days have been the hardest days of my life. I did my best to stay away when Jasper and Marcus were leaving. I knew watching Marcus leave would be more pain than I could bear right now. I know I'm doing the right thing, but the right thing doesn't always feel good. Since he left, every day has been harder than the last. I try to focus on what I need to do and bury the hurt, but nothing lessens it. All I can do is stop it from showing on my face during the day, but at night I let the tears out.

Every night I've cried myself to sleep, letting myself feel the icy cold that has latched itself around my heart and the empty space inside me where the other half of my soul was meant to be. If this is how I feel now, I can't even fathom what rejection will feel like, no wonder it kills some wolves. Honestly, I think death is the Goddess's way of sparing us a lifetime of pain without our soulmates. In which case, I think she deserves a thank you.

To keep myself busy, I have been integrating the new members into our pack and helping others move out. There's been a lot of transitions taking place since the Vernal Ball – people who found their animai had to settle on whose pack they would be living in. The ones who left had to sever their link to me and my pack and be initiated into their new packs, and the same

Including Vitali's animai Eric.

Eric is fitting in great already and I'm thrilled that Vitali won't be alone in the Beta suite. Vitali and Eric have marked each other, but Vitali says they haven't mated yet. He's a bit nervous, which is perfectly understandable. There's no rush, so the two are taking their time to just enjoy each other and get to know one another. Either way, Eric has been integrated into our little group as if he's always been here, and I know that's made Vitali incredibly happy.

I made a public announcement to the pack informing them of my poisoning. Everyone was shocked, to say the least, and rumours about me being unstable quickly turned into gossip about me being so tough, not even five ranked wolves could knock me down. I have to admit, my self-esteem really needed that. There are still some pack members who aren't fond of me being their Alpha and I'm carefully monitoring them. I can't have pack members I can't trust, and right now, they are suspects in the attempt on my life.

Grandpa and grandma have changed their travel plans and will be sticking around a bit longer. They're back in their cottage not far from the packhouse. It seems they and my parents feel the need to keep an eye on me. They aren't saying anything or asking questions, but I see and feel their sympathetic eyes on me. I know it's from a place of love, but honestly, I hate it. It reminds me of everything that's going on and makes me feel worse. Makes me feel like a failure.

Running a pack is easy. Relationships are freakin' brutal.

Mum and dad still plan to move out, but their cottage is still being constructed. They were also supposed to spend time travelling and enjoying retirement but have also chosen to stick around. No doubt to also hover. Yay me.

Outside of me spending my days being depressed but trying not to act depressed, life has been normal. I mean, that's how it goes right? Doesn't matter how much pain or loss you experience; the world will continue to spin. I have no choice but to spin with it as I mentally prepare myself to reject my animai. But let's face it, no level of mental preparation can ever make you ready to rip away half your soul.

I've continued to train Mei and she's getting stronger and faster by the day. I'm incredibly impressed with how far she's come. She still has her triggers, and they may take a very long time to overcome but seeing her embrace her natural instincts and all the gifts that come with what she is, makes me feel proud. If she can go through all the pain and suffering she has, and come out the other side as this strong, lovely woman, then that gives me hope for myself.

Zara has been mostly quiet, but I've been making sure we shift a couple times a day, so she has a chance to get out and get some air in hopes she'll feel a bit better. I know this is harder on her than it is on me. Fact is, my animai couldn't accept me as I am, but hers could. I didn't get to meet him, but I know Ace loved us. He wanted us, title and all. Now she's going to lose that because Marcus is a narrow-minded jerk and I hate that. I hate it to my very core.

It's been five days since Marcus left and I know I should be getting ready to visit and go through with the rejection, but for some reason, I can't bring myself to do it yet. Am I scared? Do I think I'll change my mind if I see him? I don't really know. My mind is just a storm of unwanted thoughts, and I can't seem to focus on work, so I decide to go for a walk.

Getting up from my desk, I turn everything off and step out as the door automatically locks behind me. I leave the packhouse and just wander around aimlessly. I don't really care where I'm going, I just focus on the sound of my feet against the pavement; letting the simple rhythm of my steps calm me. Heel-toe, heel-toe; one foot in front of the other.

I look up when I hear the sounds of children squealing and realise I've made it to one of the parks. It's small with a decent jungle gym for the kids and is right near a lake. Parents like to bring their pups to come and feed the ducks. Surprisingly these ducks aren't afraid to be near us. They must be mighty ducks...

HA, mighty ducks! Get it? Like the movie?

Thank Goddess these lame jokes are only in my head.

"Lucky me, I get the privilege of hearing them," Zara cringes.

"Sorry Zara, I'll try and keep the bad jokes to a minimum," I apologize.

"It's not so bad. You should share your bad jokes with the rest of the world. Let people see just how normal their Alpha is," she teases.

"Great idea, they can add a terrible sense of humour to the list of reasons why I'm not fit to be Alpha," I say sarcastically.

"If humour was a requirement to become an Alpha I'm pretty sure most Alphas would lose their candidacy. You've met these guys, what a bunch of fuddy duddies," she rolls her eyes.

"There are a lot of words I'd use to describe most of these Alphas, 'fuddy duddies', however, was not on that list," I say, amused.

"Well, it's on mine," she tells me.

As I scan around the park I notice the temporary addition to my pack, Landry Green. Officially a member of the Alpine Pack, he is serving out community service in my pack due to the fact his thoughtless rejection of Jennifer nearly resulted in her death. He's adapting rather well surprisingly, though I'm sure not being allowed to shift is making him and his wolf antsy.

It's a rare thing for an Alpha to command a pack member to not shift. Some describe it as feeling like bugs crawling under your skin. Many of us can go long periods without shifting, but for some reason being denied the chance to shift bothers us physically. It's not painful, just uncomfortable.

Landry is sitting on a park bench, and he's focused on something in the distance. I look over and see Jennifer smiling and playing with a group of children. She's been recovering nicely from the incident, far better than anyone expected. I'm sure it's still taking a toll on her, but she's not showing it. She just pushes forward like the cheerful person she is. Seeing Landry watch her so intently has me intrigued and hopeful. Curiosity gets the better of me, so I decide to walk over to him.

"This seat taken?" I ask.

He jumps in surprise and looks up at me wide-eyed, "I-I… I was just… I mean… I swear I wasn't slacking off," he stutters nervously.

I chuckle and sit beside him, "I'm not here to lecture you, you're allowed to take breaks. I don't expect you to become our slave. Besides, Maggie has kept me updated and says you're doing very well."

He relaxes a little bit, "She can be a little scary sometimes."

I laugh, "She is indeed a force to be reckoned with. She's quite lovely when you get to know her, but she puts a lot of pride into running the packhouse and likes things done a certain way."

"Yeah, I noticed," he frowns.

"Something wrong with that?" I ask, quirking an eyebrow.

His eyes shoot up and he waves his hands defensively, "No! No! Not at all, I just… she's not what I expected."

"Care to elaborate?" I query.

"She's not an Omega, is she?" He asks me.

"You're correct, she's not an Omega."

"It's just… I thought only Omegas do things like cooking and cleaning. My dad always said that's all they're good for. Serving stronger wolves," he admits quietly.

I suppress a growl. His dad has done a number on him. But I don't think he's like his dad. He's making observations and he's not offended by them. He's curious. That's a good sign.

"Some packs do view Omegas that way, unfortunately. Believing that, because they can't shift, they are useless and hold no other value than to work in servitude to 'stronger' wolves. We don't agree with that here and I know Alpha Lucas doesn't either. Any member of this pack can work in the packhouse doing cooking and cleaning. It's a paid job like any other job. You make money, meals are provided and if needed, there's a living quarter as you know. We don't treat Omegas as less than anyone else. In fact, my best tracker, she's an Omega and my grandmother, the former Luna of this pack; she was an Omega too," I tell him.

His head snaps to me full of shock and surprise, "The Luna was an Omega? No way!"

"Way. And she's one fierce lady. Even now that she's retired, she's still very respected. No one dares piss her off because she'll make you sorry," I say with a chuckle. Grandma Sorrell can be scary when she wants to be.

"The Alpha never considered… you know… rejecting her?" He asks swallowing nervously. I understand where his mind is on this.

"Not for a single second. He firmly believes animais are given to us for a reason and to reject them is foolish," I inform him, seeing him wince out the corner of my eye. We're quiet for a couple of minutes, just watching how everyone is enjoying the park. "I was told you visited Jen while she was sedated."

"I... I'm sorry. I shouldn't have. I just..." he trails off.

"Wanted to see her," I finish for him with a gentle smile. "I don't think that's a crime. It may have even helped her get better." For a moment, I see hope shine in his eyes.

"Do you really think that?" He asks quietly.

"I can't be sure, but I like to believe so. You are her animai after all," I say with a shrug.

"Was her animai," he says glumly, looking down at the dirt.

"You sound as though you regret it," I observe.

"I never meant to hurt her," he says, and I can hear the regret in his voice. "When I saw her I thought she was the most beautiful girl I'd ever seen in my whole entire life. I couldn't believe someone so beautiful existed. But then, I could tell she was an Omega and all I could hear in my head was my dad's voice screaming about how useless Omegas were. How they ruin lives and make strong wolves weak. I didn't think. Before I knew it the words were out of my mouth, and she was screaming." He wipes the tears from his eyes.

"Should never judge a book by its cover. Or in this case a wolf by its rank. Jennifer is a very special young woman."

"People keep saying that, but no one will tell me why," he asks curiously.

"She was our miracle pup," I tell him with a warm smile.

"Miracle pup?" He asks, cocking his head to the side.

"When her mother was pregnant with her, she'd gone for a walk one day. During her walk, she was attacked by curs. They mauled her savagely. By the time the pack warriors found her, she'd already lost so much blood. They rushed her to the pack hospital and had to perform a C-section to get the baby out. The mother was losing blood fast and the baby had been deprived of oxygen for too long. They were able to save her mother but when Jennifer came into the world she wasn't breathing, and her heart wasn't beating," I say. I was only two at the time and barely remember this, but I've heard the stories. Landry is listening intently. "Doctor Richard refused to give up on her though. He worked and worked and worked and after fifteen minutes everyone listened as she let out the loudest cry they ever heard. Doc said it was like she was screaming that she wanted to live. But even though he was able to revive her, her vitals were terrible. He was certain she wouldn't make it through the night."

"So then what happened?" He asks eagerly as he keeps glancing over at Jennifer.

"Night came and went and even though she wasn't doing good, she was holding on. One day become two, two became three and by day six, her vitals finally started to improve. Doc says it had nothing to do with medical science. She lived because she had a strong spirit, she lived because her will wouldn't let her die. To the entire pack, it was a miracle. This tiny baby, who by all reason should have died, beat science and fate. That's why she's our miracle pup. Watching this innocent baby fight for the will to live left everyone in awe of her. Watching her grow into this beautiful, bright, bubbly young woman has made everyone very happy," I tell him, smiling as I watch how she interacts with the children. "She works in the day care and pre-school. She absolutely adores kids, and they adore her."

"I can tell," he says, a wistful smile on his face as he watches her. Eventually, he slumps with his head in his hands. "I screwed up. I screwed up so bad. I threw away the greatest gift the Gods could have ever given me and for what? How could I be so stupid?"

I'm trying not to smile like a moron. This is what I was hoping for. I knew he was a good kid underneath everything. I knew he made a rash mistake.

"I won't lie. You definitely screwed up big time. You made one hell of a mistake. The question now is, what are you going to do about it?"

He looks up at me; tears streaking his face, "What do you mean what am I going to do about it? I rejected her, she accepted it. There's no going back from that."

"Come on now. Do you think a God would go out of their way to create the powerful magic that is soulmates and leave no possible way for them to be together?" I ask rhetorically.

His eyes widen in surprise. "Y-you think there's a chance I can get her back?" He asks me, hope coating his words as he looks over at Jennifer longingly.

"Do you want her back?" I ask with a cheeky smile.

"Yes! I'd do anything. I've felt empty since she accepted my rejection. I don't feel like I'm living anymore. It's like she was my reason for existing and even though we never got to know each other, losing her feels like I lost a reason to live. I don't even know her, but I miss her. I miss her so much," he says sadly.

"Then fight to get her back. It won't be easy, and it won't be overnight. But if you want her, earn her back. Make it right," I encourage him.

"But what if she wants nothing to do with me?" He asks nervously.

Fair question, but honestly, knowing Jen, she'd give him a second chance. She's always seeing the good in people and I don't see her not doing the same for Landry. He was chosen for her after all.

"Risk you're just going to have to take," I shrug.

He thinks for a moment and then takes a deep breath, stealing his shoulders. "I'm going to do it. I'm going to win her back," he says with so much conviction that I genuinely believe he can pull this off. Then his face slips into a frown. "But how do I start?"

"Got a phone?"

He looks confused by my question, but nevertheless hands over his phone. I take it, open Google Maps, and set directions to a nice restaurant in the city and then hand it back to him .

He looks at the screen confused, "What's this?"

"Directions to the restaurant you'll be taking her to for your date. Though I recommend calling ahead and making a booking," I say getting up and dusting my pants off. "Let me know when the date is, and I'll let you borrow my car... you can drive can't you?" He nods fervently. "Perfect. Then you let me know when you need it. I'll hand over the keys and I'll loan you my credit card. But don't go crazy... eh, screw it, go nuts."

He just stares up at me in shock, "Why are you helping me? I thought you hated me."

"I don't hate you. In fact, you seem like a good kid. You made a mistake and I believe people deserve a chance to fix their mistakes."

A small smile spreads over his face, "Thank you, Alpha. For everything."

I smile back and excuse myself. He's got a date to plan, so I decide to let him be.

While I wasn't able to salvage my bond with my own animai, at least I could help fix theirs. Truthfully, I think Landry and Jennifer will make a cute couple. Just because I'm miserable doesn't mean everyone else deserves to be. I have to admit, helping Landry fix his bond did make me feel a little better. But with that distraction over with, I now need a new one. So, with that in mind, I make my way back to the packhouse.

Once inside I tie my hair up in a bun, roll up the sleeves on my flannel shirt and make my way to the laundry room. I grab a bunch of cleaning supplies and head to the staircase. I drop to my knees, line up the products, and get to work cleaning the stairs, making sure to give extra attention to the banister and the wooden fixtures of the railing. Time and thoughts float away as I focus on the task at hand.

"Amelia... I didn't know things were that bad," comes a sad voice.

I look up at the top of the stairs to see Evalyn looking down at me with a sorrowful look in her eyes. She looks nice today in a cute lilac sweater, jean shorts that go down to the knees and tennis shoes. Her light brown hair in two braids that hang over her shoulders.

"Huh?" I ask confused.

"You clean the packhouse when you're really upset," she perches herself on the top step.

"Is that so?" I ask absentmindedly as I continue to clean.

"Yes. Last time you did this was after you went with your dad to that Alpha meeting that was held at the Tenebris Luna Pack. You spent the two days after you got home scrubbing the place from top to bottom," she frowns.

I grit my teeth at the memory. "Goddess I wanted to wring that Alpha's neck. What a disgusting low life," I snarl.

Evalyn nods in agreement. "Anyway, I came looking for you because we're going to have a movie night and we'd love for you to join us."

I love my friends to death; they are my family. But I really don't want to be around three couples right now. This would be one of the bitter moments.

"I appreciate the invitation, but maybe another night," I suggest.

Her frown deepens, "That's what you said last night."

I sigh. "I know you're trying to help but being a seventh wheel is not going to improve my mood right now, Eva."

She nods sadly and her face softens, "I understand, just know we're all here for you, whatever you need."

I look up at her, smiling softly. "I know, and it mea– " my words are cut off as a cry of pain leaves my lips and I cup my mouth. I'm not sure if I'm crying out from the pain or the shock. My lips feel like they're on fire, not spicy food fire, but actual fire.

"Amelia, what's wrong?" Evalyn asks in a panic, getting to her feet.

"I don't kn–" I'm cut off again by a new wave of pain that knocks me back as I clutch my ear and cry out. The pain is travelling. It's moving from my ear down my neck, and it feels like someone is taking a branding iron to my skin. Just when I think it can't get worse, I'm proved wrong. I cry out again and fall backward as the pain moves south straight for my vagina. At the same moment Zara starts howling, it's full of pain and as soon as I hear it, I realise what's going on and my heart feels like someone just split it in half with an axe.

Evalyn manages to catch me before I fall down the stairs. Her arms are around me, but all I can focus on is the pain.

"Amelia! What's happening?" Evalyn cries in panic.

"Pain," I pant.

Evalyn must have linked Tyson because next thing I know, he's at the top of the stairs looking down at the both of us with worry.

"Shit, what the fuck happened?" He asks, rushing down to both of us.

"I don't know, we were just talking and then suddenly she was in pain and these blisters started appearing on her skin," Evalyn says in a rush, and I can hear her trying to hold back a sob.

Tears prick my eyes as the pain continues, I can feel my flesh at the apex of my thighs burning and blistering just like my neck, but it doesn't compare to the pain in my heart. Tyson is watching me carefully, then his eyes widen in realisation, and I want to die.

"That motherfucker!" He seethes. "I'll fucking kill him," Tyson scoops me up into his arms and all I can do is whimper and try to bite back the pain.

"Kill who? Ty, what's going on?" Evalyn demands.

Tyson rushes me to my room with Evalyn right on his heels. "Her animai is being intimate with someone else, that's what's happening to her. It's causing her physical pain," he says through clenched teeth.

I knew it as soon as Zara started to break down but hearing it out loud makes this so much worse. I can hear Evalyn gasp, and I just want to curl up and hide.

Just as Tyson gets me to my room and lays me down on my bed, the pain stops. I can still feel the blisters on my skin, but the travelling pain and its intensity is dying down, meaning whatever Marcus was doing, has now stopped.

I know he didn't have sex, but does it matter? Even this much was bad enough. Why would the Goddess do this to people? Why punish someone for someone else's infidelity? Did she believe that knowing they'd cause pain and injury to their animai would dissuade them from their actions? Or do some Gods just like to watch the rest of us suffer for their own amusement? I would really like to fucking know.

"Amelia? Are you okay? What can I do?" Tyson gently asks in a worried voice.

I wipe away my tears and sit up, wincing as I feel the pain of the blisters between my legs. I feel like I'm going to throw up.

"It stopped," I deadpan. There's no emotion in my voice, maybe because I don't know how I'm supposed to feel right now.

"Oh, Amelia," says Evalyn as she climbs on the bed beside me and pulls me into her arms. I let her. I just don't have the energy to push her away.

I was going to reject him, could he not have waited? Was he that desperate? Did I mean so little?

"I could use a stiff drink," I tell them.

"I think you could use several, I'll go get the good stuff," Tyson announces, and he is off in record time to get me what is going to be the first in a long night of drinking.

Chapter Sixteen
Marcus

I want to die. It's been nearly a week since Amelia kicked me out of her pack with promises of rejection and each day kills me a little more. Ace has completely stopped talking to me, I haven't even been able to shift – not that I want to.

I'm in a total state of apathy. I just don't give two fucks about anything; how can I? Everyone was right. I never took the time to understand Amelia. I didn't even really try. I just kept making one dumb assumption after another and look where it got me. My animai, the person chosen for me by a higher power, nearly died and I didn't even know about it. And if that wasn't bad enough, I tore her down while she was recovering from a near-death experience. No one can hate me more than I hate myself right now, it's just not humanly or supernaturally possible.

When her Beta told us what had happened and I realised just how badly I fucked up, I broke down. I sobbed like a little baby. I felt like a piece of me was dying and it was my own fucking fault. Ace was clawing away inside my head, part of him wishing he could rip me to pieces and the other part wanting to go and take care of Amelia. I wanted to take care of her too, but it was too late. I was being kicked out and there was nothing I could do.

Some nights I cry. I don't see the point in denying it. I never knew there was a pain like this and right now I'd do anything to be free of it. I don't know when Amelia is going to show up to reject me, but I keep going over in my head what I can say or do to make her reconsider. It might be pointless, but I have to try. Picturing a future without her is more than enough of a wakeup call to realise I need to change my thinking because if I don't, I can welcome this pain for the rest of my life.

"Yo, tune in Marcus!" I hear Calix's voice. I lift my head up and see Calix, Aiden, and Jasper's eyes all on me, full of pity. I fucking hate it.

"What?" I say in a flat tone.

"Jazz asked how the repairs at the school are going," Aiden says, the pity never leaving his eyes.

I get it, I'm fucking pathetic. They don't have to keep rubbing it in with their sympathy.

"Oh. Um, fine. They estimated it will be finished by the end of the week," I tell them.

A couple teens got into a brawl at our pack high school, a fight over a girl it would seem, and it resulted in both the guys shifting and causing some serious damage to the school. They've both been suspended. Teenage wolves tend to be more hot-headed than the rest of us and can be a major pain in the ass, but stuff like this is too common to be a cause for expulsion.

"Marcus, I think you should go take it easy for the rest of the day," Jasper sighs.

"Why?" I ask with a raised eyebrow.

"This isn't the first time you've zoned out during a meeting; your head isn't here, and I need you here. No one can blame you for being in a bad way right now, but you're no good to me like this, so just go take the rest of the day off," he says softly.

Great, now I'm being fucking babied.

"I don't need to fucking take it easy, so you can cut that shit out," I scoff.

"We're just trying to help," says Aiden sympathetically.

"I don't *need* help, so back off," I say through gritted teeth.

"Fuck, Marcus, just stop!" Jasper yells as he slams his fist down on his desk. We all jump. "This is what I'm talking about. You're unfocused, you're moody and you're taking it out on your friends who are just trying to help you."

"How is looking at me with sad eyes fucking helping me?" I spit.

"You don't want us looking at you that way, then do something about it. You have no one to blame for the mess you're in but yourself. I warned you. I repeatedly warned you and you didn't fucking listen. If you don't want things to be this way, then stop moping around and do something about it. Consider this an order from your Alpha; go and take the day off and think about how you can fix the mess you made." He lets out his Alpha Spirit, the force of it leaving me no choice but to obey.

"Yes, Alpha," I grit, getting up and storming out of his office and straight to my suite.

Before meeting Amelia, I never realised how empty and lonely this room was. I always knew I wanted my animai, I always knew a part of me was missing without her. I just never knew how big that part was until I met Amelia. Sweet, strong, beautiful Amelia.

I walk over to my bed and flop down onto it and just let the tears fall. Who the fuck cares about dignity? I feel lost and lifeless without her. I feel like I'm dying. I want her, I want her so fucking bad I can't think about anything else. I have to get her back, I don't know how, but I won't give up. I can fix this; I just have to. There is no future for me without her. At some point, the emotional exhaustion gets to me, and I finally fall asleep.

***

The sun is shining off the lake that's just on the edge of our pack lands. The water is calm, the breeze is gentle, but I'm captivated by the scent of mango and pineapples. The best scent in the world.

"Penny for your thoughts?" Amelia asks me, a smile lighting up her face. The sun bouncing off her golden hair.

"I was just thinking about you and how lucky I am to have you," I tell her as I tuck her hair behind her ear. Her eyes flutter closed, and she relaxes into my touch. She couldn't be more perfect. Her eyes open and they are shining with so much love my heart might explode. She leans in and captures my lips in a heated kiss, and I eagerly kiss her back, wanting nothing more than to taste her lips till the end of time.

Catching me off-guard, she pushes me down onto the picnic rug beneath us and starts trailing slow, passionate kisses along my jaw to my ear. My hands find their way to her hips, and I grip them tightly, my dick straining against my jeans.

"I knew you wanted me," she whispers, her tongue teasing my ear. There's something different about her voice... since when does Amelia have an accent?

Her tongue and lips are going to town on my ear and neck, and I breathe erratically. My hands travel and cup her perfect ass, giving it a firm squeeze. Fuck, she feels so damn good. Her hand reaches down into my pants and starts stroking my dick. A guttural groan leaves me as I throw my head.

"That feels so fucking good, baby," I groan as I squeeze her ass harder.

"I know what you like," she says in a seductive voice as she keeps stroking my dick. She's driving me crazy. But again, there's something off about her voice.

Our moment is interrupted when a large russet-coloured wolf runs up to us. I don't feel fear, I know this wolf... wait, how is this possible? How the fuck is Ace here? Amelia doesn't stop pleasuring me, she doesn't even seem to notice him.

"Marcus, wake up!" He shouts in my mind desperately.

"What are you talking about? I am awake," I say confused, gulping as Amelia's pace picks up.

"WAKE THE FUCK UP, NOW!" He roars.

His words reverberate through my head, bringing me back to my senses. My eyes shoot open, and I realise I'm in my room laying on my bed. I must have fallen asleep. Fuck, it was just a dream. A really fucking good dream. Wait... something's wrong.

As my senses come back to me, I realise I'm not alone, there's someone else in the room with me and they're... fucking hell, they're playing with my dick! What in the fuck?! I look down to see a woman with cream skin and long, brown, curly hair and caramel highlights lying next to me going to town on my dick. I catch a whiff of her arousal and her scent. Lilies. Anger and disgust course through me and I sit up, grabbing her shoulders and yanking her up with me. My eyes glow with rage as I stare down the amber eyes looking back at me.

"What the fuck do you think you're doing, Davina?!" I shout with a snarl.

"I was just making you feel good, baby. Don't act like you weren't enjoying it," she smirks, her voice husky. It does nothing for me. My hard-on has completely vanished and I'm fucking enraged. I toss her across the room with no remorse as I jump off the bed. I look down at myself and my fucking dick is hanging out of my pants. I quickly tuck myself away as I shoot Davina a deadly glare. How dare she fucking touch me? I don't want anyone touching me but Amelia. How the fuck did she even get in here?

"What the hell is your problem?" She shouts, her Israeli accent thickening. She gets to her feet.

"You're my fucking problem!" I storm over and grab her by the throat. She's scratching at my hand to try and get free, but I barely even feel it, I'm too consumed by my anger. "You think you can just sneak into my room and have your way with me? You're even crazier than I thought. I found my animai and even if I hadn't, I told you I want nothing to fucking do with you," I hiss at her, desperate to rip her throat out.

Tears fill her eyes, but I'm past caring. "You don't mean that Marcus, I love you! I know you love me, too."

"I never loved you; how many times do I have to tell you?" I growl. I'm done with this bitch. *Get to my fucking room now, before I go on a rampage,* I link to Jasper, Calix, and Aiden. "You're going to regret this and I'm going to enjoy every second of your punishment." I drag her out of my room by her neck and into the hallway tossing her to the floor like the trash she is.

Jasper, Calix, and Aiden appear in record time looking around fully alert until their eyes settle on Davina. Their expressions morph into anger and contempt.

"What the hell is going on here?" Jasper demands.

"I woke up and found this crazy bitch in my room stroking my dick like it was a fucking genie's lamp," I spit, my eyes never leaving her. I don't trust her for a second.

Angry growls erupt from the guys, but Jasper is the most livid as his dark brown eyes start to glow.

"You were forbidden from ever returning to the packhouse, Davina. Not only did you return, but you broke into your Beta's room and sexually assaulted him?!" The floor and walls around us to shake.

Wait, did he just say, 'sexual assault'? I wouldn't call this sexual assault... would I?

"WHAT?!" She screams. "I didn't assault anyone! How can you even say that? I love Marcus, I was just showing him how much I love him and making him happy." She looks up at me, "Tell them! Tell them how much you were enjoying it! You were moaning for me; you were telling me how good it felt." Her tone changes from pleading to flirtatious and she licks her lip seductively.

I think I'm going to be sick. Once upon a time we dated and had the occasional hook-up, but that was before I met Amelia; before I met the other half of my soul. I could never picture being with anyone but her, in my dream it *was* her. The thought of another woman touching me is disgusting. Even looking at Davina does nothing for me now, she can't compare to my Paradise.

"I was unconscious! I didn't even know you were there, and in my dream, I was picturing my animai, not you. I would rather roll around in lupine than ever have you touch me again."

She shakes her head adamantly, refusing to hear what I'm saying. Why did I ever think hooking up with crazy chicks was a good idea? I really am a fucking idiot.

"I tried to tell you that," says Ace.

"So, you're officially talking to me now?" I ask. Truthfully, it's a huge relief hearing his voice again. Not having him just made this whole thing worse.

"You needed my help. I wasn't going to let her keep doing what she was doing," he says, but his tone is surprisingly caring. It's making me feel a little choked up.

"Thank you, Ace. For waking me up," I say sincerely.

"Don't mention it. Can I finally kill Davina now?" He says wagging his tail excitedly. He's always hated her.

"We'll see what Jasper says," I tell him. He huffs and flops down.

"Marcus, why are you lying? Why won't you just tell them the truth?" Davina begs.

Aiden lets out a low whistle, "The woman is utterly mental."

"Enough, Davina! I have had enough of your shit, and this is the final straw. I will not tolerate this behaviour in my pack! Davina Cozbi, I, Alpha Jasper Clyborne, hereby banish you from the Aurum Obscuro Pack. Pack your things and leave immediately," he declares, his Alpha Spirit stretching out over all of us. I watch with great satisfaction as Davina lets out a cry of anguish, clutching her head as her link to the pack is severed. Good fucking riddance.

"Calix, escort Davina back to her home and have two warriors stay with her as she packs her things, and then have them escort her off our territory," Jasper orders.

"Yes, Alpha," Calix says with a nod. He walks over and grabs Davina by her arm and starts dragging her away while she's literally kicking and screaming. I rub my face in exhaustion. Karma is seriously kicking my ass this week.

"Are you okay?" Jasper carefully asks as he walks over and puts a hand on my shoulder.

"I swear I didn't invite her over, you have to believe me," I tell him in desperation.

"I believe you, it's okay. Don't worry about that, but are you okay?" He asks, his face gentle and full of concern.

"I feel disgusted. I feel…" I trail off, not sure what word I'm looking for.

"Violated?" Aiden carefully offers as he walks over.

I frown. Now that he said it, yeah, I feel fucking violated, but that reminds me of what Jasper said. Was this a sexual assault? And if it was, just how weak of a Beta am I?

"Don't," Jasper says sternly.

"Don't what?" I ask.

"I know you; this doesn't make you weak. Man, the psycho molested you while you were asleep. That's not your fault. As soon as you woke up and realised what was going on you took care of her and now she's gone for good," he squeezes my shoulder.

I take a breath and try to let his words sink in. How can I not feel weak? I'm a six-foot-five Beta and these muscles aren't decorative. How the hell did I let myself get one-upped by a five-foot-seven she-wolf?

"Listen to our Alpha. You weren't one-upped, she took advantage of you in a vulnerable moment. But it all worked out. Besides, given what you were dreaming I can't blame you. It was a nice dream," says Ace sadly.

Tears prick my eyes at the memory. It felt real, I wanted it to be real. I want to be that way with Amelia, and I may never get to have that ev– FUCK, Amelia! Dread rolls through me and I swear I just about shit my heart out of my ass.

"Jasper I need your phone!" I shout in a desperate rush.

He looks taken aback. "What, why?"

"Amelia!" I yell in a panic. His brows furrow in confusion, but quickly widen in alarm as realisation sets in.

"Oh, fuck…" says Aiden, now looking as wide-eyed as Jasper.

"She would have…" Jasper starts to say.

"Felt all of it! She's going to think I was unfaithful to her. Please, I know you have her number, I have to call her and tell her that's not what happened, I would never do that to her." I'm nearly crying in a panic. How much pain did this cause her? Fucking hell, even when I'm not trying to hurt her, I still find a way to hurt her.

When you meet your animai, the bond instantly snaps into place. Even without marking, you would be able to feel if your animai was being intimate with someone else, or in this case, if someone was fucking getting you off in your sleep.

Jasper doesn't hesitate, he grabs his phone out of his pocket and video calls Amelia's number. I start getting jittery. I've never felt a stronger urge to vomit.

"Alpha Jasper?" Greets a familiar voice. I look confused, why is Amelia's Beta answering her phone?

"Beta Vitali, I need to speak to Alpha Amelia, it's an emergency," he says, not even trying to hide the urgency in his voice.

"Um, Amelia is a little… indisposed right now," he says hesitantly.

"WOOHOO! Crack open another bottle!" Shouts a voice in the background. A voice that has every nerve in my body reacting.

"Did you just finish that entire bottle? Amelia! That was Tezus brew, are you nuts?!" Yells another voice in the background, it sounded like her Delta.

"Yeah, I know, weak as shit," she scoffs. If this situation weren't so fucked up, I'd be laughing. I've never seen or heard Amelia drunk before, but she sounds hilarious.

Tezus is a special alcoholic brew made for supernatural beings. It's made in a distillery based in Rome that's run by a family of makkares. A makkari is what humans would call 'witches.' They use magic to make their brews more compatible with our bodies. You can get pretty wasted off a couple glasses super-fast. If she just downed an entire bottle then I'm amazed she's still standing.

"Indisposed? She sounds Gods damn wasted," Jasper says with a raised eyebrow.

"That's another way of putting it," Vitali says casually. I step next to Jasper so I can try and see what's going on. Unfortunately, Amelia isn't in the frame. I badly want to see her.

"And why is your Alpha wasted?" Jasper questions.

"Ask your fucking Beta," Vitali spits with hatred while glaring daggers at me.

"It's not what you think," Jasper says in my defence, though I'm not sure I deserve defending.

"I find that hard to believe," he scoffs. "I saw the blisters on her lips and neck, don't even try to deny it," he seethes. My stomach twists into a painful knot and Ace starts whimpering in my head. I knew an animai feels the pain of their soulmate's betrayal, but I never knew it was this severe. I'm tempted to run out, find, and kill Davina for causing my Amelia this kind of pain.

Hell, I want to kill myself for causing her this kind of pain.

"Please let me talk to her. It wasn't like that, and my Alpha can confirm it. Please, I have fucked up so much, but I would *never* hurt Amelia like that, I swear. She's... she's everything to me," I say with tears in my eyes. I used to laugh at guys who cried, now here I am constantly weeping like a little bitch. But honestly, this is all worth weeping over.

Beta Vitali looks surprised at my display of emotion; yeah, me fucking too. He looks torn until a guy – who I think was introduced to us as his animai – walks over and puts his chin on his shoulder and kisses his cheek.

"Let him speak to her. Whatever's going on they need to talk about it, regardless," the guy says. Thank the Goddess for this dude!

"She's not exactly in a state to be having this conversation," Vitali scowls.

"She's an Alpha, she should be fine. Just put her on the damn phone," yells Aiden in annoyance while he rolls his eyes. These guys can be pricks sometimes, but they're the best friends I could ever ask for. Even with all my shit, they still have my back.

"One second," the Beta sighs. I feel my heart rate skyrocket as nerves take over. "Amelia, someone's on the phone for you," he says gently.

"Okay!" She yells. I then hear stumbling and the sound of a thud. "Shit. Fuck. Dammit," she mutters in the background as Vitali shakes his head.

Coming into frame is my beautiful Goddess of an animai. She plops onto the sofa, next to Vitali. Her cheeks a deep shade of red – no doubt from the booze – and her hair is looking wild and sexy. She's even more beautiful than I remember. Ace has perked up in my mind and is watching her through my eyes, desperate to be with her and I know how he feels.

I suck in a sharp breath when I see red marks down her gorgeous neck and some swelling still left on her lips. Her healing has kicked in, but I can still see the signs of the marks that had been there and the sight of them is like a sucker punch to the gut. My poor Amelia. Hasn't she been through enough lately? Do the Gods hate her or something? First, she gets saddled with me, then someone tries to kill her, and now this.

"Amelia..." I say softly to get her attention as I take the phone from Jasper. Her inebriated eyes find their way to me. I expected to see rage on her face but instead all I see is hurt... so much hurt and it's killing me. In the small time I had with her, I learned Amelia is good at controlling her emotions and she doesn't show people when she's hurt. But I guess the alcohol in her system is making it hard for her to hide how she feels, because it's all over her face. Ace is cowering and whimpering, and I want to join him.

"Why?" She whispers sadly.

I feel the tears start to fall, "I didn't. I swear to you, I didn't. I would never, I *could* never. I know I've done a bad job showing it, but you mean more to me than that."

"Amelia?" Jasper says trying to get into frame. "You know I wouldn't lie to you. Marcus is telling the truth. A she-wolf in my pack broke into his room and... tried to have her way with him while he was asleep. She had been banned from the packhouse for attacking an Omega just the other month. She... she has an unhealthy obsession with Marcus. I have banished her from the pack for her actions. What happened to Marcus and what you felt, was not consensual."

Amelia goes rigid and her Beta is looking disgusted. I look away in shame. I've never felt more pathetic in my life. Just wait till the pack finds out. I hate to think what they'll say. I shudder at the thought.

"Who the fuck is she?" Amelia growls. My head snaps up and I see her beautiful turquoise eyes glowing.

"No one you need to worry about. She's being escorted off my pack as we speak," Jasper assures her.

"Not good enough. She assaulted my animai and inflicted pain upon me. Did she know he had an animai?" She asks menacingly.

Wait, she just called me *her* animai.

Does that mean I still have a chance? Fuck I hope so!

"Yes, Alpha. She knew," says Aiden.

"While you may have banished her, if I ever see her, I'll personally rip her heart out," she says with a scary glint in her eyes. Fucking hell, my animai has a side that's bloodthirsty. She really is full of surprises... and to be honest, the blood lust in her eyes is actually turning me on.

"Make that two of us," pants Ace.

"She's not my problem anymore, so do what you want with her," Jasper shrugs.

"Amelia, can we maybe talk? Tomorrow when you've sobered up. Please?" I beg. I'll even get on my knees if that'll sway her.

She's quiet for a moment, her eyes returning to normal as she looks at me through the phone. Finally, she sighs and slowly nods, "I'll call you sometime tomorrow."

Relief unlike anything I've ever felt floods me and I almost pass out from it. "Thank you," I breathe out.

"Are you okay?" She gently asks; nothing but concern in her voice and on her face. After everything I've put her through, she still manages to have concern for me. I so don't deserve this woman.

"Not really, if I'm being honest," I tell her. She slowly nods, but her nod is a little wobbly. Really, how is she upright and speaking coherently? Woman can handle her liquor.

"We'll speak tomorrow," she says, and with that, her Beta ends the call. My chest tightens not being able to see her face, but I feel hopeful knowing she's going to let me talk to her tomorrow. Tomorrow is my chance to win her back, I will do whatever it takes. I will not fuck it up this time. Not even the Gods can stop me from winning over my animai.

Chapter Seventeen
Amelia

As I wake up, I am painfully aware of the thudding in my head. Yeah, I definitely drank far too much last night. If I had been drinking human booze I'd be waking up like nothing ever happened. But Tezus liquor will knock you on your Gods damn ass, and that's definitely what it's done to me.

Come to think of it I should be feeling better by now. I had stopped drinking after I found out what happened to Marcus... Oh Goddess, Marcus. Some filthy she-wolf laid her hands on my animai. I have no idea who she is, but I promise the Gods she's a dead woman if I ever see her.

I knew they were telling me the truth; Jasper would never lie to me and Marcus... I saw the shame on his face. It hurt me to see it. I'm not sure which was worse; thinking my animai was with another or knowing someone was sexually assaulting him. There isn't a winning scenario here. They both have my stomach flipping and my heart clenching in pain.

For a moment, I blamed myself, thinking if I hadn't kicked him out of my pack this never would have happened. But if he hadn't been an asshole, I never would have kicked him out. So instead of dwelling on what sequence of events lead to that moment, I'll just stick to blaming the nasty little bitch whose days are definitely numbered.

Sitting up, I feel a hand drop from around my waist. I look behind me and see Evalyn curled up behind me with Tyson spooning her. What on earth? I look around the room and down on the floor on my side of the bed is Vitali snuggled with Eric and over on the couch is Chris snuggled with Mei. A soft smile spreads across my face knowing my friends stayed with me through this ordeal. No matter how many bad things are thrown at me, just knowing I have them is more than enough to keep me going.

Carefully, I get up and tiptoe to the bathroom and get in a very needed cold shower. My head is still thumping, and my skin feels hot and itchy. I've gotten drunk plenty of times and never felt like this the next day. I guess this is why you shouldn't drink when you're upset.

Once I finish my morning routine, I creep back into the bedroom to find everyone still fast asleep. I shrug, they were kind enough to stay by my side, the least I can do is let them sleep in a little more. I walk into my closet and put on a pair of black slacks, a purple satin button-down blouse and some black ballet flats. I skip blow drying my hair, and instead, put it up in a clip. With one last look at my sleeping angels, I smile and step out of the room quietly closing the door behind me.

Mum and dad aren't here. I remember they were going to their cottage early this morning to see how it's coming along. I'm glad I don't have to explain to them what happened last night. I love them to death; I just don't want to sit down and explain more drama in my life. You get to a point where there is so much constant drama going on that just having to rehash it over and over again becomes more exhausting than the drama itself.

I make my way down to the dining hall and make myself a plate of everything and then take it up to my office to get started on today's work. I'm halfway through my breakfast when the buzzer goes off. I hit the button under my desk and the door opens. To my very pleasant surprise, Landry walks into my office and closes the door behind him.

"Landry, what can I do for you this morning?" I ask him, wiping my mouth with a napkin.

"I, um, well… I came to take you up on your offer," he says nervously.

"I take it you have a plan in place then?" I answer cheerfully.

He nods enthusiastically, "I decided I have nothing to lose, so I went and spoke to Jennifer, and you were right; she's the sweetest person ever. I eventually plucked up the nerve and asked her on a date and she eagerly said yes. I called the place you suggested, and I have reservations for 6 pm tonight."

"This is fantastic news! I'm thrilled," I tell him as I stand. I unlock my desk drawer, grab my wallet and pull out my Amex Black Card, handing it to him.

His jaw drops open as he looks from the card to me and back. "I can't take that," he says quietly.

"I told you, you could borrow my credit card. I don't think you're insane enough to commit credit card theft," I smirk. He shakes his head adamantly. I walk over and place the card in his hand. "Take it and treat her to a night she won't forget. She's a size four if you were wondering." I wink at him.

He grins up at me, "Thank you, Alpha. Thank you so much."

"Amelia, you can call me Amelia. Also, go get the keys to my car from Maggie, she knows where all our car keys are kept. Ask for the keys to the Honda Accord."

Landry looks up at me for a moment, his heart rate going up and so many emotions running across his face. Before I know it, he's leaping at me, pulling me into a hug. I blink back my surprise and let out a soft chuckle as I hug him back.

"What's this for?" I ask him.

"No one has ever been this nice to me," he says, a hint of sadness in his voice.

His words make me frown, "What about your parents?"

He shrugs. "My dad isn't that kind of guy and my mum passed away when I was younger," he says solemnly.

"I'm very sorry about your mum."

"She'd have really liked you," he announces happily.

I smile, "Thank you for saying that. Now enough shooting the breeze with me, you've got a date to get ready for." I playfully push him out the door.

He laughs and waves, "Thank you, Alpha!"

I smile shaking my head. At least someone's romantic life is looking up. Just as I'm about to shut the door, three scents waft my way: oranges, violets, and saltwater taffy; a very unique combination. I open the door as Vitali, Tyson, and Chris walk in.

"Imagine our surprise when we wake up, and a certain Alpha is missing," pouts Vitali.

"Aww I'm sorry guys, but you all looked so cute. I didn't have the heart to wake you," I tell them with a cheeky smile, shutting, the door.

"We are pretty cute; I will give you that," says Tyson nodding in agreement.

"How are you feeling?" Asks Chris with concern.

"Not that great to be honest. My head is killing me and I'm feeling hot and itchy," I tell them as I return to my side of the desk.

"You should be feeling better by now," points out Chris.

I just shrug. "That'll teach me not to scull magical booze," I joke.

"So, you told Marcus you'd speak to him today. Are you still going to?" Tyson asks, taking a seat in front of my desk and reaching over to steal a sausage off my plate.

I snarl and grab his hand before it can reach my plate, "You touch, you die," I say menacingly.

"Dude, when will you learn not to try and steal her food? It's a quick way to lose a hand," Vitali warns, sitting on the edge of my desk.

"It's not my fault if she leaves it sitting there, looking so inviting," he says defensively.

"Go and get your own," I tell him as I pull my plate closer. No one steals my food. No one.

Mum said I was an aggressive baby when it came to food. Apparently, when I was a toddler, I saw my parents having an intimate moment and I kicked my dad in the shin for kissing my mum's chest, telling him he wasn't allowed to touch my food. Mum found it hilarious. Dad was annoyed, especially since I was no longer being breastfed at the time, so I guess I unknowingly cockblocked my dad. But he was also impressed because he said, for someone so small, my kick was nice and strong, so that part made him proud.

"To answer your question, yes, I am still going to call him," I tell them as I sit down.

"I can't believe that happened. What kind of sick person would do a thing like that?" Chris asks in disgust as he takes the remaining seat in front of my desk and puts his wet hair in its usual bun.

My fists clench in anger at the mere thought of someone touching Marcus, I can't even imagine what he's going through right now. A large part of me wants to bathe in this bitch's blood for daring to lay a hand on him in any way. Another part of me wants nothing more than to go to him and make sure he's okay.

"We should find the slut and kill her," snarls Zara, though she sounds tired.

"Are you okay, Zara?"

"Just a bit tired, but I'm fine. I'm worried about Ace and Marcus," she says meekly.

"Me too," I sigh.

"Are you still going to reject him?" Tyson asks cautiously.

"How can I reject him at a time like this? That would be far too heartless and cruel," I say shaking my head. The very thought of it makes my heart break.

"I don't think you want to reject him at all," Vitali says flatly.

"Of course, I don't want to reject him. He's my soulmate for crying out loud," I shoot back. How can anyone think this is what I truly want? I wanted a happy life with Marcus.

"Then don't," Vitali shrugs. "It kills me to admit it, but he looked really worried about you. So talk to him and see where things are at." We all look at him with our mouths hanging open. He looks around at us. "What I say?"

"Since when are you on his side? I thought you hated him," I say with suspicion.

"Oh, I still hate him; the guy is a dick. But Eric put some things in perspective for me, and I think he's right. You two should at least talk it out," he says, making me smirk. "Now what?"

"I told you you'd finally found someone who could tame you," Chris teases with a smirk.

Tyson and I snigger.

Vitali rolls his eyes, "He has not 'tamed' me."

"Oh, he has definitely tamed you," I chuckle.

"You know what? I think you guys are just a bunch of meanies," he says crossing his arms.

We each laugh at his childishness. Goddess, I love these guys.

"Okay, that's enough. We've got a lot to get through today, so let's get to work," I say. With that everyone straightens up and settles in for a long day of work, work, and more work.

***

"So I think that's settled. We'll build the new homes on the west side of the territory," I say while pointing to the map laid out on my desk. "But we'll have the trees transplanted to the east side instead of completely cutting them down," I say as I wipe a hand over my forehead, feeling a couple drops of sweat. I've been feeling hotter by the hour.

"When should we get things started?" Chris asks.

"I think we can start construction this month. All the leg work has been done, now it's just a matter of implementing it," I say.

"The new couples are going to love this," Vitali says proudly.

It's very common when a mutolupus finds their animai that they move out and get a place of their own. With so many newly mated and marked couples, and therefore new additions to the pack, we had to start expanding and building new cottages, which is easy. The issue was finding which plot of land on the territory was the most suitable. Not to mention land and nature are very important to us, so it's also a balancing act of building new homes while also preserving the nature and land we live on. But we seem to have managed just fine.

Tyson is folding up the map when an alarm starts blaring all around the pack, causing our heads to shoot up immediately. This alarm sound is a warning for pack members to seek shelter immediately.

"Incoming! Wolves on the south-east border!" Shouts one of the patrols through the pack-link.

Not missing a beat, I throw my office windows open and the four of us leap out, shifting mid-air. We don't have time for stairs and a four-story drop is nothing to us.

Searing heat spreads through me and my clothes are torn from my body as I bring Zara forward. Zara lands at a run. For some reason she seems a little lethargic, but she doesn't let it stop her. She races to the south-east side as fast as she can with Angel, Axel and Blaise flanking her.

"Border patrols, hold your positions, be on alert for other points of attack. Available warriors to the south-east border immediately! Triage unit, I want you set up at a safe distance from the south-east border," I command to the necessary pack members while Zara races ahead.

As we make it to the south-east side, we can see wolves everywhere, the fight already in full swing. The four of us don't hesitate to jump into the fray. Zara pounces on a large black and grey wolf who is going for one of our warrior's throats. She clamps her jaws around its neck, yanking them off the warrior and proceeding to shake her head violently until there's a snap and the wolf drops dead. Our warrior is back on his feet with only minor injuries and we're quick to fight with the others.

There must be at least thirty wolves attacking us, which is highly unusual. The only time you'd see a large number of wolves attacking is if another pack had declared war. There's something strange about these wolves, Zara and I can feel it. They're definitely not curs, but they seem far more savage than the average wolf.

Zara is taking on two wolves at once, but she's starting to slow down. I can feel us burning up and I don't think this is hangover symptoms.

"I'm sorry Amelia, I'm not going to be able to keep fighting," she tells me, the exhaustion so clear in her voice. I've never heard her like this, and honestly, I feel just as tired, and we've barely even started to fight.

Zara manages to sink her teeth into the neck of one wolf while kicking the other with her hind legs. As the wolf trapped in her jaw chokes to death on its own blood, the other wolf goes flying into a nearby tree. Its body breaks and bends around the tree in a sickening way before crumpling, lifeless to the ground.

Suddenly, without trying, I find myself shifting back into my human form and I'm now all too aware of just how many wolves have their focus on me, not just the invading wolves, but some of my own pack. I know why the moment agonising pain rips through my lower abdomen and spreads like liquid fire throughout my body. I drop to the ground and let out a blood-curdling scream.

"Amelia! You're in heat!" Zara cries in a panic, but there's nothing she can do. When a mutolupus goes into heat, she's unable to shift. It's something the human side goes through and there's nothing the wolf can do; the wolf is basically drained and handicapped until the heat is over.

I look up through tear-filled eyes to see dozens and dozens of wolves locked on me, their eyes piercing with hunger and need. The scent of a wolf in heat taking over their self-control, their primal instincts overriding, telling them to mate.

Oh, like I fucking need this today.

Immediately Vitali, Tyson, and Chris have me flanked and are snarling at the wolves around me. Each of them is marked, so my heat doesn't affect them. But every unmarked wolf in a three-mile radius is going to lock onto my scent and come running. Never rains but it sure as fuck pours, I swear to the Gods.

"Amelia, get to the bunker!" Tyson shouts through the link as he intercepts a wolf lunging towards me.

Another scream escapes me as another wave of pain hits me and I swear it feels like someone is stabbing me in the uterus with white-hot pokers while I roll around in hot coals. I've never felt something so agonising in my life. I thought the pain last night was bad, but that's got nothing on this, but then again no actual sex occurred. If Marcus had actually had sex… I hate to think what that kind of pain would have been like.

This fight has gone to utter shit, and now I'm putting my own pack members at risk. Heat or not, I'm still the fucking Alpha and I will not let this beat me… even though I feel like my insides are being ripped apart.

"ALL UNMARKED WOLVES RETREAT TO YOUR HOMES, NOW!" I command through the pack-link; my Alpha Spirit rolling off me like a blast. They may be heat-crazed, but they still have to obey an order from their Alpha.

My fists dig into the dirt, trying to grab onto something to get me through this pain as I watch my unmarked pack members fight between instinct and command. Command eventually wins and they all run off as fast as they can. One problem down, one to go.

"Amelia we're outnumbered, we'll try and hold them off, but you have to get out of here. You can't command these wolves," Vitali says in a panic, taking on three wolves who are trying to get through him to get to me… this gives me an idea.

Summoning what little strength I have left, I get myself to my feet, gritting my teeth so hard I feel like my teeth will break through my jaw. Every ounce of my body is screaming in protest. A deep unyielding need to mate is wreaking havoc on my body, my heart is erratic, my skin is on fire, my arousal is in the air and not getting a release is making me feel as though every part of me is being whipped with barbed silver whips laced in lupine.

"Stop! I'm going to use myself as bait. Their wolves are going feral, the need to mate is overpowering them. Let them chase me while the rest of you catch them off guard," I order my remaining warriors.

Vitali, Tyson, and Chris keep fighting but each of their wolves' heads snaps to me, and I can see the horror in their eyes.

"Are you out of your fucking mind?!" Tyson screams.

Yeah, probably. But I can either let my heat jeopardize my pack or I can put this agony to good use and that's what I'm going to do.

"Come on, boys come, and get me!" I call out as I take off at a run. I'm nowhere near my normal speed, and each step is like razor blades through me. But no matter how bad it hurts; I keep pushing forward. I can sense the wolves behind me, my Alpha blood the only thing keeping me ahead of them. I can hear the sounds of my pack members taking out the enemy one by one. I just need to hold out a little longer.

"Make sure you take one of them alive!" I order just as I feel a sharp pain

slice down my back. I cry out as my body goes tumbling. The metallic scent of my own blood fills the air as I feel it pour down my back.

Great, because I'm not in enough pain.

I look up and see a large brown, black and grey wolf stalk its way over to me, a deranged look in its eyes. I shudder. The fucker has me cornered and between the pain of my heat and the claw marks down my back, there's no way I can outrun him.

Torie suddenly zips in front of me, her two favourite silver daggers making contact with the wolf's throat as she comes to a stop in front of me. I sigh in relief. Thank you, Morrtemis! The wolf drops and starts flailing around as its blood coats the forest floor. Torie turns to me and squats, looking down at me with concern.

"Alpha, you're hurt," she says in a worried tone.

"I'll live. Thanks… for the save," I manage to say through gritted teeth. Oh, and I'm still very naked, though I am way past the point of caring right now. She reaches out to touch me, but I shake my head. Another shitty aspect of heat; if anyone other than my animai touches me, it'll only make the pain worse.

Was I fucking cursed at birth or something? Because what the fuck?!

As I struggle to my feet, I see Chris' 6'1" black and brown wolf Axel walking towards me. His demeanour quickly changes and faster than my impaired senses can register, Axel has leapt behind me and is suddenly yelping in pain. I turn to see a very pissed off looking man – who looks like he's seen better days – standing in front of Axel, who drops to the ground writhing in pain. The man is holding a strange looking dagger in his hand, and it's covered in blood.

With a new rush of adrenaline coursing through me, I get up, push forward and grab the man, snapping his neck unremorsefully. I turn back in time to see Axel shifting back into Chris as he cries out in pain. I quickly kneel at his side and even though I know it's going to cause me more pain, I reach out and stroke his hair to comfort him. I look down and see an open wound in his chest – the one he got protecting me. But it's not the stab wound that has me worried… it's the black veins spreading out from the wound.

What the hell is that?

"Chris, listen to me, it's going to be okay," I tell him, though each word is coming out breathless. I grit my teeth as hard as I can as another wave of hot stabbing pain radiates through me. I'm trying to ignore it but fuck me it isn't easy. Torie comes up and hands me a shirt and helps me slip it on, doing her best not to touch my skin.

"You're still bleeding," she says with worry.

"Heat slows down the healing process," I tell her. Yeah, and male wolves like to say female wolves are fucking weak. I'd like to see them go through this shit every three months and see how they like it.

"A couple of wolves managed to get away," Tyson says, sprinting over in his human form. It's a good thing we wolves don't care about nudity. His brows knit together with worry when he sees the sight of Chris writhing on the forest floor.

"Vitali, grab a warrior and get Chris to the pack hospital right now. Don't touch the wounded area. Tyson, do a headcount of our warriors, and get those in need to the triage unit asap and only then assemble a crew to collect the dead bodies. Torie, get one of the ATVs and track the wolves who got away, I want to know where the hell they came from," I order, struggling to see straight.

Tyson and Torie both nod and sprint off. Vitali shifts back into his human form and rushes over with a warrior at his side. They carefully pick up Chris and start heading for the pack hospital. Whatever he was stabbed with is going to need more than a triage unit, I know it. I turn to one of the warriors still in wolf form.

"Sonja, collect that dagger and... have it sent off to the lab for testing, but be sure not to touch the blade," I pant.

She nods and, though I can tell she doesn't want to leave me, she obeys her Alpha's orders. With great difficulty, I get to my feet and start walking towards the pack hospital. I'm wobbly and every breath feels like I'm inhaling shards of glass. Every minute, the burning, stabbing pain emanating from my uterus intensifies and I don't know how much more I can take.

Inside the pack hospital, I notice I'm dripping blood through the corridor, but there's not much I can do about that. I follow Chris' saltwater taffy scent and before I make it to the room, I can hear his screams. Using the wall for support, I make my way into his room and see Doctor Richard looking down at Chris with a pale, horrified expression; Vitali is watching in anguish and nurses are hovering in the doorway unsure what to do.

"Why the fuck aren't you helping him?" I grit as I enter the room.

"Amelia, I've told you, you have to get to the bunker," Vitali says with worry.

"I'm not leaving while Chris is like this!" I shout at him. I glare at Doctor Richards. "Why are you just standing there?" I demand.

"Alpha, I… I can't help him," he says in a pained voice. My chest tightens

"What do you mean you 'can't help him'?" I question, gripping a nearby trolley for support and grinding my teeth together.

"There's only one thing that can do this to a mutolupus. The object used to stab Delta Chris had to have been made from wolfram."

At that moment, it's like my entire world has come crashing down around me. Funny enough I almost don't notice the pain of my heat or the blood seeping through my shirt from the claw marks on my back. All I can see is my Delta and best friend screaming and writhing in pain as disgusting black veins spread throughout his body. Hot tears prick my eyes as I walk over to Chris and look down at him. This can't be happening. That wound was meant for me. This was mine to bear, not his.

"What the fuck is wolfram?" Vitali asks in frustration, though I can hear the pain in his voice.

"Wolfram is a metal also known as tungsten. It's a thousand times worse than silver. A mere cut made by wolfram is enough to kill a mutolupus in hours. The metal is poisonous to our kind… and there is no cure for it," Doctor Richard answers regretfully.

Vitali stumbles back in shock, tears filling his eyes. He shakes his head, refusing to believe what he heard, but there's no denying it. The proof is right in front of us. I've read about wolfram. It's an agonising death for any wolf who comes into contact with it. They can't even give Chris anything for the pain, the poison is too strong. I reach out and grab his hand, not caring how much pain it causes me. I'm not abandoning my friend. At that moment I have to make a choice and I know it's the right one.

"Mei, I know you can feel what's happening to Chris. Get to the pack hospital as fast as you can. He needs you," I tell her urgently.

"What's happened to him? Is he going to be okay? He's in so much pain, I can feel it," she sobs through the link.

"I know he is in pain, but he won't be once you get here, so hurry," I instruct her and feel her cut the link. I don't know whether to thank Goddess Morrtemis or Goddess Zarseti or both of them for creating a pairing that will save my friend, but whatever God is responsible; thank you, thank you, thank you.

"Mei is on her way here. Once she is here shut the door and close the blinds. What happens next does not leave this room," I order them letting my Alpha Spirit roll off me. Doctor Richard and Vitali bow their heads in submission.

"What is going on, Alpha?" Doctor Richard asks.

"We just so happen to have a cure," I announce.

Doctor Richard's eyes widen in surprise, "But… forgive me, Alpha, but that's not possible," he says.

"I assure you it… is," I say clutching the bed, my knees giving out as another wave hits me. Fuck this fucking heat, I swear!

At that very moment, Mei storms into the room, chest heaving, tears pouring down her face. A cry of anguish breaks from her when her eyes land on Chris. She's over to his side before any of us can catch the movement. Her species is twice as fast as a mutolupus, and since she's been training, she's been coming into her speed and strength more and more. Now I need the rest of her to be ready.

"Chris. Chris, I'm here," she sobs, clinging to him.

Vitali is quick to shut the door and close the blinds as I instructed, just as Chris starts to seize and foam at the mouth. Mei wails – I can only imagine how much this is triggering her, but right now, it's time for her to be strong. My own strength is nearly depleted, but I use what's left to get to my feet and grab Mei by the shoulders. Shockingly, touching her skin doesn't increase my pain. Will try to remember that later.

"Mei, Chris needs you. You're the only one who can save him. So, I need you to focus and heal him, do you understand?" I tell her in a firm tone, or at least as firm as I can manage in my state.

Mei looks me in the eyes, and I can see the emotional battle she's going through. But one look back at Chris and she finds her resolve. She breaks away from me and closes her eyes, placing her hand on his chest. When she opens her eyes again, golden reptilian eyes have replaced her brown ones and a soft, warm yellow light spreads from her palm and through Chris.

The light seems to have a mind of its own because it starts moving towards every black vein, healing the poison that has spread through his system. It then heads straight for his wound, sealing it closed. I've never seen anything like it in my life. Both Vitali and Doctor Richard are watching in shock and awe. I'd be in more awe if my insides weren't trying to murder me right now.

The light vanishes once Chris is finally healed, his heart returning to its normal rhythm, and he slowly opens his eyes to look up at Mei. "You're the most amazing creature on the planet," he whispers in awe as he pulls her down onto him and buries his nose in her neck. She clings to him, once again sobbing, though I can tell her sobs are no longer anguished.

"Don't ever do that again," she weakly scolds him. He lets out a soft chuckle.

"Never, xingan baobei. I promise," he coos before taking her lips in a deep kiss.

Doctor Richard is watching them as if he just witnessed a miracle, which, in a way, I suppose he did.

"How did she…"

"Mei is a nagata and one of the few with healing abilities," I announce as I clutch my stomach. This gets the doctor's attention. I can see his astounded expression wanting to know more about Mei, but his doctor instinct is kicking in.

"Alpha, you can't go on like this," he says, his brows furrowed in concern.

I wave him off, there's nothing he can do. "What you have seen does not leave this room. Outside of a select few, no one can know what Mei is or what she can do," I say sternly, though I'm trying not to scream.

"Yes, Alpha," Vitali and Doctor Richard say in unison.

Mei pulls away from Chris and looks at me gasping. "Amelia! You're hurt! Why aren't you healing?" She asks in a panic.

I force a small smile. "It's just slowed down for the time being," I reassure her. She shakes her head and moves closer with a look of determination in her eyes. She places a hand on my back, and I feel a gentle tingle spread through my back, replacing the pain from the claw marks until I don't feel them at all. I look at her with relief and appreciation.

"Thank you, Mei," I say sincerely, grateful she was able to alleviate some of my pain.

She frowns, "You're burning up and you're still in pain, why can't I heal it?" She asks with worry.

"Because I'm in... heat... and you... can't fix that," I pant as another wave hits me. Chris is now off the bed and he's looking at me with concern too. Well, this is fun.

"Come on, I'll help you to the bunker," Vitali says gently. I nod in agreement. Now that Chris is okay, it would be safer for me and everyone else if I am locked away for the time being.

Vitali escorts me to the bunker under the packhouse that has an emergency room for wolves in heat. It's basically an icebox that is cut off from everything. Air can come in, but it has filters in place to stop my scent from leaving the room. It has a bed, and a small fridge so the person inside will be okay, though I don't think a snack and some water makes that much difference.

While we walk to the bunker I can sense Vitali's worry and sympathy as I struggle with each step. I know he desperately wants to reach out and help me, but he knows he can't. This is unbearable in so many ways. I make my way down the steps as a whimper slips past my lips. My fever is running so hot, I've barely been able to see in front of me; everything is coming in double.

Vitali gets the door open, and I step in; the below-freezing temperature of the room only alleviates the fire in my body by a small fraction, but I'll take what I can get.

"I've had some of the staff pack the fridge with water, Gatorade, and plenty of snacks. I'm so sorry this is happening, Amelia. Just link me if you need anything," he says solemnly.

I nod and lay down on the floor, letting the cold floor soothe my burning skin.

Vitali sighs and closes the door behind him. The latch on my side automatically locks once it's closed. I wait a couple minutes and then let out the ear-piercing scream I've been suppressing as I give myself over to the unbearable agony I've been fighting to hold back. It's about to be a rough couple of days.

Chapter Eighteen
Marcus

I wasn't able to sleep a wink last night, but to be fair, I haven't had a decent night's sleep since before I met Amelia. If I hadn't been such an asshole the night we met, I could have spent that night with her wrapped in my arms. Every night, my soul cries out for her and I know I won't have peace until I'm with her again.

All night I went over in my head what I would say when I talked to Amelia again. I can't express how happy I am that she's willing to talk to me and best believe I'm going to take that opportunity by the balls and use it to win back my animai. I was thinking I'd send her a bouquet of flowers. It might be corny, but at least it's a start.

I eventually get up and head down and join everyone for training. During sparring, I take my anger over the whole Davina thing out on every warrior willing to spar with me. After I TKO the third warrior, Jasper decides it would be best I fight him instead. It's great – I don't have to hold back with him and that's what I need right now.

After training, I'm downing some water when Jasper comes up and slings his arm around my shoulders. "Feeling better?" He asks.

"A little bit," I nod.

"You may have taken me down a couple times today, but you know I'll

"I'll be ready for you," I chuckle.

"Any idea what time she'll call?" He asks as we walk back towards the packhouse.

"No idea and the waiting is killing me," I say, running my fingers through my hair.

"Look man, I hate to sound like a broken record here…"

"You don't have to say it. First, she was going to reject me because I'm an asshole, then I'm sure she was ready to reject me thinking I was banging some she-wolf, not giving a fuck what it would do to her. The fact she's willing to talk to me at all is a miracle and I'm not going to take it for granted. I won't make any more assumptions and I'll try to be more understanding and talk things through with her," I tell him.

He blinks at me, stunned. "Wow… that's the smartest and most mature thing you've ever said."

I roll my eyes, "Fuck off, if I wasn't smart or mature then why would you make me your Beta?"

"Peer pressure. Sheer peer pressure."

"Asshole," I mutter.

He laughs as we head back into the packhouse and go our separate ways; me heading to my suite to go get a shower. As soon as I step into my suite, a growl escapes me. Davina's scent is still lingering in my room and it's pissing me the fuck off. I slept on my couch last night because no way am I going near that bed again. I've already torn off the sheets with the intent of burning them. Might burn the whole bed while I'm at it. Just looking at it makes me feel sick. Not just because of Davina but because I realised how many women I've had in this bed. I don't know where things are headed with Amelia, or if she'll ever visit here, but just in case, I'm not letting her near a bed that other women have been in. She deserves better than that.

I jump in the shower, freshen up and once I'm out I comb my hair and trim my beard a bit. I let it get too wild for my liking the last few days; I just didn't have the energy to care about it. When I finally have myself looking presentable, I head down to Jasper's office and let myself in. He's sitting at his desk with his son, Blake, sleeping on his chest.

"Bit young to start his Alpha training, don't you think?" I joke.

"Funny. Izzy had a meeting with the education board, so that leaves Blake with me," he says, smiling down at his son.

Jasper and Isabelle only leave Blake with a sitter if it's absolutely necessary. Other than that, they make sure one of them is with him at all times. Everyone can see how much they adore that boy. Even I'm pretty fond of the little tike.

Aiden comes in a few minutes later and then we're sitting around waiting for Calix, who is unusually late. We get started without him and after twenty minutes, he finally rocks up and straight away we know why he was late.

"You reek of sex, man," Aiden complains as he blocks his nose.

Calix shrugs. "Too bad. I like the smell of my woman on me," he says proudly, flopping down onto the couch.

"Yeah, but do the rest of us have to suffer?" I ask.

"You're just jealous. I bet when you finally get with Amelia, you won't shower for days," he smirks.

"I would totally shower. I'd just make sure she's in there with me when I do," I smirk back. That may just be wishful thinking, but it's all I have to hold onto right now.

"We'll make it a reality. Once we have her, we're not leaving the bedroom for at least a week. Minimum," Ace declares. I'm glad he's speaking to me again. I need his optimism.

"That is something we can both agree on," I tell him.

We get back to business and catch Calix up on what he missed while he was busy doin' the deed. During the entire meeting, I can't sit still. Ace is getting antsy and there's this uncomfortable prickling sensation radiating up from the base of my spine. I keep scratching my lower back to try to relieve the feeling, but it doesn't do anything.

"Dude, what is with you? You're acting like you've got ants in your pants," says Calix and Aiden chuckles.

"Maybe I do," I say, shifting uncomfortably yet again.

"Huh?" He asks in confusion.

"What's wrong?" Jasper asks with concern, looking up from feeding Blake his bottle.

"I don't know. I just feel restless and so does Ace. My spine feels all hot and prickly," I tell them with a hint of irritation in my voice. Each of them goes stiff and throw each other panicked looks and now I'm worried. "What? What is it?"

"Um, Marcus... I'm pretty sure Amelia is in heat," Aiden says cautiously.

I stare at him like the dude has lost his damn mind, then throw my head back and laugh. "That's a good one. No way would she be in heat. We haven't even marked each other yet."

"Exactly," says Calix, confusing me.

"Marcus, Amelia is an Alpha. The instinctive need to mate is much stronger in an Alpha because our packs depend on us. The bond clicked in almost a week ago and you haven't mated or marked each other. Her heat could be coming on as a way to speed up the process," says Jasper, sombrely.

I look at them all and see how serious their faces are. They're not fucking with me. I shoot up out of my chair, my panic now at Defcon One.

"Why the fuck didn't anyone tell me sooner?!" I shout and start pacing, yanking my hair in agitation.

"How the hell were we to know? And she was supposed to reject you, remember?" Says Calix.

Asshole just had to throw that in, didn't he?

Shit, Amelia is in heat and she's all alone. She's going to be in so much pain... what if some wolf gets his hands on her? Unmarked wolves go crazy when a she-wolf is in heat. Their wolf will do anything to mate with them. I start growling and shaking.. She could end up raped, all because I couldn't just accept her from the start. My stomach rolls at the thought and I can taste bile rising up my throat.

No one is touching our animal! Get to her now! Ace growls in my head.

Again, I'm in agreement with him.

"I have to get to Amelia," I declare.

"It's an hour by car to get to her pack," Aiden points out..

"I'll shift and run. Ace can get us there in thirty minutes, maybe twenty with the way we're feeling right now," I tell them, already throwing off my shirt.

"Marcus, wait. What will you do when you get there? Just storm in and mate with her then and there?" Jasper questions.

Fuck, he's right. I can't do that to her. That's not how I want our first time together to be. Just because I have been around the block when it comes to women doesn't mean I don't want my first time with my animai to be special. She deserves that. Not a quick fuck because she's in heat.

"Of course, I wouldn't do that. I'll figure something out, either way, she needs me. Just being close to her can ease the pain and I need to do at least that much for her," I tell him, desperation coating my voice..

He stares at me for a minute and nods, "Go. I'll call the pack and let them know you're coming so they don't hold you up."

I sigh with relief, "Thank you!"

I run out as fast as I can, and I hear the guys shout 'good luck' behind me. Once I get to the front of the packhouse, I throw off the rest of my clothes and let the heat roll over me as I shift into Ace. I give Ace full control and he takes off like a bat out of hell, as desperate as I am to get to our animai. He's weaving through trees and leaping over logs, not letting anything get in our way. The scenery around us becomes nothing but a blur as he keeps his eyes forward.

"We can't mate with her, Ace. I know our instincts will be screaming at us to do it, but we can't. It can't be like this. We'll be there for her and help her through this, but I need us to work together to stay in control," I plead with him.

"I know, Marcus. It will be difficult, but she's our everything. I won't do anything that risks us losing her, again. I promise I will rein myself in." I can hear the love in his voice, and I can feel the strength of it through our bond. I trust him. He's been protective of Amelia from the start. He accepted her before I did. He won't let us hurt her.

"I'm sorry for the mess I made. I swear I'll make it right. Starting now. I refuse to put her through more shit," I vow to him.

"Glad to hear you've come to your senses," he says proudly.

This is the most in sync Ace and I have ever felt, and I swear I physically feel our bond strengthen. Somehow it gives him a boost of energy that has him racing at record speeds. I'm not complaining. Whatever gets us to Amelia faster is fine by me.

In twenty-three minutes, we're crossing into Invictus Pack territory and straight away I can pick up Amelia's scent. It's perfuming the whole damn territory and has the hairs on our body on end. Ace falters for a second when her scent hits us but he forces himself to shake it off and keeps sprinting to our woman. Border patrol sees us but doesn't stop us, so Jasper must have done as he said and let them know we were coming. Seriously, they do not want to get in my way right now.

Her scent is everywhere and it's messing with our head, so not knowing where to go, we go straight for the packhouse. The front doors are open and Ace leaps right in, letting me shift back into my human form. I can see a group of people down towards the back of the packhouse and I recognise some of them as ranked members. They've all got their heads turned to me, so I storm over to them. I'm panting and trying to catch my breath after running faster than I ever thought we were capable of.

"Where is Amelia?" I demand.

Before I even know what's going on, a woman with auburn hair storms over to me and sucker punches me right in the jaw making my head snap to the side.

Fucking hell! What the hell was that for?

"You have some nerve showing up here! My daughter is going through hell right now because of you!" She yells.

Daughter? Oh, this must be Amelia's mother and the former Luna.

"Nothing like meeting our mother-in-law with your junk out. Great first impression," says Ace sarcastically.

Am I currently standing in front of everyone baring all? Yup. Do I care? Not in the fucking least.

"Easy, Fleur." says a man who is radiating Alpha energy, I can assume he's Amelia's father. I can see she got her blonde hair from her father, but she got her mother's eyes. He pulls the woman into his arms and kisses the top of her head while she looks at me like she wants to rip my dick off and here

I am, naked as the day I was born, making it way too easy for her.

There's another woman to the side who only looks a little older. She's short, with a bob haircut and is smirking nodding in approval... I think at the fact I just got decked. That Luna can throw a punch, I'll give her that. I can still taste blood in my mouth.

"No, I will not go easy, this sorry excuse of a man is why our daughter is suffering," she says and while her face still looks angry, I can see how worried she is for her daughter.

"Believe me I know. But I'm here to make it right. Please just tell me where she is, she needs me. You keeping her away from me is only hurting her more," I argue. I am sure they all hate me, but I'll take them all on to get to Amelia, they are not keeping me away from her.

"Here," Beta Vitali walks over handing me a pair of shorts. I guess he was prepared for my arrival.

"Thanks," I say, quickly pulling them on. Every fibre in me is screaming to go be with Amelia. Her scent is driving me crazy.

"Aunt Fleur, we all feel the same way, but he's right. He's her animai, he's the only one who can help her right now," says Delta Chris, holding his own animai, Mei, tight in his arms. She nods in agreement.

"I swear, I won't hurt her," I promise.

"Well, maybe not hurt her, but I really don't think this is how Amelia pictured losing her virginity," says a slender woman with long brown hair.

"Eva!" Gamma Tyson groans as he facepalms.

"Whoops... Did I just say that out loud?" Says this Eva woman guiltily.

I turn still as a statue. Amelia is a virgin? Fucking hell. Was she saving herself for her animai? For me? My chest fills with pride at the very thought of her waiting for me and knowing no other man has touched her – not that I would be disgusted by her if she had a few experiences. This just makes Ace and I even more determined to resist the pull of her heat. I will *not* let her first time be like this. Over my dead body.

"I would prefer we not stand around talking about my daughter's sexual history or lack thereof," says the former Alpha. Elias, I think his name is. His eyes focus on me as he stares me down and while my instinct is demanding I bow in submission to him, I fight it. Alpha or not, he's not getting between me and my soulmate. "You do anything to my little girl without her consent and I will personally chop your balls off, put them in a blender and feed them to you through a straw. Do I make myself clear?" He says in a deadly tone.

"Alpha, if I hurt Amelia ever again you won't get the chance to end me because I'll have done it myself," I say flatly. He quirks an eyebrow at me.

"Kid's got spunk. It's going to be fun seeing how these two will be together," smirks a man who looks just a little older than the Alpha, but he is also throwing out Alpha energy, so I'm going to go out on a limb and say that's Amelia's grandfather. At least he doesn't seem to hate me.

"I agree, dear. Zarseti knows what she's doing," says the woman with the bob, moving into his arms. Grandmother, I take it.

"You realise now our animai's parents, grandparents and all her closest friends have seen your dick before she has, right?" Ace sniggers.

I sigh. When he phrases it like that it makes me feel like shit. He's such a fucking asshole.

"Takes one to know one," he says, snidely.

"Look, you can all give me the third degree later, but right now can someone just please take me to my animai!" I growl, getting frustrated by all this time-wasting bullshit.

"Vitali, take him to the bunker," the former Alpha instructs. Vitali nods and kisses his animai's cheek before nodding for me to follow. We go out the back of the packhouse where I notice Amelia's scent is stronger.

"There's something I should tell you. Our pack was attacked a little while ago. Amelia was hurt, but she's fine now. Point is – you're going to see her in a very bad state, and I don't want you to get a shock," he tells me.

A lump grows in my throat. Can my animai not catch a fucking break? Like seriously.

"Are you sure she's fine?" I ask nervously.

"I promise. She was stubborn, but amazing, I've never seen or heard of anyone doing what she did," he says, full of pride for his Alpha.

"What did she do exactly?" I ask curiously.

"Thirty or so wolves attacked; we have no idea where they came from. We captured one and we'll wait for Amelia to decide what we'll do. Anyway, her heat hit while we were in the middle of fighting, and it was fucking chaos. I don't think I have to tell you what happened," he says, looking at me carefully.

I shudder knowing exactly what would have happened. Every unmarked male wolf around her would have become her enemy, even her own pack members. I gulp back the bile rising in my throat.

"We tried to get her to go to the bunker, but she refused. She ordered all her unmarked warriors to leave the fight and then used herself and her heat as a distraction so we could kill the remaining invading wolves. She was injured, she was in heat and still, she put her pack first. I've always been proud of Amelia, but today I've never been more proud to call her my Alpha," he tells me, and I believe him.

My Amelia, my animai, took on an army of wolves during her heat and not only endured the pain; she turned it into a fucking weapon. Tears prick my eyes and pride swells in my chest. The Goddess gave me someone amazing and I nearly threw it away over stupidity. I don't know why Goddess Zarseti thought I was worthy of someone like Amelia, but I'm going to prove her right.

"Damn right we will!" Ace declares.

Vitali leads me down into an underground bunker, down a long hallway under the packhouse and to a reinforced door. He pulls out a key and unlocks the door.

"Good luck," he says giving me a pat on the back before running off.

I put my hand on the door handle and brace myself. With one deep calming breath I open the door.

Okay, all the mental preparation I did on the way here meant fuck all. Nothing could prepare me for this. Amelia's scent has smacked me in the face like I just jumped off a fifty-story building and landed face-first into the concrete. It's strong. It's intoxicating, and I can taste it on my tongue. Her arousal is in the air like the world's strongest and most delicious perfume and it's making my dick painfully hard. Ace is pacing and thrashing his head, trying his hardest to fight his instincts.

I focus on breathing through my mouth – which barely helps – as I step in and shut the door behind me. Amelia's heart is pounding in her chest, her breathing is ragged, and I can feel her fever from across the room. They call it heat for a reason. I take slow steps towards her, fighting the animalistic need to plunge my cock deep inside her wet walls and fill her with my cum… fuck, those thoughts are not helping.

I crouch down next to her as she lays on the floor whimpering in the foetal position. Just seeing her like this breaks my heart. I reach out and stroke her cheek; her skin feeling like fire, but at the same time, the contact sends electricity through my body and directly to my dick. I bite back a groan. The sensation is a thousand times more powerful than last time. She shudders at my touch and her heart rate increases as her eyes shoot open to look up at me in shock.

"M-Marcus," she croaks.

"I decided a phone call wasn't sufficient," I joke softly.

She looks at me as her eyes turn glassy with tears and it makes my heart clench. My strong, beautiful soulmate has been through way too much. I should have been by her side being her support, not another problem.

Trying to focus on anything but the throbbing in my dick and my aching blue balls, I take a better look at her. Fucking hell, Vitali wasn't wrong. Her shirt is soaked with blood, though it looks mostly dry, and her gorgeous skin is covered in blood and dirt. Safe to say, she's had a rough fucking day.

"It's okay, baby, I'm here. It's going to be alright," I coo, stroking her cheek. I'm thrilled when I see her lean into my touch and close her eyes. "Amelia…" I start to say. She opens her eyes to look at me and I can see the apprehension in them. "I promise I won't do anything; I won't take advantage of you like this, but… I think it would help if our skin were able to touch. Would you be okay with that?"

A tear falls down her cheek and I can't tell if it's good or bad, but she nods, so that's something. I carefully pick her up in my arms and her overheated body curls into me. I don't care how much pain my dick is in; it's fucking worth it. To finally have her in my arms and seeking comfort from me is better than I ever could have imagined.

I carry her to the bed and lay her down. She cries out in pain the second my contact is gone. It's like a switchblade to my heart, but it means my touch does in fact help. I carefully help her out of her shirt. I was trying so hard not to look at her body, but it just happened, and this just got a lot fucking harder.

Even covered in blood and dirt she looks like a Goddess. Her white skin is flushed from her heat making her look irresistible as fuck. Every inch of her is toned; her hourglass shape is even more perfect than I realised. She has the most fantastic breasts I've ever seen, and I have to clench my fists together to resist reaching out and kneading them – she's got to be at least a C cup. Her nipples are hard and begging to be sucked on, her pretty, pink areolas are larger than I would have expected and something about the size of them is making my dick twitch.

I'm telling myself to look away, but I can't. She clenches her thighs together and the action draws my eyes straight to it. I swallow the saliva building up in my mouth as I see the state of her. Her juices are soaking her thighs, making them glisten and the sight of it has me desperate to dive my head between her legs and lick up every last fucking drop. My dick throbs and twitches to a painful degree and I swear I nearly come just at the sight of her arousal.

I close my eyes and try to summon all the willpower inside of me. Once I think I've got myself under control, I lay beside her and pull her into my arms, wrapping my legs around her. I breathe in her euphoric tropical scent that I have missed so much and relish in the electricity that sparks everywhere our bodies touch. She presses up against my dick and it takes my everything not to rub against her, seeking friction.

"Is this helping?" I ask her, softly.

I feel her relax a bit and bury herself against me and I swear I've never been so happy in my whole life.

"It's helping, thank you," she whispers, breathing in my scent. I gently kiss her forehead and softly run my fingers up and down her back.

"I heard you kicked ass today," I tell her, hoping I can distract her a little bit with conversation.

She looks up at me quizzically. "Who told you that?" She asks.

"Your Beta," I say. She nods in understanding. "I'm so proud of you," I tell her sincerely. This time her head snaps up so fast, I thought she might accidentally break my nose.

"You're proud? Of what?" She asks in disbelief.

"Of you. No one could have done what you did. I'm in awe of you," I say earnestly, pressing my forehead against hers. She looks at me with shock and suspicion. I fucked up big, I don't blame her for being hesitant to believe me. "Being separated from the other half of your soul and fearing you'll lose them forever really knocks some sense into a guy," I tell her with a soft smile.

She returns my smile but then her face crumples up, and another cry of pain passes her lips. I pull her into my arms tightly, trying not to think of how good her hard nipples feel brushing against my chest. This is by far the hardest thing I have ever done, but she's worth it. After all, she's the one copping the worst of it. If things had gone well that first night, this wouldn't be happening, and if it were happening she'd be crying out in pleasure, not pain.

An idea comes to me. I am definitely insane for thinking this, but watching Amelia suffering is killing me, and fucking her like crazy is not an option right now.

"Amelia, I have an idea," I tell her as I rub her back.

"Wh-what idea?" She asks through clenched teeth, breathing heavily. Ace is whimpering in my head; he hates this as much as I do.

"Our animai is so strong," he says.

"You've fucking got that right," I agree.

"You know how you can share your strength and healing with pack members?" I ask. She nods, looking confused. "Maybe you can share your pain with me." I place a soft kiss on her nose.

She shakes her head adamantly, "No. You don't need to prove a point, Marcus and how would I even do that? You're not a member of this pack."

"But I am the other half of your soul. We're already connected, I felt that you were in heat from back in my pack. Just try, please? I can't bear to watch you in pain. If I can take even a little of it, then let me," I try to convince her.

She takes a breath and nods, "I'll try.

"Look at it as a bonding experience," I tell her cheekily.

"Did you hit your head recently?" She queries and I chuckle.

"Jasper may have gotten in a few hits during training, but I assure you there's no permanent brain damage," I say, smiling down at my beautiful woman. Fuck she's perfect.

"I think I'd like a test to determine that," she teases.

I've wanted this so fucking much; holding each other, teasing each other. The circumstances are shit, but I'm still happy I get to experience this, especially when I thought I'd lost my chance.

She closes her eyes and wraps her arms around my waist. I clench my teeth at the way my dick is screaming to be inside her, ignoring it. Two minutes later ignoring my dick becomes incredibly easy when I am hit with pain, unlike anything I have ever felt in my whole entire life. My grip on Amelia tightens and a whoosh of air leaves me like I just got kicked in the gut.

Fucking hell, am I dying?

Is this what death feels like?

What the fuck is this shit?

I feel like someone is stabbing me repeatedly in the lower abdomen with a knife made of lava and then twisting it for good measure. At the same time, it's like silver shards are in my blood and are scraping my insides. Is this what Amelia has been going through all this time? No, this is only *half* of what she's been going through.

Oh, fuck off!

"Are you okay?" She asks me, still strained but a little more relaxed sounding.

I nod, unable to find the words to speak. How the fuck has she been able to string two words together?

"I can pull it back; you don't have to do this," she says in a worried tone, but instead I tighten my hold on her.

"Don't you dare," I grit and take a breath. "If you could endure twice as much, then I can handle at least half. You're made of fucking steel, babe," I tell her as I bury my nose in her neck and breathe in her scent. I can feel her silently laughing as she snuggles into me.

I regret anything I ever said about a woman not being strong enough to be an Alpha. I apologise on behalf of my gender. Marked she-wolves go through this every three months? How are they not dead? And how did Amelia not castrate me the first time I accused her of being weak? I'm lucky to be fucking alive. I take back everything I ever said, throw it in a chest, seal it with chains, weigh it down with bricks and toss it into the depths of the ocean. I could not have been more wrong, and my woman truly is a fucking Goddess.

Chapter Nineteen
Amelia

These have been the best and worst three days of my life, if that makes any sense. Worst because every minute was consumed by agonising pain and best because I've never felt so safe and content. I spent three full days in the arms of a man who I thought didn't want me. He rushed to my side, and not for sex, but simply to look after me. He even did something I never expected and asked to share my pain. I didn't think I could, but when I tried I could feel my tether to his soul, from there I was able to share my pain. I felt guilty; I didn't want to hurt him, but he refused to let me pull back. The gesture was so touching it brought me to tears.

There's a lot about Marcus I didn't know, which doesn't surprise me. I would never have thought of him as the romantic gentleman type, but here we are. Aside from when he took off my shirt, he kept his promise and didn't try anything. His hands caressed my back and arms to soothe me and never strayed. Every now and then he would place a kiss on my cheeks, nose, forehead, or crown, but never my lips. Everything he did showed me how treasured I was and how much he cared for me, and, despite the pain I was still in, having that made it a bit more bearable.

Sleep didn't come easy and feeling Marcus' constant erection was not helping to quell my own need for him, but we both resisted. Sometimes about the attack on my pack and went over the details together so that I could hit the ground running when my heat was over. In those moments, I felt like I had a real partner. Someone who could run this pack at my side and that filled me with hope.

Waking up I'm relieved to feel not an ounce of pain anywhere and my temperature is back to normal. Thank the Goddess! Though maybe I shouldn't be thanking her, maybe I should go to the temple we have on our territory and cuss out Goddess Morrtemis for putting us she-wolves through this shit. Then again I don't feel like getting myself cursed and the Gods are notoriously as vengeful as they are benevolent.

As my eyes flutter open I'm aware of the strong arm wrapped around my waist and the muscular body curled around my back. My animai. I smile to myself. He's here, and he's amazing. Who says you can't teach an old wolf new tricks? I snort with laughter at my own joke and cover my mouth realising I did that out loud.

"Just what are you laughing about?" Comes the sexy sleepy voice of my animai.

His voice sends instant shivers through me. How was I able to resist him? I should win a medal for that.

"Thought of something funny," I say nonchalantly.

He places a soft kiss on my shoulder blade that causes my breath to catch as electricity shoots through me.

"How are you feeling?" He asks groggily, clearly still waking up.

"Much better. The heat has stopped," I inform him looking back at him. His eyes pop open now fully awake.

"That's great news! I'm so relieved," he exclaims, pulling me closer to him.

"Me too," I giggle. I turn over to face him and we just spend a moment staring at each other. I've missed his forest eyes more than I thought possible. "Thank you for everything you did for me," I say sincerely.

He gives me the sweetest smile and shakes his head, "Don't ever thank me for that. I will always be here for you; I give you my word."

I can feel my cheeks heating up. My eyes dip to his full lips and all I can think about is kissing them. He must be thinking the same thing because I notice his eyes also dip to look at my lips.

"How about we get out of here and have a much-needed shower?" He suggests.

"Together?" I ask nervously with a gulp.

His eyes widen in surprise. "No! I mean… it's not that I wouldn't love to, but I meant individually," he sighs running his fingers through his luscious hair. Part of me feels a little disappointed he didn't want to shower together. "Let's get cleaned up and then I'll explain myself, okay?" He asks, stroking my cheek. I can tell he's a bit nervous and he's already done so much for me, so I nod and agree to his simple terms.

I get up and stretch myself out, feeling my strength coming back to me. I hear a subtle groan from Marcus, and it gives me some satisfaction knowing he enjoyed the view. It further proves how amazing what he did for me was. He resisted every primal instinct he had, all for my sake. I feel beyond lucky to have a soulmate like him. I open one of the nearby chests of drawers and throw on a dress that's inside. Just something to keep me covered till I get to my suite.

"Shall we?" I say turning to Marcus to see he's already up.

"Lead the way," he instructs.

I reach out and take his hand and lead him out of the bunker. I can feel him give my hand a light squeeze and it makes my insides flutter.

As we walk into the packhouse I can hear chatter and as we pass people, they start to whisper. A smart person would just use the pack-link. We get to the third floor and are met by Tyson and Evalyn.

"You're back!" Evalyn screams as she throws herself at me. "Goddess, I was so worried," she says, hugging me like her life depended on it. I chuckle and hug her back with my free arm.

"Did you two…" she says through the pack link.

I shake my head smiling, *"He was a controlled gentleman. I mean it was utter hell, but honestly, it brought us closer I think."*

She pulls back looking at me wide-eyed and then looking over at Marcus appreciatively, then grinning cheerfully. Marcus raises his eyebrow at me. I shake my head in amusement.

"Thank you for taking care of our Alpha," says Tyson.

"Like I said to Amelia, don't ever thank me for that," he says, yanking me into his side and kissing the top of my head.

I blush. Since when do I blush? This is embarrassing. Evalyn is bouncing with excitement and Tyson is smirking.

Jerks.

"Never thought I'd see the day you blushed. Didn't even think you knew how," Tyson teases.

I narrow my eyes at him but ignore the comment, "Marcus, allow me to formally introduce you to my Gamma's Tyson and his animai Evalyn. Ty, Eva, this is my animai Marcus," I introduce them.

Marcus looks down at me in shock before his face morphs into one of pure happiness. I think he might even cry. He holds me even tighter, and I bask in the electricity that runs through me.

"It's nice to finally meet you properly. Like, originally, I wanted to kick you in the balls, but now you seem like a decent guy," chirps Evalyn, making me snort.

"Couldn't have said it better myself," says Tyson as he kisses her temple.

Marcus laughs. "It's good to properly meet you both too and thanks for not kicking me in the balls."

"I never said I wouldn't," Evalyn points out menacingly.

"Can we not talk about damaging my soulmate's balls, please?" I tell them.

"It's okay babe, besides, your father's threat to my balls was the superior one," he reminds me.

Oh yeah, Marcus had told me about how dad threatened to put his balls in a blender and knowing my dad, he would absolutely do that. Grandpa would even help. Hell, so would grandma.

"Should we expect you later?" Tyson asks.

"Yeah. I'll meet you at the cells in thirty minutes. Just let me get freshened up and then we can get to work," I tell him.

"Thirty minutes it is. Come on, Firecracker," Tyson says as he tugs

Evalyn along. She happily follows, smiling widely at us.

"They seem nice," Marcus says earnestly.

I smile and guide him to my suite, "They are and have been my friends since we were pups."

"Same with your Beta and Delta?" He asks.

"Mhmm. Chris is Evalyn's older brother," I tell him. I can see the surprise on his face. "I know they don't look very alike, but hey, that's genetics for you."

"What about Mei and Vitali's animai?" He asks. I really love that he's showing interest in my friends.

"Eric and Vitali met the same night we did, and Mei has only been with us a couple of months. Chris found her at another pack where she'd been kept as a slave," I inform him. That is private information, but this is my animai and the one who may potentially run this pack with me. I'm pleased when I hear him growl and see his forest eyes glow.

"Which fucking pack?" He seethes.

"Albus Mons."

"WHAT?!" He roars, bringing me to a halt. "Are you sure?" He asks quickly.

"Of course. Chris and his dad went there because they hadn't RSVP'd to the Vernal Ball and weren't taking our calls. That's when Chris found Mei," I answer, "Why? What's wrong?"

"We have fucking trade with that pack, but we had no idea they had fucking slaves. I have to call Jazz and let him know right away," he says with urgency.

I nod in understanding. An alliance or agreement with a pack with loose morals reflects badly on your pack. Jasper would be disgusted to learn he has ties to a pack that practices slavery.

"Let's get cleaned up. I'll leave you my phone and you can call Jasper and handle things with your pack while I go down and ask our prisoner some questions. Sound good?" I ask.

"Sounds perfect," he nods, smiling. "Though I had hoped to join you for the interrogation," he says as we walk into the Alpha suite.

"Why's that?" I inquire.

"Just an excuse to be close to you," he confesses with a cheeky smile.

I can't help but giggle, "We can get together afterwards and eat?"

"I can't wait," he says, looking around and taking in the room.. "I like it," he comments.

I veer to the left past the lounge area and lead him into my room, grateful that it's been cleaned.

My room isn't overly big, I don't need that much space. I have a queen-size bed to the left with a white and purple duvet, with white, purple, and grey pillows to match the light shade of grey walls and carpeting. There are dark grey nightstands and lamps, and opposite the bed is a floor to ceiling window framed by thick purple curtains with a charcoal three-person sofa in front of them. There's a white desk to the right of the door and double doors opposite the main door, that leads to my walk-in closet. There's also a door on the left-hand side of my bed that leads to my bathroom. The widescreen TV is on the ceiling but pulls down with a remote control, that's probably the only lavish feature in here.

"Not what I was expecting," he says looking around, his eyes lingering on the mirror that reflects my entire bed. I wonder what's so special about that.

"What were you expecting?" I ask curiously.

"More green. I thought green was your favourite colour," he says.

I smile knowing he remembered. "I love green, doesn't mean I want to be surrounded by it twenty-four, seven. Bathroom is through that door," I point. "You can use my bathroom while I go use my parents. You and Tyson look roughly the same size, so I'll have him bring up some clothes for you to wear."

He surprises me by pulling me close and kissing my forehead; my body jolting to life at our contact. "Thank you," he says softly against my forehead.

I don't think I could ever get tired of this.

"I'll meet you back here in a little bit then?" I ask looking up at him. I can't help the level of hope that is coming off me. Things have been going so well, I don't want anything to ruin it.

"I'll be here waiting for you," he tells me with a swoon-worthy smile.

Be still my wolfy heart! I grin, reach up, and kiss his cheek, then dart off into my closet to grab a change of clothes before racing off to my parent's room to use their bathroom.

"I'm going to come right out and say it, our animai is damn fine and if you don't tap that soon I'm having you committed, because there is clearly something wrong with you," Zara says.

"Good morning to you too, Zara, I'm doing very well, thank you for asking," I say sarcastically.

She lowers her head. *"Sorry, Amelia. I know how horrible the last three days were. I hated being unable to do anything to help you,"* she says remorsefully.

"It's not your fault, just the cards we were dealt. I take it you and Ace had time to bond," I say. She nods excitedly.

"He's perfect Amelia, I can't wait to meet him. Ace says Marcus has really had sense knocked into him, and I believe him," she tells me.

"I believe it too. He's... different. But in a good way," I say.

I jump in the shower and finally scrub off the dry blood and dirt from my skin. How Marcus put up with me in this state is beyond me. While I'm in the shower, I ask Tyson to leave a change of clothes for Marcus and have him collect my phone from my office and leave it with the clothes, along with a note telling Marcus what my passcode is.

When I'm finally clean and refreshed I dry my hair and get dressed in black stretch slacks – I may need extra room for moving around today – a tight black spaghetti strap tank top with a black mesh long sleeve top over that. I zip up some emerald crocodile skin pointed toe stiletto ankle boots and give myself a final once over. I look ready for business... and maybe I'm hoping to impress Marcus a little bit, so sue me.

I step out into the living area and don't see Marcus; I assume he's still in my room. I badly want to peek in and just see him and hear his voice again. The bond is like he's a magnet and I'm a jar of those colourful paperclips getting yanked in his direction. It is hard to fight against that kind of force. Him being an asshole made it easier to resist. However, now that he's being the model animai, I find myself not wanting to fight the pull.

But I am again forced to resist the pull of our bond and I step out of the Alpha suite and make my way to the cells to meet Tyson. When I get there he is waiting patiently outside.

"You look ready to rock and roll," he says with a grin.

"I've got three days to catch up on. Any major injuries during the fight?" I ask with concern. Casualties are a part of war, but I know no one died. I'd have felt their death, had it happened.

"A couple of gnarly ones, but they've all since healed. Chris had it the worst, but as you know he's completely fine" he informs me. I nod, once again grateful to the Gods for pairing him with Mei.

"Has anyone spoken to our new prison mate?" I ask.

He shakes his head, "We were waiting for you. But he's received food and drink. The guards didn't attempt to talk to him, and he didn't attempt to talk to them either."

"Well, let's see if he feels like having a chat now."

Tyson opens the door and ushers me in. Once inside, we walk over to the main security hub for the cells and sign the logbook. I nod a hello to Tatiana and Caleb who are on guard duty.

"Everything alright with our guest?" I ask them.

"Nothing bad has happened, if that's what you mean," Tatiana says.

"Could you clarify that for me?" I ask curiously.

"He seems totally out of it. We didn't do anything to him, of course. Sometimes he grunts but, aside from that, nothing," she says, sounding a little unnerved by the man we captured.

"Thank you, Tatiana," I tell her. I quickly glance at Tyson as we step into the elevator and head down to the underground cells.

The cells are essentially cages made up of four walls of silver bars that are reinforced into the concrete ceiling and floor. Being surrounded by silver will weaken him. When the doors open, I can smell burnt flesh – a sign that he's also wearing the silver cuffs that keep him from shifting and linking anyone.

While we stand in front of his cell, I watch as the man just sits on the floor against his cot looking completely spaced out.

"I am Alpha Amelia, are you ready to talk?"

The man looks up at me but all he does is snarl. Not the reaction I was expecting.

"Why did you attack my pack?" I demand.

Instead of answering, he jumps up and throws himself at the bars, reaching his arm through to grab me. I don't flinch and simply watch as he pulls his arm back crying out as the silver bars burn his skin.

Tyson and I look at each other, confused by his behaviour. There's something off about his scent. He's not a cur, that much I can tell. When a wolf is banished or leaves their pack, their scent develops an earthy undertone. His doesn't have that quality, but something about it is definitely confusing me.

My eyes glow as I push my Alpha Spirit towards him at full force; Tyson takes a step back, his body shuddering from feeling it second-hand.

"Who sent you?" I command, but I get no reaction from him.

"*Zara...*" I start to say.

"*I don't know, Amelia. That should have knocked him on his ass. He doesn't even seem to notice it,*" she says in shock.

I may not be his Alpha, but an Alpha Spirit can force most wolves into submission, . When you use the full weight of your Alpha Spirit, it can actually cause physical pain. It should feel like someone cracking your skull open. I went all out, and he seems completely oblivious.

"Why isn't he responding?" Tyson asks in stunned confusion.

"I have no idea." I try again, pushing my energy forward with all my strength. Tyson is whimpering just being in proximity to it, but again the man doesn't react. Something is not right.

I walk over and grab a pair of gloves off the wall and put them on.

"What are you doing?" Tyson asks apprehensively.

"Going in there," I say flatly.

"Amelia, are you sure that's a good idea?" He asks with uncertainty.

"If it was a bad idea, I wouldn't do it."

I open the gate and step in; Zara whimpering as soon as we're surrounded by silver, but we resist as best we can. I walk over and take the cuffs off the man and grip him by the neck, looking into his eyes. He tries to fight back but he's too weak from the effects of three-day contact with silver. He bares his canines and I continue to watch his eyes as I tighten my hold on his neck.

"Speak," I command pushing every bit of my Alpha Spirit on him, but again, nothing. "Fuck," I mutter as I let him go.

I quickly put him back in the cuffs and step out closing the gate. I then link the pack hospital instructing them to send a nurse to retrieve a blood sample from the prisoner and test it immediately.

"What's going on?" Tyson asks.

"I'm having someone come and take a blood sample," I tell him as I put the gloves back.

"What for?" He asks with surprise.

"I have a theory I want to test out. I'll tell you once we get results," I say as we make our way out of the cells. I just really hope my theory is wrong.

"*Torie, I want to see you in my office ASAP,*" I link to Torie.

"*Right away, Alpha!*" She says.

"*Vitali, Chris, meet me in my office,*" I instruct

On our way out I inform the guards someone will be coming to take some blood, then Tyson and I make our way to my office. I don't want to rush my work, but I'm extremely eager to get back to Marcus.

"*Me too, this is the only downside to being an Alpha,*" Zara sulks.

"*THIS is the only downside?*" I ask incredulously.

"*Okay, there's the whole people wanting us dead, and the disrespect for our gender and the early onset of heat, but I didn't think those were significant enough to mention,*" she says breezily. I bite back a laugh.

We're heading towards the packhouse when my ears prick up as I hear the tail end of a conversation somewhere in the distance. The last words I heard were: 'I've told you everything I know, what the hell more do you expect me to do?' followed by silence. I don't know what that conversation was pertaining to, but it was enough to make me suspicious. The fact the voice was Ryker's is just the cherry on the suspicious cake.

We walk into the packhouse and make it to the fourth floor when I'm tackled by my Beta and Delta. I could be wrong, but I think they missed me.

"Are you okay?" Chris asks, clinging to me.

"We missed you like crazy. Don't leave me in charge again!" Vitali begs, also clinging to me.

I chuckle and hug them back. "I'm fine, and no promises on not making you work hard again… hang on," I take a whiff of Vitali and then pull back with wide eyes. "Did you and Eric…" He nods enthusiastically with a stupid grin on his face. "Vitali! That's amazing! Congratulations," I say, hugging him tighter. "Figures I'm the one who went into heat and you're the one who got laid," I tease. The guys laugh.

"Well, I was certain you weren't going to, so someone had to," he winks at me. I raise a questioning brow at him. "Come on Amelia, you didn't even let your own heat get in the way of protecting this pack, I doubt you were going to let your heat ruin your virtue."

"I'm not sure how I feel about that comment," I pout as I usher them into my office.

"It's just good to see that animai of yours finally stepping up and doing right by you. We were impressed," Chris says happily.

"Eva maintains she will kick him in the balls if he does anything stupid again," Tyson says proudly.

"Sounds like her. But can she just avoid anything below the waist?" I say as I move behind my desk.

"Don't want anyone damaging his baby maker. We hear you loud and clear," Vitali winks, throwing himself onto the couch. The guys snigger and I roll my eyes.

Torie walks in a moment later and shuts the door behind her. Chris takes a seat in front of my desk, but Tyson and Torie remain standing in full warrior mode.

"First, Tyson, I want you to have Izac tail Ryker," I order, surprising him.

"May I ask why you want our best spy following that twerp?" Vitali asks.

"Because on our way here I heard him talking, I think on the phone, to someone. The conversation may have been benign, I'd rather jump to conclusions than not jump to conclusions and regret it later. Between what happened with his parents, the constant threats, an attempt on my life and now the pack being attacked, I'm not dismissing anything."

"I'll have him get started immediately. Do you think he might be the traitor?" Tyson inquires.

"He very well could be. It would not surprise me. But Ryker has a brain the size of an acorn, so he would not be the mastermind behind all of this. I want to know who is. I can't risk losing a potential lead or him warning who he is working with, so for now, I want him followed. I won't pull him into an interrogation just yet," I inform them. They nod in understanding. "Torie, tell me what you found when I sent you off the other day," I instruct.

"Yes, Alpha," she says stepping forward, "I tracked their scents to the river and then lost it. I crossed the river on foot to try and pick it up on the other side but there was nothing. I travelled along both stretches of the lake thinking they had kept to the water and travelled down or upstream and crossed somewhere else but again, I was unable to pick up a scent. I found tire tracks, so I believe there was a getaway vehicle. I followed the tracks, but once they hit the road I lost them," she says in irritation. "Also there was something just not right about their scents. I'm not sure what it was, it was just... different," she says her brows set in a deep frown looking like she's trying to solve a complex puzzle.

"I noticed that, too. You did your best and it's all I could hope for. Thank you for your efforts," I tell her. "I have questioned our prisoner and gotten nowhere. I have requested some blood work and am hoping to find some answers from it. Safe to say there was a lot wrong with our little interaction," I inform them as Tyson frowns.

"Wrong how?" Chris queries.

"He was immune to Amelia's Alpha Spirit," Tyson says. Everyone looks shocked.

"That's impossible," Vitali argues.

"And yet it happened. I will speak on my theories once I get the blood results back," I sigh, rubbing my face. "Chris, how are you holding up?" I know Mei healed him, but what I know about the nagata comes from books, so I don't know if maybe there were side effects from the wolfram.

"Never better. I feel good as new, thank you for asking," he chirps.

I relax. "Thank you for saving my life," I say as gratitude swells in my throat. "That blade was meant for me, and you and Axel saved me. Zara and I will forever be grateful for what you both did."

He looks a little choked up himself, "You're my Alpha, my best friend and like another little sister to me. I would never let anything happen to you,"

I smile with appreciation. I got lucky with these guys that's for damn sure.

I dismiss Torie and have the guys catch me up on the last three days. Once that's done, I find my parents to have a quick catch up with them, which turns into them asking too many questions about Marcus. I try to hurry it up because I want to get back to Marcus as quick as I can. I know he'll be there, but I can't stop this nagging feeling that maybe he changed his mind and bailed.

I know I'm not being rational, but I spent my whole life fearing that my animai wouldn't want me because I was an Alpha. Then I met Marcus and that fear became a reality. While I can see Marcus has made some changes and has taken some massive steps in proving himself to me, it's going to take some time before this insecurity of mine is completely put to bed.

Chapter Twenty
Amelia

Heading back to my suite, I take a breath when I reach the door; bracing myself. I push it open and, sitting on the half-circular sofa watching something on the TV is my animai, looking clean and handsome as ever. The delicious combination of his caramel scent and the smell of food wafting in the air have me salivating. I'm not sure which one I'm hungrier for.

"I know which one I want more," Zara says, licking her chops. I roll my eyes at her.

Marcus' head turns to me as soon as I enter and the brightest smile spreads across his face. He's up and over to me before I can even blink and has pulled me into his arms, spinning me around. His nose is buried in my neck, inhaling my scent. I giggle as I relish the incredible currents of delight that spread through me. A woman could get used to this.

"You're back!" He exclaims, kissing my forehead as he sets me down.

I kick the door shut and grin up at him, "I promised I would be. Did you order food to be brought up?"

"I went down and got a bit of everything for us, I wasn't sure what you'd like. I thought we could eat up here… is that okay?" He asks, appearing uncertain.

I nod eagerly and smile. "That's perfectly fine, and I love everything."

He relaxes and guides me over to the sofa, pulling me down next to him. "How did everything go with Jasper?" I ask while he hands me my plate.

"He was as pissed off as I was. We honestly never had any suspicion anything like that was going on," he says frowning.

I squeeze his arm reassuringly, "I believe you. Though I'm surprised they hid it from you. Because the way Chris and his father described it, they weren't in the least bit remorseful and made no attempts to hide it. But then again, we didn't have any agreements with them."

His frown deepens, "Disgusting bunch of fuckers. Jasper isn't hesitating to end our trade with them. But that now leaves us with a problem."

"Which is?" I ask.

"Well, we purchase produce from their crops. So without that, we're left with a food supply problem," he explains. That is definitely a problem. We may be wolves, but if we relied solely on hunting and eating in our wolf form, the wildlife population would deplete fast and that would screw up the entire ecosystem.

"May I make a suggestion?"

He nods with his mouthful and quickly swallows, "Please do."

"Try reaching out to Alpha Lucas of the Alpine Pack. I know they're a little further away, being based in Montana and your pack based in Washington, but his pack produces some of the best organic food in the country. My pack uses them, and I can assure you, they don't have slaves," I smile.

My heart skips a beat when he gives me another smile. For real though, who told this man it was okay to have such a killer smile?

"Thank you, Amelia. I will gladly let Jasper know and hopefully, a new agreement can be made. Anything that means we don't have to deal with those other fuckers again," he says with disgust. He shakes his head and relaxes. "How was everything with you? Get anything out of your prisoner?"

I sigh and shake my head, "Things are a bit complicated. There may be some potential developments, but I can't confirm that yet. I'll let you know when I have some solid information." He looks confused but lets it go. for now.

We finish our food in comfortable silence, but once both our plates are empty, he turns his full attention on me, and that bubble of insecurity starts rising to the surface.

"I promised you an explanation for earlier, with the shower thing," he says, rubbing the back of his head anxiously.

"Go on," I say, trying to remain composed.

"I want you to know, turning that down may have been even harder than resisting you during your heat," he laughs nervously, and I blink in surprise. "Don't get me wrong, resisting your heat was pure hell, but the thought of our first time being like that... well that was enough reason to resist. With it over, I don't have that excuse," he says sheepishly.

I smile softly, understanding what he's saying. I'm actually feeling the same way. If that had been my first time... well I would not have ever been able to look back on that memory fondly. But, since my heat ended, I find myself struggling to come up with reasons not to complete our bond.

"I understand completely," I reassure him, squeezing his hands.

"Amelia..." he says taking a breath as he holds my hands. "I can never take back the hurtful things I did or said. I wish to the Gods I could, but I can't. I can, however, vow to never hurt you like that ever again. Thinking I'd lost you was the worst pain I have ever experienced. First, I thought I lost you when you said you'd reject me, then I thought I lost you when that psychotic bitch Davina did what she did," he says the she-wolf's name with so much hatred and I clench my jaw remembering what she had done to my soulmate. How dare she think she can just go around laying her hands on someone without their permission? She's a sick, pathetic bitch.

"I mean it, she's dead if I ever see her," I remind him.

He gives me a proud smile, "I think I might enjoy that." His face turns serious and nervous again, "I want to do this right. I want a chance to start fresh with you and go about things the way I wanted to, had my big fucking mouth not gotten in the way. So, Amelia... would you do me the honour of going on a date with me?" He asks, and suddenly the big, tough Beta looks like a nervous teenager asking out his crush.

"Date? You're asking me on a date?" I squeak in surprise.

"I am, and I'm hoping you'll say yes. Let me show you that I can be the man you need and deserve. Let me prove to you I can be at your side as your equal, to be the one to lift you up instead of tearing you down. In the blink of an eye, you have become my world – my slice of paradise – and if I have to fight to keep you, then I'm prepared to declare war on the whole world," he says with more conviction than I've ever heard anyone use.

His words have rendered Zara speechless, her jaw literally hanging open along with mine. Never in my wildest dreams or fantasies did I ever think I would hear such a declaration from Marcus, or any other person for that matter. His words are running through my ears, tears are pricking my eyes and my heart could rivel a hummingbird right now. I can't find the words to say to him, so I do the only thing I can think to do. I throw myself at him.

My arms wrap around his neck and yank him to me as I crash my lips onto his. I try to convey every bit of passion, want, and need I have for this man into my kiss, and with it, I bear my insecurities and fears. I kiss him not holding anything back, basking in the electric shocks coursing through me. To my utter joy, he wraps his arms tight around me groaning against my lips as he returns my kiss fervently.

He's holding me tight against him and yet it's not tight enough. My fingers are tangled in his thick, luxurious hair as our lips battle for dominance and I'm enjoying the fight. He brings one hand to cup the back of my neck and angle my head so he can deepen our kiss and I gladly let him as his beard tickles my face in all the right ways. As our kiss deepens, a deep moan makes its way up my throat; my walls clenching so strongly I can feel it in my stomach.

My arousal is filling the air and next thing I know he has me pinned to the couch; his plump lips trailing passionate kisses down my jawline and down my neck. My breath catches in my throat as his hot tongue glides against my heated skin, causing me to bite back a moan. My hands have found their way up his back under his shirt, and I revel at the feel of his smooth muscles flexing under my touch. I want to feel more of him.

"Fuck... Amelia," he groans into my neck as he presses his very prominent erection against my core. I can feel my panties dampen, and I know I'm going to need a change of clothes before I leave this room again.

His mouth continues its assault on my neck making its way to my marking spot and as he starts to suck, pleasure I didn't even know was possible spreads through me. I cry out as I buck my hips against him, desperate for more. He's driving me crazy, and I don't want him to ever stop.

"Don't stop," I beg as my body writhes underneath him. His lips find mine again and we resume our battle. Just as I feel his right hand slide up under my top I feel a link opening in my mind, and I want to cuss out whoever is ruining the best make-out session of my life.

"Alpha, I have results from the blood you had taken from the prisoner that I would like to discuss with you in person," comes Doctor Richard's voice.

Damn, damn, damn. I can't put this off, it's too important.

"Please meet me in my office," I instruct. I open my eyes to see Marcus staring down at me patiently; chest heaving, lips swollen, pupils dilated and his hair tickling my face.

"Important pack-link?" He asks with not an ounce of anger or disappointment.

"That was Doctor Richard, he has results for a test I requested," I say, breathless. Marcus's face flashes with panic and I realise he thinks the test is for me. I smile up at him and brush his hair back out of his face. "It's not for me, but it is important. I need to go speak with him. You're welcome to join, only if you want to." I chew the inside of my cheek, nervously.

His face flashes with surprise and then softens, "You trust me that much?"

"I want to. I want you in there with me," I tell him kissing his lips softly.

He returns my kiss and smiles down at me. "I would be honoured," he says as he slowly moves off me, but I stay still. "What's wrong?" He asks with concern.

"I uh… need to go change," I answer awkwardly.

"Why?" He asks curiously.

"You ruined my underwear," I admonish him.

His eyes widen and then a sly smirk forms on his face, "And I should feel bad about that because…?"

Damn him for being so sexy!

"No, damn that doctor for ruining a fun time. What a twatblock," Zara scoffs.

I nearly lose it completely hearing that. *"Zara!"* I chastise, trying to hold in my laughter.

"What? It's true," she shrugs and flops down. I roll my eyes at her and get up, but as I do Marcus gets up and yanks my back to his chest, making me yelp.

"So was that a yes?" He whispers in a low sexy voice in my ear making me shiver as the wetness between my legs increases. Gods dammit.

"Yes," I whisper with a gulp.

"Brilliant! Now go get on a new pair of panties so I can ruin those too," he says cheerfully, landing a light smack to my ass.

I jump with a loud squeak and throw him a glare, but the happy jerk is grinning like an idiot. It's not fair, guys don't need a change of underwear when they are turned on. Guys can lose an erection, but women can't get unwet. Thank the Gods this wasn't in public, or I'd be walking around very uncomfortable. Not to mention, everyone would smell the state of me. That thought is mortifying. I know it's normal for our species, but this is new territory for me, and I also don't need more reasons for pack members to look down on me.

Zara growls in my head. *"If an Alpha walked around with a hard-on, everyone would just call him virile, but you would be considered a slut. It's not just unfair, it's not right!"*

"I know that; I share your feelings. Change takes time Zara, we can't reverse thousands of years of thinking in a matter of weeks, no matter how much we wish we could," I remind her, soothing her through our bond.

"Yeah, well, I still get to grumble about it," she huffs.

"Grumble away my feisty wolf," I say playfully.

Once I have changed my underwear, and my pants which were also ruined – damn that sexy, sexy man – I return to Marcus.. As soon as he sees me his eyes trail over my body slowly, biting his lip, his eyes filling with desire. It takes me a minute to steady my breathing.

"Shall we?" I say, embarrassed when I hear my voice crack.

He smirks and holds out his hand, "Gladly. Did you change your pants too?"

I can hear the amusement in his voice. His face, however, looks proud as hell. I walk over taking his hand nearly sighing at his touch.

"Yes, you ruined those too," I admonish through narrowed eyes.

"If you're looking for an apology, it's not going to happen," he says, still smiling like an idiot.

"Why do I get the feeling you're going to be bad news for my wardrobe?" I sigh.

Images of him ripping my clothes off and having his way with me are swirling around in my head and it's not doing anything to calm these raging hormones.

"The fact you're saying that makes me feel extremely optimistic for our future," he says cheerfully.

I have to admit his happiness is infectious. Whenever I see him smile, it makes me smile, too. With our hands clasped we walk down the hall to my office as I link Vitali, Tyson, and Chris. It's a good thing I love these guys so much or seeing them so often would get old really quick. I let us into my office and as soon as we step in, I feel Marcus go stiff beside me. I look up to see a sad look on his face, his brows pinched together.

"Marcus? What's wrong?" I move closer and rub his hand, letting our bond soothe him, even if it's not fully in place yet.

"The first and last time I was in here I said some fucked up shit that nearly made me lose you forever. The memory just caught me off guard, was all," he says looking down with a sad smile.

"We can make new memories," I reassure him.

He nods and kisses the back of my hand and damn does it feel good. I walk around to my side of the desk, refusing to let go of his hand.

"Where do you want me?" He asks. Such an innocent question, and yet it has me picturing him sitting on the couch while I ride his dick. Holy crap! I wasn't even having these erotic thoughts while I was in heat. "Amelia?" He gently prods. I look away feeling my cheeks become as hot as the sun. Please don't notice. His free hand comes up to cup my chin and tilt my face up to look at him, my heart thudding as our eyes meet. He examines my face for a moment before that sly smirk returns. "Was my sexy little Alpha having dirty thoughts about me?" He teases, again looking very proud of himself.

Butthead.

Wait, did he just call me sexy? ...DID HE JUST CALL ME ALPHA?

"Noticed that huh?" Zara sniggers.

"Oh, shush," I retort, but she just laughs at me. "So what if I was?" I say nonchalantly, though my heart is pounding. My animai not only just called me sexy he acknowledged me as an Alpha for the first time.

"Then I would say getting to take up real estate in your mind makes me one lucky son of a bitch," he says matter-of-factly.

That shuts me up. I was expecting him to tease me, and instead, he said something like that. I think I'm a goner.

Before I can say anything else, Vitali, Tyson, and Chris all file in. Marcus lets go of my chin most unwillingly and that makes two of us, because I nearly whimper at the loss of his touch. When did I become this woman? The guys look very surprised to see Marcus, but their surprised faces quickly turn into smirks.

"Monopolising our Alpha I see," says Vitali.

"Only as much as she'll let me," Marcus says proudly, pulling me into his side. I shake my head but wrap my arm around his waist and breathe in his sweet, delicious caramel scent.

"Your first official meeting as Amelia's animai, does this mean you're considering joining and helping to lead the pack?" Chris asks.

It was an innocent and fair question to ask, but it has Marcus and I both going rigid. We hesitantly look at each other and panic sets into my bones.

We haven't talked about it; in fact, I've been avoiding even hinting at it. I just wanted to be with my other half without something ruining it and I was afraid any discussion of what to do with the Luna position would end in harsh words. My heart can't handle that. I'd rather fight a hundred wolves while in heat than go through that again.

"One thing at a time. First let's see what the good doctor has to say," I reply doing my best to deflect the question. I feel Marcus relax beside me, much to my relief.

Doctor Richard walks in a few minutes later closing the door behind him. His face is set in a deep frown, and I feel bad for him. I seem to be giving him a lot of reasons to frown and worry over the last week, far above the norm. I should encourage him to take a holiday when this threat is over.

"Doctor Richard, allow me to introduce you to my animai, Beta Marcus Hayda," I say proudly. I can feel Marcus oozing pride beside me and damn does it feel good.

"Beta Marcus, it's an honour to meet you formally. How is the collarbone?" He asks in his usual warm tone.

Marcus rubs the back of his head shyly and mumbles, "It's good".

So the good doctor treated his broken collarbone… yeah, I don't want to think about that day.

"You have some results for me," I prompt.

Doctor Richard gives me a pointed look, "You knew what I would find, didn't you?"

"Depends what you found," I say, keeping an even tone.

He sighs, rubbing his forehead, "The wolf enzymes are not binding to his red blood cells. They continue to bind and then detach constantly."

His words knock the wind out of me. Fuck, fuck, fuckity, fuck.

I let go of Marcus and rest my hands on my desk. "I was afraid of that." I sigh, closing my eyes. What shit storm have I gotten into now?

"Someone want to fill the rest of us in on what the hell that means? We're not all book worms like Amelia here," Vitali quips.

"Alpha, how did you know?" Doctor Richard asks curiously.

"He doesn't have a wolf spirit," I announce. This causes everyone else in the room to gasp in shock. "He was completely unresponsive to my Alpha Spirit. I kept trying to get a sense of his wolf, but I felt nothing. At first, I thought it was because of the silver, so I took the cuffs off, but even then… nothing," I explain. Doctor Richard nods gravely.

"What does that mean 'he doesn't have a wolf spirit'?" Tyson questions, his body tensing as if sensing danger.

"The young man you have in the cell is human," Doctor Richard announces.

Silence falls on my office for a moment before it's broken by Chris, "Far be it from me to question your skills as a medical professional, but we all saw him shift from his wolf form. I assure you he's a mutolupus."

"He wasn't born one," I whisper.

All heads turn to me as I say this. Those four words feel bitter on my tongue, and I have a strong urge to be sick.

"What are you saying?" Marcus gently asks.

I rub my face realising I have to tell them something. Something that, while it is not forbidden knowledge, is not something one casually shares.

"There's something else that separates an Alpha from other wolves. An Alpha wolf has the ability to bite a human and turn them into a mutolupus," I tell them. Everyone but Doctor Richard steps back in shock.

"Why have we never heard of such a thing?" Vitali asks still in shock.

"Because it's supernatural law to only use it under two conditions: to save a life or, in the case of a mutolupus being fated to a human, the human wishing to live an equal lifespan with their animai. Outside of these conditions, the Delegation made it law that no Alpha was to turn a human. The punishment for doing so is death," I tell them.

"Have you ever…" Chris asks, looking at me curiously.

I shake my head, "No, but my dad has."

"What? Who?" Vitali questions, unable to contain his interest.

"Brian's animai, Melissa. It was before I was born. But Melissa was a human and my dad turned her into a mutolupus. He had requested permission from the Delegation first, of course, given these were permittable circumstances."

"Holy shit, Melissa? Spitfire Melissa was human? But I don't get it, she has a wolf spirit," Tyson points out in confusion.

"One of the reasons turning a human is a crime is because the change doesn't always take. Have any of you heard of the Beast of Gévaudan?" The doctor asks, looking at everyone. I'm the only one to raise my hand which elicits eye rolls from my best friends.

"Nerd," coughs Vitali.

"Excuse me for picking up a book every now and then. At least I take the time to read and learn," I snap.

Marcus wraps his arm around my shoulders, kissing my temple to let me know he's here. It relaxes me instantly.

"Hey, I read!" Vitali says defensively.

"I don't think comic books count, dude," Tyson sniggers.

"Comic books can be very educational," Vitali argues.

"Enough!" I say, silencing them. "Please go on Doctor Richard."

He smiles in amusement but nods, "For three years, starting in 1764, an animal, humans called the Beast of Gévaudan, terrorized the general area of the former province of Gévaudan, which is now called Lozère, in south-central France. Over eighty men, women and children were said to have been killed by the beast," he says gravely. Doctor Richard is a great doctor. He values all lives and so the loss of life always bothers him, even if the person is unknown to him. I respect that about him a great deal.

"I take it this beast was a mutolupus?" Marcus deduces.

"Yes and no. Humans didn't have all the facts. What actually transpired was an Alpha had declared war on another pack, wishing to take their land for his own. He began kidnapping and turning humans in neighbouring cities in order to build a larger army. It was pure madness and chaos. Many individuals did not survive the transformation. Some survived it just fine and became a mutolupus no different to you or me. But then there were the other cases. Cases of those who were turned and became trapped between two states, a biological limbo, if you will. Their human-self was lost and while they could turn into a wolf, they had no wolf-spirit. So, they were only left with mindless animal instincts," Doctor Richard explains.

Tyson's eyes widen in understanding as he looks over at me, "Just like the guy in the cell. It's why he didn't speak and why you felt no wolf-spirit."

I nod affirmatively.

"Yes, it would seem your prisoner is one of those very unfortunate cases, made evident by his blood," Doctor Richard says solemnly.

Chris flops down into a seat rubbing his face processing the news. "We killed humans," he whispers.

The silence in the room is deafening. My hands are shaking and if it weren't for Marcus's arms around me, I would have thrown up. It's against the law to harm a human, but even if it wasn't, we'd have no reason to. The weight of Chris' words has hit everyone hard. We just killed dozens of innocent human beings. History seems to be repeating itself. There is a small, very small chance that people like the man in the cell consented to the change but that would still make it illegal. Truthfully, I don't believe they were given a choice in their transformation. Now I understand why their scent was off to me and Torie. We could smell the clear markers that make them a mutolupus, but the scent hiding underneath that was confusing us was the scent of a human. We just didn't know it.

"The massacre that was created by that Alpha is what prompted the Delegation to create a law about turning humans and, until now, it seemed to have been upheld. Like Doctor Richard said, there's a lot of risk turning a human, and most don't survive. Though in the cases of a human animai being turned, they always seem successful, which I think is a sign that our Goddess permits the change for the sake of the bond. But that's just a theory of mine," I explain.

"I would agree with that theory," the good doctor smiles warmly.

"The man we have in the cell is a potential victim, there has to be something we can do for him," Chris says compassionately.

"He didn't seem like much of a victim when he was trying to strangle Amelia," Tyson scoffs.

Marcus stiffens and looks at me in alarm as anger flashes over his face. Nice one Tyson. "He didn't touch me," I reassure Marcus, before turning my attention to Tyson. "And that wasn't his fault. When someone is turned into a mutolupus, they are physically bound to their maker. It's stronger than an Alpha command because the Alpha's DNA now runs through their veins. They cannot disobey an order from their Alpha. So, if he was ordered to kill me, then that's all he can focus on until I'm dead, the command is removed, or the Alpha who made him dies," I explain.

Marcus's hold on me tightens as he sucks in a breath, "So what happens now?" Marcus asks.

I sigh running my fingers through my hair, "I'll have to make a call to Yildiz, she'll have to come and assess the situation."

Marcus looks confused, but Vitali goes stiff, "Yildiz?... She wouldn't bring Nuray... would she?" He asks, his voice becoming unusually high.

"Probably, they tend to travel together. Why...?" My eyes narrow as he fidgets avoiding eye contact. "Vit, tell me you didn't."

He says nothing but Tyson starts laughing and Chris groans.

"You just can't keep it in your pants, can you?" Chris says with disgust.

"Please let me be there when you explain this to Eric," Tyson says between laughs.

"Ty, don't be an ass," I tell him, then look back at Vitali. "I can't believe you had sex with a member of the Delegation, are you out of your mind?" I question with displeasure.

Marcus looks at Vitali in surprise, while Doctor Richard shakes his head as if he's too old for this nonsense. He's actually seventy-three, though he doesn't look a day over forty.

"What happens between two consenting adults is no one else's business," Vitali argues though he looks embarrassed for once, which is not like him.

"You're on a first-name basis with Delegation members?" Marcus asks me with incredulity. I shrug. "Now I know something we can further discuss during our date," he whispers in my ear, though they clearly heard him, and their stupid goofy smiles are making that obvious.

Receiving threats was bad. Being poisoned was incredibly unpleasant. My pack being attacked; now that pissed me off. But this Alpha-son-of-a-bitch destroying the lives of humans so he can build an army to take me and my pack on? That has me sick to my stomach. I swear when I get my hands on this asshole, I'm going to give him a slow agonising death that would make those involved in the Spanish Inquisition look away in horror.

Chapter Twenty-One
Marcus

The longer I'm around Amelia the more captivated by her I become. Every new thing I learn about her just makes me love her more.

Did I just say 'love'? Yes, I did because I fucking do.

I love this strong, sexy woman more than all the stars in the universe. Maybe it's too soon to say that to her, I don't know. I fell for her the moment I saw her but being locked in a room with her for three days confirmed it, she is all I could ever want or need.

Sitting in on her meeting had me learning shit I never expected. I can't believe Jasper at no point thought to tell me he can turn humans into wolves. I get why this isn't public knowledge, but we've been like brothers since we were pups, so you'd think he'd have mentioned it at some point in the last twenty fucking years.

I nearly sprinted down to the cells to pummel the guy who tried to lay a hand on my animai. He's lucky he didn't actually touch her and that I feel bad for what happened to him. Otherwise, he'd be choking on his own dick right about now.

If that wasn't enough information to shock my system, then I think the phone call my sexy minx is on right now sealed the deal. My soulmate is on a first-name basis with members of the Delegation and by the sounds of the phone call, they're actually good friends.

Who is this woman the Gods have chosen for me?

The Delegation is an organization – you could say – made up of beings called irshiusts that are in charge of law and order among supernatural beings. I think Goddess Zarseti is a fixer because everything she seems to have created is with the purpose of fixing shit other Gods fucked up. Species were running around hating each other and fighting over who was superior, so she created animais to bring everyone together. It didn't solve everything, but it helped and I'm sure as fuck not complaining.

Then she saw how out of control people were becoming even among their own kind, so she created irshiusts who formed the Delegation. Their only reason for being is to keep the rest of us in line. I think there's like a hundred or more of them, I've never personally met one, but I've heard a lot about them. I was shocked to hear Amelia's Beta actually slept with one. For some reason I always viewed them as nuns. Dedicated to their mission in life and never getting close to people, but I guess I was wrong and Vitali must have some killer moves. I was also surprised because his animai is a man, so I just assumed he was gay.

Amelia finishes her phone call and starts rubbing her temples. I don't need to be bonded to her to know how stressed out all of this has made her. Who wouldn't be stressed? So I walk over and rub her shoulders, which calms me as much as it calms her.

"They'll be here in a couple of days," she tells me. I freeze for a second when I realise I'm going to meet some of the Delegation, one of the few beings who still have direct contact with a God.

Fucking hell.

"You really aren't like other Alphas."

"What do you mean?" She asks, turning her head to look at me.

"You have the Delegation on speed dial and you're on a first-name basis with them. Any other Alpha would use that as a major fucking flex, not to mention use it as intimidation against anyone who was pissing them off . But instead, you just shrug and are like 'all in a day'," I say, shrugging for emphasis.

"They're my friends and I wouldn't use our friendship like that. I'm only contacting them because a law has been broken and that is specifically their territory."

"You're proving my point, babe. You don't see them as an asset or an ace up your sleeve, which most Alphas would. You have a better heart than they do," I tell her, leaning down to kiss her cheek, smiling as a beautiful shade of pink spreads across her cheeks. How did I ever fucking think she was incapable of being an Alpha just because she's a woman?

"Because you're an idiot. But fortunately, you're making up for it and I approve. However, I would like to go back to her room and finish what we started earlier," Ace says, wagging his tail.

"Not yet, but I have a plan. I just hope she likes it," I say a little nervously.

"It's a fantastic plan and she will love it. I'm excited!" He yips. I don't think I've ever seen him so excited in my life, but I'll take it. At least he's not cussing me out. *"Screw this up and I'll do more than cuss you out,"* he threatens.

"Can I ask you something?" I say, leaning against her desk and folding my arms over my chest. I don't miss the way her eyes follow the movement of my muscles, and I fucking love it. So does Ace, by the way he's preening in my head.

"Ask me anything," she says, turning in her chair to face me, giving me the perfect view of her cleavage through her mesh top.

Fuck, I want to bury my face between those perfects tits. Fuck, focus!

"Is it true what they say about irshiusts? That they can compel you to tell the truth?" I ask nervously.

"Why? Worried they'll make you confess something?" She smirks.

"Well, yeah. What if they made me reveal something I did when I was twelve or something?"

"Did you do something when you were twelve?" She asks with a quirked eyebrow. She's enjoying this.

"No," I roll my eyes. "It's just an example."

She chuckles and the sound is heavenly, "To answer your question, no. That's not how their gifts work. When you're around them, they give off this calming aura that makes everyone feel serene and at ease. This is supposed to keep tensions from rising; it's their natural state. But they are walking lie detectors. They themselves aren't even able to tell a lie and if someone lies to them, they know immediately."

Well, that's not so bad, just keep your mouth shut. "What about if you tell a half-truth?"

"They would pick up on the elements that were true and the elements that were a lie. But, if someone didn't know they were lying, then there would be a problem," she clarifies.

I nod taking in the new information. "So how come you're such good friends with them?" The curiosity is killing me. No other Alpha has ever been able to call an irshiust a friend, at least not as far as I know.

"I met them when I was shadowing my dad when I was little. They were always very friendly and welcoming to me, which was a huge contrast compared to how most other Alphas treated me. They always told me they were excited for when I would become Alpha. I don't know, maybe it's because there are no male irshiusts. Their entire species is made up of women, so I guess it's a women supporting women type of thing. Us ladies gotta stick together," she says playfully.

This is news. I actually had no idea that the Delegation was made up of only women. That makes a lot of sense that they would gravitate towards Amelia as the first female Alpha. To them, she was probably a breath of fresh air. I sigh internally, realising the fucking Delegation welcomed my animai with open arms and I fucking couldn't. Could I be a bigger prick?

"Yes, but let's not try it, okay?" Says Ace.

"Trust me, I don't plan on it."

I focus back on the beauty in front of me, "So, do you have much work to do?"

"Just need to check a few emails, call a couple local businesses for a check-in, and speak to my dad about the recent developments. Not much overall."

"Would it be okay if I left you to your work for a bit?"

"Sure... is everything okay?" She asks, a nervous edge to her voice. I notice the closer we get, the more open she is about showing her emotions. I didn't realise just how walled up she was when we met, but the fact she's thawing around me is a great sign.

"Everything is fine," I say, taking her hand in mine. I will never get tired of how it feels just holding her hand. "But I do have a date to plan, and I have someone bringing me my truck and a packed bag from home."

Her eyes widen with surprise. "Does that mean you're sticking around for a bit?" She carefully asks.

"I'm still the Beta of my pack, but I'm not ready to leave you and Jasper understands that. Amelia…" I take a breath running my fingers through my hair. "We have a lot to discuss and go over, but for now, I just want you. I want you to be mine and me to be yours. Can we focus on that for now?" I ask gently.

Her breath catches in her throat and for a second, I think she's going to argue but instead, she nods her head. I let out a breath and relax, not realising how tense my shoulders were.

"When is this date exactly?" he asks me.

"I was hoping tonight; unless you have plans." Maybe I should have checked first.

"Actually yeah, I do have plans," she sighs. Fuck, I knew I should've checked.

"Oh. Well, that's okay. What are your plans?" I ask, trying not to sound as dejected as I feel.

"Nothing major. Just a date with my animai," she shrugs, the ghost of a smirk playing on her soft lips. I narrow my eyes at her. Why that little minx!

"That was just mean. I say we spank her for that," Ace says with a wicked glint in his eyes.

"I actually agree with you on this," I tell him.

"That's a dangerous game you're playing," I say in a low voice, pulling her chair close and resting my hands on the armrests, caging her in. "I may have to punish you for that." I lean into her heady tropical scent. Fuck me, it's divine.

"You could try," she teases, her eyes glued to my lips.

Well, fuck. For a virgin, I was expecting her to be more timid, but she continues to surprise me. I can tell she's always going to keep me on my toes and the thought fucking excites me.

"Oh, believe me, my sexy Alpha, I would love to try," I tell her as I capture her lips with mine. I kiss her slow and passionately, giving her just enough to taste, but not enough to satiate her need. As I pull back, she leans in for more and I chuckle.

I kiss the tip of her nose. "To be continued," I promise, standing up straight. She gives me the cutest and sexiest pout that makes my dick twitch. As much as I would love to continue devouring her lips and exploring her body right now, I need everything perfect for tonight. So with one more kiss on her forehead I pull myself away from her.

As soon as I'm in the hallway, I take in lungfuls of clean air. Instantly, I feel empty inside. We're not even marked but being away from her is unbearable. I'm going to be a fucking mess once I've finally marked her. But enough of that. I'm a man on a mission.

I make my way downstairs and keep my eyes open, hoping to find a few particular familiar faces. I wander around the packhouse until I end up in what looks like an entertainment room.

It's massive with a large black sectional and a black coffee table facing a large plasma screen TV on the left-hand wall. There are beanbag chairs, boxes with toys, an air hockey table, and a pool table with a scoreboard on the right-hand wall next to a dartboard. Shelves that flank the door are filled with books and movies and there are large sliding glass doors that make up the entire back wall. I see the people I'm looking for sitting on the couch laughing.

"Hey, I hope I'm not interrupting," I say, while in fact interrupting them. Evalyn looks up and gives me a wide smile, so I guess my balls are safe. For now.

"Marcus! Hi. Oh, this is Mei, Chris' animai and my sister-in-law," she says proudly, making Mei blush. "And Eric who is Vitali's animai," she introduces.

I offer my hand to each and shake them.

Mei seems a little reserved and hesitant , but now knowing about her fucked up past, I can't say I blame her. What that pack did to her was a fucking disgrace and I don't even know the extent of what they did.

"It's really nice to meet you guys," I tell them.

"At least you're dressed this time," Eric teases with a smirk.

I forgot they've all seen my dick. As a wolf, that shit wouldn't bother me, but knowing they've seen me naked, and Amelia hasn't, makes me feel bad.

I shrug and sit down, "Actually, I need some help and I thought you guys would be the perfect people to help me."

"What kind of help?" Evalyn asks, her interest clearly piqued.

"It involves Amelia."

Mei sits up a bit straighter and scoots closer, "Is she okay? Is she hurt?"

My face softens. I don't know much about this girl except that she's strong and fast as fuck. Not a mutolupus, and even in proximity of her scent, I have no idea what she is. I know she was once a slave; a fact that fills me with rage. I can hear a hint of a Chinese accent, but it's very faint, so I would guess she was not born here but grew up here. I also now know she cares deeply for Amelia and well, that makes her good in my book.

"Amelia is just fine, I promise. Actually, I need you guys to help me with the date I plan to take her on tonight."

To my surprise, all their faces light up and Evalyn starts squealing.

"And here I thought my day was going to be boring," Eric says. "What do you need us to do?"

I didn't think he'd be so interested. I really need to stop making assumptions.

"I want to take her on a romantic date, but I don't know any restaurants around here. So I need help finding a restaurant, preferably outside pack territory; I'll need to make a booking. I also want to get her something new to wear for the occasion. It should be green and fitting of a fancy restaurant, nothing casual. I also want to arrange a romantic set up in her room for when we return." Evalyn squeals again. Bundle of energy this one. "Calm down, I'm not pushing for anything, but I still want to do something nice for her regardless of how the night turns out. I just… I want to show her that she's important to me and I'm committed to making this work."

I've never been a sappy bastard; I've never done the romantic gestures and all that stuff. It's not that I've been a heartless asshole... well, not entirely. It's just, I always imagined saving that stuff for my animai. Now that I've met her, I'm pulling out all the stops.

"I think it's very sweet, what you're doing for her," Mei tells me in a soft voice.

"Sweet? It's romantic as hell!" Evalyn swoons. "When you say romantic set up, what did you have in mind? Tell me your vision."

Not only do Evalyn and Chris almost look nothing alike – except maybe the fact they both have long hair – they act nothing alike either. He's more reserved and proper. She's feisty and loud.

"Lots of candles, nothing too over the top. I don't want to come off like I'm trying too hard. This might be hard, but do you think you can find somewhere that sells green roses?"

"Now this I can help with!" Eric chimes in. "My cousin is a florist; I'll give her a call and see what I can do. How many were you after? If I can find them; those don't sound very common." .

"Just one. I was originally planning to send her a bouquet of green roses before this whole heat thing happened. So now I'm just re-working my original idea," I explain.

"I've never even heard of green roses. Are you sure you didn't make it up?" Evalyn questions with uncertainty.

I roll my eyes. "I looked them up, they are a very pale shade of green. If you can't find them, then one red rose will do."

"Can do Lu... Beta Marcus," Eric quickly says.

Everyone stiffens for a moment including me. Was he just about to call me 'Luna'?

They're each nervously watching me and I'm just frozen. This is what I've been avoiding with Amelia. A Luna is a woman's position. They're seen as the mother figure of the pack. I'm not a woman or a fucking mother figure. I want this to work, I really fucking do, but the idea of being this pack's Luna just doesn't sit well with me. Maybe I sound like an asshole, but I just feel like that would rob me of my masculinity. Ace snorts in my head.

"What?"

"I didn't say anything," he says defensively, sitting back on his hind legs.

"Just spit it out," I say in irritation.

"Marcus..." he sighs. *"I'm okay with being called a Luna. If mother Morrtemis and Goddess Zarseti have chosen me for that role, then I would fill it with pride. You're making it a bigger issue than it needs to be. Isn't the important thing to just be with our soulmate?"*

He sounds sad and it makes me feel fucking guilty. *"I'm not you, Ace. My whole life I was raised to be a Beta. I was raised to be strong, to be a warrior, now I'm supposed to do what? Plan events and play with the pups while my soulmate is on the frontlines?"* I shake my head in frustration.

"No one is asking you to do that, you're making assumptions and you just agreed you need to cut that out. Just... just don't overthink it. Put it on the back burner for now, but don't dismiss it. For me?" He pleads.

Fuck. Since birth Ace has never begged or pleaded with me for anything. I guess it's the least I can do for my wolf and best friend.

"I can do that," I promise, sighing.

"Thank you," he says with relief.

I look up at the others who are watching and probably waiting for me to blow a gasket, but I shake my head, clearing it,. "So, think we can get this done?"

"Absolutely," Evalyn speaks, thawing the atmosphere. "But what about you? You came here butt naked."

"I already contacted my Alpha; my car and clothes should be here soon."

"Then we have our marching orders and shall get to work. Come on guys, we have an Alpha to help woo," she chirps excitedly.

Evalyn gets up with Mei and Eric and they head off to help me put together a first date that Amelia will never forget. I won't assume or push for anything tonight; I just want her to feel happy and cherished. If anything more than that occurs, then I'll consider myself one lucky motherfucker.

With Amelia's friends off on a mission to help me organise the best first date I can, I go and sit on the front steps of the packhouse to wait for my truck to arrive. Thankfully, with all the stuff that's gone on so far today, time is moving quickly, so I don't have to wait long. It's maybe twenty minutes before I see the red exterior of my GMC Sierra 2500 in the distance. It's good to have my baby back. I get up just as my truck pulls in with an SUV pulling in behind it. I walk over as Calix gets out of my truck and Aiden gets out of the SUV.

Here it comes.

"What are you knuckleheads doing here?" I ask with surprise as Calix comes in for a hug which I return.

"As if you'd have trusted anyone else with your truck," he snorts.

"Good point," I say, pulling Aiden in for a hug.

"So, she hasn't kicked you out yet, I see. You're setting a new record," Aiden teases.

I ignore the prick's comment, I can always deck him later. Pretty certain his daughter gets her attitude from him. Goddess, help us all when she hits puberty.

"I don't see why two ranked members had to be in charge of dropping off my stuff," I point out suspiciously.

"Oh, we didn't, we were just hoping to maybe meet your animai," Calix admits with a grin.

Fucking assholes.

"She's busy, maybe another time," I say bluntly.

"Hmm, not sure I believe you. You could just be keeping us away," Aiden says before turning his attention to Calix. "Maybe he has her tied to a bed somewhere so she can't run away, and he doesn't want the pack to find out," he says laughing at his own dumb joke. Although now I'm picturing her tied up and it's fucking hot as hell.

"Speaking of; Jasper wanted us to remind you if you do anything to hurt Alpha Amelia he's going to pummel your ass," Calix says casually.

"Well that's a nice change from everyone around here wanting my balls," I say wryly.

"Hmm, so this pack wants your balls, Jazz wants your ass and Davina wants your dick. You're just a walking all-you-can-eat buffet," Aiden jokes as Calix bursts out laughing.

Sometimes I really hate these dickheads.

"Did you assholes bring my clothes or what?"

"I'd have thought three days with your animai in heat would have mellowed you out. You seem even more uptight than usual," Aiden says, retrieving my bag from my truck.

"Not that it's any of your business, but nothing happened during her heat," I admit unashamedly.

Fuck that, I'm proud of what I did. Both of them look at me in complete shock.

"Are you serious?" Calix asks.

"No, I said that for the fucking hell of it," I spit sarcastically.

"Holy shit," Calix breathes.

"Wow... I mean, that's a huge deal. I'm actually impressed, though I can't imagine that was any fun," Aiden says coming over with a large duffle bag and a garment bag. I reach out and take the items from him, nodding my thanks.

"No, it was fucking excruciating. I had Amelia share her pain with me. I wanted to take some of the burden for her and let me tell you, it was the most horrendous experience of my life. I don't know how she-wolves do it. But going through all that was worth it. I feel closer to her than I ever thought possible without marking and mating," I say and even I know my voice has gone all airy, but I don't fucking care. Instead of teasing me they both smile and each slap a hand on each of my shoulders.

"We're proud of you, man," Calix says, full of sincerity.

"Yeah, we really are," Aiden adds.

"Have you decided if you'll be staying in her pack?" Calix asks carefully.

Great, the subject I am actively avoiding keeps coming up.

"I don't know. Neither of us wants to discuss it," I admit.

Calix frowns, "Marcus, I get why you're avoiding it and I can't say I blame you, but the longer you put it off the worse it will get. If you two can't come to a compromise and you have no choice but to reject each other, the pain will be far worse than what it would have been before."

"No one is rejecting anyone," I growl, and I know my eyes are glowing.

"I don't care what compromise we have to come to, I'm not giving her up, not now; not ever." They each step back raising their hands in surrender.

"He meant nothing by it. We just don't want to see you get hurt," Aiden says compassionately.

I take a breath to calm myself down. "I know you mean well, but things are good between us right now and I hope tonight makes things even better. As my best friends, can you two just be happy for me?"

Their expressions soften and they give me encouraging smiles.

"We really are happy for you," Calix says.

"And we want this to work out. Plus Muse and Darla are dying to meet her. Izzy has been filling them in on what she knows about Amelia," Aiden chuckles.

Great, that's just what I need.

"Do we really not get to meet her?" Calix pouts and I roll my eyes.

"A lot of shit is going on at the moment, and she should be having a serious meeting with her dad right about now. So no, not today. When things calm down, I promise to introduce you guys. But thanks for bringing my truck and my things."

"Not a problem," Calix shrugs. "The drive was a nice break, to be honest. But now I'm going to be stuck driving back with Aiden and his show tunes."

"Oh, you love them, just admit it," Aiden says, pinching Calix's cheek. Calix swats his hand away in irritation and I chuckle.

We share another round of hugs, say our goodbyes, and then the guys are climbing into the SUV and driving back home. I take a moment to really take in the sight of them leaving.

Do I want to leave my pack? Do I want to give up my position as Beta, something I prepared for my whole life, and trade it in for a role I'm not sure I can fill? Do I want to start over with a new pack and leave my friends and family behind? I know I don't want to leave Amelia, the very thought of it sucks the air out of my lungs. But I also know that, as an Alpha, she can't just give up her pack. Not even for me. At least, I don't think she would.

So much is up in the air right now and it scares the fucking shit out of me. So once again, I'm going to bury it all deep down and just focus on the fact I'm going on my first date with Amelia. Maybe after tonight, I'll have some more clarity on the matter.

Chapter Twenty-Two
Amelia

"And you don't know of any Alphas who would do such a thing?" I ask my dad while we sit on the couch in my office.

He leans forward with his elbows resting on his knees and shakes his head, "Not a single one. It's not common practice anymore and even under the best of circumstances most Alphas fear the repercussions from the Delegation."

"But as long as they act within the law, they have nothing to worry about. The Delegation isn't evil. They aren't dictators," I say, feeling a little protective of the friends I have made.

Not a single irshiust has a mean bone in their body, they weren't made that way. But I wouldn't call them pacifists either. They are trained and highly skilled warriors, stronger and faster than even a nagata. The only being I know of that can rival them in strength and speed is a God. They have to know how to fight so they can carry out sentencing and stop wars. They are essentially the earthly representatives of the Gods, or at least of Zarseti. But at their core, they are kind-hearted.

"I know, sweetheart," he says, reaching out to hold my hand, "But Alphas can be proud and stubborn, and most don't like anyone who is stronger than you feel inferior and you always taught me to be the same way," I argue.

"Yes, but not everyone is as smart or secure as we are," he says with a cheeky smile that makes me chuckle.

My dad has always had a healthy self-esteem and he was sure to pass that on to me. He knew my life would be hard and wanted to make sure I never doubted myself. He always said self-doubt can kill you faster than any enemy and, as I've gotten older, I realise how true that is.

"So no one comes to mind that could be behind this?" I ask, feeling a little defeated. My father takes a moment to think and slowly his face scrunches up. This happens when a thought pops in his head, but instead of telling me, he shakes his head as if to dismiss it. I squeeze his hand, "Tell me, it might be important. Remember what grandma always says? If a memory comes to you during a crisis it's always for a good reason. What came to your mind just now?"

He gives me a warm smile and nods, "I was remembering Mykel Mathers."

His tone is grave, telling me he doesn't have good memories of this person. Mathers? Any relation to Declan?

"Yes," he says as if reading my mind. "Mykel is Declan's older brother and my original Beta," he says acerbically.

My eyes fly open in shock. What did he just say?

Original Beta?

What the hell?

"Please explain. Why have I never heard of this Mykel person or that Declan wasn't your original Beta?" I ask, feeling a little irritated. Since when does my dad hide things from me?

"It was before you were born. We all grew up together; Mykel was more like a brother and as the son of my father's Beta, naturally, he would become mine when the time came. But as soon as he took on the role of Beta, he started sharing a lot of his ideas for the pack with me and they were… unsettling to say the least," my dad shudders.

"Unsettling how?"

"He wanted to implement harsher punishment for lawbreakers and reintroduce medieval methods for interrogations. Things our pack outlawed long ago. I naturally was against it and made it clear none of those things would happen. One day we were attacked by the Ruber Flumen Pack, whose Alpha wanted more territory. We won, but afterwards, Mykel was going on about how we needed more warriors and how we could be the strongest pack in the country if we had a bigger army. Our pack is our family, not an army, but he wasn't having it. That's when he started talking about me using my Goddess given gift and turning humans so we could grow our forces," he says through clenched teeth.

I suppress my gasps. What the hell went wrong with the Mathers' bloodline to turn them and their animals into complete and total nutcases?

"He was openly talking about breaking supernatural law," I state with disgust.

"Yes," my father nods. "And I thought it would stop, but it only got worse. Eventually, we just could never see eye to eye and to my sadness, but also my relief, he one day decided to leave the pack."

"He left? He just willingly up and left?" I ask incredulously.

"Left his pack and his family. Last I checked he was welcomed into the Ruber Flumen Pack. I haven't heard from him since."

"Wait, he joined the same pack who attacked you? What the hell?" I exclaim. I don't know this guy, but I hate him already.

"I know, I was shocked and hurt by that. But we never had anything to do with them after that and they never tried anything, so I never felt a reason to worry. Declan took on the Beta role, though now I'm seeing he was just as bad as his brother. He was just silent about it," he spits in indignation.

"Was their father a bad Beta? I can't see grandpa having someone like them as his Beta," I frown. My grandfather is a good man and was a noble Alpha – still is – he wouldn't have had someone like Mykel as his right hand.

"No, their father was a good man and like an uncle to me as James and Xander have been to you. Mykel and Declan's mother on the other hand..." he sighs, shaking his head. "A conniving bitch if ever I met one. She was mean to everyone and very manipulative; cared far more about the Beta title than the man behind the title, but he loved her dearly. She also was horrible to other pack members. I remember my father threatening that either she straighten up or he'd kick her out of the pack, even if it meant losing his Beta. He wasn't going to let a ranked member of the pack treat his pack so disgracefully," he tells me, pride in his voice. I feel proud at his words, too. You go, grandpa!

"Is it possible the current Alpha of the Ruber Flumen Pack is behind these threats and attacks? Maybe the next generation wants to pick up where the last one left off," I theorise.

"It's possible. We certainly shouldn't rule anything out. If Mykel is still a member of their pack; he may have shared inside information about ours. It would be a bit outdated, but it's still valuable," he says while squeezing my hand.

Unless he found a way to get current information...

"Like from a remaining family member," Zara says finishing my thought.

"He could be the traitor, sharing information with his uncle who is relaying it to his Alpha. It's the most plausible theory we have so far."

"I never liked that guy," she growls. That makes two of us.

"Now it's your turn to share your thoughts. What are you and Zara discussing?" He asks with a soft smile.

"Earlier today I overheard Ryker on a phone call, and something about it immediately sent alarm bells through me. Ryker is Mykel's nephew. What if Ryker is his inside man?"

Dad frowns thinking it over, "I hate to say it, but that's a solid theory. You should have someone keep an eye on him."

"I've already got Izac tailing him," I inform him, smiling proudly.

He returns my smile and wraps his arm around me, "Of course, my Little Alpha is already on the case." He kisses my temple, "Now, when are your mother and I going to have a proper sit down with Marcus?"

"Dad," I groan. "I told you before, soon. So, stop rushing me," I tell him, leaning into him.

"I'm not rushing you, sweetheart. But I am concerned. You two didn't have the best start. I am allowed to worry about you. Your mother and I raised you right, we know you're strong and you won't let anyone mistreat you. But you will always be our little girl and we will always worry about you," he says, pulling me into his arms.

"I know," I smile as I relax into my dad's embrace and hold him tight. "Thank you for always caring about me and being there for me," I tell him as I nuzzle him.

"You can count on it," he says tightening his hold and kissing my crown.

After spending some much-needed time with my dad, I get back to work, though in the back of my mind I'm thinking over what I've learned about the former Beta and how that ties into what's happening now. There are too many similarities with dad's story to not think it's related to what's going on.

I'm considering sending out a scout team to go to the Ruber Flumen Pack to see if they are able to assess the state of the pack from the borders. From what I know, the pack is based in Washington – same as Marcus' pack. They also rejected our invitation to the Vernal Ball this year. Come to think of it, I've never actually seen any of their pack members at any of the balls that I've attended in the last three years.

Once I get all my work done I exit my office and rush to the Alpha suite, eager to see Marcus again. Even though I was focused and didn't let my mind wander, it didn't mean I wasn't missing him. He was lingering in my thoughts all day. Every minute away from him harder than the last.

When I get to my suite, I fling the door open, and my jaw drops to the floor at the sight before me. Standing in all his oh-so-handsome glory is Marcus, wearing a charcoal grey suit jacket with black lapels – he seems to like black lapels – and a white dress shirt with the first three buttons undone, giving me a perfect view of his defined pectoral muscles. Which, right now, I very much would like to outline with my tongue.

"If you don't, I will. Hubba, hubba!" Zara pants in my head.

He's paired it with black slacks, black belt, and black loafers with a very expensive looking platinum wristwatch to boot. Gods take the wheel because my mouth has gone dry as a bone and my core is heating up as blood travels south fast.

"You're drooling," he says with a smirk.

"You look amazing," I admit, and I can hear how breathy my voice sounds. Well, that's embarrassing. He smiles as he walks over and cups my cheeks in his large hands; the contact sends an instant shock to the system, and I realise how much I've missed it all day.

"Thank you," he says smiling down at me. "You have some surprises waiting for you in your room. I'll wait for you to get ready, but don't take too long," he says while softly pecking my lips. I eagerly return his kiss wishing for more, but instead, I smile and walk over to my room.

When I walk in there is a garment bag on the bed, a couple small boxes, and a note on top of one of the boxes. I pick up the note to see what it says.

You better name your first pup after me
xo Evalyn

I roll my eyes. That woman is always trying to get someone to name their children after her. She's obsessed. I put the note on my desk and open the garment bag. I pull out a stunning evening dress... he got me a dress? I'm utterly speechless. I lay the dress down and open the other boxes. There are earrings, shoes, a necklace, a purse, and in the box that had the note with it... well, I can see why Eva mentioned pups; it's lingerie. I spend a moment just staring at it.

If I wear this, it means I want tonight to lead to something intimate. Am I ready for that? I could probably come up with a million reasons why I should wait, but they feel hollow. The truth is I want Marcus; I've waited my whole life for him and now I have him. My body wants him and if things were different, we probably would have mated the night we met. With that decided – and a new sense of determination running through me – I start getting ready.

I run into the bathroom and add some gentle waves to my hair, to give it a little extra volume, then when I'm done, I put on some makeup. Normally I don't wear makeup, but tonight's a special occasion and I want to knock his socks off. So I do a soft smoky eye and a nude lip, sticking to liquid lipstick because I'm going to need something that stays put if tonight goes how I hope it does.

I thought I'd be nervous but instead, my blood is pumping with adrenaline and anticipation. I've never been so excited for something in my life. If today's make-out session says anything, then I think I'm in for a hell of a night.

When the makeup and hair are done, I return to my room to strip down and put on the lingerie, courtesy of Eva. It's a black sheer mesh strapless bodysuit with thick seams stitched down the middle and across the cups to hide the nipples, making it a little more enticing. It's a perfect fit and rides up high on my hips. It's also surprisingly comfortable. I then put on a pair of silver high heels with diamante straps. The jewels on them catch the light perfectly. When those are on, I slip on the dress and look myself over.

The dress is emerald-green silk with thin straps and a tasteful billowing neckline. It pulls in at the ribcage and fits tight to the body, falling just below the knee; a thigh-high slit on the right side. I absolutely love it and it fits like a glove. I add a thin platinum chain necklace and a pair of platinum Celtic dangle earrings with emerald teardrops. I transfer all my essentials into the slim black velvet envelope style clutch purse, only now realising Marcus still has my phone.

I give myself a final look over in the mirror. I feel and look amazing! I can't believe Marcus did all this for me, I don't even want to know how much it cost him but I feel giddy, in a good way. I take a breath, steel myself and step out into the living area. He's leaning against the kitchen counter but stands straight and turns when he hears me.

He's holding a single green rose and is looking at me with a mix of awe and lust. He looks like he wants to both worship and devour me, and it has my heart thumping away. We stare at each other in silence, his eyes slowly trailing over my body, drinking me in like he doesn't want to miss a single detail.

He takes a slow breath and makes his way over to me, holding out the rose, "You look absolutely exquisite."

I feel my cheeks heat up. I take the rose and sniff it instinctively. I'm surprised when I can smell that it's real; there's no colouring chemicals. I had no idea green roses even existed. It's a very soft green, a kind of tea green shade, but it's beautiful, nonetheless. I smile up at him in awe to find him still staring at me.

"I can't believe you did all this for me, thank you, Marcus. I don't know what to say," I tell him as I feel myself getting choked up with emotions.

"That was all I needed. Besides, just seeing you like this is reward enough," he smiles and holds his arm out for me, "Shall we?"

I nod eagerly and wrap my arm around his, "Lead the way."

He leads me out of the suite and down the stairs. As we hit the main floor I am aware of whispering, but I ignore it because I'm riding a high at the moment. I'm going on my first date and it's with my soulmate. Finally, something good is happening. We walk outside and he leads me to a mammoth-sized red four-door truck, opening the passenger door for me. Though he knows I'm strong enough to get myself in, he helps me in anyway, and I have to admit, I'm loving the chivalry. Women who get mad at this are insane. He moves quickly to his side, jumping in with a look of excitement on his face. His excitement is feeding my own.

"Where are we going?"

"I'm taking us into the nearest city for a romantic dinner," he tells me, my smile somehow growing wider.

"I can't wait," I tell him eagerly.

He grins and starts up the engine and quickly we are taking off.

The nearest city is only a forty-minute drive away, so not too far and I can't say being in a car alone with him for so long is a negative. The inside of his truck smells just like him, though I pick up another scent – honeysuckle – I assume that belongs to the person who dropped off his truck.

"How did you manage to pull all this off in a short amount of time?" I inquire.

"I may have enlisted the help of a few people who were more than willing to ensure their Alpha has a terrific date. I don't know what kind of dates you're used to, but I'm hoping this one beats them all," he says proudly.

I chuckle, "Well that won't be hard, there is no competition."

"Were they that bad?" He asks sympathetically.

I smile shaking my head, "No, this is my first date." His foot slips off the accelerator and the truck jerks for a second before he regains control. "What?" I ask, laughing as he repeatedly glances between me and the road, a look of shock on his face.

"You're joking, right?" He asks.

"Wouldn't be a very funny joke, now would it?" I smirk.

"But… you…" he sucks in a deep breath. "Amelia, I know you're a virgin, Evalyn let it slip. And, while I was surprised, I understand a lot of she-wolves wait for their animai. But… not even a single date? Why?"

I'm not fazed by Evalyn telling him I'm a virgin. I'm not ashamed, nor do I care who knows. He'd find out eventually. I guess that was part of why he fought my heat so hard and honestly, that just makes me appreciate and respect what he did even more.

"I wouldn't say I was saving myself for you, but I wasn't not saving myself for you either."

"Explain," he says, sounding confused.

"Ideally, yes, I would prefer my first time be with the one who shares the other part of my soul, but had an opportunity presented itself, would I have taken it? Possibly, though I doubt it. As for dates and anything that could have been a result of those dates, I honestly just never had the time. I made time for my friends and family, of course, but dates were hardly crucial and so I never found a need for them," I shrug.

He watches the road in quiet contemplation and I wonder what he's thinking. If we were marked, I'd at least have some idea.

"I wish I'd waited for you," he whispers. Now I'm the one who looks surprised. I never expected him to say that.

"You know I don't hold it against you, right? I'm not upset you're not a virgin. Would it be a lovely gesture if we waited for each other? Sure, but I'm not going to cry that you had a sex life before me. What matters is that we're together now," I tell him, reaching out to hold his hand.

Instead of calming him, my words seem to make him frown more. "Ace always wanted to wait, he would always get mad that I was intimate with women who weren't you and now I wish I'd listened to him. I was always excited for the day I'd meet you, I wanted you more than anything. I just wasn't patient."

I don't love hearing about his sex life, it sets off an animalistic, territorial side of me that does not feel pleasant, but I tap it down.

"Marcus, why are you beating yourself up over this?" I softly question, squeezing his hand.

"Because I know how over the moon I was when I found out you were a virgin. Knowing no one else has touched you has Ace and I more thrilled than I can describe. I wouldn't care if you weren't, but knowing you are, makes us feel honoured and proud and kind of special and I hate that I can't give that to you. I hate that because I couldn't control my own hormones, I robbed you of that," he says dejectedly.

I just sit there blinking rapidly. He feels bad because he feels he robbed me of the experience I'm giving him… is this man for real? Is this the same guy who a week ago was calling me weak and not capable of being an Alpha? Now he's planning romantic dates, showering me with gifts and making declarations that have my head swimming. I feel tears pricking my eyes, but I force them back. Otherwise, I'll end up looking like a racoon instead of a wolf.

I bring his hand to my lips and kiss the back of his hand and each of his knuckles. "What you just said is one of the most touching things anyone has ever said to me. I don't want you hating yourself and feeling like you have robbed me of something. I want us to find firsts we can share together. I'm sure we can."

He glances over at me and, slowly, his frown turns into a smile. He pulls my hand to his mouth and places a slow lingering kiss on the back of my hand that I can feel in my core. "I am so lucky to have you," he whispers against my hand.

"You say that now," I wink, making him chuckle.

Chapter Twenty-Three
Amelia

It's not too long before we're approaching our destination and he's parking against the curb on a side street. He gets out, zipping over to my side at lightning speed and opens my door for me. He holds out his hand and I don't hesitate to take it, stepping down from the truck. He shuts and locks the car, but this time, I wrap my arm around his before he even has a chance to offer.

Marcus looks down at me like a child who found out Christmas arrived early and I instinctively smile back up at him. It still amazes me how my emotions feed off of his – both positive and negative – even though we haven't marked each other. Is it just us, or is it all animai? Maybe no one notices because most couples don't hesitate to seal the bond. I'll have to ask Chris since he held off longer than anyone I've ever known.

We walk arm in arm around the corner and, in a few short steps, he's opening the front doors of the establishment we've stopped in front of. We step in and I'm surprised by the ambience, or should I say lack thereof? The restaurant is all shades of white and black. Every wall is painted the darkest shade of black and square tables are scattered all around with white tablecloths and black velvet chairs. The only lights illuminating the rather dark interior are single fluorescent globes embedded into the ceiling, pointing directly over each table. I've never seen a restaurant like this before.

If it weren't for the pops of light over each table, the place would be bathed in darkness. And apart from those designated spots, it practically is. If I came here with friends or family, I would consider this place too dark and moody for an enjoyable night out. But being here with Marcus gives it an entirely different vibe. Instead of moody, the dark element makes the atmosphere feel seductive and enticing.

We're only having dinner and yet between the ever-growing tension between us, the electricity set off when our skin touches, and the shadows that curve around the room, I almost feel as though I'm participating in something illicit. It's compounding the excitement that has been steadily growing the whole drive here.

We wait patiently for the maître d' who finds Marcus' booking and leads us to our table. As we walk through the restaurant I breathe in the intoxicating smell of French cuisine and my stomach instantly snarls in response. I haven't eaten since lunch and right now I could inhale another moose.

Marcus softly giggles – no doubt hearing the sound of my stomach. Once brought to our table at the far end of the restaurant, Marcus pulls my chair out for me and, with a smile on both our faces, I take my seat. He gently kisses the top of my head, breathing in my scent before taking his seat opposite me. The host places two menus in front of us and lets us know someone will be along with our drink orders shortly.

"What do I smell like?" Is the first thing I think to say once the maître d' is gone.

Marcus looks at me with amusement twinkling in his beautiful green and brown eyes but clearly understands my question. "It's very tropical, like mangos and pineapples," he tells me in a dreamy tone.

How fascinating! My dad has always said I smelt like fruit punch to him. It makes sense though; our soulmates are supposed to smell appealing to us.

"What do I smell like?"

"Like caramel. It's my favourite flavour," I say, licking my lips.

His eyes darken as they follow the action of my tongue. I suppress a gulp. I've never had anyone look at me the way he does, and it has my mind swirling with thoughts and images that are rather shocking because I have no idea where I plucked them from.

I look down at the menu and, to my dismay, realise the entire thing is in French. Of course, from the smell, I can tell it's a French restaurant. But how can I order if I don't know what I'm ordering?

"What's wrong?" Marcus asks.

I look up to see a look of concern etched on his face. "I don't understand the menu," I admit.

"I can order for us if you like. Do you have any preferences or things you'd like to avoid?"

I shake my head. "If it's edible, I'll eat it," I announce, smiling.

He grins, "A woman after my own heart."

Eventually, our waiter comes to take our drink orders – Marcus orders a bourbon and coke and I order a gin and tonic for myself. He then goes ahead and orders our meals for us and I watch absolutely enraptured as he reels off the items he's picked for us, repeating them in perfect French. My animai speaks French!

"Voulez-vous coucher avec moi ce soir?" Zara says while wagging her tail flirtatiously.

"Are you saying that because you want him to sleep with us tonight or because that's the only French you know?" I quip.

"A little from column A, a little from column B," she says bouncing her head from side to side causing me to chuckle.

"What did Zara say that's so funny?" He asks with a smile once the waiter leaves.

"She was just testing out her French skills, which are nowhere near as impressive as yours. When did you learn to speak French?" I quiz with great interest.

"Jasper's mother, Luna Fayette. She's French and was born in France in the Lumière Stellaire Pack. She was kind enough to teach me the language, and I owe her my thanks since now I get to use it to impress you," he winks, and I can't help but giggle. "There's no rush but I would love to meet your wolf. I know Ace is dying to meet her."

"Zara is very eager to meet you and Ace too. Perhaps tomorrow we can let them out for a run. I feel bad since they seemed to connect right away and yet they haven't had a chance to be together yet," I frown.

"I think a run tomorrow is a great idea," he says with delight.

"I'm not upset; I can be patient. The human is in the driver's seat for all this, we understand how this works, but thank you for caring about me," Zara says while nuzzling into my mind.

"Of course, I care about you, you deserve to be happy too. I promise you'll get to see Ace tomorrow," I say, leaving no room for doubt.

"Thank you, Amelia!" She cheers, bouncing around. She can be so cute sometimes.

"So, tell me more about you," I say leaning forward on my elbows. "Are you from a long line of Betas?"

He nods and I can see pride fill his body, "Six generations so far. My dad – Beta Jerome – and mum – Beta Jessica – did great work as Betas of our pack and all my life I hoped that I could do them proud. Serving my pack and Alpha is an honour. Jasper being my best friend is an added bonus," he says, his chest puffing up and his posture straightening. Pride always radiates off him when he speaks of his pack and his title. I admire that. I just hope he can one day feel that way about my pack.

"That's amazing. Is your mum of Beta blood too?" I ask just as the waiter returns with our drinks.

Marcus raises his glass in the air and connects his eyes with mine sending a thrilling shiver through me. "A toast, to our first date and hopefully many more to come," he beams and my heart stutters with hope of more nights like this with him.

"To many more to come," I echo as we clink our glasses and sip our drinks; the cool liquid soothing my parched throat. We could drink several of these back-to-back and not even feel buzzed, sadly.

"To answer your question; no, my mother was not of ranked blood. Just a regular she-wolf who was fated to a Beta."

"Have you told them about me?" I ask, sipping my drink to avoid chewing the inside of my cheek.

"Oh yeah, I told them all about you. My dad chewed me out big time and prayed Goddess Morrtemis would take pity on me," he chuckles dryly.

"And your mum?" I prompt only for him to rub the back of his head; something I notice he does when he's nervous or flustered.

"She…" he hesitates, struggling to pick his words carefully. This can't be good.

"Give it to me straight, I'm not a baby."

"No, you are most definitely not," he says, his eyes dipping to my chest. He sighs and rubs his beard. "My mum agreed with me. She couldn't make sense of a woman being an Alpha." He looks as though it caused him physical pain to tell me this. I simply nod. "Amelia, I don't feel that way anymore. I was so, so wrong and I see that now. Please don't be upset," he begs, his words coming out in a panicked rush.

I reach out and take his hand, squeezing it to give him reassurance, "Breathe. I'm not upset. Your mother is entitled to her opinions, but they make no difference to me. Your opinion mattered because you're my other half, so hearing you say the things you did cut me deeply. But really, I couldn't care less what your mother thinks on the matter."

He relaxes and gives me a relieved smile, "Thank you. She'll come around. I know once she meets you she'll go as crazy for you as I have," he assures me.

I would love to have a healthy relationship with his parents – his dad seems like we might get along – but if it doesn't happen, I won't cry about it. I'd still be civil for his sake, though.

"She's a traditionalist, I take it."

"Big-time," he sighs. "I guess I got some of my more offensive views from her. She may be a Beta Female but she's still of the belief that women are there to take care of the men and the pups and they don't belong on the battlefield." He winces, "For the record, I don't agree with all of her opinions. I'm all for female warriors. If someone is willing to fight for their pack, then you should let them. A pack is stronger when it works together; holding members back just because of their gender is detrimental to the pack as a whole."

I'm stunned. Am I ever going to be able to figure this man out? I guess he's not as sexist as I once thought. It's just the dynamics of Alpha and Luna where his mind can't break from tradition and I can understand that. It's never been any other way.

"She is aware the Goddess who created us was a warrior, right?" I question with a raised brow.

"Yeah, but she always dismisses that saying she's a God, so it doesn't count," he chuckles, shaking his head. I see she'll be a tough nut to crack. "What about your parents? I know your dad was the Alpha, was your mother of Alpha blood? She sure throws a punch like she is." He absentmindedly rubs his jaw.

I chuckle remembering how he told me my mum had delivered him a fresh knuckle sandwich, "No, she's of Gamma blood. Grandpa Kiernan and Grandma Erina were the Gammas of the Argentum Montem Pack which is where my mum grew up."

"Were?" He asks cautiously.

"Grandpa Kiernan died when I was little. He died fighting for his pack. Sadly grandma just couldn't live without him and she passed away a few months later. My Uncle Zeke is the current Gamma until they can find someone to take his place," I explain.

"I'm sorry about your grandparents," he says sympathetically, giving my hand a gentle squeeze.

"Thank you," I say appreciatively.

"Does your uncle not have a son... or daughter?" He quickly adds 'daughter' for good measure.

I have to admit it's amusing the way he's trying to catch himself from putting his foot in his mouth.

"Aunt Brianna was never able to have children and I know they had options, but neither of them had it in them to adopt. They just didn't feel they could give a child that wasn't their blood the love they deserve and that's fair; not everyone can. They have been happy with just each other, even if it took some years to get there. So, unfortunately, no heir, meaning the current Alpha will have to look elsewhere in the pack for my uncle's successor."

"So, you don't have any cousins?" He checks.

"Nope, just me," I grin. He smiles and sips his drink, never taking his eyes off me.

Our food arrives in record time and I'm immediately salivating. For me, Marcus has ordered pan-seared sea scallops in a ginger-lime sauce, which looks and smells to die for. For himself he has ordered chicken breast tenderloin sautéed with garlic, leeks, tomatoes, capers, and white wine; equally delicious.

"Is what I ordered satisfactory?" He asks with amusement; clearly seeing how I'm eyeing up our food. I nod enthusiastically and quickly dive in, taking a bite of a scallop. I can't stop the moan that bursts out of my throat as the exquisite flavours dance on my tongue. I open my eyes to see Marcus squirming in his seat.

"Are you okay?" I ask, swallowing the delectable food.

"I'm conflicted. On one hand that sexy sound from you has blood rushing south, on the other hand, I'm a little jealous that one bite almost gave you a When Harry Met Sally moment," he teases.

I cover my mouth as I laugh, trying to not spit out my food. I won't lie, the food is rather orgasmic, but I can't believe he just openly admitted my moan is giving him an erection. The thought of him getting hard right now because of me, and his brazen way of saying it so openly, has my cheeks flushing like a stop sign. Though, stopping is the last thing I want him to do. I actually love this quality about him.

We happily dive into our food, stealing glances at each other between bites and it makes me feel like a teenager being all silly with her crush. I never thought I was this person, but I rather like it. With things going better between us, I feel myself opening up and relaxing around him more instead of being guarded.

"There's something I've been dying to ask you," he says after taking another sip of his bourbon and coke.

"Should I be scared?"

"I don't think so," he chuckles, "I just can't for the life of me figure out what Mei is," he says, making me freeze with my fork near my mouth. I frown; I wasn't expecting this question. "Is it that bad?" He asks with a worried tone.

"No, it's not that. It's just not public knowledge and only a select few know what she is. I've been doing my best to keep it that way. I wanted to make sure she was strong and able to protect herself before we let it be more public."

"Oh. I can understand that," he concedes.

I chew on the inside of my cheek debating what to do. It's not my secret to tell, but he is my soulmate and I hope the person who will run this pack with me. He would be someone who would protect her... I guess I should dive in and find out.

"Mei is a nagata," I tell him.

His eyebrows practically disappear into his hair, "I thought those were a myth."

"So are we, technically."

"Good point. So, you're saying she's a snake?" He clarifies.

"That's correct," I nod. "Though I haven't seen her snake form. She's actually never shifted. Her form is there though; I've seen it in her eyes."

"That explains Chris' mark," he muses to himself. "Only thing I remember reading about nagatas is they are powerful and often guardians of royals or other powerful figures like that. How the hell does one end up a slave in a wolf pack?"

"Her father was a wolf; part of the Tian Pack in China and her mother was a nagata. Her mother was killed by their Alpha when Mei was only five and they fled here. Her father was killed by the Albus Mons Pack while seeking asylum and they took her in as a slave not knowing what she was," I say in a strained voice. No matter how many times I've heard it or said it, Mei's story shatters me.

For a brief moment, Marcus' eyes start to glow before he closes them, gripping the table tightly; his body trembling with anger so palpable I can feel it from here. I reach out, placing my hand on his, hoping our bond will calm him and his wolf down. Slowly but surely, his breathing evens out.

"How is that pack still standing?" He asks, his jaw clenched.

"Hardly, the Delegation was contacted, and the pack was reported. Last I checked their Alpha was taken into custody to receive punishment. Not sure what the punishment was, but I'm sure it was fitting," I assure him.

He takes a breath calming down a little more and nods, "Good. I fucking hope so," he takes a long sip of his drink. "So Mei's a hybrid?"

"Funny enough, no. She had full blood work done when she joined us because of her poor state of health. Not a trace of mutolupus DNA, which I thought was odd. But I guess the nagata blood is stronger, though our doctor was unable to identify her blood when he saw it due to having never encountered it before. Mei is stronger and faster than we are, and unlike us, nagata have three forms instead of two," I inform him.

"Three?" He asks with surprise.

A manage an 'mhmm' as I swallow my food. "We have human and wolf. Nagata have their human form, their snake form and then a third form that is half human half snake. I am very eager to see her shift, but I won't push it. It has to be when she's ready."

"And she's okay answering to you and being in your pack? I only ask because that would be like expecting an Alpha to be content serving under an Omega, given she's described as superior to you," he asks with nothing but genuine curiosity.

"She seems to be very happy as she is. Besides, she was fated to a Delta. I don't think Zarseti would have put them together if it were going to be a problem," I point out.

"Fair point," he agrees.

Overall dinner has been going very well, the atmosphere has been light – for the most part – with conversation flowing freely, which is why I'm so acutely aware of a shift in the air. Call it magic, intuition, or wolfy senses, but right now the hairs on my arms and the back of my neck are on end and Zara is already crouching in my head with her hackles raised. We both sense danger nearby. What that danger is we don't know, but it is present.

I know something is definitely wrong when Marcus goes completely rigid, his hands balling up into fists and his nostrils flaring. He's not just mad, he's positively furious. Before I can ask him what's wrong, the unpleasant scent of lilies invades me. Ugh, I hate lilies.

Marcus

What in the actual fuck is this bitch doing here? Here I was having what can only be described as the single greatest date of my existence and it was all shot to hell the moment I caught a whiff of her scent. The only thing keeping me in my fucking seat is knowing we are in a human establishment surrounded by humans. If not for them, I'd have shifted by now.

Is this psycho slut stalking me? How the fuck did she find me? Because I'm not stupid enough to believe her being here is a coincidence.

"Marcus! Oh my Goddess, I can't believe it's you!" She screams giddily as she rushes over, throwing her arms around my neck; the bile in my stomach already making its way up my throat, searching for the nearest exit.

"Let me out! I want to rip the bitch to shreds!" Ace roars in my head. I can feel my body trembling. I haven't had to fight so hard against the urge to shift since I was sixteen.

"ACE! Calm the fuck down! We're around humans, so stop trying to force a fucking shift!" I growl at my wolf. He's baring his teeth at me, but he steps back trying to calm himself down, which helps me calm down.

"Get your fucking hands off me, Davina," I order in a low growl with my Beta Spirit. She's no longer a member of my pack, so my command doesn't work fully on her, but she's still a lower-ranked wolf so it should at least make her back off.

She lets out a small whimper and lowers her arms. Thank fuck for that. I look over at Amelia, worry clinging to my bones. She's sitting up straight and proper, her face a mask of calmness. Fucking hell. I know that expression. It's forever burned into my brain and I don't fucking miss it. First time I saw it, I stupidly mistook it for my animai calmly listening to my words and planning to do as I said. Being the fucking moron I was, I didn't realise that this is the face of Alpha Amelia.

Alpha Amelia is not like other Alphas I have ever encountered. She doesn't resort to her baser instincts; she doesn't lash out or act on the emotions that no doubt run rampant inside her – as with any other Alpha – no she's a whole other breed of Alpha. She becomes calm, reserved, patient, with an air of regality to lull her prey into a false sense of security before she unleashes the full weight of her wrath.

When she did it to me, it threw me for a fucking loop and resulted in my ass getting the old heave-ho out of her pack and a promise of rejection. Here she is; that impossibly calm demeanour has returned and I can't tell if it's me or Davina who is going to be on the receiving end of what is to come. Amelia is both the calm and the storm and I fear the wreckage the storm she unleashes will cause.

"So, you're Davina," she says in a saccharine tone.

Fuck, here it comes.

"Oh, you've heard about me. All good I hope," Davina says with a smug expression, still in my personal fucking space.

"I wouldn't call sexual assault 'good' and, if you do, well that says all I need to know about you," Amelia says as if she's a CEO shutting down a bad business proposal.

I am both intimidated and turned on as fuck.

Davina's amber eyes flash for a split second. Most Alphas walk around happily projecting their Alpha Spirit to intimidate strangers. Amelia keeps hers restrained, even around her own pack members. I'm not sure why; I think it's why I didn't realise who she was when I met her. Point is, Davina has no idea she's openly challenging an Alpha and, speaking from experience here, she's fucked. Which makes me thrilled.

"I don't know what you think you heard, but I can assure you it was between two consenting adults," Davina says, venom dripping from her lies. Ace is barely containing himself. I glare up at her, ready to call her out on her bullshit, when Amelia jumps in.

"Enlighten me. How does one give consent while asleep? Have you perhaps mastered aspects of the pack-link I am unaware of?" Amelia asks.

I let out a snigger. If I hadn't spent time getting to know her and examining everything she says and does with great interest, I'd stupidly mistake her tone for one of genuine curiosity instead of the sarcasm it really is. She finds a way to keep her sarcasm so subtle that dimwits around her don't pick up on it; myself included. Davina is the biggest dimwit of them all, but still, she can't find a decent response.

"How the fuck are you here, Davina?" I spit at her. She turns to me, ignoring Amelia, to give me this gross puppy dog pout. All I see is a puppy I want to kick.

"It's kismet, what are the chances of bumping into each other here of all places? I've missed you so much baby," she says reaching to touch me again.

I grab her wrist, gripping it firmly - almost to the point of snapping it. But we're in public, so I hold back, yet still use enough strength to make her face contorts in pain.

"Kismet, my fucking ass. Are you following me? You were already banished, you're lucky to be alive," I hiss, tossing her hand away from me.

"Why can't you just admit you miss me? Miss us," she says with crocodile tears, holding her wrist to her chest.

"Why would I waste time missing a psychotic ex, who was an ex for a reason, when I can be enjoying a date with my soulmate?" I say, smiling proudly at Amelia, hoping she can understand how much I wish this weren't happening. I reach out for her hand and am thrilled when she takes it.

"Your what?" Davina growls while staring silver daggers at Amelia. "You're supposed to be his soulmate?" She scoffs and tosses her long brown curls over her shoulder. "I guess the Goddess doesn't have good taste anymore."

"Must not, since she paired your parents together and gave us you," Amelia deadpans.

Davina's jaw drops and her face turns the colour of flaming hot Cheetos. I don't even attempt to hold back my laughter. Even Ace has doubled over, rolling around laughing his tail off. Watching Amelia kick ass with wit and intelligence alone is getting my dick seriously hard right now.

"Who the fuck do you think you are?" Davina growls, slowly stepping towards Amelia. Amelia casually sits back and meets Davina's stare without so much as blinking.

"Someone who would have ripped your heart out of your chest by now if it weren't for the fact we're around humans. Consider yourself very lucky, because these lovely people around us are the only reason you're still breathing," she says calmly, but there is murderous intent in her eyes. She's an Alpha, I'm a Beta, I should be terrified, but my dick is jumping in my fucking pants seeing her like this.

"How da– "

"Please do us the courtesy of fucking off. You're ruining my night," Amelia waves her hand dismissively, bringing her drink to her lips.

Though we were speaking low enough that no one around us could hear, Davina's presence has garnered enough unwanted attention. The maître d' comes over and encourages Davina to sit or leave, and unfortunately, she picks the former. At least it's around the corner where I can't see her. Seriously, how the fuck did she track me here? I cautiously look over at Amelia; if my heart beats any faster, it'll fucking explode.

"Amelia? Are you okay?" I ask softly. She looks up giving me her warmest smile and starts drawing patterns into the back of my hand, the electricity it sends through me once again just adds a new level of stiffness to my now aching dick.

"I am perfectly fine, are you okay? Seeing her after what happened..." she sucks in a deep shaky breath. "She had no right to do what she did to you. Regardless of whether you are mine or not. And if her showing up here was kismet, I'll suck on a fucking lupine flower."

I blink, feeling tears start to build in my eyes. I have never been a crier, not even as a pup. But Amelia has me bearing all to her, and why not? Why should I have to hide from my very soul? This Goddess of a woman wasn't shaken because of the pain she endured by Davina's night visit; she's shaken because she hates the idea someone took advantage of me. Which, as true as that is, it's hard for me to accept.

"I don't think sucking on lupine will be necessary. I agree something is going on, and I'm so fucking sorry that it's ruined our first date." I run my fingers through my hair and down what's left of my drink.

"Our date isn't ruined," she consoles me. "It just took a detour; we can get it back on track," she assures me, her words easing my mind almost instantly.

"I don't know what I'd do without you, Ma Reine," I say lovingly as I kiss the back of her hand.

"Ma Reine?" She echoes, cocking her head to the side with a curious smile on her gorgeous face.

"It means 'my queen,' because the way you handled that and the way you hold yourself, in general, is not like an Alpha; It's like a fucking queen."

Chapter Twenty-Four
Amelia

Zara was snarling uncontrollably the entire time *Davina* was in our presence and if it weren't for the fact I've had twenty-one years of practice maintaining my composure, I would have leapt across the table, ripped the lying bitches tongue out and fed it to her.

I was fully aware of Marcus' rage; I could even taste it on my tongue. But I also noted his fear and panic. Not of her but fearing her presence would scare me off. I held no anger towards Marcus over this, but I'm glad we are both in agreement that something is amiss. How did a banished wolf follow him all the way to a human restaurant in another state?

"She's still here, and no doubt listening to our conversation," Zara growls. Her rage still very prevalent.

"I know, I can feel her. Let her listen, I'll deal with her when the time comes," I assure her.

Fortunately, I was able to calm Marcus, who I could tell was struggling to stop Ace from shifting. I could only imagine how Ace is feeling right now, but I'm sure Zara is doing her best to console him, even though their connection is weak since Marcus and I haven't mated or marked each other. I, on the other hand, am still reeling from what Marcus said. He called me his queen.

Saying it in French just made it sound like silk caressing my ears. A week ago, I was struggling to gain his respect and have him accept and acknowledge me as an Alpha. Now he's calling me a queen. Those walls are crumbling terribly fast. I was afraid to admit it, but I think I really am falling for him.

Once we were both calm, we ordered dessert and resumed enjoying our evening, though I was keeping a keen ear out for the little sex offender. We may be around humans, but the fact she's here would indicate she has more brains in that head than others may think and for that reason I'm not letting my guard down.

When dessert is over, we decide it's time to head back to the pack. My stomach flutters, thinking over what is to happen next.

"I just need to use the bathroom," I inform Marcus as we rise from our seats.

"I'll wait here then."

With a smile, I quickly dash off to the lady's room, and take longer than I anticipated thanks to the bodysuit. Bodysuits and bathroom needs do not mix.

When I'm done and everything is back in place, I step out of the stall, place my purse on the sink, and wash my hands. I hear the door open behind me and before I even catch her scent, I know who is behind me. I take back what I said about her having a brain.

"You're going to reject Marcus; do you understand me?" Davina growls and I hear a lock being latched. I proceed to rinse and dry my hands.

"*Oh, this bitch just messed with the wrong wolf,*" Zara says, rolling her neck.

"I will be doing no such thing," I say casually, throwing the paper towel in the trash and turning to face her. She's very beautiful, I'll give her that. Healthy, bouncing loose brown curls with caramel highlights that compliment her creamy skin and amber eyes. Even her thick Israeli accent is alluring. Too bad she's certifiable.

"Honey, you have no idea who you're dealing with," she threatens, as she stalks forward.

"And you seem to be mistaking me for someone who cares," I retort in a bored tone.

"He's mine!" She snarls. A growl rumbles in her chest, her amber eyes glowing, and her left hand is a fist aiming for my face. A cold smirk forms on my face as I catch her fist effortlessly. The impact it makes with my palm is barely even felt. She looks surprised and then annoyed as she tries to pull her hand back, but I tighten my grip, locking her in place. Without a moment's hesitation, I push forth my Alpha Spirit and let it crash down on her like a meteor falling to earth.

Fear and realisation take up her now wide eyes while she whimpers from the pain of the weight of the energy rolling off me. My glowing eyes stay on hers and the blood lust I keep buried is itching to come to the surface. Oh, I am calm and unbothered under pressure, but that took time and effort and wasn't without side effects. You can't bottle up your emotions and not expect something to go wrong.

For all the calm I can summon, there is a side of me that hungers for the hunt. Yearns to see the fear in my prey's eyes; a primal part of me that lurks deep in the darkest recesses of my mind thirsting for blood, and Davina here just woke that beast. A beast I am more than willing to let come out and play.

"Who were you calling yours?" I ask in a low threatening voice that's wrapped in a growl. Her head is bowed in submission, her body shaking uncontrollably with fear as sweat clings to her brow. The scent of her fear is tickling my nose and egging me on.

"Wh-wh-what are you?" She stammers.

"You know exactly what I am."

"Tha-at's not possible. You're a woman," she whispers in disbelief.

"Observant aren't you? Now time for a little chat, woman to woman." At breakneck speed, I pin her against the wall by her throat while my other fist keeps her hand in a vice grip. "First question, what pack are you a member of?"

"What?" She asks in confusion.

"Alpha Jasper banished you, and yet you don't carry the scent of a cur. So, what pack do you belong to?" I ask pressing my Alpha Spirit on her. She lets out a small cry of pain that I relish. She tries to fight against the weight of my power, but she's just not capable.

"I… I was accepted into the Roanoke Pack," she rushes out while trying to catch her breath. My brows knit together. Roanoke? I know the names of every pack in North America, there is no pack called 'Roanoke'.

"There is no such pack," I argue, though my words lack certainty. She certainly smells initiated, but she could be lying about the pack's name to protect them.

"Shows what you know," she says smugly. I growl and tighten my hold around her neck. Her eyes start to bug as she uses her one free hand to fruitlessly pry my hand off her.

"Who is your Alpha?" I order in a threatening tone. Again she tries to resist but that just causes her more pain, which I am all for.

"I can't tell you," she says through gritted teeth. "He found me and promised he could help me get back Marcus, all I had to do was join his pack and help him! By Alpha order, I'm forbidden to say his name!"

Her face is contorted in pain. Well, that's highly suspicious but anything else I can learn on my own. So onto the next matter at hand.

"Next question," I say, as I raise her left hand. "Is this the hand you used to touch my animai without his consent?" I ask coldly. Her eyes flick from me to her hand and back, panic setting in as her heart thunders in her chest. "I'll take that as a yes."

In a flash, I cover her mouth and snap her wrist like a twig, shivering at the sound of her muffled scream harmonising with the sound of her carpals snapping and breaking through flesh. The smell of blood tickles my nose and the beast is loving it. Zara's loving it too.

Davina weakly struggles against my hold, though mine doesn't ease up for a second.

"Listen and listen well. Marcus is mine, but mine or not, you had no fucking right to touch him. The only reason you get to live today is because I don't need humans investigating the mutilated corpse in the women's stall of this restaurant." Tears fall from Davina's eyes as a strangled sob is muffled by my hand. "That being said, if you ever touch, come near, or speak to my animai ever again, I promise I will allow you to see your heart in my hand as you take your last breaths," I snarl as I release my grip on her and step back.

Davina slumps to the floor cradling her hand as sobs of pain and fear wrack her body. I walk over to the sink and collect my purse and turn to grace Davina with a bright smile.

"Do enjoy the rest of your night," I say saccharinely. I walk over and unlock the door and step out to be enveloped by the sweet scent of caramel. I turn and my eyes lock on the forest gems of my animai. He's breathing heavily, his pupils are dilated, his fists are balled up and there is a very obvious tent in his pants. Holy hell... I quickly gulp down the saliva building up in my mouth.

"Mar–" I start to say before I'm cut off as he takes my face in his hands, looking in my eyes with an intensity that would make even the sun blush.

"I heard everything. I know you can handle yourself, but when I saw her follow you in, I was so worried," he breathes pressing his forehead against mine, the contact sending a delightful and calming zing through me. The bloodthirsty beast retreats back into my mind. "But then I heard how you handled it and..." he swallows audibly, "Fuck, Amelia, I've never been so turned on in my life," he groans, closing his eyes.

My heart starts to pound, and my eyes automatically dip down to the shape in his pants. A very big part of me wants nothing more than to reach out and touch it, but I fight it back.

"Maybe we should do something about that," I whisper in a husky voice I don't recognise.

His eyes fly open as he leans back looking stunned, "I... I didn't mean... I wasn't suggesting anything, Ma Reine, I swear." The pads of his thumbs skim across my cheeks, causing my eyes to flutter shut.

"I know," I breathe, smiling up at him, "But I wouldn't protest if that's how the night ended," I confess. His jaw slackens and he just stares at me like I've grown a third breast. "Shall we get back?" I offer.

He nods and adjusts himself before wrapping his arm around my waist and escorting me back to his truck.

We're driving for a few minutes before Marcus starts up a conversation. "I take it from what I heard that you broke her hand?" He asks with a malicious smirk.

"She's lucky that's all I did," I deadpan.

"Were you that jealous?" He teases.

"I only get jealous about things that matter," I say dismissively. The atmosphere in the truck becomes uncomfortable all of a sudden.

"Are you saying I don't matter?" He whispers. My head snaps to his and I can see the hurt all over his face.

Fuck. Shit. Dammit.

Great, now I'm the one putting their foot in their mouth.

"Why the hell did you say that?! Fix it!" Zara yells in a panic. Neither of us wants to see Marcus hurt and it upsets me to know I did. That wasn't my intention.

"That's not what I meant," I quickly say.

"Then what *did* you mean?" He asks tersely.

I rub my face taking a deep breath to think of how to phrase my words. "Have you ever felt jealous or envious over anything?"

He frowns thinking over my question, "No, I haven't."

"Well, I have. You have no idea how inadequate those emotions make you feel. They suck. I'm an Alpha. That title was always guaranteed to be mine but that didn't mean I had it easy. I'm jealous of my dad and other Alphas because they had the love of their pack members so effortlessly before they even took over, whereas I had to work to earn most of their love and still do. I envied how easy other Alphas and ranked wolves and their progeny had it because that sure as shit wasn't how it was for me," I tell him while painful memories and emotions flash through my mind.

Marcus' frown deepens, his eyes trained on the road, but he continues to listen.

"The reason I can be so calm while someone like Davina lies to me, insults me, and makes a move on you, is because I've had two decades to master not letting people see how they affect me. Someone looks at an Alpha wrong and they go on a rampage; no one so much as blinks because that's just how Alpha's are. I do it and I'm called hormonal and unfit to be an Alpha. You can't even argue that because you accused me of the exact same thing," I quickly add when I see him go to interject.

He clamps his mouth closed.

I lean my head back taking another breath to find my centre. This subject is hard.

"When I said I'm only jealous about things that matter, it didn't mean you don't matter to me. You *do* matter to me, more than anything. I don't fear someone like Davina can steal you away nor will I be made to feel inadequate by someone like her, because I trust that you are mine. Because I'm putting my faith in us enough to believe no one can take you away from me. I would never want to make you feel jealous or envious and I would hope you wouldn't want the same for me."

Silence.

He says nothing, or more accurately he has nothing to say. I can almost hear the cogs in his head turning . More minutes pass before either of us speak again.

"I'm sorry," he whispers.

"What for?" I ask in confusion.

"For ever making you feel inadequate," he says remorsefully.

I reach out and take his hand and pull it into my lap, "I'm sorry for making you think you don't matter to me," I say, kissing his hand.

He gives me a small smile, then sighs, "I was an idiot that day... Okay, I was an idiot every day. Every day I managed to find a new way to insult you or put you down. I swear I wasn't trying, but that doesn't excuse it. The day I stormed into your office I was scared," he confesses.

"Scared? Of what?" I gently ask.

"I listened to the way those stupid punks talked about you. The way they were disrespecting *you*, their *Alpha*, so openly. In front of another Alpha no less. I was seething at how disrespectful they were, Jasper had to keep me from doing something stupid but even he was disgusted with them. As a Beta, I was angered that any pack member could brazenly insult their Alpha like that. But as your animai, hearing him say you cracked under pressure was hearing my fears come true," he tells me in a strained voice.

"What fears?" I ask, rubbing his hand to soothe and encourage him.

"I feared that you would get hurt, that people would come for you and your pack, seeing you as an easy target. I feared that the pressure would be too much and it would only hurt you in the long run. I made bad assumptions instead of getting to know you or even learning what happened."

His eyes turn glassy with unshed tears and I can see how hard this is for him to say aloud, making me appreciate him saying it all the more.

"When your Beta told us what happened to you, I felt my heart shatter. My soulmate nearly died. Someone tried to kill you. You had been laying in a hospital bed and I should have been there, I should have been there to help you recover. I nearly lost you and I didn't even know it. But there you were, back at work like the queen you are, and me? I stood in front of a woman who just hours prior fought for her life and won, accusing her of being too weak for her role. When the fact she was standing before me and breathing at all was evidence to the contrary," he tells me as tears slip from his eyes.

I reach out and brush away his tears with the pad of my thumb, feeling tears pricking my own eyes, "It hurt me so deeply. I wanted nothing more than to seek comfort in your arms and in that moment I had to accept I wouldn't get it.,"

Marcus pulls over and turns off the car. He unbuckles his seatbelt and turns to face me, tears still filling his eyes. "I can never forgive myself for hurting you like that, for not being there when you needed me. You're the other half of my soul, Amelia, I'm nothing without you. I did and said a lot of dumb shit, but I'm learning. I want to be better, for you, for me, for us. I love you, Amelia, and I swear to the Gods I will spend every day I have on this earth and the life after showing that to you," he says with conviction.

The tears that were stinging my eyes make their escape. This gorgeous – and at times infuriating – man, just bared his heart and soul to me. He loves me. I can see the guilt in his eyes for his past actions, but I see the love too. His words feel like a blanket of protection and promise of a beautiful future, one I desperately want. I want him, and I refuse to let him go.

I reach out, capturing his face, pulling his lips towards mine so they connect in a searing kiss. I kiss him with fierce abandon, our lips gliding and massaging against one another, speaking to each other of passion, longing, and love because I love him too. I loved him the night we met and I've loved him every day since, which is why his words and actions broke my heart.

I don't know how long we sought comfort from each other's lips. Breathing didn't even seem necessary. When we finally do break for air – which turns out we did need – we rest our foreheads against one another and breath in each other's scents.

"You're right, I don't want you to feel inadequate, especially not over a psycho like Davina," he says, hissing her name.

"I could never feel that way over someone who felt she had a claim to you just because you gave her a couple of orgasms," I scoff. Marcus starts to say something and quickly presses his lips together. I raise a questioning eyebrow, "You were going to say, 'more than a couple,' weren't you?"

"You can't prove anything," he says defensively, putting his seatbelt on. I throw my head back and laugh while he starts the car back up and resumes the drive home. I love that I get better at reading him each day, the fact that we feel so connected without marking or mating is incredible and has me excited for what that experience will be like.

Once we arrive back at the packhouse and as soon as Marcus turns off the engine, I reach over and give him a soft peck on the lips.

His face splits into a wide smile that takes my breath away, "What was that for?"

"For the best first date ever. Sans psycho exes," I tease.

He laughs while rubbing the back of his head, "I hope to avoid those on our next date."

"And if not, prepare for some bloodshed," I shrug. He gets out and comes around, opening my door while I collect my purse and rose – can't leave that behind.

"Why does you getting all bloodthirsty make me thirst for you?" He queries as he helps me from the truck.

I chuckle and shrug, "Must be your kink."

"If it is, it's one I only have with you," he says, nuzzling me.

I sigh contentedly as we walk towards the packhouse. To my surprise, coming out of the packhouse hand in hand is Jennifer and Landry. They both look up at the same time and see me.

"Alpha!" They cheer simultaneously.

I smile, shaking my head, "Jen, Landry, what are you two doing here at this hour?"

"We were playing some games and watching movies in the entertainment room and time got away from us," Jennifer admits shyly.

Landry looks down at her with nothing but adoration, "It was worth it," he says, planting a kiss on her temple.

She turns scarlet. Aww! I see they are hitting it off as I thought they would.

"Jennifer, Landry, this is my animai, Marcus. Marcus, this is Jennifer, a member of my pack and Landry, of the Alpine Pack," I introduce.

"It's nice to meet you both," Marcus smiles and nods. Jen, being Jen, squeals with delight and jumps up and down, much to Landry's amusement.

"I knew the rumours weren't true! I just knew it! Oh, Amelia, I'm so happy for you!" She cheers, throwing her arms around me in a warm hug.

I smile and gladly return the hug placing a gentle kiss atop her head. I don't know what these rumours are, nor do I care.

"Thank you, Jen," I say appreciatively.

"Oh! We should let you two be, we don't want to interrupt," she quickly grabs Landry's hand, "Let's go, Lan!"

He chuckles and smiles like a giddy little boy, "One second, Pixie," he says tugging her hand. He reaches into his pocket and pulls out my credit card – I'd forgotten all about it. "Thank you for lending this to me, Alpha. I owe you... there are no words," he breathes, handing me the card, his eyes full of warmth and gratitude.

I take the card and slip it into my purse. "You owe me nothing, now run along," I encourage. They both grin and run off giggling, the sound soothing my heart. I'm glad things are working out; I clearly missed their development while going through my heat.

I'm about to climb the packhouse steps when I notice Marcus looking at me suspiciously.

"What?" I ask.

"I'm pretty good with faces, isn't that the girl who got rejected at the Vernal Ball *and* the kid who rejected her?" He inquires.

"That would be them."

"Why did he have your credit card?"

"I lent it to him so he could take Jen out on a date," I shrug.

Marcus blinks with surprise then smiles, shaking his head, "So now you're coming for Zarseti's gig," he jokes.

I snort with laughter. "Hardly, more like supporting and aiding in her wishes," I say while pulling him into the packhouse.

"Why? I mean, why help them after all that?" He questions curiously.

"Because Jen deserves to be happy and loved and that boy is just a young kid who made a mistake because of a bad influence. I knew he regretted it and I believed he deserved a second chance. They both did. Don't you think people should get second chances?" I ask pointedly.

"Oh, I am a *huge* believer in second chances," he says nodding eagerly. "Even thinking of starting up a club for it," he jokes.

We both head up the stairs laughing along the way, each step feeling like I'm floating on air. I never want this night to end, and frankly, I hope this isn't goodnight.

Chapter Twenty-Five
Marcus

I was so sure that Davina's sudden appearance had ruined my date with Amelia and our progress altogether, but that was not the case. Instead, it help me understand Amelia better, all while wracking me with guilt for all the shitty things I said to her when we met. Everything she said in the car pierced my heart and soul.

She's controlled and level-headed because one impulsive word or act would be detrimental to her position as an Alpha. She was right. I made the same argument against her, so I know I was no better, but hearing her talking about what it was like for her growing up had me thinking about what it was like for me growing up.

I never had to fight hard to be the Beta. Jasper and I were like brothers, so it was a no brainer. I just had to train to make sure I was the best Beta I could be. Jasper always worked hard because he loves and cares for his pack, but not once did anyone question if he would be a good Alpha because of his gender. The pack rejoiced the day he was born, the day they had their new heir. I can picture a screaming baby Amelia coming into the world and instead of rejoicing, her pack might have felt upset and slighted because she wasn't a boy. Like that's even her fault.

She is smarter and stronger than most Alphas I've met, she's patient and caring and wants everyone to be the best version of themselves. She's helping a victim of abuse deal with trauma. She's helping two rejected animals find love with each other. And, she's even giving me a second chance while also fending off one of my exes. Not to mention, she's doing all of this while defending herself and her pack from an unknown threat.

I said it before and I'll say it again, Amelia's not an Alpha, she's a fucking queen. *My* queen and tonight – if she'll let me – I'm going to worship her body like a queen deserves.

Heading up to the Alpha suite my heart starts to pound faster with each step we take. What if she hates this surprise? What if she thinks I'm pressuring her or thinks that I expect sex for the date? Which I don't! Guys like that are fuckers. They're the same dumb fucks who don't give a shit if their woman gets off. Selfish cocksuckers.

When we enter the suite, my anxiety level goes through the roof. Evalyn said she'd make sure Amelia's parents weren't in the suite tonight and for that I'm grateful. I owe that woman a lot, she was nothing but helpful with putting this date together. She followed my instructions to the letter and it was clear how much she wanted her friend to be happy. She's good in my book.

"Just let me put my things in my room," Amelia says warmly.

I nod mutely while trying to control my breathing. Amelia walks over to her room and opens the door and I hear her gasp as she freezes in place.

Is that a good gasp or a bad gasp?

"Go over and find out. But I bet it's good. You're trying to show her you care, I'm proud of you, Marcus," Ace says sincerely.

Fuck, now my wolf is choking me up, *"That means a hell of a lot coming from you."*

"I can't criticise you all the time," he teases.

Oh, but he would if he could.

Taking Ace's advice I walk up behind Amelia, breathing in her tropical scent to calm me as I place my hands on her hips.

"Do you like it?" I ask nervously.

I look around and see her room littered with tealights. It looks romantic and sensual, but not too over the top.

"Wha-… How did you do all this? *When* did you do all this?" She looks like she's in a trance.

"I texted your friend Evalyn while you were busy putting the fear of the Gods into Davina, letting her know we were on our way home, so she'd know when to get to work," I answer smoothly, though the nerves are still overwhelming me.

"You just called this place home!" Ace rejoices.

Wait, did I?

Amelia walks further into the room placing her purse and the flower on her desk while she looks around in wonder.

"Marcus, this is… it's so beautiful," she says turning to me, her eyes lighting up with so many emotions; the candles around the room are reflected in her turquoise eyes making them sparkle like she has stars in her eyes. Or maybe she does. If you told me she's actually a Goddess, not a mutolupus, I would believe you. "The clothes, the jewellery, the date, now this… I have no words," she gushes with a bright smile on her face that makes my heart soar.

I walk over and take her beautiful face into my hands; I sigh as soon as our skin makes contact and I feel those delectable electrical currents.

"I'm not pushing for anything; I don't expect anything. I just wanted to do something to show you how much you mean to me," I tell her as I brush my nose against hers.

Amelia keeps her eyes trained on me while slowly pushing my suit jacket off my shoulders till it drops on the floor. I don't dare break my eyes away.

"I don't want this night to end," she breathes.

Fucking hell! Is she…?

Wait, does she really mean what I think she means?

"Are you sure?" I ask tentatively. I have to know; I need her to be sure.

"I am very sure," she says confidently, nodding.

Fuck, this is really happening!

I let out a big whoosh of air. "You can always change your mind, please know that," I reassure her. I don't care if it was right before I was about to come, if she told me to stop, I'd fucking stop.

"I know, I trust you, Marcus."

The way she says my name sounds like a chorus of angels. I pull her close by her hips, sliding my arms around her and capturing her lips in a slow and passionate kiss. Her lips move against mine and it's like I never knew what kissing was before I met her. My tongue lightly teases her lips, eliciting a shiver from her that has me itching for her. Our lips continue to move against one another, her hands gliding up to the opening of my shirt to slide over my pecs, and the moment I feel her fingertips against my chest, my body shudders with delight.

I move my hands down her back until I feel the zip of her dress and then I gradually pull it down, sliding the straps off her shoulders and inching the dress down her body. I can feel something under the dress and curiosity gets the better of me. I break from our kiss so I can look at her and my mouth goes dry at the sight.

Fuck. Me. Dead.

She's wearing a strapless, black sheer bodysuit that reveals just enough to be tantalising but hides enough to be tasteful, and she looks fucking terrific. I groan at the sight of her and my dick strains against my pants, eager to break free.

"Fuck... I think you're trying to kill me," I say as my hands roam her bodice.

"Do you like it?" She asks nervously, chewing the inside of her cheek in that cute way she does.

I pull her closer to me pressing my erection against her. "I think this should tell you that I don't like it - I fucking love it," I growl into her ear as I nip her earlobe.

She moans, clutching my shirt and instantly her arousal perfumes the air. Fuck me, she's intoxicating. I place soft kisses across her shoulder and tease the crook of her neck with my tongue – the spot I'll place my mark. Her breathing is increasing, along with her heartbeat and her soft little moans are driving me wild.

"I want to undress you," she whispers.

I love that my woman knows what she wants and goes for it.

"Be my guest," I smile down at her. She smiles, licks her lips and gets to work unbuttoning my shirt. She takes her time and lets her fingers graze my skin. She may be a virgin, but she knows what she's doing. Suddenly the reality of the situation hits me like a bolt of lightning and a wave of nerves I didn't expect crashes over me.

I've never been with a virgin; I never wanted that responsibility. I love that Amelia is untouched but, now I feel like there is so much pressure on me to perform well. I have had experience – more than I care to admit – and she knows I'm not a virgin, so she'll expect me to know what I'm doing. I want her first time to be incredible, I want *our* first time to be memorable, and now I'm fucking scared shitless I'm going to fuck it up somehow.

What if I can't make her come and she thinks I'm lousy in bed?

What if I can't get it up? No, wait, the aching in my dick is a reminder that will *not* be a problem.

While I'm having my internal meltdown, Amelia is sliding my shirt off my body making sure to keep contact with my skin. She places a slow kiss on my chest and a growl of approval rumbles in my chest. I kick off my shoes and socks as Amelia unbuckles my pants with surprisingly steady hands. I gulp as she yanks my pants and briefs down, letting my dick spring free. I hear her suck in a breath as she trails her eyes over my body.

My flesh tingles everywhere her eyes trace and her hungry eyes on my dick has me twitching. She reaches for it, but I press her body against me and capture her lips in a searing kiss. She moans against my lips and the vibration is sinful in all the good ways. Her arms wrap around my neck and her fingers tangle in my hair. She gives it a gentle tug and I groan with pleasure into her mouth.

I lift her by her ass and on instinct, she wraps her legs around me. Gods I can't tell you how good it feels to have her wrapped around me like this. Her arousal is getting stronger and it's enough to drive me to madness; a madness I want to disappear into. Our lips never part as I walk us over to the bed and gently lay her down.

My hands explore every curve and dip of her toned body, just the way I pictured the night we met. My lips form a path of kisses down her jawline, her neck, all the way down to her cleavage. Fuck, she's gorgeous. I run my tongue along the swell of her breasts and find myself grinding against her very wet core. She's soaked through her lingerie and her juices are lubricating my dick. Her breathing is laboured as she writhes under me, her pussy rocking against my dick seeking friction – friction I am all too willing to give.

"Can I take this all off?" I ask, gently nipping the tops of her breasts, my tongue tracing over her Alpha's mark and causing her breath to get stuck in her throat.

"Please," she says in a moan as she arches into me; my dick is throbbing right now, but I'm not rushing this.

I sit back on my heels and give myself a second to take in the beauty splayed out in front of me. She is the sexiest sight that not even my wildest dreams could make up. I gently claw my fingers down her thighs, watching her groan as her eyes roll back. I could watch her reactions forever. I lift her leg and kiss down her calf to her foot as I remove her heels, making a mental note to have her keep them on next time.

I nestle back down between her legs, letting my hands trail back up her body. She's panting and can't stop wriggling beneath me, and I'm loving every fucking second of it. I reach back to find the zip and quickly unzip her bodysuit and peel it off her. My brain short-circuits at seeing my love completely bare to me. Her physique is indescribable, but you'd never guess how strong she is from looking at her. Her pink nipples are erect and begging me to suck them, so I decide to help myself.

I dive forward and clasp my mouth around her right nipple, my arms circling around her, holding her to me. Her fingers return to my hair and as she moans, I flick her nipple with my tongue. Fucking hell, how is it she tastes tropical too? I can't fucking wait to taste her pussy.

"M-Marcus... Oh, Marcus," she moans breathlessly as I suck and tug her nipple. I trail kisses to her other nipple and pull it into my mouth. As I do I glide my hand down between us heading straight for her pleasure centre. She's completely shaved and we're going to have to have a talk about that later, but I'm not bringing that up now. I'm not a complete moron.

My finger glides effortlessly between her slick folds to find her swollen clit and I gently apply pressure to it. She mewls, throwing her head back as her hips buck and I smirk around her nipple, "I love how responsive you are, my Sexy Little Alpha."

"Your hands feel so good," she pants, her hands fisting and tugging at my hair.

Oh, she has barely experienced what my hands can do.

I slide my finger down her folds, seeking her entrance and just as I reach it, her hand – at the speed of a snake's strike – reaches out, grabbing my wrist to stop me.

Fuck. I freeze looking up at her, trying not to show panic.

Did I hurt her?

Is it too much?

Has she changed her mind?

"It's okay if you want to stop," I say pulling my hand away and resting it on her hip as I stroke her hair with my other hand. "I can just hold you," I assure her. She smiles shaking her head. She takes my face in her hands and plants a deep kiss on me that I return and moan into. I think I'm getting drunk on her kisses.

"I don't want to stop, I just..." she trails off, looking embarrassed.

Amelia? Embarrassed?

Holy fuck, this is a first.

"Just what? You can tell me, baby," I encourage while placing soft kisses all over her face. She sighs in contentment and the sound has Ace preening in my head. I love hearing and feeling her so relaxed with me.

"I just don't want your hand to be the first thing I feel inside me," she says sheepishly.

I look at her wide-eyed, my heart ready to break out and fly to the fucking moon. How amazing can this woman get? She wants the first thing she feels inside her to be me, not my hand, not a toy, but my dick and fuck does it make my ego feel good.

"I can do that," I say softly as I caress her cheek.

She smiles leaning her face into my hand. I will never get tired of that.

I'm not the biggest in terms of length, I'm a very decent six inches. But what I lack in length, I make up for in girth. Even my own hand has a hard time reaching around, so right now I'm a bit worried about how much this might hurt her. But then again, this is my badass woman who took on a pack of mindless wolves while in heat, so if anyone can handle me, it's her. After all, she was fucking made for me.

"I'll try to be gentle, tell me if it's too much," I say, kissing her cheeks. She smiles, running her fingers through my hair. I never liked people playing with my hair until her.

"I can take it, I want it," she says confidently. I smile looking down at her as I slowly rub the tip of my dick up and down her wet folds. She whimpers with pleasure, wrapping her legs around me, urging me on. I guide myself to her entrance and make the call to do this in one thrust – it's a good thing she's soaking wet. If I drag this out, I'm prolonging her discomfort. I kiss the tip of her nose, wrap my other arm around her and in one quick thrust plunge my dick inside her.

OH FUCK!

She sucks in a sharp breath scrunching up her face, her fingers digging into my shoulders. She's holding her breath and I'm holding mine. I press my forehead against hers while I try to focus. She's the tightest thing I've ever felt in my fucking life; her warm, wet walls have a vice grip on my dick. I almost came just entering her.

Fucking hell!

I stay still giving her a chance to adjust, but also because I'm afraid if I move, I'll blow and there is no fucking way I'm letting her think I have quick-release issues. I have one hand fisting the sheets as I try to get a handle on myself, at the same time I place more gentle kisses on her face; her eyelids, her nose, her lips.

"I've got you, you're okay. I love you, Amelia," I say nuzzling her.

She finally exhales and wraps herself tighter around me, "I love you too, Marcus," she says. My eyes snap to hers, searching for any sign I just hallucinated her saying that, but I see nothing but a sparkle in her gorgeous eyes. She loves me! She fucking loves me!

My lips crash down on hers and I wrap my arms tight around her and, as our lips move, I start to move inside her. I keep my movements slow, still letting her adjust. She lets out a small groan against my lips, her hands fisting my hair, but she doesn't protest. In fact, she tightens her legs around me. I can take the hint. I keep up a steady rhythm while trying not to get too lost in our passionate kiss. Gradually I start to pick up the pace of my thrusts and her groans morph into salacious moans.

"I love you so fucking much," I breathe against her lips. I try to keep my thrusts gentle but as her moans reach my ears and her hands roam my body, I find myself pushing in and out a little harder and a little faster. I shift a little, pulling all the way out and plunging back in, filling her up to the hilt. She arches back crying out in pleasure as her nails claw down my back. The sensation has me twitching inside her. My muscles tense and I will myself not to come.

I latch onto her nipple, sucking and flicking it as I thrust into her at a moderate pace. The room is filling with the scent of sex; her mango and pineapple scent consuming me. Her moans are the sweetest music my ears have ever heard and the clenching of her warm walls around me is like finding my nirvana. This is paradise. *She* is my paradise and I want to bask in her forever.

"Oh, Marcus! Oh Gods, Marcus! Please don't stop!" She cries my name like a prayer. A shiver runs through me. My muscles are coiled, and heat is building in my lower abdomen, but my woman is coming first if it fucking kills me.

"I'll never stop, baby," I promise in a pant as sweat coats our bodies. I kiss her hard and she kisses back just as hard.

"Mark me," she moans. I slow down my thrusts, looking at her for uncertainty, but once again I find nothing. Just undiluted need, passion and… love.

"Only if you mark me," I say cheekily. She giggles but nods enthusiastically. I grin like a fucking kid given the keys to the candy store and pick up the pace.

Her face contorts as her cries of pleasure echo around the room, I feel the sweat building on my brow as I pump into her fast. My canines distend and I watch as hers distend as well. Just seeing them sends another rush of blood to my dick, making me harder than I already was. I don't hesitate, I sink my canines into the crook of her neck and taste her blood on my tongue. She screams in euphoria as her pussy clenches and locks around my cock. Her orgasm breaks through her. In the same moment, I feel her canines pierce the flesh of the crook of my neck.

"FUCK!" I cry out with a groan as my orgasm bursts through me and with a hard thrust, I empty inside her in the most intense, mind-blowing orgasm of my life. My vision blurs, my toes curl and I'm groaning into her neck, my teeth still embedded in her flesh as I continue to release into her. I've never come like this in my life. I retract my canines and lick away the blood from her neck, eliciting another moan and a shiver as her pussy pulsates around me, milking my cock. I feel her retract her canines and lick the flesh she marked and I too shiver.

We're panting, holding each other tight and as our marks heal, I feel the tether to each other completely lock into place. Like two jigsaw puzzle pieces were finally put together. A wave of happiness, love, and excitement crashes into me and it doesn't take me long to realise it's coming from Amelia. I smile and bury my nose in her neck, breathing in her scent. I can feel what she feels now.

"You're mine," I link to her.

She strokes my hair nuzzling into my neck, her grip on me never slacking. *"As you are mine,"* she links back.

Fuck it's amazing, feeling her in my mind. It's like I finally became whole. That empty spot inside me that was always there is finally filled, and it's filled with the only person it ever belonged to. Amelia.

I don't want to pull away, but I know I should. So I slowly pull out and lay beside her, drawing her into my arms. She turns on her side to face me and snuggles into me. I can't help my shit-eating grin. I just mated and marked my animai. She's finally mine and no one can take that away from me.

"How are you feeling?" I gently ask as I smooth her hair out of her face.

She smiles up at me with those incredible, clear, beach water eyes. "You tell me," she smirks.

I chuckle, "I can feel how happy and content you feel, but I still want to hear it" I kiss her nose and stroke her back. The electricity felt from our touch is now a thousand times more potent. I can feel myself getting hard again. I guess I'm going to be walking around with a permanent erection.

"I've never felt happier than I do right now. That was the single most amazing thing I've ever experienced, and I can't wait to do it again," she beams.

I throw back my head and laugh, "I think I've created a monster."

"I think so. But I'm *your* monster," she says with conviction.

I smile down at her with nothing but love and pride, "You sure are." I place a long, tender kiss on her lips that she returns with a moan.

"Was I... um... okay?" She asks hesitantly.

I blink in surprise. Oh no, I'm not letting her assume that for even a second. I capture her chin and tilt her head back, forcing her to look at me.

"That was the most mind-altering, most transcending experience I've ever had and don't you dare think otherwise for even a single second. You were fucking fantastic and I am honoured that you let me have you," I say, brushing my thumb against her lips.

She smiles and relaxes, "Thank you. Though if you'd said I needed some work, I'd have been all up for more practice."

Oh, this little minx. "Well, I am all for practice." I roll her onto her back. "Practice does make perfect," I continue, kissing her bright red chest, still flushed from her orgasm. I love this colour on her.

"Mmm I've heard that, too," she breathes, running her hands up my back.

"Can I ask you something? And please don't get offended, I swear I'm not trying to be an asshole," I say quickly.

"Okay..." she says with apprehension.

"Do you wax or shave?"

She stares at me for a second before her brows dip in confusion, "Um, shave. Why?"

"Would you be comfortable to stop doing that?"

"Huh?" She says, looking more confused.

"It's your body, so ultimately your call and I will respect what you do, but… I would love it if you let it grow naturally," I admit

"Can I ask why?" She inquires, no judgement in her tone, thankfully.

"Because, when I watch my cock pump in and out of your wet pussy I want to feel like I'm buried in my woman, not a little girl. You are definitely not a little girl," I growl against her ear.

Her emotions are an interesting mix of surprise, contemplation and my favourite, lust. If that wasn't clear from her body language, then the scent of a new wave of arousal reaching my nostrils would be the dead giveaway. What I said has her getting wet for me again. I smirk leaning in and kissing below her ear.

"Does my queen like dirty talk?" I whisper huskily, cupping her breast with my hand and giving it a gentle squeeze. Fuck she fits into my palm perfectly.

"Ye-yes," she admits, arching into my hand.

"And does that mean you will consider my request? If not, that's fine," I say, kissing her neck.

"Can I at least keep it trimmed? So it's not too uncomfortable," she says in a breathy voice, her leg brushing up and down mine.

"I think that's a perfectly reasonable compromise," I grin. Look at us discussing shit and finding a middle ground. We're off to a good start.

"Then I don't mind," she smiles, kissing my cheeks.

"You're so fucking perfect," I growl running my tongue over my mark on her neck. She moans, wrapping herself around me.

"I was thinking that about you," she says, licking my mark. My dick gets hard instantly.

Who the fuck needs Viagra? Fucking hell.

I can feel her pussy soaking my dick again as I rub my length against her, making sure to apply enough pressure to her clit.

"Tell me what you want, baby," I instruct as I suck and kiss my way down her neck.

"You. I want you inside me, Marcus. Please," she pants, rocking her pussy against me eagerly.

"Whatever my queen wants," I tell her as I sit up and back on my heels, grabbing and angling her hips to drive my cock deep into her pussy.

"Fuck!" I grunt as her hungry pussy swallows me whole, still tight like a python.

"Marcus!" She screams, gripping the pillow under her head like a life raft. But I can feel through the bond I haven't hurt her, no, she fucking loves it. That's my girl.

"That's it, Amelia, take my cock," I say, ploughing into her hard and fast with abandon, watching as her perfect tits bounce with each thrust, her chest flushed that sexy shade of red. What we did a few minutes ago was making love in the purest form imaginable. This; this is straight-up fucking.

Her screams of pleasure spur me on, her hands fisting her pillow till her knuckles turn white. She's a fucking remarkable sight. Seeing her in the throes of pleasure like this is gasoline on the fire. Her body is glistening with sweat, new and old, and I can feel the sweat trickling down my back. Every muscle in my body is wound up, seeking its release the only way it can, through Amelia.

"Tell me how it feels," I grunt, as I thrust into her harder.

"It feels... so... fucking... good... baby AH!" She struggles to say each word as I thrust in and out of her wildly, her head thrashing from side to side. I can feel how overwhelmed by pleasure she is and I've barely even scratched the surface. I yank her up, pulling her body flush against mine, her eyes widen, then roll back as she feels me deeper this way. Her pussy is like warm silk and she fits like a fucking glove. I just want to stay inside her forever.

"Move your hips, baby," I encourage her as I wrap one arm around her back and guide her hips with my other hand.

She swallows a moan as her eyes connect with mine, fire – burning hotter than lava – shines in her eyes and without much prompting from me she starts riding my cock. I groan and clench my jaw at how fucking good she feels.

"That's it, fuck, keeping doing that," I tell her.

She picks up her pace and, to my surprise, starts bouncing on my cock. Oh, fuck yes!

Her arms are tight around me, and I have a firm grip on her hips as I watch her pussy come down and repeatedly devour my cock. The sight itself is orgasmic. Heat builds in my spine and I feel my balls tighten. Her walls are quivering, her moans are overlapping and becoming strained and I can feel through our bond, she's close. I grip her hips a little firmer and thrust up into her, meeting her movements.

"Marcus! Oh, Marcus! Marcus, I'm gonna come!" She cries as she grips my hair.

"That's it, Amelia, come on my cock," I say through gritted teeth. I'm barely holding on; I just need to hold it a little longer.

"I... I... FUCK! MARCUS!" She screams coming down on my cock hard. Her walls clench around me as her orgasm breaks through her.

Holy, fucking shit.

Between her clenching pussy and feeling her orgasm through our bond, it breaks all my control and brings on my own orgasm, forcing it to crash through me like a fucking tsunami.

"AMELIA!" I cry, wrapping my arms around her burying myself deep inside her warmth as I come long and hard, twitching inside her.

We stay like that, wrapped in each other, panting, neither willing to let go.

"I really love practising," she says breathlessly. I laugh into her neck. Gods I love this woman.

Chapter Twenty-Six
Amelia

Waking up, I have never been so glad I'm a mutolupus. Last night was the most mind-blowing, vigorous, euphoric, and romantic night of my life. For hours I lost myself in Marcus and him in me, neither able to get enough of each other. He took me to heights of pleasure I didn't even think existed. It was a delicious mix of making love; which was slow and tender; and fucking so hard and so fast I felt like my soul was being blown out of my body. If it weren't for fast healing and supernatural stamina, I would be dead to the world right now.

Marcus is wrapped around me, just like he was every time I woke up during my heat, but this time is different. Now that we're marked, I can feel everything he feels and I have a direct link to his mind. I can see his dreams now! Should I? Maybe that's an invasion of privacy. But then again, we are bonded now…

I take a little peek into his mind and my heart does somersaults. He's dreaming about me! It's not even a sex dream, shockingly. He's dreaming of us laughing and playing in a lake, just completely enraptured by each other. I pull out of his dream and tighten my hold on the arm he has around my waist. I feel like the dam in my heart is about to burst, this is all I wanted. To find my other half and have him love and accept me. And he has. I can feel it. I feel his love for me. I can't see the tears that are in my eyes. I'm not usually this emotional.

Marcus stirs behind me, and I can feel him wake up and pull me closer to his chest, "Amelia, what's wrong?" He whispers, and I can both feel his concern through our connection and hear it in his voice. I shake my head and wipe away my tears. But he's not having any of that. He quickly turns me to face him and analyses my face. "Why bother lying when you know I can feel what you feel? Talk to me," he softly encourages.

"I'm just so happy. Growing up, you were all I ever wanted, but I was so sure when I found you that you'd reject me; not wanting a female Alpha for an animai. Then with everything that happened… I just never thought we'd end up here and knowing we have, I'm happier than I know how to handle," I confess.

His face softens and a small smile plays on his lips, "I was a prick, but please know this, Amelia. Whatever backwards opinions I had, there was not a single part of me that wanted to reject you. That wasn't even an option for me and even knowing you were going to come to my door and reject me - I had no intention of accepting it."

"You're so stubborn," I chuckle, snuggling into the warmth of his chest.

"Look who's talking," he scoffs, wrapping his arms around me.

"Hey, I am not stubborn. I just know what I want," I huff.

"Oh, I've noticed, and I love it," he says, kissing my forehead. "Let's go have a shower. As much as I love you covered in my cum, I can't keep you that way forever," he says bluntly.

His words have my insides clenching with need and straight away I feel myself getting wet. How does this man get me going with just his words? It's not fair.

"Oh, as if you're actually complaining. You love him and his dirty words," Zara yawns.

"And good morning to you too. How are you feeling?"

She yips and wags her tail excitedly, *"Terrific! We're marked, I can finally connect with Ace much better now. But I'm not the one who lost their V-card last night. How are you feeling?"* She asks with genuine concern.

"Never been better," I beam hugging her through our bond. I feel her

nuzzle my mind and it soothes me.

"Good morning, Zara," Marcus says, his forest eyes glowing. I grin, feeling my eyes glow as Zara pushes forward a little.

"Good morning, Ace," I say.

"I see our wolves are in a good mood," he grins, getting up. My eyes immediately linger on every muscle and dip in his gorgeous body. His defined biceps, his chiselled pecs and abs that look photoshopped because, surely, they can't be real. My eyes dip lower landing on my favourite piece of his anatomy, his semi-hard cock. Bless the Goddess for creating this specimen.

I admit when I first saw it, I felt a bit nervous. Look, I know if I can push out a pup, then obviously I can fit his cock, but it was my first time. It was going to be a lot to take the first time. It hurt, no doubt about that, I felt like I was being ripped open. But after handling the pain of my heat, it was like a papercut by comparison. It was also pretty easy to ignore while Marcus showered me with kisses and told me he loved me. All pain vanished after that and was replaced with pure ecstasy.

"If you keep eyeing my cock like that, we won't make it to the shower," he teases.

I clench my thighs together. Something about the way he says the word 'cock' that has my body tingling as if I can feel it inside me already.

"Threats aren't supposed to sound so erotic," I tease back, getting up.

I only just realise how sticky and gross I feel. Between my legs is a fucking mess, sticky, dry, and wet. Oh, this is not pleasant at all, and yet I want to do it all over again. I want to get clean so he can dirty me up again.

I brush past Marcus and into the bathroom, turning on the shower. I step in under the water, letting the heat cascade over my body and loosen up every muscle. I'm not alone for long when I feel Marcus' arms snake around me, his face nuzzling against my mark.

I sigh as electric tingles pulse through me, "How does it look?"

He brushes my hair aside and gives it a tender kiss, making me shiver. "Absolutely perfect, just like you," he says with such reverence, it almost knocks me off my feet.

I turn to face him; my eyes homing in on his mark. A small silver paw print – Zara's paw print – shining as the sunlight in the room bounces off it. It looks perfect and a territorial growl slips out of my lips at the sight of it. I can feel Marcus' amusement and… desire.

Instinct takes over and I press him against the shower wall, pinning his hands at the sides of his head as I lick and nip at his mark. My pussy is getting wetter and I can feel my juices spreading to my thighs.

"Fuck, Amelia," he breathes as I feel his erection press against my stomach. I know what I want, and I want it now. I've never done this before, but it's not rocket science.

I take my time kissing down his body, letting my tongue tease and caress his firm but silky skin. He even *tastes* like caramel; oh I am so done for. I work my way down, until I'm on my knees, my tongue tracing every single ab, committing each ridge to memory.

"Amelia, you don't… have to do this," he says through clenched teeth as he fights between his desire and care for my wellbeing.

Since he returned to the pack, he's done nothing but be considerate of me and my feelings and now that we're marked, I can feel how genuine it is. It fills my heart and soul with a warmth I can't begin to describe.

"I know, I'm doing this because I want to," I smile up at him. "Do you actually want me to stop?" I raise an eyebrow.

"Fuck no, I just only want you to do it if you're comfortable," he says softly, reaching out to stroke my cheek.

I close my eyes leaning into his touch. I love when he does this. I open them again to eye my prey. Although, from the size of it, it is definitely a monster. His dick has my mouth watering as it twitches before my eyes, precum glistening at the tip; the scent of it driving me to the brink of insanity. But for him, I crave that insanity. He's thicker than most I've seen but none of them have ever had my thighs quivering the way his does.

I reach out and wrap my hand around the base of his dick, he immediately jerks his hips as a groan of pleasure escapes his mouth. The sound of it sends pleasurable jolts through my body. I can barely fit my hand around this beast, and it's starting to look angry. I best tame it then. I stick out my tongue and slowly lick the precum from the head of his dick and the taste of it is like the sweetest dessert I've ever had.

Marcus hisses when my tongue makes contact, but I can feel his pleasure through our bond and it fuels my own. I slowly run my tongue up and down his shaft, relishing how it tastes against my tongue. I watch as his eyes roll back. With both hands, I begin stroking his dick and I'm amazed by the feel of it, it's firm like marble but soft as velvet and I'm in awe of the sensual beast in my hands. Marcus' hands are balled into fists at his sides, and I can feel his eyes on me now.

I was confident sooner or later my pussy would fit him, that's what it's built to do, but my mouth is another matter. I'm not a python, I can't unhinge my jaw and by the looks of this thing I may require that ability to achieve this. I don't have a very big mouth. This was proven when Vitali and I competed over who could fit the most grapes in their mouth; he won of course, and now I think I know why.

As my hands firmly stroke him, I suck the tip of his dick and flick the slit with my tongue.

"Holy mother of fuck," he says through gritted teeth as he fists my hair.

I let out a pleasurable groan as the feeling of him gripping my hair has my walls pulsating for him. Okay, so apparently I like having my hair pulled. Learning a lot about myself.

"You like that, baby?" He pants.

I nod as I continue my task. He smiles down at me, and his smile has me eager to please. I want him to feel as amazing as he's made me feel.

So what if I break my jaw? I'll heal. As they say, jaws were made to be broken.

What? Literally, no one says that. Are you nuts? Says Zara, looking at me like I've gone mad.

Whose side are you on?

Hey, you do you. I just had no idea you were this cock hungry, she sniggers.

I slowly take him into my mouth, trying to keep my jaw relaxed so I can take as much of this beast as I possibly can.

"Sweet fucking Gods, Amelia!" He cries, throwing his head back while fisting my hair into a ponytail. His cry of pleasure mixed with the way he's playing with my hair has me moaning around his dick and, from the way he reflexively thrust his hips, I'd say he liked that.

I feel galvanised at the sight and feel of his pleasure. I start sucking his monster of a dick, managing to fit about half of him in my mouth. My hands have to help me with the rest. I'm looking up at him through my lashes, his face contorted, and I want to take a picture of it and keep it forever. He looks so fucking sexy like this! I keep my pace slow, but I'm sucking him like I'm trying to suck the alcohol out of a deodorant stick.

His moans of pleasure are everything my ears didn't know they needed; I feel like the sound of them alone is going to make me come. His pleasure gives me pleasure and I can't keep from moaning around his dick. He looks down at me, his hands still keeping my hair back. His eyes are dark with lust, but I see that softness around the edges that still hold love for me.

Gods how I love this man!

He doesn't give me instructions or tell me what to do, he lets me have my fun, test the waters, and explore him. I start sucking a little faster, stroking the rest of him with both hands in a twisting motion. I can see his thighs going taught as every muscle in his body tenses. I can feel how close he is and I badly want him to come in my mouth. I want to taste him on my tongue and feel him down my throat.

Wow, Zara's right. I really am cock hungry.

His grip on my hair tightens and I can tell he's resisting the urge to thrust deeper into my mouth. He wants his release and I want to give it to him. So, like the cock hungry woman I have apparently become, I give myself over to my carnal desire. I suck and stroke his thick cock like my very life depended on it. I am barely aware of my surroundings; all I feel is him and me and this overwhelming need.

"Fuck, baby…. oh fuck… keep going, I'm gonna come," he says through gritted teeth, "Fuck, fuck, fuck, fuck, f…UCK!" He cries throwing his head back as his orgasm crashes through him and he unloads into my mouth. His dick continues to twitch and spurt cum into my mouth, and I quickly swallow it down. I pull back slowly and run my tongue all around his dick.

Marcus pulls me up by my shoulders and crashes his lips down on mine in a bruising kiss. It's heated and mind-numbing and I love it. I wrap my arms around him moaning into this kiss, not able to get enough. We slowly break apart and we're both panting, hearts racing and it's heavenly.

"Have you... have you done that before?" He asks apprehensively. I shake my head. His eyes widen in disbelief. "I'm your first for that too?"

"You think I didn't have time for dates, but I had time to go around giving guys blow jobs?" I ask incredulously. I will chalk up the dumb question to his brain being fried from his orgasm.

He chuckles and rubs the back of his head, "That's a good point, sorry," he says, kissing my nose. "It's just you were fucking amazing."

"Even though I couldn't take all of you?" I pout.

He smiles softly, brushing his thumb over my lips, "You took way more than I thought. I'm not mad if you can't fit all of me, you have other places that can do that," he smirks while squeezing my ass. I gulp, feeling it in my core and it makes my pussy clench. "Hair pulling and ass grabbing huh? You really are made for me," he teases, picking up on my arousal.

I lightly smack his chest and get back to the point of getting in the shower. He chuckles and moves closer to wash my body and I let him. Marcus takes his time washing and kissing every inch of me. I wanted to do the same to him, but he said we'd wasted enough water.

Once we're finished, we get out, dry off and I head into my closet to get dressed. I decide today will be a casual day; light blue skinny jeans, black tank top and a pair of Nike Air Jordans in pink, red and black. To my pleasant surprise, Marcus has his bag stored in my closet, so he changes with me. He puts on a stretch navy blue t-shirt, black ripped jeans with tan pull up boots. I lick my lips at the sight of him. He's all-around grade A material and one hundred per cent all mine.

I quickly run off to brush my teeth, but he follows behind me with a toothbrush so he can do the same. This is so weird! But the good weird. It's like we've already stumbled into a routine, yet we haven't even been mated and marked a full day. I'm not complaining, of course. This is amazing and feels unbelievably natural.

"Always a pop of colour down south huh?" He muses while combing his long locks.

I cock my head quizzically at him.

"Your shoes. Almost every time I've seen you, you've had shoes that make a statement, even sneakers," he explains.

I shrug. "At least ninety percent of the time. Easiest way of adding colour to my attire without really trying."

"I love learning new things about you," he admits, and once again I feel heat rising in my cheeks. "See, like that. You don't blush out of embarrassment; you blush when you're happy over something romantic or aroused." He brushes the back of his hand against my cheek softly.

"Explains why I never blushed until you entered my life," I inform him.

Oh, he liked hearing that. If his smile got any bigger, you'd see it from space.

I grab his hand and lead him out to the living area. The scent of my parents in the room is barely there, which means they weren't here last night – for the best.

"Do you want me to have breakfast sent up or shall we go downstairs to eat?" I ask. Before he can answer, the doorbell goes off. "Hold that thought," I say kissing his cheek. I walk over and open the door to be met by a very flustered looking Vitali.

"I really screwed up and need your help!" He exclaims in a rush.

"Whoa, slow down. Start from the beginning," I instruct as I pull him into the suite and shut the door.

"I told Eric about Nuray. I didn't want to, but then I remembered irshiusts can't lie and I didn't want it accidentally coming out in front of Eric. So, I told him, and he had a bit of a meltdown and now I don't know what to do. I shouldn't have told him." He's waving his hands around, getting more flustered by the second.

"You absolutely should have told him. Think of how hurt he'd be if she showed up and everyone knew you two had slept together but him. You did the right thing by telling him," I assure him as I walk over and rub his shoulders.

"Yeah, but now he won't speak to me and he locked me out of our room," he says despondently.

"And you were hoping I would talk to him for you," I surmise. I know I'm right when Vitali looks up at me with puppy dog eyes.

"Would you? I don't want to burden you; I know you've got stuff going on," he comments.

I wave a hand dismissively, "Hey, the day we signed up to be best friends was the day your bullshit became my bullshit and my bullshit became yours. You've been fielding my bullshit for the past week, now it's my turn."

He chuckles and sighs with relief. "You really are the best, Amelia. Really, I would talk to Eric myself, but I was afraid of pulling a Marcus," he says nodding his head towards Marcus, who has been standing quietly to the side.

"And just what the fuck does 'pulling a Marcus' mean?" Asks Marcus, disgruntled, crossing his arms over his chest.

I swallow as I watch his muscles strain against his shirt.

"Putting your foot in your mouth. You're quite notorious for it," Vitali says offhandedly.

Marcus looks like he's about to argue but purses his lips. It's true, Marcus does suffer from Foot-In-Mouth Syndrome.

"But we still love him," Zara cheers happily.

"We sure do," I agree.

"Yeah, well, I'm a reformed foot-in-moutherer," he huffs indignantly.

Vitali looks dubious while I can't help but laugh. Is 'moutherer' even a word?

"Okay, boys, back to your corners," I say.

I notice Vitali's eyes narrow at Marcus, widen, and then snap to me. "Holy shit you guys marked each other! And you…" he takes a quick whiff, and his eyes nearly bug out of his skull. "No way! You two mated? Just how good was this date?"

"It was the best ever," I say, grinning at Marcus. He grins back and walks over, wrapping his arms around me and pressing his nose into my hair. I giggle and wrap my arms around his waist inhaling his rich caramel scent. "Though I think it had more to do with the company," I admit.

"Oh, it was definitely the company," Marcus agrees, kissing my lips softly.

I eagerly return his kiss. Can I just kiss him forever?

"Wow, in that case, congratulations to you both," Vitali says warmly, walking over and offering his hand to Marcus. Marcus looks surprised but quickly shakes his hand.

Seeing them getting along makes me happy.

"However, hurt her in any way and I promise they will never find your body," Vitali vows.

And then he has to say that.

I roll my eyes, "I know everyone means well, but the next person who threatens my animai is getting a beating from me." My voice deepens and my eyes glow as I let my Alpha Spirit push forward.

Vitali immediately bows his head, but Marcus doesn't flinch. Pride swells inside me. Marcus is my other half, my equal. Now that we have marked each other, my Alpha energy doesn't affect him at all.

"I make no promises," Vitali retorts.

Jerk.

"Can you guys get along while I go talk to Eric?" I ask looking up at Marcus.

"Go do what you have to do. I'll have food waiting for you when you get back," he promises, kissing my nose.

I smile and nod.

Okay, cheer up my other Beta and then fill my tank with my animai so we can talk about the rest of our day. I quickly dash out and walk down the hall to the Beta suite, aware of the extra pep in my step today.

"I wonder why; couldn't be all that dick you got, could it?" Says Zara, cheekily.

"Subtlety is not your forte," I quip.

Oh, I before I forget! *"Vit, don't you dare go interrogating Marcus while I'm gone, I mean it. He's been nothing but amazing since my heat, please don't meddle,"* I implore through our link.

"I promise. I want to try and get to know him for your sake. Last thing you

need is your Beta and animai feuding," he reassures me.

That kind of logic is why I made him my Beta in the first place.

Reaching the Beta suite, I ring the bell and patiently wait. Fortunately it's not too long before Eric comes to answer the door. My heart sinks. Poor thing has puffy bloodshot eyes and tear-soaked lashes and his nose looks a bit stuffy. He's been crying. I got here just in time.

"Hey, Eric," I say gently.

"He sent you, didn't he?" Eric sniffs.

I shake my head. "Technically I volunteered. Can I come in?"

He heaves a sigh and takes a seat on the couch, leaving the door open. I walk in, closing the door behind me.

The Beta suite is very similar to the Delta suite. It has an identical layout and rooms, with the only difference being that Vitali wasted no time redecorating it, settling for corals and soft blues with pops of black. It's very him; soft with minor, hard edges.

I walk over and sit next to Eric on the sectional, "Vitali is freaking out; he hates that he's hurt you and he doesn't know how to fix it. He's scared to say the wrong thing and that says a lot."

"What does that say, exactly?" He asks tiredly.

"That he cares about you a great deal. Vitali has always been the type to say what he thinks and damn the consequences, but with you, he doesn't want to take the risk of hurting you."

Eric sighs rubbing his face.

"What was it about what he said that upset you so much? It can't be that he was sexually active before you, as I know you both weren't virgins," I say, nudging him playfully.

He gives me a wry smile. "It's not that. I'm not sitting here wishing he'd been a virgin."

"Is it that it was with a woman?" I ask carefully.

"What?" He frowns, "No! I don't care that he's bisexual, that's not it either. It's the *what* that bothers me."

Now it's my turn to frown, "I'm not following."

"He slept with an irshiust! A Delegation member! These perfect, near god-like beings. How the hell am I supposed to compare to that?" He says, dejectedly.

My face falls. I wrap my arm around him, "You can't compare. There is no comparing because none of them were his animai. *You* are. You're the very thing he needs to live and he loves you more than anything. That I can say with absolute certainty. I wasn't happy to learn who he'd slept with, but he's an adult so I can't dictate his life for him. But I know that no matter what they had together it will never come close to what he feels when he's with you," I say trying my best to comfort and reassure him. "Do you doubt his feelings? Eric, you're marked, you should know he's genuine just as you should know he's freaking out right now."

This makes him flinch. "No, I don't doubt his feelings. I... I doubt that I'm good enough for him," he says sadly.

"Why don't you think you're good enough for my airhead of a friend?" He shrugs.

"There's a reason you feel this way, please tell me," I encourage while giving his arm a squeeze.

"It's what my ex used to tell me," he says in a whisper, but I hear him just fine.

"What did your ex used to tell you?" I ask cautiously. I'm not going to like this.

"That... I was good enough to fuck but not good enough for a relationship. That my animai would be so disappointed to find out I was his that he'd reject me and run," he says with a shaky breath.

I tap down my emotions and keep myself composed. "I see, and does this ex have a name and a pack?" I ask casually.

He looks at me carefully, "Why?..."

"No reason. Just curious," I shrug. Curious about where I can find him so I can rip out his trachea with my bare hands and ram it up his piss hole. Zara falls over laughing in my head. I guess she found that amusing.

Eric's face contorts in discomfort and before I can ask anything, Vitali storms into the room, chest heaving and face full of rage, "Who is this fucker? Where can I find him so I can beat the ever-living shit out of him?"

Vitali seethes.

"You were using our bond to listen in?" Eric accuses, through narrowed eyes.

"Of course, I fucking was, now who is this motherfucker?"

"It doesn't matter, Vit," Eric sighs.

"Some asshole made the man I love feel not good enough for me, that shit fucking matters to me, Eric," he states firmly.

I bite back a smile. Vitali has always been protective of those he loves and that's only increased for Eric.

Vitali walks over and kneels in front of Eric; I scoot away a little to give them some space. Vitali grabs Eric's face, forcing him to look at him, "What that asshole said is a load of shit. When I ran the night we met, I was running from me, not from you, and I'll regret that till the day I die. I love you, Eric. You make me a better man; you make me feel proud and confident in who I am and there's not a moment I spend with you that doesn't have me in total awe of you. If anyone isn't good enough, I'm good enough for you."

Well, if that wasn't the most romantic thing I've ever heard Vitali say. I almost had tears in my eyes. Actually, Eric does, in fact, have tears in his eyes. Oh, these two are so cute.

"I love you too, Vitali. I'm sorry I got so upset," Eric apologises.

Vitali shakes his head adamantly, "You have nothing to apologise for. Nothing. Do you hear me?" He plants a searing kiss on Eric.

Eric's eyes widen before closing contentedly as he slides his fingers into Vitali's hair, returning his kiss. Okay, now I feel like I'm intruding. I quietly get up and step back to let them be alone. Just as I make it to the door, Vitali stops me. So much for a quick escape.

"Amelia, wait. I was coming to get you anyway. Your parents have returned to the suite and are setting up lunch for the four of you," Vitali says.

"Oh," I say with surprise. "I guess that was inevitable. Thanks for letting me know."

"Aunt Fleur is dressed in all black," he says in warning.

My body goes stiff. Fuck, fuckity, fuck.

Chapter Twenty-Seven
Amelia

This is bad. This is so very bad. You see, my parents balance each other out very nicely. My dad is rational, level-headed, and thinks before he acts. Traits he passed on to me. My mum, on the other hand, can be pretty volatile. Something, if I'm being honest, that was also passed on to me. Oh, for the most part, she's charming, delightful, and upbeat. But upset her in any way and you're up shit creek without a paddle.

As I've mentioned, my mum is the picture of elegance when she dresses and, usually, she sticks to more earthy tones – maroon being her favourite. But anyone who knows my mum knows that when she wants to interrogate or intimidate someone, she pulls out all-black attire. So Vitali telling me my mum is in the Alpha suite all in black with my animai, who she recently sucker punched, has sirens in my head screaming 'mayday.'

"Babe, just how fucked am I right now?" Comes Marcus' voice in my mind.

"I won't lie, it's not good. But I'll be there in a second."

True to my word, I zip out of the Beta suite and back to the Alpha suite at full speed and arrive in no more than three seconds. I compose myself and step into the room. Dad and Marcus sit opposite each other at the dining table, and it looks like they've left a spot at the head of the table for me, which I appreciate. Mum is plating up food for everyone, indeed all dressed in black. A black turtleneck, black slacks, black stilettos, and a diamond tennis bracelet for good measure, because why not? Her auburn hair is piled up perfectly on top of her head, not a strand out of place. How much hair spray did she use? I lock eyes with my father.

"I tried to stop her, sweetheart, but you know how your mother is," he says through the link and I roll my eyes.

"Amelia! Come, join us. You're just in time for lunch," mum announces in an overly cheerful tone.

Oh boy, here we go.

"I wasn't expecting this, this is a pleasant surprise," I say walking over and sliding my arm around Marcus' shoulders. His broad, perfectly sculpted shoulders that can pin me and…

"Amelia! Focus!" Zara shouts.

Right. Wow. That train really derailed. I lean down and kiss Marcus' cheek, but I notice him holding back a smirk. Damn, he knew I was thinking about him.

"I love that I'm on your mind, baby. If I survive this lunch, I hope to be in more than your mind later on," Marcus teases and I feel my heart kick up a gear.

Oh, this man!

I sit at the head of the table and take Marcus's hand when he reaches out for mine. It was only a few minutes, but I already missed being close to him. I never saw myself as clingy, but this damn thread tying us together has a mind of its own. Though I'm hardly fighting it.

Mum finishes serving up the food and takes her seat to dad's left. "So, I see you two marked each other," my mother says while taking a sip of her water.

And we're off, ladies and gentlemen!

"Yes, we did," I smile proudly at Marcus who has the same expression on his face as me. Yeah, we're marked and I'm proud as shit.

"Congratulations, sweetheart," says dad genuinely as he gives my other hand a squeeze. "And welcome to the family, Marcus," he says warmly to Marcus, offering his hand across the table.

Marcus smiles humbly and returns the handshake. At the end of the day, my dad just wants me to be happy, he trusts my judgement and I know he'll be nothing but welcoming to Marcus.

"Hmm, and whose idea was this?" My mum asks.

"Spur of the moment. I asked him to mark me, he asked me to mark him, and here we are. Not much else to say," I shrug and start digging into my food.

"Why did you mark my daughter?" My mum asks pointedly at Marcus. Oh, good grief.

"Fleur…" my dad warns, but she just waves him off.

"Why did you mark Alpha Elias?" Marcus retorts.

Dad snorts and tries to cover it with a cough while I snigger.

Mum's turquoise eyes glow for a second before she reins herself in, "I marked him because I love him, I'm not so sure you love my daughter after the hell you put her through."

"That was then, this is now. This is your first lunch meeting Marcus as my animai and our being together as a family. Can we please not do this?" I implore, but she's hell-bent on ignoring me.

"No disrespect, Luna Fleur, but you don't know the first thing about me or my feelings for your daughter. Not to mention, she's a grown woman with a good head on her shoulders, which no doubt is thanks to the two of you. If you're questioning her judgement on giving me a chance and letting me mark her, then you're saying you have no confidence in how you raised your daughter."

Fuck me that was hot! Even dad is looking impressed.

I'm starting to like this young man. I can see why he was chosen for you. He doesn't cower or back down," my dad shares, and I can feel his approval through our link.

I smile at him, *"Oh, he is full of surprises."*

Mum, on the other hand, has frozen, unable to form a response. After a long pause, she narrows her eyes at Marcus, "How dare you? I have nothing but faith in how I raised my daughter. I trust her. It's you I don't trust."

Marcus rolls his eyes.

"Enough!" I boom, letting out my Alpha Spirit to get my point across.

"Mum, I love you dearly, but I will not sit here and have you disrespect myself, my animai, and a future leader of our pack." I hope. "He and I are linked now; I feel what he feels, and I feel how genuine his feelings are for me. I understand you two need time to get to know each other and that's fine, but do not sit here and give Marcus the third degree on matters you don't have all the facts on. I'm not stupid and I don't make frivolous choices, so you either trust me or you don't. Which is it?"

If I don't put a stop to this now, it sets a bad precedent. It says I don't have Marcus' back and it makes me look bad as an Alpha. I won't have it, not from her of all people. People already look down on me, if people knew my mum was disrespecting me and my animai, I'd be fucked.

Mum looks at me, cowering slightly. While my dad and mum are the former Alpha and Luna, those titles were relinquished when I took over. Which means, while they still hold authority over other wolves in terms of hierarchy, I now outrank them. I can't order them around, but I can make them submit or back down. I never wanted to have to do that, but if my mum keeps this up, she'll leave me with no choice. She loves and cares for me, I know that, but if she makes me choose between her and Marcus, it's an easy choice. He's my soulmate.

"Amelia…" mum sighs, "I'm just worried about you. You know I always hoped you'd find your animai. Knowing how he treated you…."

She glances at Marcus who squirms in his seat. I can feel his guilt through our bond. I don't want it. I want that crap in the past, so I project my love and trust through our bond and immediately feel him relax.

"I get it, I really do. But a lot can change in a week. A lot *has* changed this past week, so please, for me, give Marcus a chance, because this," I say, pointing to the mark on my neck, "isn't going anywhere."

Dad reaches out and rubs mum's back to soothe her.

She sighs and looks at me guiltily, "I apologise for disrespecting you and Marcus." She sighs again, but looks at Marcus, "You see, I always hoped and prayed to Zarseti that Amelia would find her soulmate. I was so excited for that day. Amelia hasn't had an easy life, and I thought the one thing she'd never have to struggle with was meeting her soulmate."

I sigh, understanding her logic. At the end of the day, she's just being protective of her pup. Marcus keeps his eyes on my mum, but his fists are clenched, and I can feel his remorse.

"I wish and hope for you two to be happy, I truly do. I just don't want to see my little girl get hurt," she tells him.

Dad pulls her close kissing her cheek and I stroke Marcus' forearm. I don't want him to keep blaming himself. He said some dumb shit, but that's all he did. It's not as though he assaulted me or cheated on me. So, I don't think the matter is worth holding a grudge over.

"Amelia, I know you've forgiven me, but I'm still so, so sorry for everything I said and did. I..." he says in a broken voice.

I press my finger to his lips to silence him, "It's in the past, you have more than made up for it. We can only move forward, so let's do that, okay?" I caress his cheek, his beard tickling my palm.

He closes his eyes and holds my palm in place as he inhales my wrist, "I can do that."

"Good. Now let's enjoy this delicious food because I'm hungry as hell," I chirp.

Marcus and dad chuckle, mum gives me a gentle smile, and we settle into a more comfortable atmosphere.

Lunch was actually great after that little debacle. Mum was her usual charming self and she and Marcus were quickly getting along. I can see dad already viewing Marcus as the son he never had. I don't say that bitterly. I know my father has never for a moment wished he had a son; he loves me unconditionally. Marcus talked about his pack, his family, and even his first shift. It was one of the best lunches I've ever had. I can only hope it goes smoothly when he meets my grandparents or when I meet his parents. I fear his mother and I are going to clash like oil and water.

After lunch, we make our way downstairs hand in hand and, as cliché as it sounds, I feel like I'm walking on air.

"That went a lot better than I expected ," Marcus says.

"If that was considered 'better,' I hate to think what you actually expected."

"More punches, that's for sure. Your dad seemed to like me," he beams proudly.

"Dad definitely likes you," I smile. "He respected the way you stood up for me and for us."

"Even though I was talking back to his Luna?" He asks dubiously.

"He knows what mum is like and he wasn't on board with her interrogation plan, he made that clear to me when I came in."

He nods as we continue to walk. "So, what's next on the agenda?"

"I do believe we both agreed to go for a run," I smile playfully.

His face splits into a wide grin, "I vaguely remember that."

"Finally! I haven't been let out in days!" Zara says in exasperation.

I feel bad for that. I do my best to let her out every day, but what with going into heat and getting distracted by Marcus, I never managed to find a moment.

"Don't feel bad, I'd say getting distracted by our animai and that bitch of a heat are pretty good excuses. You still let me out more than most mutolupus'," she shrugs.

"Thank you for understanding, but I think it's time you got to be with Ace," I tell her.

I kid you not, she did a backflip. A freakin' backflip! This wolf has got her jumping over backwards and they haven't even met yet – officially.

"Is Zara as excited as Ace?" Marcus asks in amusement.

"Oh, you have no idea," I chuckle. We make it to the back of the packhouse and I start unbuttoning my jeans.

"What are you doing?" Marcus asks in a disapproving tone.

"Taking my clothes off?" I say, cocking my head to the side.

"I don't want everyone to see you naked," he huffs, "That's for my eyes only."

I roll my eyes, "They've seen me shift before. Come on, Marcus you know our kind don't care about nudity." I take my top off, putting it with my shoes.

"Yeah, well, you weren't a marked woman then," he argues, though he's eyeing me hungrily.

"Uh-huh. Just out of curiosity, how many women have been up close and personal with you and your naked glory?" I question, folding my arms over my chest.

His body tenses and I can feel both guilt and annoyance coming from him, "I thought you didn't judge me for my past."

I sigh and run my fingers through my hair, "You can feel through me that I'm not judging you. I'm just pointing out that while people have and will see me naked before and after I shift, there has never been anything sexual about it. Whereas I'm guessing many women have seen the most intimate sides of you. I understand being territorial, but this is in our nature. Or would you rather I ruin my clothes every time I shift?"

He sighs in defeat, "Why do you always have to be so logical about everything?"

I chuckle and move closer, wrapping my arms around his neck and shivering as he wraps his arms around me. "That's just the woman I am. But I do like you being possessive of me," I say as I capture his lips in a long, slow, passionate kiss. He growls against my lips and for a moment we're lost in the movements of our lips as they caress each other.

Best. Kisser. Ever.

We break for air and he presses his forehead down on mine, "Time to shift my Sexy Little Alpha."

He squeezes my ass and it sends pleasure straight to my core. Why does that feel so damn good? He's got that stupid smug, sexy smirk on his face again. Damn him.

I finish taking off my clothes and let Zara push forward. A burst of searing heat and my jaw elongates, canines protrude, bones rearrange, nails turn into claws and fur sprouts all over my body. As usual, I let Zara take the reins and feel as she shakes out her fur. She wastes no time as she walks over and licks Marcus' face.

Flirt.

"Hi there," he chuckles as he reaches out to stroke her fur. She lets out a low, contented grumble, enjoying how his hand feels in her fur – heavenly. "You're a beautiful wolf, Zara," he says in awe as he looks her over and gives her a kiss on her snout.

She yips, licking his face and then tackles him to the ground, pressing her snout against his chest. As much as she wants to play with Marcus, she is eager to see Ace. Can't say I blame her. She's probably cock hungry too.

"*I heard that. You should wash that foul mouth out with soap,*" she tsks.

"*What?! Who said it first?*" I ask pointedly.

"*I don't know what you are referring to,*" she says, feigning ignorance. Cheeky thing.

"I get it, I get it, you want Ace," Marcus chuckles, rubbing her neck. "I'll shift before Ace gives me a headache.".

Marcus makes quick work of undressing and, in a flash, he's on all fours in his wolf form. Goddess, he is the most gorgeous wolf I have ever seen! He has the most vibrant russet coloured fur from nose to tail. His fur is a bit thicker around his neck and he still has those amazing spring-forest eyes. He's perfect! Oh, and he's only a fraction shorter than me, not very noticeable.

Zara is absolutely elated. I've never felt her this happy. Twenty-one years together and while she's always been a happy wolf, right now she feels whole, and I am thrilled for her. For us. Ace strolls over to her and nuzzles her. She gladly nuzzles him back. Aww, these two wolves make me want to cry. Ace starts grooming Zara in a way that is so loving and tender, it warms my heart.

"*I think they're happy,*" comes Marcus' voice in my head. I keep forgetting we can link now.

"*Very happy,*" I agree.

"*How often do you let Zara be in control?*"

"*Always. It's an agreement we made long ago. Zara has full control in this form unless there's an emergency, and vice versa.*"

"*Wow. I don't know many wolves, let alone Alphas, who so easily give total control to their wolves,*" he says.

I can feel a mixture of awe and concern emanating from him. "*Most wolves and Alphas aren't as in sync as we are,*" I respond.

It's not long before Zara and Ace are bounding off into the woods together; chasing and nipping at each other, tugging each other's tails. They are having the time of their lives and I'm thrilled. At some point their playfulness shifts and before I know it, Ace is making his intentions clear and Zara is presenting to him.

Oh boy.

I don't hesitate to retreat further back into our shared mind. It's a peaceful, quiet place. Like being in a state of meditation, only far more effective. I'm vaguely aware of everything going on, but it's easy to tune out. I want to give Zara and Ace their time together, just like she did for me and Marcus.

I don't know how long they were at it, but eventually, I feel Zara tugging me back, which is her way of giving me the all-clear. I let myself come forward and am aware of Zara and Ace snuggled up on the forest floor together. My heart is melting!

I can hear a deep rumbling laugh echo in my head. *"Who knew you were so excitable, Amelia,"* comes a new, teasing voice. Oh! Ace! Now that he and Zara have mated, I can speak to Ace and Marcus can speak to Zara.

"What can I say? I just love you two to bits," I coo, making him laugh. I hear him sigh. *"What's wrong?"* I ask, concerned.

"I'm sorry for everything Marcus put you through. I hope you know I don't share those views and neither does Marcus anymore," says Ace gently.

"You don't need to apologise for him, Ace," says Zara echoing my thoughts as she nuzzles Ace. He licks her snout.

"Zara's right. Not only aren't you to blame, but it's in the past. Dead and buried. I'm over it and I want you to be too," I say firmly.

"Ace has nothing to apologise for, but I do. I'm so sorry, Zara. I know you and Ace clicked instantly and my dumb ass got between you too. I'm sorry that my words and actions hurt you and Amelia," Marcus says solemnly.

"It's true, you were a dumb ass," Zara says in casual agreement and I roll my eyes. *"But you have made up for it, so I forgive you."*

Marcus chuckles but I can feel his relief, *"Thank you, Zara."*

As much as I would love to let these two hang out in the forest all day, I have to check in on things, especially the start of development on the expansion. With great reluctance, Zara gets up and Ace, along with her. They begin trotting back towards the packhouse keeping close, so their fur is always touching. Ace really is the most gorgeous wolf.

"Oh, stop," says Ace shyly, *"You're going to make me have a big head."*

"She's going to make you have a big something," Marcus teases.

"No one asked you, jerk. Our animai was giving me the compliment," Ace says haughtily.

Zara and I both chuckle. *"Are you two always like this?"* Zara asks.

"Oh, yeah," says Marcus.

"For sure," says Ace.

Zara and I chuckle some more. These two are definitely going to keep things interesting.

We're strolling at a leisurely pace when Evalyn's panicked voice forces its way into my head. *"Amelia! Something is wrong with Izac! Kylie was cleaning the dining hall and she dropped screaming in pain. She's saying something has happened to Izac. Whatever it is, it's still happening, I can't calm her down,"* she cries.

Fuck, I had Izac following Ryker. If someone – especially that little shit Ryker – has done something to him, I'll fucking rip them limb from limb. I reach out through the link to try and get a sense of where Izac is and I find nothing but static on the other end.

"Send for someone from the hospital to see what they can do; I'll try and find Izac." While I'm giving instructions to Evalyn, Zara is filling in Ace and Marcus as she takes off at a sprint with Ace following at her side. Two heads are indeed better than one. *"ATTENTION ALL WARRIORS!"* I boom through the pack-link to my warriors, *"Something has happened to one of our own, Izac Mallod. Patrols start scanning your designated locations. Remaining warriors fan out to your respective quadrants. I want Izac found now!"* I order.

"Yes, Alpha!" They shout and I can feel their determination through our link.

A cold chill creeps down my spine and Zara picks up the pace, a sense of urgency humming between us. Something bad is happening. Very, very bad. As Zara's sprinting through the territory, pain lances through me like someone just pierced my heart and it's quickly followed by a snap. The snap of a pack member dying. Zara lets out a howl of pain, loses her footing, and goes tumbling across the forest floor. She whimpers but forces herself to her paws as Ace rushes to her side, nudging her with his snout to help her up.

"What's happened?" Marcus asks in a panic.

I can't even form the words to answer him, neither can Zara. She pushes away the pain and the feeling of emptiness and takes off again, now with more determination.

"Alpha, we found him," comes the devastated voice of one of my warriors.

We pick up on his location through the link and race towards it. As we approach, the scent of death is on the wind and something rotten. Zara's footing slows down the closer we get until we approach two warriors standing by a large tree with their heads bowed and their fists balled at their sides. Zara walks over to where the warriors are standing what we see has the blood in our veins turning to ice.

Chapter Twenty-Eight
Marcus

A ce is acting like the cat that got the cream since he and Zara mated – multiple times.

"Hey! Do not call me a cat, that's racist!" He shouts indignantly.

"Calm down, Cujo, it was just an expression," I say rolling my eyes.

He gasps, *"Now you're calling me a rabid dog, the insults just keep coming."*

Believe it or not, this is Ace in a good mood. Damn wolf is practically ng on air, and I know the feeling. Being connected to Amelia and Zara redible. I'm thrilled I get to talk to her wolf now and Ace can talk to ia. Naturally, his first topic of conversation with her was throwing me the bus. My wolf is such an asshole.

o not say it takes one to know one!" I exclaim cutting Ace off before he eak. He's quick to clamp his muzzle shut. Yeah, I know him too well. e're returning to the packhouse when suddenly we feel panic radiating Amelia as Zara comes to a standstill. Ace nudges her shoulder letting hine of concern. Something has happened.

ack member has collapsed in pain screaming that something has happened nimai. Amelia is assembling the warriors; we need to find him," Zara to us. Zara doesn't wait for a response from either of us, she takes print much faster than the speed she was running when she was ith Ace. At first, I didn't think Ace was going to be able to keep up with her, but to my surprise, he's keeping up with her very nicely.

"Of course, I am. We've marked and mated with an Alpha, that's made us stronger," Ace scoffs. Huh. Completely forgot that's how it works, but then again I never expected to rank up… though I don't really know what my rank is anymore.

For some reason, Zara starts running even faster, which I didn't think was possible. She's in the zone, focused on her task, I can feel hers and Amelia's determination and dread. Suddenly Zara lets out a howl filled with pain and anguish. We can feel a slight echo of that pain through the bond – an uncomfortable snapping sensation. Whatever it was, Zara and Amelia took the brunt of it, causing Zara to lose her footing and topple headfirst. She's whimpering – though not from the fall – and trying to push herself up. Ace is at her side in a heartbeat to help her up. We're both fucking terrified because we don't know what's going on.

"What's happened?" I ask Amelia and Zara urgently.

Neither respond. Instead, Zara just gets up and takes off in another direction with Ace quickly following. We're not leaving her side, not after all the shit that has happened lately.

As we run along, we pick up the scent of blood, death, and something almost rotten. Not like garbage – It's not something we've ever smelt before. Zara slows down and approaches two very naked warriors who have their heads bowed. They're keeping their composure, but I can tell they are distraught. A horrible icy chill spreads through us and it's coming directly from Amelia. We follow to where Zara is standing and pale at the sight before us.

A young man, with short blonde curly hair and fair skin, has been bound naked to a large tree and I wish that was the worst of it. I've seen a lot in my time as Beta, but never have I seen anything this gruesome. He's covered in blood and large black veins are protruding all over his body. There is a wide gash across his abdomen that looks like it's infected. Black blood is pouring from the wound, resembling tar. The smell has Ace and me heaving.

If that wasn't bad enough, the words 'see you soon' have been carved into his chest and I know immediately who the message was intended for.

Black, tar-like blood is pouring from the poor man's mouth, eyes, nose, and ears and, even though he's dead, there's nothing peaceful about him. His face is contorted in unimaginable pain. Whatever was done to him, it was clearly a slow and agonising death.

Zara shifts back into Amelia. She's looking up at the body; her own body rigid, her face stoic, and her eyes cold as glaciers. She's in complete control, but with us now bonded I can feel exactly what's going on under the surface. Fucking hell, I knew she kept her feelings hidden, but I never realised the extent.

She is simmering with rage, disgust, pain, sorrow, and even guilt. It's a storm of emotions swirling around inside her, crashing into one another and yet on the outside, she remains calm. Is this what it's always like? Every time she has that calm mask on her face is this what she's hiding inside? How the fuck is she able to hide all of that? Seriously, not a single crack in her façade.

However, I am getting better at reading her. When she was confronting Davina, her eyes were calm; almost bored. But the look in her eyes now is cold and murderous. There's something else under all those other emotions, something lethal and thirsty for blood and it's clawing to get out. Not going to lie, it's kind of scaring the shit out of me.

I want to hold and comfort her, but the threat may still be near so Ace keeps his form and stays close to Amelia so he can protect her if something happens. I've never seen Ace so worried before. He's staying close and brushing against Amelia to try and give her comfort through contact.

"Hospital staff are on their way to collect the body. No one touches him until they get here," she says in a monotone voice that makes me shudder, and not in the good way.

"You want us to just leave him like this?" One of the warriors asks incredulously.

If I were in their position, I'd probably react the same way, but I can feel how sick Amelia feels. She hates that she's doing this.

"Yes. I know what killed him and if there are traces of it left on his body and you touch him, you'll end up the same way," she says flatly.

What the fuck *does* something like this? But I understand, she's trying to protect anyone from meeting the same fate. The colour drains from the warriors faces as they take a step back from the body.

Amelia never takes her eyes off the young man's body as we wait for people to arrive. Soon enough a team in full hazmat gear arrive, get the man down from the tree and place him in a body bag. As they cart him off, Amelia dismisses the warriors but continues to stand there, frozen. Ace lets me shift back and I quickly step closer and pull her into my arms. I've never seen her like this, and I don't think I ever want to see her like this again. It's unbearable.

"I'm right here. It's going to be okay," I whisper into her hair as I stroke her back. But not even my touch eases her tension.

"It'll be okay when I find the son of a bitch who did this," she says in a low, primal voice that has the hair on the back of my neck standing on end.

⬥Amelia⬥

There's so much rage inside me that everything around me is just a haze. Any other time Marcus' touch would soothe or excite me, but not right now. I feel the electricity, but it is doing little to settle the beast stirring within.

Izac was tasked to follow and monitor Ryker. Now he's dead. I don't believe in Santa Claus or coincidences; I want that son of a bitch to answer to me. No more defence. I reach out through my link to my pack until I find my tether to Ryker.

"RYKER MATHERS, AS YOUR ALPHA, I COMMAND YOU TO RETURN TO THE PACKHOUSE IMMEDIATELY!" I growl as I project every ounce of my Alpha Spirit through the link. I'm not giving him a fucking choice. I shift back letting Zara take over as we make a dash for the packhouse. I feel Marcus shift back into Ace and follow us.

"Amelia, please talk to me. You're worrying me," Marcus says, his deep concern piercing me.

"It's okay to show how you feel with him. He's our soulmate, you don't have to bury the emotions anymore. Not from him," Zara says gently.

While I show a lot to my friends and family, there are parts of me I never let anyone see, and as far as Marcus and I have come, I just don't know if I'm ready to share those parts with him just yet. But he deserves to know what's going on and I appreciate him not prying into my mind.

"His name was Izac; he was our best spy. Yesterday I assigned him to follow the former Beta's son. Now he's been killed using the same substance that one of the wolves attacking us the other day tried to use on me, and his body left as a message for me," I say matter-of-factly.

"What is this substance?" He asks, but I could feel his anger and fear when I mentioned the threat to my life.

"Wolfram. A highly poisonous metal for our kind, symptoms of which are incurable. Someone tried to stab me with wolfram, but Chris took the hit for me. I watched as he screamed in agony and those black veins spread through his body." The memory of Chris on the brink of death cuts me deeply. I swear I'll make whoever did this pay.

"If it's incurable, how did he survive?" Marcus asks in confusion.

"Mei's gifts as a nagata saved him," I tell him, not specifying that she has the ability to heal people.

We arrive at the packhouse, Zara letting me shift back as I find our clothes and make quick work of getting dressed.

"Amelia, Kylie is in one of the guest rooms under heavy sedation and Ryker just arrived at the packhouse. He keeps trying to leave, but he just ends up screaming in pain," comes Tyson's voice in my head.

"Because he's under my command. Have him taken to an interrogation room in the cells and restrained. I'll be there soon," I instruct.

"Yes, Alpha," he says before cutting the link.

"I have to go to the cells and interrogate someone," I explain to Marcus as he gets dressed.

"Do you want me to come with you?" He asks cautiously.

I ponder that for a moment. On one hand, I do want Marcus close, but I'm not ready for Marcus to see this side of me. Not to mention, while we may be marked, Marcus hasn't acknowledged my pack yet, nor has he acknowledged his position in the pack I just know when that conversation finally arrives, it'll go over about as well as a fart in a car.

"I need to do this on my own, but thank you," I say trying to convey my sincerity, but I don't think it's coming out in my words. Everything I say or do right now is laced with rage that I am barely keeping tapped down.

Marcus comes closer taking my face in his hands and tilting it up to his. His vibrant forest eyes looking into mine, full of love and concern. "Link me if you need anything. I will be right here," he says as he places a slow kiss on my forehead.

I want so badly to get pulled into the sensation that his skin on mine causes me, but I have a traitor to find and an enemy to kill, so that will have to wait.

"Thank you," I whisper as I kiss each of his palms and pull his hands from my face.

With that, I turn on my heel and head straight for the cells. With each step I take, I let the beast inside me make its way to the surface. I let the bloodlust course through my body, breathing life and strength into every limb. I'm going to enjoy what comes next.

Chapter Twenty-Nine
Amelia

I am greeted by Caleb as I enter the cells. He nods solemnly while I sign the logbook. As usual, news travels fast.

"Gamma Tyson has the prisoner in interrogation room one."

I nod and make my way down the hall until I get to the hallway that houses the interrogation rooms. I see Tatiana standing guard outside room one on the right-hand side. She gives me a quick nod and opens the door for me. I nod and step inside.

It's a small white square room with a reinforced titanium table in the middle that is bolted to the floor with a chair on either side facing each other, which are also bolted to the floor. There's a two-way mirror that runs the length of the wall on the right-hand side. On the other side of the mirror is the observation room, but we won't be needing that today. The only source of light in this room is a single lightbulb in the ceiling, which isn't overly bright, but the white walls make it seem brighter. But with wolf eyesight, it could be pitch black and we'd see just fine.

Ryker is sitting in a chair at the table facing the door, his hands chained to the table in silver cuffs that are burning into his flesh. Tyson is leaning against the wall on the back of the room, burning holes into the back of Ryker's head.

"Why the fuck am I here you crazy bitch?!" Ryker screams. His quick jerk causes the cuffs to bite into his skin making him cuss in pain.

"That's Alpha to you, dipshit!" Tyson growls grabbing a chunk of Ryker's hair and tugging his head back. "Watch your fucking mouth," he warns in a seething tone, then roughly lets go of Ryker's hair.

"First thing's first, did you kill Izac?" I ask flatly, pushing my Alpha Spirit on him full force.

His body starts to buckle under the weight of it as sweat beads form on his brow. "No!" He shouts, panting through clenched teeth.

"Do you know who did?" I continue. He tries to fight against answering my question, but the more he fights the worse the pain becomes.

His face is turning red, and his dark brown eyes appear almost black, "YES!" He screams collapsing onto the table. "Please stop!" He begs with tears in his eyes.

"I imagine that's what Izac said as he was dying. He probably begged for the pain to stop as it ravaged his body, turning his blood into poison," I say coldly, feeling my anger festering.

"I already said I didn't kill him! Go torture somebody else!" He says in a rush.

I step closer, planting my hands on the edges of the table and lean into him and feel satisfaction at his whimpers of pain from being so close to my energy. The closer I am, the more it hurts him, and I want this to hurt.

"But you did say you know who did. So next question, who killed Izac?" I calmly ask. Once again, he fights with his wolf, trying to resist the urge to obey his Alpha. An ear-piercing scream breaks from him as the pain becomes too much. I'm surprised he's fighting it at all. I pegged him as too weak for that.

"My uncle! It was my uncle!" He cries, panting harder. His breathing is becoming more laboured by the second. Tyson and I exchange a look.

"Mykel Mathers? How do you know that?" I question.

"Because he found out… Izac was following me, so he… got him out of the way so he wouldn't spoil his… plans," he says, trying to catch his breath.

"And yet killing Izac resulted in the same thing happening. Now all he's done is successfully pissed me off. Next question, what are your uncle's plans? Is his Alpha behind the attacks on my pack?"

Though his face is contorted in pain he shockingly starts laughing maniacally. Tyson glances from Ryker to me with a worried look. I just know what I'm about to hear won't be good.

"His Alpha?" He snorts weakly. "You're so oblivious. My uncle *is* the Alpha," he says with a smug smirk. Tyson's head snaps up in shock and, while I am shocked and confused by this revelation, I don't let it show.

Ryker isn't lying, he can't while under command, so let's break this down. Mykel left our pack after conspiring to break both pack and supernatural laws. He joined the Ruber Flumen Pack, an enemy pack, and after that neither were heard from again. Since he wasn't born an Alpha, the only other way to become one is by challenging and killing one in combat, thereby inheriting their pack and power. It would explain why that pack went radio silent all these years.

"Mykel is the current Alpha of the Ruber Flumen Pack," I conclude.

"Well, he wasn't a fan of the name, so he changed it," he shrugs. He's trying to act tough and nonchalant, but he stinks of fear. As if his liquorice scent wasn't bad enough.

A thought bursts to the front of my mind and a new level of anger erupts through me. It must have seeped into my energy because Ryker is immediately weighted down by it, writhing in pain.

"Is the pack's new name 'Roanoke'?" I ask in a low voice. Ryker can hardly move or lift his head, but his eyes snap to me and they are wide with alarm.

Bingo.

That sick motherfucker recruited by animai's ex into this bullshit. What, is she plan C, D or E? I'm definitely killing that slut the next time I see her.

"How did you know that?" Tyson asks in confusion.

"Just so happens Marcus' crazy ex was banished from her pack only to be welcomed into a pack I'd never heard of. The Alpha ordered her to never say his name and promised that if she helped him, she would get Marcus back. I'm going to go on a limb here and guess that helping him and getting Marcus means killing me," I say impassively.

"Why the fuck is he doing all this?" Tyson asks, rubbing his face.

"Good question," I grip Ryker's face in my hands. My eyes are glowing as I let Zara's claws come forward and tear through his skin. His eyes bulge with fear as he groans in pain. I bet he's never seen a partial shift before. They're incredibly hard and incredibly rare. "Why is your uncle doing this? I assume he's the one who sent the threats, I'm even going to guess you were the one who poisoned me," I say, leaning close enough to hear Ryker gulp.

"H-he wants your pack! He wants revenge against Alpha Elias for siding against him, and he wants you dead so you can't ruin and weaken our species. My parents were always sharing information with him, but then you killed them, and he had to move his plans forward. He had me slip you the wulfenite, but you survived, so he attacked your pack," he forces out.

"You filthy little traitor. All you Mathers' are fucking sick in the head," Tyson spits.

"I guess I'm not as weak as you all thought. At least I'm not turning innocent humans into mindless monsters and using them as cannon fodder," I say menacingly.

Ryker looks confused, "What are you talking about?" Ryker asks quietly.

"Didn't you know? Your uncle has been using his status as Alpha to turn humans into a mutolupus so he can build an army. Yet you claim I'm the one ruining our species," I scoff, shoving his face away as my claws retract. The holes my claws put in his face are dripping with blood; his injuries unable to heal due to the silver.

"You're lying. My uncle would never do that," he argues.

"Oh, he would and he did. In fact, it's one of the reasons he left the pack in the first place. I see your beloved uncle hasn't been sharing all the facts with you," I say in mock sadness.

"Fuck you! My uncle will kill you, but I hope he drags it out. I hope he captures you and tortures you for years. I hope he tears into your tight little pussy and makes you his bitch until you die," he says with sadistic glee.

My stomach is heaving, but my face once again remains neutral. Can't say the same for Tyson though as his pale blue eyes start glowing and a murderous snarl rips out of his chest. He reaches out, wrapping his hand around Ryker's throat, squeezing until his face goes red.

"What. Did. You. Just. Say. To. My. Alpha?" He says slow and menacingly as Ryker gasps for air.

"Let him go," I order.

Tyson quickly lets Ryker go and steps back, his chest heaving. Ryker coughs and splutters. Weak excuse for a mutolupus. He's all bark, no bite.

"If you would be so kind, please go and get my kit," I instruct.

"Gladly," Tyson smirks as he steps out of the room.

"Kit? What… kit?" Ryker asks.

"I'm glad you asked. You see, you have a long list of crimes. Conspiring against your pack, conspiring against your Alpha, poisoning your Alpha, and aiding in the murder of a pack member. If you thought you were leaving here, you were sadly mistaken," I tsk.

"If you're going to kill me, j-just k-kill me already," he stutters, his voice betraying his fear.

I let out a cold chuckle, "Who said anything about killing you?" I relish watching the blood drain from his face.

"Y-you c-can't," he tries to argue.

"Oh, but I can." At that moment Tyson walks in, handing me a black pouch. "Thank you. Please stand outside," I instruct.

"Ame-" Tyson begins to protest, but I wave him off.

"I said, stand outside," I order. I listen as he sighs and steps out, shutting the door behind him. "Now, time to have some fun."

I place the black pouch on the table, pull the drawstrings, and watch it unfurl. Inside, are various torture tools I keep – only for extreme circumstances. This calls for it.

"Wait, I told you everything! I answered all your questions!" He fights against his restraints, groaning and crying out as the silver burns.

"That you did, right before saying you hope your uncle rapes me till I die, if I'm not mistaken. Or did I mishear that?" I quiz.

He gulps, glancing between me and the tools, perspiring furiously now, "Please, I'll do anything."

"Anything?" I ask, putting on a pair of leather gloves.

413

"Yes! Anything! I swear!" He cries.

I nod thoughtfully as I put a set of silver knuckles on each hand, "Then let me hear you scream."

I hear the sizzle as I land a vicious punch to his face, the silver connecting with his skin. His bones crunch and blood spurts from his mouth and splatters against the white walls. I let the beast take over as I throw right hook and left hook, over and over. The more blood I draw the more I crave. I'm in a complete blood rage. I'm landing punch after punch, to his face, his ribs, his stomach. Anywhere I can reach.

I can feel his blood on me and I crave more of it. His screams and grunts are sounds of sweet delight and I need more. For the pain he caused me. For making me hurt my friends. For betraying me. But most importantly, for Izac.

Izac's deformed, rotting corpse carelessly tied to that tree, with words carved into his flesh, will be forever burned into my mind. He was a good man; he was a kind and loyal man. He loved Kylie more than life itself. They were planning to try for their first pup. He had goals and dreams and a future and now, it's all gone. This sick son of a bitch and his sick psychotic family took that from him. They took his life; they took his future and they destroyed Kylie. For that I want him to suffer, and whatever I do to Ryker, I will do to his uncle tenfold.

Time seems to lose all meaning. I don't even feel fatigued. I just keep unleashing my wrath upon Ryker, wanting him to feel every ounce of pain Izac felt, I'm not even in control anymore.

"Amelia, stop!" Comes a voice that lights up every nerve in my body.

The sound of it breaks through the blood rage and I find myself looking down at Ryker, my chest heaving. What the fuck have I done? I step back, shocked at the scene before me. Ryker is barely breathing and he's no longer recognisable. He's just a mangled meat-suit, all bloody, bruised and broken. Only now am I aware that I am covered in blood.

Large arms wrap around me and pull me close. I breathe in the delicious scent of caramel and feel the tension slowly leave my body.

"It's okay. You can stop now. I've got you," Marcus coos against my ear while stroking my hair.

I never wanted him to see me like this. But instead of being disgusted with me, he's comforting me. He's calming and quelling the blood lust inside and I'm letting him. I give myself over to our bond and let myself escape into it, desperately needing a reprieve.

Chapter Thirty
Marcus

Leaving Amelia alone didn't feel right. It felt wrong as fuck. But I could feel that she needed to handle this without me, so I reluctantly gave her space. That doesn't mean I'm not tuned into her emotions though. Never been more grateful for our bond than I am right now.

Walking into the packhouse the atmosphere is desolate. There are pack members scattered around consoling each other, some are angry, some are sobbing; just a mix of emotions that I completely understand. Losing a pack member is never easy. Packs are tight-knit; it's how we thrive and survive. A wolf needs a pack, so losing a member of our pack hits us all hard.

I didn't know the guy, but his death has affected even me. I feel angry that someone could do that to him. Just thinking of how painful his death must have been, has me grinding my molars together. Looking around at all the despondent faces cuts right through me. I want… no, I *need* to help these people. I can't explain it, but I feel protective of them.

"Really? You can't think of a single reason why you might feel protective of these people?" Ace asks sarcastically.

"No. They're not my pack, I'm not linked to any of them, so it's weird," I explain.

Ace rolls his eyes and flops down. *"Just when I thought you'd finally seen the light,"*

"What's that supposed to mean?" I snap, but he decides not to grace me with a response. Ever the asshole.

I head upstairs hoping to find one of Amelia's friends and end up finding Chris and Mei whispering in the hallway of the third floor.

"But I could have saved him, you know I could have saved him," Mei says in desperation, tears in her eyes.

"It was too late. Listen to me, my love. You can't save everyone. It's not your responsibility either." he says gently, cupping her face.

"You won't even let me try. What is the point of all these gifts if I can't use them to save good people?" She sobs into his shirt as she fists the fabric.

Amelia had mentioned it was Mei who saved Chris from ending up like that warrior but didn't specify how, but now I'm extremely curious. What gifts does snake lady have exactly? I still can't fucking believe nagatas are real. Did not have that on my supernatural bingo card.

"Is everything alright?" I ask, walking over to them.

Chris looks up while he has his arms protectively around Mei. He gives a curt nod, "We'll be fine. This is just hard for all of us."

"I'm sorry for your loss," I say sincerely and he nods.

"Where's Amelia?" Chris asks with a hint of worry in his voice.

"Interrogating the person she had your warrior shadowing," I answer as Chris snorts. "Is there a problem?" I ask curiously.

"I'd be surprised if Ryker survives, let's just say that," he says stiffly.

"If he was behind what happened, then I don't see the problem. Whoever did this deserves to fucking die," I spit with more aggression than I anticipated.

"Oh, I completely agree, he's not who I'm worried about," he says with a frown.

"You're worried about Amelia," I conclude.

"Is she in danger?" Asks Mei as her head whips up to look at Chris. For a brief moment, her eyes flash, stunning me. They were the eyes of a snake! Bright golden yellow eyes, not a trace of white to be seen, and a long black pupil down the centre. Now that was fucking cool.

Chris smiles and tucks Mei's hair behind her ear, the action so gentle, I wonder if she even felt it. "She's not in danger, my love. I swear," he reassures her.

I really do love how much she cares about Amelia; I like this young woman. Though I wonder why she's so protective. According to Amelia, it was Chris who saved her, so why does she have such a strong allegiance to someone who biologically is inferior to her? No disrespect to my woman.

"But?" I ask.

He sighs, "Nothing. I shouldn't have said anything."

"Too late, it's out. Now speak," I say firmly, crossing my arms. Fat fucking chance I'm letting him backtrack. Sweet little Mei's eyes narrow at me. Guess she doesn't like me speaking down to her man. Too bad.

"You've seen Amelia when she's upset, how calm she becomes," he reminds me.

I nod, "I have become very familiar with it, it's impressive."

"It is, but that's just one version of upset Amelia. That version is like the appetizer before the main meal, and no one wants the main meal. She hides it, but some of us have seen glimpses of it, and it's kind of terrifying."

I frown but think over his words. I detected a side of Amelia that is bloodthirsty, and I could feel it simmering under all her emotions when she found Izac. Now that I focus back on my link to Amelia I can feel that same rage almost boiling to breaking point. Like a volcano on the brink of erupting. It's hard to picture Amelia as terrifying, but I know there's a dangerous side to her. I heard it when she broke Davina's hand. I'll be the first to admit hearing her threaten and maim Davina got me hard, but what I'm feeling from her now, has me worried.

"But it's not like she'd just unleash that on innocent people," I clarify.

"Of course not, and if Ryker is guilty then I hope she makes the little dickwad suffer," his comment makes Mei giggle. Chris doesn't seem like the type to curse or get angry much, so I can understand why him calling someone a 'dickwad' would be funny.

"I will never get used to you swearing," she says sheepishly.

"I hope not, I would hate to taint such beautiful ears with such vulgar language," he replies, kissing each ear and making her blush scarlet. These two are clearly very in love. "Oh, congratulations by the way," Chris says with a wide smile.

"Congratulations?" I repeat with confusion.

"On you and Amelia completing your bond," he says jutting his chin towards my neck. On instinct, my hand fly's up to the left side of my neck where Zara's paw print is printed on my skin. Just touching it sends tingles through me.

"What?!" Mei shrieks then turns to me, looking at my neck. Her eyes widen and she starts bouncing up and down with glee. Either she's warming up to me, or she feels safer with Chris around. Whichever, I'll take it. It's amazing to think this young woman bouncing up and down without a care in the world suffered such disgusting abuse. The world is a fucked up place sometimes and treats even the purest souls like trash.

"Calm down, xingan baobei," Chris chuckles wrapping his arms around Mei pulling her back to his front. Her face has gone bright scarlet again. I have no idea what he just said, but I'm guessing it was something sweet.

"Welcome to the pack!" Mei cheers happily.

"Oh, I haven't joined the pack," I clarify making her frown.

"But you and the Alpha are marked now," she says meekly.

"He hasn't been officiated into the pack yet. They'll figure that out in their own time," Chris explains gently while kissing her cheek. She relaxes into his arms though she still seems deep in thought. I give Chris an appreciative nod.

I don't regret marking Amelia; I couldn't be happier. But am I ready to leave my pack? Do I want to be a part of this pack? What would I even be to this pack? The only thing I know for a fact is that I want to be with Amelia always. It's every other fucking thing I can't figure out for life nor money.

Just as I'm in the middle of having yet another stupid battle with my fucking conscience, I feel white-hot rage surge through me so strongly it nearly knocks me off my feet. I grab onto the wall for balance to stay upright.

"Marcus, are you okay?" Chris asks, grabbing onto my shoulder to steady me.

Am I okay? Fucking hell… that feeling wasn't coming from me, that was Amelia. I focus more on her and what I feel is hard to process. She feels feral… there's anger and grief colliding inside her and erupting in this primal, feral rage that just craves pain and blood. The strength of it has me shuddering and feeling a little queasy.

"I have to get to Amelia. Excuse me," I say as I race back down the stairs and out of the packhouse. I follow the pull of our bond and it leads me to where the cells are.

I see myself in and some guy – I assume a guard – looks me over suspiciously, "Who are you and what are you doing here?" He questions aggressively in an attack stance.

"Your Alpha's animai, now where the fuck is she?" I growl.

His eyes nearly fall out of his head. "I-I'm so sorry, I didn't know," he bows his head in submission. "She's in interrogation room one, it's down this hall, then take the hall on the left and it'll be the second door on the right… you have to sign the logbook though."

I roll my eyes but decide to follow protocol. It's there for a reason. After I sign my name, I take off at top speed. I get to where he told me to go and I can feel I'm in the right place. There's a woman standing by a door with Gamma Tyson pacing near her. His head snaps up when he hears me coming. I don't ask questions. I don't ask permission. I don't give two fucks right now; Amelia needs me and that's all that matters.

I yank the door open and step into a small white room… well, I'm sure it *used* to be white. There's blood splattered all over the fucking walls and ceiling like a Jackson Pollack painting, but that's not what shocks me. What shocks me is the sight of my sweet little Alpha – my queen – pummelling the fucking shit out of some guy.

Her breathing is ragged, her eyes look far away, and her Alpha Spirit is radiating off her like she's gone nuclear, though it doesn't seem to affect me like it once did. She's wearing gloves and what looks like silver knuckles. She's covered in blood and the guy she's demolishing doesn't even look alive anymore, he looks like fucking roadkill. From the looks of her, she's not even tired. She just keeps landing punch after punch to his beaten body. It takes me a moment to snap out of my shock and find my voice again.

"Amelia, stop!" I shout, and she does. She freezes like my voice has snapped her out of a trance. Her hands drop to her sides, and she steps back examining everything around her like this is the first time she's seeing it. I can feel her shock along with the rage and blood lust she had a second ago, subsiding, leaving behind nothing but the sorrow she was feeling.

I rush over and pull her to my chest, hoping my touch and scent will calm her and I feel her relax, which relaxes me in turn.

"It's okay. You can stop now. I've got you," I whisper in her ear as I stroke her hair. I feel her surprise and her relief but also shame. I need to get her out of here. I keep her wrapped in my arms and pull her out of the room with me. I look up at Tyson who is now looking down at Amelia with concern.

"Whatever the protocol is in these situations, do it. I'm taking her to get cleaned up," I instruct. He doesn't argue, he just nods and steps into the interrogation room.

I pull Amelia with me, but I can feel she's walking on autopilot, so without hesitation, I pick her up and race to the Alpha suite. As I enter, I see Amelia's parents and grandparents sitting on the sofa talking. As soon as they see the state of Amelia, they're up on their feet.

"What happened?" Asks Elias quickly. I can hear the panic in his voice.

"She's bleeding!" Her mother gasps, rushing over to take her out of my arms. I tighten my grip, not bothering to stop the growl that erupts out of me. No one, and I mean fucking no one, is taking her out of my arms. Her mother steps back in surprise, but she's not afraid, which isn't shocking.

"It's not her blood," I state firmly. "She was interrogating your Beta's son," I say looking at Elias. "I guess she got the answers she needed because when I went in, she was beating him half to death. But after the state your dead warrior was left in, I can't say the little fucker didn't have it coming." I say defensively, just in case they disapprove of her actions. I won't say what happened didn't shock the fucking shit out of me, but I don't disapprove. As Alpha, these are the kind of things that fall on your shoulders. She hasn't done anything wrong, at least not by supernatural standards. Humans might disagree, but fuck 'em, what do they know?

Elias sucks in a deep breath and I swear my words make him age rapidly. He runs his hands over his face.

"I told you. I told you that making Mykel your Beta was a bad idea and I told you that brother of his was no better. Mykel and Declan were too much like their bitch of a mother Romona and nothing like Lark. Ryker clearly didn't fall far from the tree; both his parents were traitors too," Amelia's grandfather spits in disgust.

"Really dad? Now is not the time for 'I told you so'," Elias retorts.

"He's right, dear. It does no one any good," says the former Luna, Sorrell, as she places a calming hand on her animai. Yeah, I was paying attention at lunch.

"Mykel..." Amelia whispers.

"What is it, my Little Alpha?" her father asks as he moves closer.

Thank fuck I say 'sexy little Alpha' instead of just 'little Alpha' or the bedroom is gonna get awkward real fuckin' quick.

"Let me get her cleaned up and then she can fill you in," I say pointedly.

Elias looks up at me with a brief flicker of annoyance until he looks over his daughter and frowns. He nods in agreeance, "You're right, it can wait." He steps back, wrapping his arm around Fleur. I expected him to fight me on that. He's not as hard-headed as most Alphas. I can see where Amelia gets it from.

I dash into Amelia's room and take her straight to the bathroom, setting her down on her feet. Her eyes are cast down and I can feel her shame.

"Ma Reine? Look at me," I say tilting her chin up. She reluctantly looks up at me and her eyes are unreadable. It makes my heart clench. Even Ace is whimpering. "I need you to take the knuckles off, I can't touch them," I tell her gently.

Realisation flashes in her eyes and she hastily pulls the knuckles off, tossing them in the sink, quickly followed by the gloves. Good, we're making progress.

"Can I undress you?" I softly ask. She looks at me and gives me a slow nod. I give her a smile, hoping it relaxes her a bit. Carefully I rid her of her clothes and toss them in a hamper in the corner of the bathroom leaving her in her bra and panties. Any other time I would be worshipping her body, but there's nothing sexual about this. This is just me trying to look after my woman because I can feel right now, that's what she needs.

I am about to put on a bath for her when suddenly her hands are undoing my jeans. My brain temporarily short-circuits as I freeze, watching her in confusion, "What are you doing?" I ask like a moron.

"Seriously, I want to talk to your parents and find out just how many times you were dropped on your head. What does it look like she's doing, jackass?" Ace mocks.

She doesn't answer me, she just proceeds to lower my jeans and my briefs exposing my dick. I gulp as she moves onto her knees giving me the most incredible view. My gorgeous woman, on her knees for me, in red lacey matching underwear. Fuck, that's my favourite colour on her. Wait, no. I should stop this. I should stop this, right? This is wrong. She's not in her right mind.

"Please, let me do this," she quietly pleads.

The desperation in her voice fucking guts me. I look down at her to see her waiting patiently for my response. I can feel her need for a distraction, her need to feel something other than what she's feeling. If this is what she needs right now, who the fuck am I to say no? Seriously, as long as she's okay with it, so am I.

"Okay, baby," I say while softly caressing her cheek. I feel her relief and I too relax a little.

Instantly she wraps her hand – or tries to – around the base of my length and electricity shoots through my dick and up my spine making me jerk my hips and groan. Gods, how can a single touch be this fucking good? While holding me with her perfectly firm grip, she traces the veins of my cock with her tongue, and it causes me to roll my head back.

Fucking hell, for a woman who is only doing this for the second time, she's a mother fucking pro. Her tongue swirls around the head of my cock and teases my slit, her actions have me harder than granite. My dick is so fucking hard right now it could put a dent in steel. She gingerly sucks on the head and fire spreads through my body.

"Fuck, Amelia," I hiss as I put my hand on the basin counter for support. I have to resist the urge to shove my cock down her throat. I don't want to hurt her. But maybe she is reading my mind – which is possible now – because she starts taking my hard length into her warm, wet mouth, inch by fucking inch and it's sweet, sweet torture.

Her mouth starts working my cock, her movements slow but deliberate as her tongue strokes the underside and I'm unable to hold back my grunts of pleasure. The feeling of her pretty mouth wrapped around my cock is unlike anything else. As she works my length, she takes in more and more of me, like she's slowly working on stretching herself out to fit me. She's not actually going to try and take all of me, is she?

With slow, steady movements I watch in blissful awe as more of my cock disappears into her perfect mouth. She keeps going until her nose presses against my lower abdomen and I can feel my cock in her throat. She swallows and the sensation of her throat muscles squeezing my cock is…

"Fuck!" I cry out. "Fuck your mouth feels so fucking good, baby," I pant as I look down at this incredible woman. I wrap her hair around my hand holding it into a ponytail and as I do, she starts going to town on my fucking cock. "Sweet fucking Gods…. yes… oh, that's it," I moan as she sucks my dick like she's a dying woman and my dick is the only thing that can save her.

She looks up at me through her lashes; drool dribbling down her chin from the speed at which she's devouring my length, her pebbled nipples straining against the fabric of her bra, and I'm completely enraptured watching her. There's something about having this sexy Alpha on her knees swallowing my cock that has me feeling more powerful than I could have ever imagined. It sends pleasure coursing through every cell in my body and I feel more alive than I ever thought possible. No one has ever made me feel the way she has, and no one ever will.

Every muscle in my body is coiled in anticipation, my balls are tightening, and my ass is so clenched, it could crack a walnut. I can't stop groaning and grunting, she has me feeling too good to keep quiet, and I notice how much she loves it. Every sound I make increases her arousal. It fills the room, the scent of it driving me to completion. But it's the moan she lets out around my dick that does me in. The vibrations of her sexy fucking moan shoots through me, pushing me over and on autopilot, I tighten my grip on her hair and shove my cock in her mouth until it hits the back of her throat as I explode in wave after wave of mind-numbing pleasure, causing black spots to dance around my eyes.

"AMELIA!" I cry as I come down from this unbelievable high, she continues to take me on. She slowly pulls back, letting me fall out of her mouth with a pop as I stand there trying to catch my breath. "Fucking hell you're incredible," I say reverently. No fucking way she isn't a goddess, I refuse to believe otherwise.

I help her to her feet and capture her lips in a bruising kiss that she eagerly returns as she wraps her arms around my neck. I can taste myself on her and it is fucking driving me wild, I feel ready to go again. But I don't want to be greedy, I just can't help what she does to me.

"Are you okay? I didn't hurt you did I?" I ask concerned, as my lips brush against hers.

She smiles against my lips as she runs her fingers through my hair, "You didn't hurt me, I enjoyed it," she says planting another kiss on my lips. I smile and relax. I mean, I am sure I'd have felt her pain or discomfort, but then again maybe I'd have been too out of it to notice. Her blowjobs fuck with my head. Aww hell, *she* fucks with my head. But fuck, do I love it.

"Come on, let's get you in that bath," I coax her, kissing her forehead. I step out of my shoes, socks and pants and toss my shirt off and turn the bath on. I notice some bottles of bubble bath so I add a bit and splash the water to get the bubbles to appear quicker.

I turn back and help her out of her bra and panties, which are once again soaked through. Fuck do I love what I do to her, maybe even more than I love what she does to me. I can't stop myself. I look her dead in the eye as I pull her panties to my face and inhale deeply, letting the glorious scent fill me up. Her eyes widen as she watches me, but her pupils dilate, and I feel her desire grow. Another wave of her arousal perfumes the bathroom and I know she's getting wetter. We're going to have to do something about that.

I help her into the tub and step in behind her. I grab her loofa and I take my time washing her body, being gentle with my movements. I just realise my woman gave me a killer fucking blowjob while she was covered in blood like the mastermind behind a massacre, and if I'm being honest there was a part of me that was more turned on for it. Maybe that's sick, but what the fuck ever.

"Amelia?" I call her name getting her attention.

"Hmm?" She hums.

"You don't have to tell me, but I wanted to ask what happened in the cells." Her body stiffens and I feel her become nervous. Hold up, nervous? She's nervous? Somehow nervous and Amelia just don't go together. "Baby, listen to me. I'm not disgusted or scared of what I saw, I'm just worried about you. What I felt coming from you... I can't describe it. I just want to understand." I pull her against me. I grab a washcloth and gingerly clean the blood off her beautiful face. She sighs relaxing into my touch.

"I never wanted you to see me like that; for anyone to see me like that," she says apprehensively.

"Why? You wouldn't be the first Alpha to beat or torture a criminal, it's a natural part of your job," I gently reassure her as I work on wetting and washing her hair.

"Sometimes that side of me scares me, but what scares me more is..." she trails off with a shaky voice.

"How much you enjoy it?" I guess is where she was going.

She nods. "I have a theory. But I'm no psychologist, so maybe I'm just making up excuses."

"Tell me your theory," I prompt as I massage her scalp. I always imagined doing things like this with my fated half. While the conversation is serious, I'm still thrilled I get to do this with her.

"I told you how I had to learn to repress my emotions. I don't believe emotions are a weakness, but some people reading those emotions can be dangerous, especially when they want to use them against you. When some Alpha or Alpha heir would come along and give me shit or try to goad me into proving myself – which was really them looking for a way to put me in my place – I always had to squash the need to beat the ever-living shit out of them," she growls.

"I would pay good money to see you put those fuckers in their place, baby. Just picturing it is hot," I say, kissing her mark.

She shivers and lets out a soft giggle. Gods I love that sound.

"Point is, I could never react. I never wanted to give them the satisfaction no matter how badly I wanted to react. Over time, when I would get angry, I could feel this part of me stir, a part that craved blood and pain; that wanted to crush my enemies and bathe in their blood," she takes a shuddering breath. "Sometimes the intensity scares me, other times I thrive on it. I love how strong it makes me feel, I love how it… excites me."

I grab her hips lifting and turning her around so she's straddling me. She yelps in surprise as I rest her on my thighs while trying hard not to think about how close my length is to her core. It's harder than you may think. Way fucking harder.

"Listen to me. We may have a human side, but even without our wolves, we are still more animal than human. Hunting, fighting, those things are ingrained in us. We all have this strong animalistic side to us; I think it's weaker in some wolves than others, but can come out with the right trigger, like seeing your animai hurt. Pretty sure that would fucking do it," I say as I gently rub her thighs, her eyes staying on mine. "If I had been there the day you were attacked and I saw that fucker trying to kill you, I guarantee I would have revelled in tearing him to bloody pieces and dancing in his entrails." My Sexy Little Alpha smiles and laughs. I'm glad to see she's relaxing. "There's nothing wrong with you, and what you said makes sense. You can't repress your emotions without them erupting into something catastrophic. That being said, I don't think badly of you for it. It shocked me, I can admit that, but since we're giving confessions, here's mine: seeing you blood-crazed, beating someone within an inch of their life while covered in their blood… it's a fucking turn on." There, I said it.

I watch as her eyes widen in surprise, but her surprise quickly vanishes and all that's left is raw carnal desire. Fucking hell, even through the water,

I can smell her arousal. Just how potent is this? I don't have time to think as she grabs my face crashing her lips down on mine in a hungry kiss. I kiss her back with as much hunger; growls erupting from both of us. I pull her body flush against mine, her hard nipples rubbing against my chest, sending blood straight to my dick.

I buck my hips rubbing my length against her folds and relish the moan it elicits from her pretty mouth. Her breathing increases as she trails passionate kisses down her neck down to my mark. She bites and tongues my mark, sending hot pleasure through my veins as I groan into her shoulder. I tighten my hold just as she starts rubbing her sweet pussy against my dick.

"That's it, baby, make yourself feel good with my cock," I growl as I capture one of her nipples into my mouth, sucking and teasing with my tongue, occasionally giving a gentle bite and tug. She throws her head back, moaning. I grab her hips and urge her to keep moving against me, but it's not enough. I want more. As I keep sucking her pert nipple, flicking it with my tongue, I guide my hand down between us and find her little nub. I apply a little pressure as I start rubbing it in circular motions.

"Oh fuck!" She cries, digging her fingers into my shoulders. Fuck how I love seeing her like this. No one will ever know this side of Amelia; her pleasure is just for me. "M-Marcus," she pants, her face and chest flushed with her ecstasy.

"You like me touching you, baby?" I ask, captivated by the way her body moves, the way her tits rise and fall as she pants.

"Yes, so much," she breathes. I capture her other nipple in my mouth and begin my assault on it, her fingers buried in my hair, tugging it in the way I now fucking love. I halt my movements on her clit and she whimpers in disappointment. I try not to chuckle. I slide a finger over her entrance and just tease her opening with small flicking motions.

Her body squirms as she mewls. I can feel her craving the pleasure I'm giving her and needing more. The combination is driving her wild and I feel powerful knowing I'm the one doing it to her. Said it before and I'll say it again, any man who doesn't want to see his woman like this ain't no fucking man.

I decide to give her what we both want. I slide one finger into her warm walls and I groan around her nipple at the feel of her. She shudders, letting out a long salacious moan. Oh, we're not done. She's so fucking soaked, I get no resistance. I insert another finger and begin pumping into her at a steady rhythm. I cup the back of her neck with my other hand and lock my eyes on hers.

"Keep your eyes on me, baby, I want to see you when you come," I instruct. My words make her walls clench around my fingers. I hiss at how good it fucking feels. My lips are on hers as my fingers move in and out of her, her moans vibrating through my lips. I capture and suck on her bottom lip. "You like my fingers inside you?" I ask in a husky voice. She nods breathing heavily. I release her neck and give her right breast. a hard squeeze. She yelps.

"Use your words, I want to hear you," I order as I wrap my hand back around the back of her neck.

"Yes! I fucking love your fingers inside me... fuck... Marcus, it feels so good!" She cries, her words making my dick throb and twitch almost painfully.

"That's what I wanted to hear," I growl. I tighten my grip on her neck, my eyes on hers as I curl my fingers in a come here motion as I start finger fucking her hard and fast. She squeals in pleasure, her eyes clamp shut, her body going taught and her hands fisting my hair for dear life. "That's it, come on my fingers, baby, let me see you shatter," I coax as my eyes never leave hers.

She forces her eyes open to look at mine just like I'd instructed, her jaw is slack, her breathing laboured, and I can feel her walls fluttering as her orgasm nears. I increase my pace and I know she's close as her breathing stops altogether. Her muscles are locked, her thighs are quivering and like a floodgate unlocking, she screams in ecstasy, her body convulsing as her orgasm rips through her, her walls clenching around my fingers like a fucking vice. I continue my assault on her little pussy, riding out her orgasm until her body collapses against mine. She takes in deep lungfuls of air.

I slowly remove my fingers as she pulls back to look at me. Her beautiful face flushed rosy, red from her climax. She looks beautiful beyond words. With my eyes on hers, I bring my fingers up to my mouth and slowly suck her juices off my fingers. I groan as my eyes roll back. Fuck me dead, she tastes like a piña colada! Oh yeah, I'm going to get drunk on that pussy.

Her eyes darken as she watches me, and I once again capture her lips with mine letting her taste herself on me. Her moans fill my mouth as my fingers knot her hair while she tugs on mine. We break apart panting, but we're both all smiles.

"Let's get out of the tub, huh?" I say, stroking her cheek. She smiles and nods and tries to get out, but I tighten my hold on her.

"I can't get out if you don't let me go," she chuckles.

"That's not true," I argue. While holding her I get up and step out of the tub, "See?" I grin cheekily. She laughs some more, gracing my ears with the sweet sound. We dry off and wrap the towels around us, making our way to the bedroom, but I notice the sheets have been changed. "Who changed the sheets?" I ask sniffing the air.

"Maggie, she's head of the packhouse staff and the only one allowed in the Alpha suite," she explains casually.

"You're not worried she'll have seen and smelt the signs of last night's events?" I ask with a raised eyebrow.

"Nope," she says popping the P. "Maggie is the epitome of professional and I have nothing to be ashamed of. I spent an amazing night with my soulmate." She shrugs and sits down on the bed. My chest puffs with pride knowing she is proud of what we did because I sure as fuck am proud too. I walk over and cup her face, placing soft kisses on her cheeks.

"Are you feeling better?" I ask gently.

"About beating the shit out of Ryker, absolutely. About Izac…" she trails off and her features become sad.

I sit down and pull her into my arms, "It's okay to be sad, I won't think less of you for it, I promise. Let it out," I say comfortingly.

I guess that was the permission my strong Alpha needed because she finally lets out her grief. Her body shakes with sobs as she cries onto my shoulder for her lost friend and warrior.

"He was a good man. He wanted to be a father and he would have made a great… one. He was loyal and compassionate, and he loved his animai more than life itself. They were so happy… and now… I don't know how she'll live without him," she cries into my shoulder clinging to me like a life raft. I hold and console her and just let her cry.

I've lost friends before and even though we know this is part of our life, that loss never gets easier. But as an Alpha, Amelia felt it. She felt the moment he died and his connection to her was severed. Even I felt an echo of it through the bond. That's not something you easily get over and, as I've learned from Jasper, it's not something that gets easier with time.

Chapter Thirty-One

Amelia

It felt nice to just let it all out knowing Marcus was there to comfort me. I didn't realise how much I'd needed that in my life, how much I'd needed him. Marcus is kind, loving, patient, protective, and he loves me. Experiencing him like this makes it hard to believe he was ever the man who tried to put me down for being an Alpha, but I'll just blame his mum for that.

After I got out my tears, we got dressed and I filled my parents and grandparents in on everything I learned from Ryker. I'm glad Marcus came in and stopped me before I killed the little turd. I don't want him dead; I want him to suffer for everything he's done. He fucked with the wrong Alpha and soon his uncle is going to learn that too. He wants me, he can fucking come and get me.

I went to check on Kylie in one of the guest rooms. The sight of her broke my heart. She was pale, her eyes looked sunken, and she was wailing hysterically. No words of comfort or touch of affection could console her, and I didn't want to insult her by trying. She's feeling the one pain all of us fear ever experiencing: the death of our soulmate. I can't begin to fathom her pain, but I know if I ever lost Marcus, I couldn't go on. I wouldn't want to. There's no point to living if it's without him.

Marcus came with me to interview each person on patrol to try and figure out if any of them had let Mykel into the territory. I don't want to think the worst of my pack, but I'd rather think the worst and be wrong than assume the best and lose someone else.

Izac's dead body will forever haunt me. I've fought; I've seen dead people before, but nothing like that. I wouldn't even give Ryker such a brutal death and he'd actually deserve it. I wince each time I realise Kylie felt everything Izac went through, and I despise Ryker and his family all the more for it.

After conducting my interviews Marcus and I return to my office to convene with Vitali, Tyson, and Chris.

"What did you find out?" Tyson asks warily.

"Nothing. They were all clean," I inform them. They each sigh with relief.

"Thank fuck for that," Vitali breathes, running his fingers through his hair.

"So then how did this happen without anyone noticing?" Chris inquires.

"Mykel was the former Beta of this pack. He would know the territory like the back of his hand. I don't think it would be too hard for him to get in undetected, especially with his nephew feeding him information. However limited it may be, it would still have been useful."

"What happens now?" Vitali asks.

"I start the funeral arrangements," I sigh. Marcus walks over putting his arm around me and I accept his comfort.

"Has Kylie seen the body yet?" Chris asks cautiously.

I shake my head. "She's in no condition, plus they need to prep him. Make sure there are no traces of wolfram and have him look as decent as they can. I don't want Kylie to see what I saw; she shouldn't have to remember him like that." I grip Marcus' hand on my shoulder. At that moment, there's a notification on my phone. I check it and see a text that lifts my spirits marginally. "That's a text from Yildiz. She and Nuray will be arriving tomorrow morning."

Vitali groans, "Maybe I can sit this meeting out?"

"Yeah, not gonna happen. You're my Beta. You're sitting in on that meeting."

"You can't be worried Nuray will make a move on you. She's a child of Zarseti, they would never do anything to disrespect an animai bond," Chris says confidently.

"Chris is right, so what's the problem?" Tyson ask.

"I'm worried about Eric. He told me more about his ex-boyfriend and I swear if I ever find that son of a bitch, I'm going to hit him so hard he'll have to shove a toothbrush up his ass to clean his teeth," he seethes.

Marcus and Tyson have a good laugh over Vitali's colourful threat.

"That bad?" I ask sympathetically.

He nods, "I'm not worried about Nuray, she's a good person. I just don't want Eric to feel insecure because she's here. He's my first priority."

"Don't bite my head off, but maybe you should let him meet her," I say.

Vitali looks mortified and Tyson looks amused.

"Are you fucking insane?! That's the worst idea I've ever heard!" Vitali screeches, flailing his arms around.

"Wouldn't the worst idea be sleeping with a Delegation member?" Marcus says with a cocky smirk.

"Ha, good one!" Tyson says and they exchange a high five.

Chris and I roll our eyes. At least Marcus is making friends. Vitali growls at them, and not playfully.

"Are you done?" I ask Vitali in a bored tone.

Marcus snorts beside me.

"It's not happening, Amelia," he states firmly.

"Fine, don't take my advice," I shrug. "I don't think we have anything else to go over, so you're all dismissed."

They each nod and leave the room.

"I like those guys," Marcus says, leaning against my desk.

I smile, running my fingers through my hair, "I like them too, I'm lucky to have them. Speaking of friends, have you spoken to Jasper?" I move between his thighs and wrap my arms around his neck as he wraps his arms around my waist.

"I sent him a text updating him while you were filling in your parents."

"He must miss you, are you missing your pack?" I ask tentatively.

"Not as much as I thought I would, to be honest. I mean, I do love and miss them, and I miss those knucklehead friends of mine, but that doesn't compare to how I'd feel if I wasn't here with you," he says, brushing his nose against mine, making me smile.

"I don't like the thought of you leaving," I admit, resting my ear on his chest and listening to the steady rhythm of his heart.

"Good thing I'm not leaving. Not yet, anyway," he says, stroking my hair.

His last words make my heart twinge. We're both still avoiding the big conversation and we've let other things work as a distraction. But those distractions won't be there forever.

"I don't know about you, but I'm starving. Let's go get something to eat," I say, pulling back.

"We're both definitely going to need to refuel," he winks, making me giggle like a little girl. How embarrassing. Already there's an ache of need between my thighs at what might be in store for us later.

As I walk around the table, something out the window catches my eye. I walk over to the far window and look out to see Mei out in the training field in the distance. She's training with some of the other warriors. I'm stunned. When did this development take place? Though I'm thrilled to see it, that took a lot of courage on her part and by the looks of things she's kicking their asses. I smirk. I feel Marcus' arms slide around my midsection and my body becomes electrified as his scent engulfs me.

"What's my Sexy Little Alpha looking at?" He asks against my ear, his hot breath eliciting a shiver from me.

"Mei. She's getting in some after-hours training with some of the warriors, without any of us around."

He looks through the window and I can feel his awe watching how she moves, "Remind me not to piss her off."

I laugh, but feel proud, "She's lethal, I've copped the brunt of some of her punches and kicks and they hurt like a bitch, even though she was going easy on me. Which I told her not to do. But she doesn't seem to be holding back with these guys, which is good."

"You want her inflicting injuries on everyone?" He asks with amusement.

I gently elbow him making him grunt and laugh into my hair. "No. I'm just thrilled to see her embracing who she is and not being afraid of her strength," I clarify.

"That makes sense. She's definitely impressive," he compliments and kisses the top of my head. "Come on, let's go eat," he grabs my hand, pulling me away from the window and out of the office.

Making our way to the dining hall, I hear Evalyn going over the grocery budget with some of the staff – much to my surprise. She usually doesn't take an interest in that stuff, but I noticed she's pitching in more lately. Even more surprising, I see Eric consoling some of the warriors who were close to Izac. He may be new, but he's treating them like family, and I can't say how proud I am to see it. I take a moment to take in what I'm seeing as the cogs in my head start turning and an idea forms.

"I like where your head's at," Zara says approvingly.

"Do you think we can pull it off? Or is that too much change?"

"The entire mutolupus species has been living in the dark ages, it's time to step into the twenty-first century. Change can be scary, but that doesn't make it bad. I say go for it," she chirps confidently.

"When this threat is over and Mykel is dead, I definitely will."

Marcus

I'm officially not a fan of the Delegation. Amelia and I spent the entire night making love, with maybe some fucking thrown in and we'd probably still be at it if it weren't for the fact she knew we needed to get up and greet them. So yeah, they're officially on my shit list.

We're now standing on the steps of the packhouse waiting to meet our distinguished guests. I'm nervous as fuck, which isn't so bad since it means Amelia has kept a tight grip on my hand the whole time to calm me down. Vitali, Tyson, and Chris are also radiating nerves. Vitali, more than anyone else.

I can't deny standing here with them feels right, but at the same time, it makes me miss Jasper, Calix, and Aiden. I've known them my whole life, can I just give them up? But then again I can't give up Amelia. That's not even an option.

Everyone is dressed to impress – no one more than my woman though. Amelia has her sunshine hair up in a low bun that sits on the back of her neck, allowing her to showcase my mark on her neck. Fuck, I start getting hard every time I see it. She's wearing a tight, black pencil skirt that goes up to her waist with some fancy silver chain detailing in the middle of the band. She's wearing black leather pumps – which I know are Louboutin's. I may be a man, but I know what a red bottom shoe on a woman means. As for her top, there's no fucking way she chose that top fortuitously.

Last night I told her how much I love the colour red, especially on her, and this morning she's wearing a red blouse, with a sweetheart V-neck and lantern sleeves tucked into her skirt. This little minx knows exactly what she's doing. She's showcasing the Mark of the Alpha on her chest and giving me a perfect view of her spectacular tits, which I very much want to bury my face in right now.

I've gone for a black dress-shirt, but I've rolled up the sleeves, left three buttons open and paired it with tight black jeans and, with the way Amelia keeps checking me out, her desire flaring through our bond, I have no regrets. Not a fucking one.

Vitali is in a white dress shirt with a couple buttons open and beige khakis. Tyson is in navy blue slacks and a pink Ralph Lauren dress shirt with a few buttons open. Then there's Chris. I'd say he was trying hard, but from what I can tell, dressing up is just what he does. He's wearing navy blue slacks, a pale blue pinstripe dress shirt, a brown tie, and a navy blue vest. Not a wrinkle on him. He and Vitali are also both sporting man buns, which I've noticed is Chris' signature look. I rarely do the man bun, and if I do, it's only when training.

"Please try and be on your best behaviour," Amelia pleads through our link.

"When am I not on my best behaviour?" She gives me an incredulous look.

"Okay, point taken," I concede.

At that moment, a white Sedan pulls into the driveway and makes its way to the packhouse. The windows are tinted so I can't see anything, but I don't have to wait long. When it parks, two women step out and I find myself blinking rapidly. They're both gorgeous – not as gorgeous as Amelia, mind you.

The first is about 5'5" with soft mocha skin. She has thick dark-brown – almost black – braids that reach to the top of her bustline and are parted to the right. She has a dusting of dark brown freckles across her cheeks and nose, accompanied by these intense golden eyes. And I mean gold. Her irises sparkle like liquid gold and her skin is glittery – it has this natural golden glitter in it that shimmers as the light touches it.

I'm sure for humans it would look more subtle and would appear like she lathered herself in that body shimmer women like to wear – which I fucking hate. You can't kiss the body of a woman covered in that shit, it gets fucking everywhere. You ever tried to get body glitter out of your sheets? It can't be fucking done. I hope whoever invented that shit rots in hell, but I digress.

She's dressed for business, though. She's wearing a knee-length dusty lilac dress that has a black stripe down each side, sleeves down to the elbows with black cuffs and these random cut-outs near the armpits that are trimmed with black and finish in black bows on the shoulders.

The other woman is a bit taller; I'd say about 5'8". She has rich brown skin and long black braids in a half updo, the rest reaching down to her waist. She has the same liquid gold irises as the other one and the same gold glittering skin. I'm going to assume these are traits that signify they are irshiusts. She's wearing a dress that ends just below the knee and that has tiny sleeves that barely count as sleeves. It's white at the top, black at the bottom and has this weird pattern in the centre.

Sometimes I think women's clothing is just made up of subliminal messages we men will never understand. A guarded secret code meant to drive us insane. I'm broken from my conspiracy theory when both women launch themselves at Amelia. She squeals in delight, returning their hugs.

"It is so good to see you!" The one in black and white shouts with a thick accent I can't place.

"It has been far too long!" The other woman shouts with the same thick accent.

"I know, but it is so nice to see you both. I'm sorry it's not under better circumstances," Amelia says solemnly.

"We're here now. Congratulations on taking over as Alpha, we are so proud of you," the shorter of the two says and it sounds genuine.

I've noticed since they walked over I've started to feel way more relaxed. I feel almost… serene. Like everything is going to be just fine. It feels nice.

The taller woman suddenly starts screaming with glee. Jesus, are they trying to make me go deaf?

"You found your animai?! Oh, this is wonderful!" She cries, her sights now turned on me, golden eyes twinkling.

Amelia chuckles and steps back, taking my hand again. "Yes, I have. Yildiz, Nuray, this is my animai Marcus, Marcus this is Yildiz and Nuray, members of the Delegation," she says, introducing the shorter woman as Yildiz and the taller one as Nuray. Now I know which one Vitali banged.

"It's an honour to meet you both," I nod in greeting.

Should I shake their hands? Or is that rude? What's the protocol here?

"And we are thrilled to meet you," Yildiz rejoices.

"Ladies, please meet my Delta, Chris; my Gamma, Tyson; and I believe one of you has already met my Beta, Vitali," Amelia says pointedly.

Wow, she is not even a little intimidated by these women. Then again, I'm not as intimidated as I thought I'd be. The one named Nuray laughs, and it sounds so… magical? Is that a proper description? I don't know, I'm saying it anyway.

"It's very nice to see you again, Vitali, and a pleasure to meet the rest of you," she says with a warm smile. Then, her eyes home in on Vitali's neck like they had with Amelia's and she's screaming with delight again. Come on! Can she warn us first? She's going to blow out my eardrums.

"You've met your animai, too!" Nuray cheers. "Oh, this is such wonderful news. Let me guess, it's a man," she says, with a knowing smile.

Vitali's eyes nearly fall out of his head, "How the hell did you know that?"

"Yeah, how did you know that?" Yildiz asks curiously.

"Now this I gotta hear," Tyson says gleefully while Chris elbows him.

"I always knew you were bisexual. You checking out a few guy's asses gave it away," she chuckles. "As for your animai, Zarseti knows what she's doing when she makes a pairing. I figured she'd choose someone for you who would allow you to be your truest self and she did. Our mother is no fool," she says smugly.

"It's true. Her pairings are always for a reason. Though we don't presume to know what they are, we trust them," Yildiz smiles in agreement.

It's weird hearing them call a Goddess their mother, but I guess since she waved her hands and magically brought them into being, that does classify her as their mother.

"If you knew I was bisexual, why didn't you say anything?" Vitali grumbles.

"It wasn't my place. You can't force someone out of the closet, that has to be their choice. But I'm thrilled for you. It's good to see you embrace who you are," Nuray says warmly.

Vitali's face softens, "Thank you, Nuray."

"If we're done with the catch-up, shall we go to the conference room and get to business?" Asks Amelia.

"Always so professional," Yildiz quips. "Please, lead the way," she prompts.

Well, this is going to be an interesting meeting.

Amelia

I would love nothing more than to sit and catch up with these women – I can't tell you how good it is to see them again – but they are here for a reason and after yesterday's events, I can't afford to get side-tracked.

I lead everyone through the packhouse, down a hall to the right and through a set of double wood doors. We step through into the conference room, which is a large room with grey carpeting, a large, circular reinforced mahogany table, and top of the line black ergonomic chairs. The walls are lined with deep caramel wood panelling, various art pieces and a large screen at the far end of the room.

We file in and I take my seat at the far end of the table facing the direction of the door, while Chris closes and locks them. Marcus takes a seat on my right and Vitali next to him on the other side, followed by Tyson and Chris. Yildiz and Nuray take the seats to my left. I already have a folder in front of my seat waiting for me.

"Fifty bucks says Marcus puts his foot in his mouth," I joke.

Zara rolls her eyes, *"He's come a long way; I think we won't have any problems. Have a little more faith."*

Oh, I have faith. I just also know Marcus pretty well by now.

"Now you explained you have reason to believe a law has been broken, requiring our intervention. Please, start from the beginning," Yildiz instructs, her tone warm as always.

"My pack has been under threat since the day of my elevation. I only now realise the challenges made against me were just the tip of the iceberg. After that day I began receiving anonymous threats, the threats eventually held weight when I was poisoned with wulfenite."

Yildiz and Nuray gasp at my words, as does Marcus. I reach out and rub his forearm and he puts his hand over mine.

"You're lucky to be alive, Amelia," Yildiz says with concern, placing her hand over mine.

I smile graciously, "I know, and I am grateful every day. Shortly after that my pack was attacked by thirty-two wolves. During the attack, my Delta was stabbed with a wolfram laced dagger that was meant for me."

Their eyes widen in alarm and snap to Chris.

"You should be dead," Nuray states flatly.

"That's harsh," he frowns while Tyson and Vitali snigger.

"There's no cure for wolfram poisoning, so how are you alive?" She asks suspiciously.

"My animai saved my life," he says with a goofy smile on his face.

"Your aura is stronger than that of any Delta I've seen. Much stronger,"

Yildiz says with intrigue.

Nuray scans Chris until her eyes zero in on his neck. She looks shocked. "You're bonded to a nagata."

Yildiz nods thoughtfully. "Is his mark black and gold?"

"It is," Nuray confirms.

"Explains the aura then," Yildiz smiles and nods in understanding. "Well, that answers that. How fortunate you are to have such an animai. The Gods must like you."

"Wait, why does the colour of my mark matter?" Chris inquires.

"We would prefer not to answer that at this current time. Amelia, please continue," Nuray instructs.

An irshiust is incapable of telling a lie, so it's clear they don't want to answer that question. They know something but don't wish to say it and so are avoiding the question. I've learned to respect their wishes. Forcing their truth just upsets them.

"My warriors captured one alive and after a delay on my part, I was eventually able to interrogate or attempt to interrogate our prisoner. He was feral. He wouldn't speak and he didn't respond to my Alpha Spirit," they perk up, "I quickly noticed he had no wolf spirit. I had our hospital staff run a blood test that showed the young man's wolf enzymes were not binding to his red blood cells, meaning…"

"He was born a human," Nuray concludes grimly.

I nod mournfully. Knowing we killed so many innocent humans who had no control over their actions makes me sick to my stomach. Marcus must feel it as he reaches his hand out for mine and I gladly take it.

"What else can you share with us?" Yildiz asks with a sympathetic tone.

"A lot. Much has come to light since I contacted you. I've learned the person behind these attacks is the former Beta of this pack, a man named Mykel Mathers. He left the pack years ago due to irreconcilable differences and joined an enemy pack, the Ruber Flumen Pack. I have learned that, since that time, he killed the Alpha of that pack, took over and renamed the pack Roanoke. He has been using his remaining family members as spies, and has even recruited my animai's ex-girlfriend in his efforts to destroy me and my pack," I finish. Marcus' grip on my hand tightens.

"Roanoke? Well, if he was going for subtlety he missed the mark, if he was going for ominous then he hit the proverbial nail on the head," Yildiz giggles.

"That is indeed a lot. If I recall, the Ruber Flumen Pack bordered Oregon and Washington." Nuray says absentmindedly.

"Amelia, do you have what we requested?" Yildiz gently asks. I nod and open the folder in front of me handing a stapled pack to Nuray and another stapled pack to Yildiz, though I've had Yildiz's copy made in brail. They each go over their respective papers while Marcus watches in surprise and curiosity, both burning bright through our bond.

"You're blind!" Marcus exclaims in shock. I resist the urge to facepalm while Vitali throws his head back laughing.

"You owe me fifty bucks," I tell Zara.

She rolls her eyes, *"Sure, I'll just trot on down to the ATM and… oh, wait, I can't, because I live in your head!"*

"You're just mad that you were wrong, and I was right," I say smugly while she grumbles and curls up into a ball.

"Yes. Is that a problem?" Yildiz calmly asks, looking at Marcus.

"I just… wasn't expecting that. You don't look or act like a blind person," he says scrunching up his nose.

Oh, dear Gods.

"What is a blind person supposed to look and act like?" Yildiz asks with amusement.

"I… I don't know. Just not like you. Did something happen to you?" He asks curiously.

"Marcus, please stop," I implore him gently.

"No, nothing happened to me. I was created this way," she says casually.

"My sister does not owe you any explanations," Nuray spits in irritation.

Nuray is very protective of her sister; in fact, they are all very protective of each other but especially towards Yildiz.

"It is perfectly fine, sister. Do not fret," Yildiz says patting her sister's hand with a smile.

"I mean no disrespect; I was just shocked. You don't seem to need help getting around and you make eye contact with everyone. It threw me off," he admits.

"Unlike my sisters, I can see people's auras. While I can't see you as you are, or what is around you, I can, at least, through your aura see where you are and make out your shape. As for getting around, I am a supernatural being with heightened senses, minus my eyes. I can navigate anywhere just as any able body person can," she says confidently.

"That's pretty badass," Marcus grins.

Yildiz gives him a warm smile. I should have given him a heads up. But of all the things for him to comment on I didn't think it would be calling out a Delegation member's blindness. I can't tell if he's insane or has giant balls.

"You've been up close with his balls, you tell me," Zara teases.

"You, my friend, are a dirty wolf," I retort. She snorts with laughter.

"Moving back to the matter at hand, I would like to start by saying–"

"Don't say it," Nuray cuts her off, but Yildiz's smile widens.

"I told you so," she chirps, making Nuray groan. "Now while this is far from good news, I do feel validated."

"Care to fill the rest of us in?" Tyson grumbles.

"Your Alpha was able to find a missing person's report," she says waving the dossier, "that matches the man you currently have in your cells. The unfortunate news is he is a missing person we only recently flagged," she sighs.

"What does that mean?" Chris asks leaning forward.

"We monitor missing persons around the world. Very often a person goes missing and their disappearance is directly related to something supernatural. We look for the signs and try to assess if a law has been broken, or a situation requires our intervention," Nuray explains.

"A few months ago, I had free time on my hands and decided to go through and double-check various missing person cases and found a large suspicious number of disappearances taking place in Washington. Only a small number of them were flagged in our system while the others went unnoticed, and no bodies ever turned up. These missing people ranged in race, and gender but all in their early twenties. Originally I suspected it was sanguidae attacks and I had plans to come to Washington to investigate further," Yildiz explains further.

"What exactly are you saying?" Vitali slowly asks.

"Your prisoner is one of the people I recently flagged and now I know these missing people didn't go missing because of a sanguidae," she says grimly.

"It's because Mykel is building an army," I conclude.

"It would seem that way," Yildiz breathes.

"How many people are we talking about?" Tyson asks going into warrior mode.

"Hundreds," Nuray answers. We all suck in a breath sitting back.

Hundreds of innocent humans, turned and enslaved by a sadistic, power-hungry, psychopath and all for what? Because my dad didn't agree with breaking the law? How many more people have to suffer? How are we supposed to fight off an army that size? I know it's kill or be killed, but these are innocent people. I can't just kill them; they didn't ask for this. The pack he took over didn't ask for this.

Marcus and I make eye contact and just stare at each other. I find myself tracing the contours of his face, the ridge of his nose, the thickness of his beard. Every detail is now more precious to me because now I fear I'm going to lose them. I squeeze his hand and he gives me an encouraging smile.

"So, we have a pack that has changed leadership and did not inform us. They also changed their name. Both of which thereby makes them an unsanctioned pack now. And, we have a dictator Alpha who has broken the law by potentially turning hundreds upon hundreds of humans into a mutolupus. I would definitely say this calls for our intervention," Nuray summarises.

"There is some minor good news," Yildiz offers.

"Anything that can actually help?" Marcus asks with uncertainty.

"Yes and no. The good news is there is a cure to reverse the transformation caused by the bite of an Alpha. We keep a supply of it at the Kartheca and we will gladly share it with you," Yildiz informs us. Hope blooms inside me.

If we can get that cure then we don't have to kill anyone, we can just change them back.

"And the bad news?" Chris asks apprehensively.

"There's one missing ingredient. For the cure to be effective you have to include the blood of the Alpha who turned them," she says warily.

"Great, figures there'd be some stupid catch," Tyson huffs indignantly.

"The cure has to be catered to the individual turned, so the blood of the one who turned them is an important factor," Nuray says curtly.

"Send us the cure. I'll get his blood," I say firmly.

"Babe, how are you going to do that?" Marcus asks suspiciously.

"He's coming for me, so getting his blood won't be hard when I'll have access to his corpse," I say saccharinely.

Nuray chuckles. "Sounds like the Amelia we know and love. We'll have it to you within twenty-four hours along with instructions so your hospital staff can prepare it," she declares.

"I have one request."

"You can ask us anything, Amelia, you know that," Yildiz says softly, squeezing my hand. The gold glitter of her skin catches the light coming from the ceiling lights.

"Let me and my pack handle this. I understand he has broken your laws and for that, it is your duty to bring him to justice, but I request you defer that to me. It is my pack he is attacking; it is my pack he has wronged and me he has tried to kill and, just yesterday, he killed one of my pack members. This pack is owed justice and I want his head. So, I request you let me be the one to handle this. I swear should it get out of hand, or I see that I cannot control the situation, I will contact you immediately for assistance," I say calmly.

Marcus takes a deep breath through his nose while Vitali, Tyson, and Chris look satisfied. Yildiz and Nuray look at each other and then sit back, whispering. I always wanted to learn the language of the Gods, but I thought learning it might be considered offensive, so I have no idea what they're saying.

"Babe, are you sure about this? Why not just let them handle it and be done?"

Marcus softly asks, and I can feel his worry.

"This started with my pack and it should end with my pack. Not to mention the Delegation has procedures to follow. They have to do a thorough investigation, they'd have to go into his pack, establish if it was a legal takeover, assess the state of the pack and then wait for reinforcements to arrive. They follow their laws to the letter and won't deviate and in that time more people may be getting kidnapped and turned or he could attack today for all we know. We have to act fast. If they defer to me, then it becomes a pack dispute, and the Delegation will step back. This isn't a power play; I'm trying to end this quickly before more people get hurt," I calmly explain.

Marcus looks at me thoughtfully for a few moments before he sighs and kisses my hand. *"Then I have your back one hundred per cent."*

I feel tears prick my eyes as joy washes over me. Knowing I have his support, knowing he has my back means more than anything to me. I could do this on my own, but fact is, I don't want to. I want him with me. I feel stronger now that I have him. I don't feel so alone anymore.

"We have discussed it and… request granted," Yildiz says softly.

"Yes!" Tyson shouts pumping his fist in the air.

"Thank you, Yildiz, Nuray," I say sincerely as I nod to each of them.

"But we will be staying outside your territory for the time being. Should anything go wrong, and I mean *anything,* you contact us immediately and we will be here in a flash," Nuray says vehemently. "Am I clear?"

"Crystal," I grin.

"We will also personally collect the cure when it arrives, and have it brought here to ensure it makes it to you as it's supposed to," Yildiz adds.

"Thank you, we appreciate that very much."

"Gods help this man, because he is gloriously doomed once you get a hold of him," Nuray chuckles. "Thank goodness you now have your animai to rein you in."

"Oh! Speaking of animai, when is the Luna ceremony?" Yildiz asks cheerfully while looking at Marcus.

I swear all the blood drains from my face hearing those words. My brain is desperately trying to find an exit sign and escape before this gets worse.

Vitali, Tyson, and Chris snap their heads in our direction, each looking a mix of worried and cautious. Marcus… fuck, if his emotions are anything to go by, then there's no putting the genie back in the bottle.

"What Luna ceremony?" Marcus asks through gritted teeth.

I can't believe I'm saying this, but I really wish Mykel would attack right now.

"Why yours of course," Yildiz says like it's the most obvious thing in the world.

"I think we can end the meeting here," I say trying to defuse the situation, though I know it's pointless.

"What is the problem? The person fated to an Alpha is the rightful Luna. You were fated to Amelia, Amelia is an Alpha, ergo you are this pack's Luna," Nuray says casually with a shrug.

"I am not a fucking Luna!" Marcus bellows causing the room to shake as he leaps from his chair and pounds his fist into the table, though it doesn't leave a mark. And this is why the table is reinforced ladies and gentlemen. So much for an irshiusts calming presence.

Yildiz and Nuray look surprised by Marcus' outburst but don't flinch or react. Their heartbeats don't even fluctuate. The guys about jumped out of their skin, and me… all I can do is sigh and close my eyes in defeat. I knew this would happen. I knew the happy bubble couldn't last, not with this hanging over our heads. Him accepting me was easy. He accepted me because he loved me but changing all of his views that were ingrained in him; that doesn't happen in a week.

"I would appreciate it if everyone gave us the room," I say calmly.

The guys don't hesitate and make a B-line for the door. Nuray and Yildiz give me a compassionate and sympathetic look before rising from their seats and leaving the room. Now it's just the two of us, and somehow that notion isn't as exciting as it once was.

Chapter Thirty-Two
Amelia

Marcus' jaw is locked and he's glaring holes into the conference table. I can feel his anger and frustration and I can sense Ace's distress. He and Marcus are not in agreement on this. Zara is being quiet just like she was when Marcus cut us down with his words when we met. There's just no scenario where this ends well.

"Marcus…" I say slowly.

"We're not discussing this, Amelia," he says curtly.

"I think it's time we did. Marcus, we have both been tiptoeing around the subject since you came back, more so since we marked each other. We can't avoid it forever. It's now out in the open so let's address it. Nuray is right, I'm the Alpha, you're my animai, that makes you this packs Luna."

"Don't fucking say it," he says in a low voice that has Zara whimpering and I can feel Ace reaching out to comfort her. I'm glad she has him.

"I just did," I point out.

"Amelia, I love you, but I… I am not and will not be a fucking Luna. Can you not understand how degrading that is for me?" He says in frustration as he runs his fingers through his hair.

"No, I honestly can't. Please explain to me what's so degrading about being a Luna," I say as I rise to my feet. "It's perfectly fine for a woman to be a Luna, but if it's a man, that's somehow degrading. Explain that to me."

I'm trying to keep calm, but I'm not sure I want to even bother, what would be the point? He feels what I feel, so why hide it anymore?

"The Luna is the mother of the pack; she caters to its emotional needs and other typical feminine shit. I am a warrior. I fight, I don't sit around helping pups make macaroni artwork," he spits.

"Wow," I laugh humourlessly. "Say what you really mean. You see the Luna as the wolf version of a housewife, and by taking that title, it makes you one," I surmise. He clenches his molars and I feel his disgust. "I'm right, aren't I?"

"I didn't fucking say that. Don't put words in my mouth," he seethes.

"I'm not putting shit in your mouth, we're connected remember? I feel what you feel and if I want I can pluck the thoughts out of your head, but I'm not sure I'd like what I find," I take a breath rubbing my face. "You're afraid that taking on this title will somehow rob you of your masculinity. By that logic, becoming an Alpha robbed me of my femininity."

"That's not the same fucking thing, that's a higher rank," he argues.

"Last I checked a Luna is a much higher rank than a Beta," I retort.

"A Luna is a woman's role," he says scathingly, spitting the word 'Luna' as if it were the equivalent of sucking on a lemon.

"And an Alpha is a man's role, right? Is this your mother talking or you?" I say disdainfully as I cross my arms over my chest. His forest eyes start glowing momentarily as they burn into me.

"Don't you dare bring my mother into this," he says coldly.

"Why not? You said yourself these are her opinions she passed onto you. Your father doesn't have a problem with all of this, so why do you? You're so focused on this made-up idea of what a Luna is you aren't even willing to see it as anything else."

"What else is there to see?!" He shouts.

"That a Luna is the person who is equal to the Alpha! Not above and not below. They are each other's confidants, they are each other's strength and they run and guide the pack together, using their strengths the best way they can. It's just a word. A word that means whatever you want it to mean. My grandmother can't even shift and yet she was a Luna who fought for her pack. She was a warrior, so don't fucking stand there and tell me that a Luna is just someone who tends to 'feminine shit'," I say aggressively, my chest heaving.

"Maybe that's how you see it. But that's not how others see it," he retorts.

"So, you care more about what everyone else thinks of a position they'll never have, than what it might mean to me to have you take on that position and be at my side," I say quietly. "You asked me if you mattered to me, now I'm asking you. Do I matter to you?"

"How can you even ask me that?" He says hurt. "You matter to me more than anything."

"Not more than anything. You have a sexist opinion of the Luna role that your mother burned into your brain and that opinion matters more to you. I never asked you to change, I never asked you to become someone you're not. I want you for you. I want you here caring for this pack with me, but you don't want that. You want me, and you certainly want to fuck me, you just don't want everything that comes along with me," I say sorrowfully as tears prick my eyes.

"Why am I being painted as the asshole here? Maybe if you really cared about me, you wouldn't expect me to do something I'm not comfortable with," he snaps.

"Tell me, if I offered to take on the role of Luna and give you the Alpha title, would you take it?" I ask.

"Of course, I would," he says without thinking, his eyes widening when he realises what he said. "Wait, I didn't mean that," he quickly backtracks.

"Yes, you did," I smile sadly. "You're not afraid of leading and guiding a pack, you're not afraid of power and authority. You're afraid of being associated with something people view as 'feminine' because if that happens, everyone will question your masculinity, see you as weak and as your soulmate's bitch," I say and he winces, but I know my words are true. I feel it, this is what he feels at his core. "That makes you no different than every Alpha and Alpha heir who used to try and beat and threaten me to scare me out of being Alpha. Because in their eyes, an Alpha meant someone strong and masculine and if a woman took on that role, then I was going to taint it, corrupt it. Make Alphas seem weak and girly because naturally, that's what women are right? We're weak."

"You know I don't think you're weak," he says feebly.

"Maybe, but you haven't denied anything else I've said because you know you can't," I say wiping the tears from my eyes before they fall.

"It's just a word, why are you making such a big deal of this?" He groans in frustration.

"Funny, that's what I've been saying to you," I say tiredly. We both fall silent, and the atmosphere has become uncomfortable. It hurts. His words and his emotions hurt worse than anything and I feel like it's suffocating me.

"I think you should return to your pack," I calmly suggest.

His head snaps to me and I can feel his panic. "Amelia don't do this," he begs, reaching for my hands, but I pull them back while trying to ignore the hurt he feels.

"I have to focus on my pack. I have to focus on stopping someone from trying to kill me and my people. I don't have time to deal with your out-of-date views. We both need some space and time to think, so I think it would be best for you to return home. After all, you haven't acknowledged this place as your home and maybe you never will," I say sadly.

"You'd let one measly title come between us?" He asks in disbelief.

This time I glare at him. "*I'm* not the one letting their views of a title come between us, and if the Luna title was so measly and insignificant you wouldn't care this much!" I cry. I take a breath to settle myself down, trying to keep my voice from shaking though I feel like my heart is breaking in two, "Please, just go."

"Is this how it's going to be? We disagree so you kick me out? Since when do you make decisions based on hormones?" He mocks.

His words have me recoiling like I just got slapped. I can see and feel his regret as soon as the words are out of his mouth, but it's too late. They're out and he can't take them back.

"Last I checked, testosterone was a hormone and maybe if you weren't so filled with it, you wouldn't have just made a stupid remark like that one,"

I say through gritted teeth, and he flinches back. "I'm choosing my pack; I'm choosing to put hundreds and hundreds of lives first. I'm trying to be a good Alpha, but I don't expect you to understand," I say as I walk over and open the conference door. "Please, leave. I can't do this right now, because truthfully, I don't have the strength." My bottom lip quivers.

He looks at me, his eyes echoing the pain and sorrow he feels. I even detect guilt, but he's trying to bury it. His eyes are glassy from trying to hold back tears as he walks over to me.

"I'm sorry, Amelia," he whispers. The sound of his voice has tears pooling in my eyes.

"So much for having my back one hundred per cent," I say with a sad smile.

His eyes widen in realisation and all I can do is try my hardest to close myself off to our link. It's not easy, but I put up a barrier between us just as I've done with Zara for every birthday surprise, because if I have to feel more of his emotions right now, I don't think I'll ever come back from it.

He lowers his head in shame and slowly walks out the door, neither of us saying a word. Once I hear him get far enough away, I close the door, sliding back against it and let the tears fall. I pull my knees to my chest and just sob. I sob until my lungs ache and my throat feels like sandpaper. I give myself over to the sadness, the loneliness, and the feelings of rejection. I've never felt so defeated and I'm not sure how to bounce back from this.

Marcus

"WHAT THE HELL HAVE YOU DONE?! GO BACK! GO BACK AND FIX IT!" Ace screams as he claws away furiously in my mind. He wants to shift and go and comfort Amelia and Zara and it's taking everything I have in me to keep him contained.

I make my way out to the back of the packhouse and slump down on a nearby bench with my head in my hands. The tears break past the waterline and I don't bother to hold them back. Sobs wrack my body and my heart feels like someone just punched their fist directly through it and are pumping it with lupine. I knew that conversation would go about as well as trying to ice skate uphill, but it ended up being so much worse.

"Because of you! I told you repeatedly, I am fine with being a Luna. I want to be a Luna. I want to join this pack, I want to be with Zara and Amelia, but you're too busy thinking like a neanderthal. Amelia is right, your mother's stupid points of view are in your head and you're holding onto them like the universe will crumble if you let them go. You'd rather hold onto some bullshit sexist view created by humans than just embrace the path the Gods put you on and be with our animai. In case it wasn't obvious, Marcus, I fucking hate you right now. You hear me? I hate you!" He snarls and lets out a long, agonised howl.

I can't even respond to him. What can I say? I know I fucked up. I yelled at her; I snarled at her; I even accused her of being hormonal. I wince remembering her reaction to that. She's right, she's never tried to change me. All she wanted was me, so why is this so hard? I knew my words were hurting her, I felt her hurt and disappointment and still, it didn't stop me. Am I really willing to lose the other half of my soul over this?

"May I sit with you?" Says a timid voice. I look up to find the gentle eyes of Mei looking down at me with more sympathy than I deserve.

"Not sure why you'd want to," I croak.

She takes a seat beside me pressing her hands between her thighs – a nervous gesture of hers.

"Chris told me about the meeting," she says softly.

"Yeah, well, he wasn't there for the worst of it," I snort as I wipe my eyes with the heels of my palms.

"I know it's not quite the same, but joining this pack and marking Chris terrified me," she tells me.

"Given what you've been through, I think that's to be expected," I gently reassure her.

"No, that wasn't it," she says, shaking her head. "I am not just an outsider; I am a completely different species. I was afraid they'd be angry or disgusted that I was fated to their Delta, and worse, that I shared his rank. The pack doesn't know what I am. I know you do though."

"I promise your secret is safe with me," I tell her.

"I know, I am not worried," she says with a genuine smile.

"I don't know what's wrong with me. I love Amelia more than life itself, yet I keep hurting her," I grimace.

"Maybe you should try not doing that," she lightly chides.

"Yeah, that's probably a good idea," I laugh sardonically. "I keep hearing my mother's voice in my head telling me that a good man is a provider, he fights for and protects his family. Her telling me she hoped I'd find a good woman who would take care of me and give me healthy pups," I say, rubbing my face.

Mei wrinkles her nose like she smells something bad, "I grew up in slavery and even I know that kind of thinking is backwards."

I throw my head back and laugh. Then her words hit me like a sledgehammer and guilt courses through me.

"Wow, I truly am an asshole. Here you are, someone who has been through hell and back and yet you're sitting here comforting me when I'm complaining about a title. If I'd been through what you have, I don't think I'd come out the other side with the same cheery disposition. I must sound so whiney and pathetic," I say shamefully.

She smiles, shaking her head, "My life experiences don't invalidate your feelings about your own life, that wouldn't be fair to anyone. But you're right, you have a woman who loves you, people who support you and want the best for you, and you're pushing it all away. For what?" There's no judgement in her voice at all, I can see why Chris is smitten with her.

"Honestly, I have no fucking idea. Oh, sorry for the language," I say, catching myself.

"It's okay," she chuckles, "I've learned the mutolupus species have a colourful vocabulary."

"Still, I'll try to be more respectful," I assure her.

"For what it's worth, I think you'd make a great Luna. Far better than the Albus Mons Luna," she shudders and her eyes suddenly look far away. I can't imagine the horrors she lived through, And that's the thing; she was a child and she survived.

A child endured and survived abuse and Gods know what else and what am I complaining about exactly? People calling me a girl? Did I not just tell myself that women survive pain and experiences we men can't even begin to comprehend and yet I still have it in my head that being compared to a woman is an insult.

"Can I ask why you think I'd make a great... Luna?"

"You're there for Amelia. You have her back and support her, you make her stronger, but more than that, you respect packs in general. You respect how the system works and you care about all the members in a pack. You're good at reading people and, for the most part, adjusting yourself to their comfort level. The day you had us help you plan Amelia's date made that clear. You were friendly, you got to know us, you were respectful, you listened and took advice, and you were able to delegate. All the while you had a big smile on your face every time you thought about Amelia."

"And that's how you see a Luna?"

"Isn't a Luna really just the other person who runs the pack? It lets people know you're an authority figure. The way I see it, Alpha and Luna doesn't mean male or female, it means the leader who was born into the role and the leader the Goddess chose to rule beside them," she explains.

Her words strike me like a lightning bolt. Never once have I even thought of seeing it that way. In my head, the Alpha was the male, and the Luna was the female, I mean, that's how it's always been. But Amelia is right. All Alphas rule differently and so do all Lunas. Mei is right too. An Alpha is the rightful born leader of the pack, and in this case, that person was Amelia. The Luna is always the animai Zarseti made so that leader wouldn't have to do it alone. So if fate chose Amelia as an Alpha then fate chose me to be her Luna. But am I coming to this realisation too late?

"Do you think she'll ever forgive me?" I ask glumly.

"If you give her a reason to, then sure," she says brightly.

"I'm going to take Amelia's advice. I'm going to go back to my pack," I announce.

"What?!" She shrieks, mortified. "No, you can't!"

I smile and calmly take her hands. "Mei, I'm not leaving, sweet girl. Amelia needs space to focus, and I need to go back home to talk to my

Alpha. I need to let him know I've decided to stay," I say with a smile.

"You... but... really?" She asks with wide eyes.

"You're right and I'm being a pitiful prick."

"I never called you that," she says disapprovingly.

"No," I chuckle. "I'm calling myself that. I love Amelia and I can't live without her. I'm letting something so stupid ruin something so amazing. A Goddess thought Amelia would be the perfect first female Alpha, or the first one acknowledged, and then in her wisdom thought I'd be the perfect first male Luna, yet here I am more worried about what other people will think or what my mother would think. If I have any hope of being what this pack needs, I think I need to try being a bit stronger. Like you," I say as I tap her nose, making her blush.

"I'm nothing special," she says shyly.

"That's a lie. You're very special and you knocked some sense into me. I shouldn't waste energy on things that don't matter, which is something Amelia tried to teach me. It especially doesn't matter when I realise my life could be so much worse than it is," I admit.

Seriously, if Mei could face an entire pack and find the strength to take on each day after her hell, then there's no excuse for me to reject this title. I'm just being an insecure asshole. I mean, I'm still insecure. But I can at least stop being an asshole about it.

"Told you you'd make a good Luna," she smiles cheekily and I can't resist pinching her cheek, which makes her giggle.

"Let Amelia know I'm coming back, will you?" I ask.

"Why can't you do it?" She asks curiously.

"Because she either won't fully believe me or maybe she won't want to see me. I need to do this. Actions speak louder than words and if I do this it proves to her that I'm serious about her and us," I explain.

"I will be sure to let her know then," she says confidently.

"I owe you one. Or several," I say planting a kiss atop her head. I should buy her something as a thank you.

I run upstairs grabbing my phone, wallet, and keys and head straight for my truck, jumping in and flooring it to get back to my pack. Well, my soon to be former pack.

"Are you really doing this?" Ask Ace excitedly.

"I'm not saying I'm not scared because I'm scared as fuck. But I'm more scared of losing Amelia. If taking on a title and a pack is all I have to do to keep her, then I'd be the dumbest motherfucker alive to not do it," I state.

"Finally! You finally get it! You know, I really had lost all hope for you back there. I'm still furious with you for upsetting Zara and Amelia, but at least you're finally doing the right thing," he praises.

Despite how scared shitless I am, I've never felt more sure of something in my life. I feel in my bones that I'm doing the right thing. This was always meant to be my destiny, and it's about damn time I embraced it.

Chapter Thirty-Three
Amelia

I don't know how long I sat on the floor of the conference room wallowing in self-pity and heartache. The concept of time no longer mattered to me. I wanted to stay there and cry until I'd cried my soul out of my body, but a nagging voice in the back of my mind reminded me that I have a duty to my pack. My pack needs me, they need me to be strong. I can't afford to crumble now, not after we've just suffered a loss. They are all scared and sad and they need to find strength somewhere, and that strength is me. I have to be their pillar. If I fall apart, they will too, and I can't have that. I can cry when I'm alone in my room, but that's for later. Right now, it's time to be the fucking Alpha I am, even if I have to do it without Marcus.

Pain to lances through me at the thought, but I swallow it down like the bitter pill it is. I pick myself up off the floor – as I have so many times – dust myself off, rid myself of any signs of crying and march out of the conference room, ready to get to business.

"Attention Invictus Pack," I announce through the link. *"All warriors and any pack member willing to volunteer, gather at the training ground in fifteen minutes."*

I leave the packhouse and everyone I pass looks at me curiously, though many are already getting up and making their way to the training ground.

Once I reach the training ground I walk over to the nearest bench and climb up, take a power stance and wait . Within minutes, every pack warrior has assembled, along with many non-warrior pack members. I feel proud knowing that when their pack is under threat, they will answer the call to do what they can to defend it. That's what being in a pack is about. Vitali, Tyson, and Chris push through the crowd to me with compassionate eyes.

"You okay?" Chris asks.

"Want me to break his legs?" Tyson offers.

I'm trying to ignore them, but that almost has me cracking a smile. Even if the thought of Marcus getting hurt makes me feel ill, Tyson's gesture is appreciated.

"Thank you, everyone, for coming. I'm going to get straight to it. Our pack is under threat," I announce, as low growls reverberate across the crowd. "Some weeks ago, I began receiving threats against my life and this pack. I have since learned these threats, the attack, and the death of Izac, were all orchestrated by the former Beta, Mykel Mathers. Older brother of Declan and uncle of Ryker." The crowd descends into a mix of snarls and gasps. "It was Mykel who killed Izac, it was Mykel who had Ryker poison me and it is Mykel who is building an army to bring us down."

"How do we stop him, Alpha?" One of the warriors yells.

"I'm glad you asked. The army he has assembled mostly consists of humans who have been turned into a mutolupus." My words cause murmurs of shock and confusion.

"How is that possible?" Another person asks in disbelief.

"Every Alpha is blessed by Morrtemis with the ability to turn a human into a mutolupus through a bite, but this is an act monitored heavily by the Delegation and is only to be done under strict circumstances. Mykel has broken those laws."

"But you said he was the former Beta," says another voice in confusion.

"Was. Past tense. Mykel took over the Ruber Flumen Pack, becoming their Alpha. A fight is coming. It is inevitable. But we will be ready. We have members of the Delegation visiting and they have offered their aid. Now, his army consists of innocent humans ripped away from their lives and families and turned into something they were never meant to be, but there is a cure, which the Delegation will be providing us. I don't wish to kill innocent people, so training is about to change," I announce.

One by one, people step closer, intrigued. Tyson looks up at me with a quirked brow, curious as to what my battle strategy is.

"Warriors and anyone willing to volunteer; for the coming days or weeks, you will be focusing the bulk of your training on weapons. The strategy for the upcoming attack is to do your best to incapacitate the enemy instead of killing them. The goal is catch and release. You will train how to effectively use tranquillizer guns. You will use these to shoot any wolf you see with a sedative. That being said, I want everyone to prioritize their lives. You have loved ones who do not wish you dead. If the choice comes between their life or yours, then do not hesitate to go for the kill. Am I understood?" I say forcefully.

"Yes, Alpha!" They exclaim in unison.

"No one is to attempt to take on Mykel. If you encounter him, you are to back away immediately. No one will be dealing with him but me. For the time being, you'll focus on training harder, and when the time comes, we will end this threat and show the former Beta why he never should have fucked with the Invictus Pack," I declare.

The crowd lets out a chorus of howls and cheers. With their new orders, I dismiss everyone and step down from the bench, rubbing my face tiredly.

"So what's next on the agenda?" Vitali asks, keeping it business – which I appreciate.

"Tyson, I want you to see about ordering more weapons, I want everyone to have access to one. This will be easier if everyone is equipped with what they need. Vitali, head to the hospital and see to it that they stock up on sedatives strong enough to take out an Alpha. While these folks aren't Alphas, they are feral and under Alpha control, so we need something that will work strong and fast. Have them order as much as we need, spare no expense," I instruct.

"Yes, Alpha," they say in unison and rush off to see to their respective tasks.

"As for yo-" I'm cut off before I can finish my sentence as Chris engulfs me in a hug.

His arms hold me securely as he rests his head atop of mine. I fight back the tears, wrapping my arms around him and breathing in his familiar saltwater taffy scent. No words are shared, they're not needed. His hug says enough. He's here for me and he cares about me, and it means more than words can describe.

"Thank you," I whisper.

"Anytime," he smiles.

Mei walks over slowly, appraising us carefully as if she's worried she's interrupting.

"I was surprised to see you here," I tell her.

"This is my pack too; I want to help. I am faster and stronger, it would be unwise to not let me help," her voice is soft, but her eyes hold strength and conviction.

"As much as I wish I could keep you in our room and away from danger, I know you want to fight with everyone else and I know how capable you are, so I won't stop you. You have my support, xingan baobei," he says with a warm smile.

Mei squeals and leaps into his arms while he swings her around, holding her like she's the most precious thing in this world. They share a long and loving kiss and, as happy as I am for them, I have to look away to avoid the pang of hurt it causes my heart.

"Amelia?" Mei calls for my attention.

"Yes, Mei?"

"I spoke to Marcus. He's gone back to his pack, to say goodbye," she tells me with a bright smile.

"Goodbye?" I ask, holding my breath.

"He wants to prove he's in this with you, so he's gone to sort things out with his pack. He said he needed to show you how serious he is, instead of telling you," she tells me as she bites her lip to hide her smile.

"I find it hard to believe he changed his tune so quickly," I say.

"Maybe he wants to try, and this is his way of showing that," Chris offers.

"I guess only time will tell," I sigh. As I say that I can feel a link opening up to me and it's full of panic.

"Alpha, Kylie Mallod was just here saying her goodbyes to Izac and I'm very worried about her. I fear she may do something," says Doctor Richard.

His words are like ice sliding down my spine. My shoes are off and I'm racing forward, following my link to Kylie, moving so fast the hem of my skirt splits. I keep moving and before I know it I'm at the edge of the lake on our territory. Kylie is standing by the lake with her back to me; I can hear her whispered sobs and smell her tears in the air.

"Kylie…" I gently call her name.

"I can't… do… this… Alpha," she says with uneven breaths.

"I am so sorry. I can't even fathom how you're feeling, and you don't deserve it. But talk to me, okay? It might help," I offer as I take slow measured steps towards her, nothing too quick as not to make her feel threatened. I try to keep my heart rate even, but I have a terrible feeling swirling in my gut.

"Zara, are you able to talk to her wolf?"

"I tried, but her wolf has gone dormant," she whines.

This is bad.

"He was my everything," she says in a broken voice, "I can't live without him; it hurts too much. It hurts just to breathe. My soul… is gone and I can't… handle it. I can't have this baby without him."

Oh, Goddess… she's pregnant.

"You're not alone, do you hear me? You have your family and you have me, and you have this pup. I know it'll be hard, but Izac wouldn't want you to be sad. He loved you so much and I know wherever he is, he still does," I say, my voice trembling.

"I'm not strong like he was." She sounds completely bereft, "I can't go on without him. I need to be with him again… I'm sorry, Amelia."

That's when I smell the silver. Before I even have a chance to react, she raises her hand and plunges a silver knife into her heart.

"NO!" I scream as I race to her side, catching her before she can hit the ground. "No, no, no, no, no. Look at me, come on Kylie, don't you dare die on me!" I look at the knife in a panic. If I leave it in, the silver will kill her. If I take it out, she'll be dead in seconds. I cup her face and cradle her body as tears stream from my eyes. "Please don't die," I beg.

She looks up at me and her face looks more peaceful and serene than anything I've ever seen. She gives me a gentle smile as her eyes fall closed and as soon as they do, I feel the snap as my link to her breaks. I scream out in pain and sorrow until my voice is raw. Animals in the forest flee as the tears pour from my eyes, burning like acid. I pull the knife from her chest and hold her body close to mine crying into her neck.

"I'm sorry. I'm so sorry," I chant as I rock us back and forth.

In the span of twenty-four hours, I've lost two people I swore to protect and a third life that had barely even begun. I failed to keep my pack and friends safe. I know I will live with that for the rest of my days. As I gaze down at Kylie – a small, contented smile gracing her sweet face – I send up a silent prayer to any God who will listen. I pray for them to give me the strength to avenge this sweet family that never got to be and save those in my pack from meeting the same fate.

***

The next two days were torturesome. Consoling Izac and Kylie's parents, watching them grieve the loss of their children was unbearable. It shattered my heart. I didn't tell them about the baby, that was at least one pain I could save them from. No good would come from telling them in a single breath they were going to be grandparents but lost their grandpup before they ever had a chance to meet them. I couldn't do that to them.

The pack was devastated, but it galvanised the warriors and more people volunteered to help fight for the pack. They want justice and to stop more innocent blood from being shed. I know the chances of casualties are high, but I'm trying to do as much as I can to limit the death count in what's to come.

We held a joint funeral for Izac and Kylie in the Temple of Morrtemis, with a majority of the pack attending. It was a beautiful service and so many people shared happy memories of the sweet couple, myself included. For a mutolupus funeral, we wear yellow for remembrance and happiness, to honour the happy memories we had with those who have passed.

The Temple of Morrtemis resides in a deep section of the woods on our territory. It's a large stone structure with a single entrance/exit. The outside looks old and weathered and is covered in vines, but the inside is pristine; still looking newly built. It's a large geometric stadium layout with Mihrab-shaped nooks spaced around the room, fire pits burning in each. The interior is designed from smooth stone in tones of dark grey and gold and it has two golden pillars supporting the structure in the centre of the room. There is a curved stone platform at the far end of the room, with a statue of the Goddess Morrtemis in its centre.

The statue depicts her in the regalia of a God, a large shield at her side, large snarling wolves adorning its front. She stands tall and regal, looking down upon us with a gentle face. The room is filled with yellow zinnias and dahlias, and those same flowers rest on top of the two white coffins that stand in the middle of the room. I tear my eyes away from the coffins and look up at the stained-glass, barrel-vaulted ceiling. The stained-glass is actually a mural depicting the origins of the first humans who were turned into mutolupus' by the Goddess Morrtemis.

The sweet scent of vanilla and orchids reaches me as Yildiz comes to stand beside me. I continue to look at the ceiling; the rays of the afternoon sun shining through, making the mural look even more enchanting.

"Why are you looking at the ceiling?" She asks softly.

"I'm looking at the mural above us. It's a glass depiction of our origins."

"It's a touching story. The Goddess Morrtemis was tired from battling a swarm of sanguidae. When her back was turned, the creatures attacked, but a large group of humans from a neighbouring village – who watched the Goddess fight them all single-handedly – jumped in to defend her, not realising a sanguidae could not kill her. Many of the humans lost their lives, but for those who were still holding on to life, she wished to reward them and save them for their bravery. She glanced into the woods and saw the eyes of a pack of wolves and decided at that moment to bless these humans with wolf spirits. Companions to guide and protect them through life. They would be stronger and faster than any human. Strong enough to defend themselves should their village ever be attacked again. With her act of gratitude she created the first mutolupus," she finishes in a soft voice, and I can hear the smile in it.

"I guess she didn't make us strong enough," I say flatly.

Yildiz lets out a sigh, "Not everyone can be saved. You're at war, death is inevitable."

"Oh, I'm very well aware of that."

"Please don't blame yourself for what happened," she implores, placing a comforting hand on my shoulder.

"I don't blame myself. I blame Mykel for Izac's death. He's the one who killed him. But Kylie? No, I think I'll blame someone else for that," I say bitterly.

"Who? Kylie?" She asks gently.

"No. I blame Zarseti," I say bluntly.

Yildiz softly gasps and drops her hand from my shoulder, "Amelia, watch what you say."

"Why? What's she gonna do, smite me?" I ask, now turning to face her. "Why does she do this? She creates this powerful magic binding two souls together, which can be blissful and wonderfully overwhelming. But on the other side, it means when you lose your other half, your life ends." Tears fill my eyes, "You can't function. You can't live. Suddenly, a single second without them is maddening, painful torture. Your only solace is to end your own life. You're so consumed with pain and grief, with no end in sight, that you can't even live for your unborn child. A child you wanted more than anything. Why does she do this?"

Yildiz sighs sadly, "I can't speak for my mother, but great pain and suffering allows us to understand and appreciate what great love is."

"That's no excuse. They were young and innocent. Two years. That's all they had, two fleeting years," I cry as my lips quiver with every word.

"To some, two years can feel like a lifetime."

"They deserved a lifetime. They deserved to watch their pup be born, they deserved to grow old together and have pups and grandpups and great grandpups; not this. They didn't deserve this. You know, I'm starting to wonder if most of the Alphas in the world who I think are massive assholes are really only assholes because they've hardened themselves. Because they have had to feel the pain of losing too many they were sworn to protect and it becomes too much," I surmise, wiping the tears from my face.

"I don't have the answers you seek; I wish I did. I wish I could take away your pain or bring Izac and Kylie back, but I can't. I can only say that you will give them justice, I believe that with all my heart," she says confidently as she pulls me into an embrace. I give in and hold her tight, allowing her natural soothing presence to take over.

"Where is Marcus?" She inquires.

"He's back at his pack, supposedly making arrangements to leave," I shrug.

"You don't believe him?" She asks sympathetically.

"I worry that returning home will have made him realise that he doesn't want to be here. Gods only know what his mother is saying to him," I wince at the very thought.

"Have faith in him. Zarseti chose him for you for a reason. Does he know about the service?" She asks.

"I had a block up, so he was forced to call my phone; I picked up and told him everything. He insisted on coming back to be here for me, but I told him to do what he needs to do and truthfully, I needed the space. Between Izac's death, learning about Ryker and Mykel, fighting with Marcus and then Kylie's suicide I just… I needed room to breathe. I need to get my head back on straight," I explain exhaling deeply.

"That's understandable. That's a lot for anyone to deal with and while animais can bring peace and solace, they aren't a magical cure for everything," she says with a soft smile, "I believe he'll come back, and things will get better."

"I hope you're right," I say, half smiling. I miss Marcus. I'd be lying if I said I didn't. Two days without him has been unbearable, but as much as my soul and body need him like I need air and water, I have been thankful for the time to clear my head. I don't like how we left things but being an emotional wreck after Izac and Kylie's deaths, I also didn't want to end up lashing out at him and saying something I can't take back. I don't know when he'll return, but if or when he does, I hope we can calmly figure out where we stand.

Chapter Thirty-Four
Amelia

It's been five days since Kylie's death, which means it's been five days of vigorous training with the pack. No one is holding back. Everyone is excelling with target practice and learning to use guns. We've always had access to a large selection of weapons, including guns, but never have we felt a need to master them as we are now. It's mostly reserved for pack members who wish to be a warrior but are unable to shift. We train them in weapons to give them something to compensate for the lack of wolf.

Our weapons are all modified and custom-made to fight various supernatural enemies. Because of this, we have to be cautious because the weapons we use on our enemy are lethal to us as well. We can't just go into this arrogantly.

Marcus is still back at his pack handling whatever he needs to handle, but we are in communication, even if that communication feels awkward at the best of times. He insisted I take down my barrier because being unable to reach me put him on edge. I know it sounds selfish, but I did so reluctantly. Feeling his emotions all the time while he's so far away is distracting. Every time I feel something – positive or negative – I start to panic. If he feels happy, is that because he's happier where he is and that means he doesn't want to come back? If he's feeling disgust, does that mean someone brought up me and the Luna thing and he got upset again? Our bond should bring me comfort but it's putting me on edge instead.

I used to be sure of myself. I never questioned myself and I was surrounded by people that never made me question them. I had built myself into someone I was proud of. Then Marcus comes along, takes C4 to my life and leaves me in ruins. The hardest part is, I still love the bastard. I miss him, I really do. But if he thinks he can just waltz back in here like nothing happened and like his words didn't wound me, he's got another thing coming.

After today's training session, I walk over to the bleachers and grab my towel, drying off all the sweat I worked up. I've been a little paranoid since the whole poisoning my water thing, so I've had Landry put to use since he's still here serving out his 'punishment'. I guess you could say he's my water boy.

He stays for training and guards my water. Perhaps that's neurotic, but someone did try to kill me twice, so I'd rather not take any chances. The funny part was that Landry was thrilled to do it. He said he considered it his small way of paying me back for helping him win back Jen – which is going fantastically – even though I told him he owes me nothing.

Once I'm moderately dry, I take my water, dismissing Landry for the day, and walk over to catch up with Mei.

"Let's go have a chat in my office," I say as I sling my arm around her.

"Is everything okay?" She asks with concern.

"Just something I want to run by you, if that's alright."

"Of course, Alpha," she says, beaming.

"I told you, stop calling me 'Alpha'," I chuckle.

"That depends. Is this a chat as friends or as pack members?" She asks thoughtfully.

I narrow my eyes at her, "Fine! You win."

She giggles and claps her hands. It's nice how much she has come out of her shell. She's a much happier person than the woman who arrived here.

We make our way to my office; Mei taking a seat in front of my desk as I stand behind it.

"I've spent the last few days thinking very hard about what I can do to better our chances in this upcoming war. A smart leader uses their best asset and, fact of the matter is, you are my best asset," I state.

Mei perks up and scoots forward, hope shining in her beautiful brown eyes, "I wouldn't say 'best', but I do appreciate the compliment."

"Mei, you're the strongest and fastest person in the pack. That's not a compliment, that's a biological fact. I've seen you shifting now and... I'm in awe of you. I would be a raging idiot to not have you in battle. If you're willing, that is."

"I am more than willing," she nods fervently, "This is my pack, my home. I want to do whatever I can to protect it. Just tell me what you want me to do."

"According to legend, your kind were often guardians. So, I'm taking a note out of history's book – I want you to be our guardian. Mykel won't know about you, so he won't know how to fight you. Our weaknesses aren't your weaknesses, so basically you're indestructible in terms of this fight. I know I'm putting a lot on your shoulders when I say this, but..." I pause taking in a deep breath, "Your objective during the fight will be to protect and see to anyone in great need. If you see someone outnumbered, or prey to a sneak attack, take down the threat. You can cover the battlefield faster than anyone else. If you see a pack member near-death... I want you to heal them."

I don't know why this feels wrong. I'm her Alpha, so she should do as I order, but wolves respect hierarchy and I can feel that she outranks me. I don't know if it's because of her species but I know she is superior to me. Ordering her to do anything feels unnatural.

That being said, Mei's eyes light up like the Fourth-of-July, "Of course! I will absolutely do that! I know you have only wanted to protect me and shield me from danger, but I can help and I want to help. I have this gift for a reason. If we just let people die when we know I can save them, we're as bad as the enemy."

"You're right. So if you're willing, then this is our strategy. You hang back and observe. You see a place to intervene, you do so. You are only to shift if absolutely necessary. I'll instruct our warriors to stay out of your way.

If you see someone hurt beyond their own healing capabilities, step in, and help them. We probably won't be able to save everyone…"

"But we can limit the casualties. I understand," she says reaching out and taking my hands. "I'll save as many as I can. I would be honoured to be this pack's guardian."

Her snake eyes flash ever so slightly and for the briefest moment, I feel an energy radiate from her. It may have been brief, but I swear in that moment, it had me want to submit to her. There's more to Mei's strength than even she knows, but it feels as though it's starting to wake up. I think this brings her a step closer to whatever awakening is in store for her.

"You know you'll have to run this by Chris," I smirk.

Mei's face contorts into a scowl as she lets my hands go and huffs, which makes me chuckle. "He won't like it. He'll try to talk me out of it. But I'm sure once I explain my stance, he'll support me. I know he just wants to protect me, but I also know he has my back through anything," she says with love and affection shining in her eyes. A wave of envy crashes over me and I quickly push it down.

"Ultimately it's your call and he can't say otherwise," I shrug.

"Thank you for putting so much faith and trust in me, you… you'll never know what it means to me," she says with tears in her eyes.

I walk over and pull her into a tight hug, her arms snaking around my waist…

HA, snake? Get it? Because she's a snake.

I really am the worst with jokes.

"Why am I the only one privileged enough to hear your shocking attempts at comedy?" Zara quips.

"Because I don't want people to suffer," I retort.

"I've told you; you should just share it with everyone. You'll slip up one of these days, mark my words, Amelia," she playfully threatens.

"Maybe that should be my other secret weapon in this fight. Throw out a few bad jokes and watch Mykel die of cringe," I joke.

Zara rolls over laughing, flailing her legs around, *"Now that was funny."*

Mei left to break the news to Chris and I had food sent up to my office, deciding to shower later. I don't think anyone will be bothered by me working in my workout gear. Once I've eaten, I call Evalyn and Eric to my office. Eric had asked permission to set up a support group for the pack after Izac and Kylie's deaths and I thought it was a brilliant idea. It has been going fantastically. It gives the pack a chance to have a space they can share their grief and fear over everything that is happening. I'm disappointed I never thought about it myself, but I'm so grateful to Eric for establishing it. Eric arranges the meetings and checks in on everyone; they've really gotten close to him and him to them. Turns out Eric has training as a councillor, so he's putting it to use. Who knew?

With Tyson focused on training, Chris handling weapon and medical supplies, and Vitali helping me with pack procedure and battle plans, Evalyn has stepped in and helped take over the day-to-day financial needs of the pack, which I also appreciate. Fighting and training has never been her strong suit, so she's found other areas where she can be of use and it's working out wonderfully. Everyone is pulling their weight and, for the time being, we're running like a very well-oiled machine.

"I talked to Tyson about the next produce shipment, and we agreed to err on the side of caution, so I negotiated for the Alpine Pack to have their driver take a different route to the pack. Just in case someone tries to stop supplies from coming in or out of the territory," says Evalyn.

"That's brilliant thinking, we can't take any chances," I agree. "How are the meetings going?" I ask, turning to Eric.

"Good, everyone is really benefiting from it. There's another one scheduled for tonight. The meetings really seem to be boosting morale at the moment. It won't necessarily prepare them for what's to come, but it at least lets them know support is waiting for them afterwards," he informs me.

"I really can't thank you enough for what you've done. I am grateful each day Zarseti paired you with Vitali because he's not the only one who benefits from you being here," I smile.

Cute as a button, Eric blushes like a tomato. I may overdo it on the compliments sometimes just because I love watching him blush like that.

"You have to stop doing that," he scolds.

"Not a chance," I chuckle.

Once our meeting is over and they're packing up, I am debating whether or not to send Marcus a link to check in on him when the pack alarm started blaring.

"Alpha! There are hundreds of wolves coming from the south!"

"Fuck, I've never seen so many wolves attacking..."

"And these are all humans?"

My head is a cyclone of voices, all vying for my attention. I can barely differentiate who is talking.

"SILENCE!" I command through the pack-link. "Eva, Eric, you know the drill, make sure all the civilians get to the bunkers, go!" I instruct and they take off. *"ATTENTION INVICTUS PACK. All civilians follow emergency procedures and safely make your way to the nearest bunker. Triage unit, set up and remain on standby to retrieve injured and sedated wolves. Border patrol, secure the perimeter; we do not want a sneak attack. Warriors, proceed to the southern border and get into formation. Snipers, gather your weapons and take to the trees. We've been training for this, now time to show them what we're made of!"* I declare to a chorus of howls.

As I'm saying this, I dive out the window – talk about déjà vu – and shift on the way down. My workout gear is shredded, and I land on four paws. Zara takes over and sprints to the south border to join the warriors. We arrive just as the attacking wolves cross the tree line and it is a clashing of fur and teeth all around. We knew to expect this many wolves but seeing it up close is shocking, to say the least.

Every warrior is doing their best to subdue the invading wolves without killing them and while some are successful, others are forced to remain on the defensive. Snipers in the trees are taking down wolves left and right and quickly reloading. Zara is an absolute machine! She's manoeuvring around, pulling wolves off pack members who are getting overwhelmed and successfully incapacitating the invading wolves. It's like the wolf version of a sleeper hold. She's clamping her jaws around their necks but instead of going for a killing snap, she's adding pressure to the base of the skull just enough to knock them out.

"If you see a large snake-like creature, that's Mei and you are to stay out of her way," I warn my pack and I hear confused muttering in return.

Zara is about to pry an attacking wolf off a warrior when she's intercepted by four snarling wolves. They're smaller than her but not scared of her in the least. She bares her teeth and crouches as the four wolves surround her. They immediately pounce, one clawing into her right flank deeply, drawing blood and another biting into her left hind leg. Instead of howling in pain, she growls in anger.

She head-butts the wolf to her right, disorienting it, then quickly turns, sinking her teeth into the one latched to her hind leg, ripping it off her. They're hurt, but not dead. She then focuses on the two in front. She latches onto the neck of the wolf on the left, putting them in a sleeper hold while kicking the wolf on the right with her hind legs. Pain shoots up her leg, but she shakes it off. The wolf caught in her jaws goes slack while a nearby sniper knocks out the other three she took down. But there's no time to celebrate as a new group of five wolves are on her in an instant. She keeps having to take on large numbers of wolves, more so than the other warriors and we're both getting pissed off. Worse, it's tiring her out and slowly her injuries are mounting.

As she's taking on these groups of wolves, I see Mei in her human form racing around at her top speed, pulling wolves off overwhelmed warriors, and occasionally stopping to heal those who are in really bad shape. No deaths so far, but I don't know how long that will last.

While Zara is focused on the wolves surrounding her, I notice a man in the distance. He's 6'8" short black hair, glowing green eyes, ripped muscles and veins bulging through his olive skin, which I can see clearly because he is standing there butt-fucking-naked. I mean nudity is common with us, but he's making it seem weird. I don't have to guess who he is. The fact he looks like an older, more muscular version of Ryker tells me everything I need to know. Mykel joined the fight. Good, I get to enjoy killing him.

He's leaning against a tree, dick vacationing in the wind, and he's glaring daggers at Zara. His strategy is pretty obvious and annoying as fuck. Overwhelm Zara so that when he comes in for the kill she's weak and easy to take down. What a weak and pathetic excuse for an Alpha. I bet that's how he took down the Alpha of the pack he took over, by playing dirty.

Two can play that game.

"Mei! Get these wolves off me, Mykel's here and I need to get to him," I order.

"On it!" She responds.

Within seconds, every wolf surrounding us is knocked on their asses. Mei proudly salutes us, which makes me and Zara chuckle, before she zips off. Just as Zara sets her sights on Mykel – I refuse to call him 'Alpha' – we hear a large wolf coming at us from our right. Zara has taken a lot of damage to her right flank and can't afford another. I notice the smug son of a bitch is smirking, which makes me want to claw his face off.

Before Zara can pivot and catch the approaching wolf, the scent of caramel overrides our senses, and a large ball of russet fur is ploughing into the wolf that was aiming for Zara's flank, with a sickening crack. The enemy wolf goes tumbling across the forest floor and glowing eyes the colour of the forest in spring are staring at us. For just a few seconds the sounds of howls, whines, growls and the breaking and cracking of bones along with the scent of blood, vanishes and all I can see, and smell is the wolf in front of me.

Chapter Thirty-Five
Marcus

Being without Amelia before we marked was the shittiest period of my life but being marked to her and being away from her takes the fucking cake. What made it even more unbearable was she'd put up a barrier so I couldn't link her or feel anything she felt. At first, I accepted it but then it was starting to piss me off. So I texted her and kindly asked her to take it down, which she did.

I both regret and don't regret making her do it. On one hand, I'm relieved to feel our connection. But on the other hand, I can feel her sadness, her grief, her loneliness, and her anxiety. It's eating away at me. I should be with her, but I know part of her problems are caused by me.

Breaking the news to my parents that not only was I marked and mated but I was leaving the pack and joining another pack as a Luna received mixed reviews. Dad was over the fucking moon. I mean, he was radiating joy and pride. He respects hierarchy, respects our Goddess and hearing his son just ranked up and will be running a pack had him running around announcing it to all his mates. Hadn't expected that much enthusiasm, but I am not complaining. Mum, of course, was a whole other kettle of fish.

"No. No son of mine is becoming a Luna, what will people think? How can I show my face around the pack if people know my son, the former Beta is now a *Luna*," she hisses, like the word 'Luna' is dirty. Amelia was right my mother's opinions – prejudices I should say – were warping me more than I wanted to realise or admit.

"Oh, for Goddess sake Jessica! You're being ridiculous. Our son has been chosen by the Gods themselves to be the leader of his own pack and you're over here acting like he just told us he knocked up some she-wolf who he isn't fated to," dad huffs in irritation.

"It's not natural, Jerome! Our son is a man, not a girl. He needs to set this Amelia girl straight and remind her that her duty as a good she-wolf is to bare his pups, none of this nonsense," she scoffs.

That comment had me seething with anger. I love Amelia, she has brought me more happiness than I could ever wish for. I want a real-life with her as equals, fighting side by side, taking care of our pack. She's not some fucking baby factory. I was about to blow, but dad beat me to it.

"That is enough! You are the former Beta Female of this pack; I will not tolerate you disgracing this family by listening to you insult another Alpha. If the God's chose this for our son then you are not the one to decide what's natural and what isn't," my dad shouts.

My mum just blinks at him in astonishment, "How can you speak to me like that?"

"Because you are hurting our son, our pup. Not to mention this young woman is officially our daughter, she is family. We should be welcoming her with open arms, not degrading her. Keep this up and any pups they have she won't let you near," he says in warning.

"Marcus would never let that happen," she says confidently.

I snort, "Oh, yes I would. You're insulting the woman I love, the woman literally made for me and reducing her to nothing more than a walking incubator. She is more than that and she showed me how narrow-minded I've been. I love you mum, but I don't want our future pups to think the way I did, and if you're going to keep this up then no, I wouldn't let you near them. What if we had a daughter? Would you sit there and tell your grandpup she couldn't or shouldn't take her rightful place as Alpha one day?"

Her face morphs from one of shock to anger, then sadness. "I'm sure you'll have a son," she says dismissively.

"Or I'll have a daughter, or maybe both, but I won't deny my child their birth rite just because of their gender. It's not right. My mind is made up and I'm not changing it. I just hope, in time, you see things how I do. At least for my sake," I sigh sadly.

I never realised that it's not just men who can be sexist towards women. Mum is definitely a product of her upbringing. She wanted to be a stay at home mum and there's nothing wrong with that, I was glad I had her around to care for me. But that worked for her, that doesn't work for everyone. To be honest, I can't picture Amelia as a housewife, and I don't fucking want to. I like my woman and how she knows what she wants and goes for it. The thought of her only living to take care of me makes me uncomfortable.

Trying to find someone to replace me as Beta of this pack was just as hard as trying to knock sense into my mum, but eventually, we finally found the perfect person. We settled on Bryant, who is the pack's head warrior. We all have a good friendship with him and he's smart and loyal. Jasper offered the Beta role to Calix and then the Gamma role to Aiden, but they decided to stay in their respective roles and let Bryant take on the Beta position. He was sworn in yesterday and the transition has been smooth. Now all that's left is to say goodbye.

"I thought this would be harder," I say as I put the last box in the back of my truck.

"Is that your way of telling us you won't miss us?" Pouts Aiden.

"I will miss you knuckleheads a lot, but it's not like we'll never see each other again," I remind them.

"Of course not, we're coming to your Luna ceremony after all," says Jasper with a smirk.

"I know you're trying to get a reaction out of me, but it's not going to work. I'm in this one hundred per cent. I want her; I want this," I breathe.

"I know, I'm just teasing. Have you told her yet?" Jasper asks while bouncing Blake in his arms.

"Not yet. I wanted to tell her in person, not over a link. She deserves to hear it from me and see that I mean it. I've caused her too much hurt and doubt, I need to do this right," I say firmly.

"Look at you being all romantic and acting responsible like a Luna," Aiden jeers.

"Keep it up and I'll have Amelia declaring a war for disrespecting her Luna," I smirk.

"Oh, you are fucking loving this," Calix chortles.

"Ya know what? I am. I really fucking am," I grin.

"Do you have everything?" Aiden asks looking over the contents in the back of my truck.

"Everything that I need. I'd love to take you guys with me, but I guess this pack is stuck with you pricks," I smirk.

Aiden comes in for a hug, followed by Calix and then Jasper hands his son over to me. I smile and hold the little guy in my arms.

"Now listen up Blake. I won't be around anymore so I'm putting you in charge of giving your dad a hard time, okay? I expect you to annoy the hell out of him and make a mess of the packhouse. Even give him some extra stinky diapers, but I'm always going to be your Uncle Marcus, so when you're a big boy and you need advice on what not to do with women, then you come to me. Oh, and save yourself for your animai, okay?" I say kissing his cheek and giving him a big hug. I'm really going to miss the little tike. I'm a bit sad I won't get to watch him grow up and become Alpha, but I know he'll do us all proud.

"Do as he says, not as he does," Calix jokes.

I land a firm smack to the back of his head as I hand Blake back to Jasper, who is taking a deep breath.

"You ready?" He asks.

"Ready as I'll ever be," I nod, bracing myself.

"I, Alpha Jasper Clyborne hereby release you, Beta Marcus Hayda, from the Aurum Obscuro Pack," he declares in a gentle voice. Instead of a painful snap, I feel a comfortable weight disappear and leave behind a cold emptiness in its place. It's unpleasant, but I know soon enough that emptiness will be replaced by the warmth of my bond with my new pack.

I look up at my friends who are looking at me with glassy eyes and I can feel mine getting glassy too. These fuckers are going to make me cry. Jasper hands Blake over to Aiden and pulls me into a big monster hug, which I return just as firmly.

"I'm really going to miss you, brother," Jasper whispers in my ear.

"You'll always be my brother," I tell him.

We clap each other on the back and pull apart. I take one final look at the men I have grown up with and fought beside my whole life and the pack I called home for going on twenty-five years. I have so many good memories here, but now I'm ready for new ones. I climb into the truck and pull out of the packhouse driveway, saying goodbye to Washington and the Aurum Obscuro Pack.

The entire drive has had me buzzing with excitement... okay and nerves. I know I once again have to beg for forgiveness but I'm hoping proving to her I want her, and her pack, will ease tensions. I tried to tell her through texts and links that I was serious about this, but I could tell she wasn't buying it. I don't blame her. I said a lot of harsh things and made my stance on being a Luna painfully clear, but I think I've also made it clear by now I can be a bit of a moron.

"More than a bit," Ace scoffs.

"I'm making up for it alright? We're going to our new home," I retort.

"Assuming she even lets us in," Ace says sombrely.

"I'm not opposed to begging," I shrug.

We're halfway through the drive and are making our way through Oregon when sharp pain shoots down my right side and through my left leg causing me to swerve on the road. I manage to get the truck straight before pulling off to the side, panting and gritting my teeth.

"What the fuck was that?" I say through gritted teeth. I examine my side and my leg, but I don't find anything. That's when it dawns on me, I'm not the one who's hurt... Amelia is.

FUCK.

"Our animai is hurt! We have to get to her!" Ace thrashes in a panic.

Focusing on Amelia, I can feel her pain, her adrenaline, her anger, and annoyance. I focus harder on our link trying to see through her eyes. It starts coming to me, like an old television where you need to keep moving the antenna until the picture clears. Once I have a grip on what I'm doing, the picture comes through clear and easy and what I'm seeing has my heart caught in my throat. Amelia is surrounded by enemy-wolves and her pack warriors are all around her are in fights for their lives.

That motherfucker is attacking my pack again!

Oh, fuck no, no one messes with my woman or my pack. This fucker has a fucking death wish. I jump out of the truck, not even bothering to undress. I let Ace take over the shift, shredding through my clothes as we sprint off in the direction of the Invictus Pack.

My pack.

Talk about déjà vu. Ace is practically flying through the woods, his paws barely touching the ground. He has his eyes on where he's going while I am watching what Amelia is doing. She's fucking terrific! Groups of wolves keep focusing on her and she – or I suppose Zara – keeps knocking them down. But she's not going for any kill shots. This would be easier if they were going for kills. I know they're human and innocent, but I swear to the fucking Gods, if they fuck with my woman, I don't care how innocent they are. I am ripping them all to bloody pieces.

It only takes us minutes to cover the remainder of the distance to the Invictus territory. Fortunately, border patrol doesn't stop me. Either they recognise me from last time, or they've picked up Amelia's scent on me. Since we marked each other, a piece of each other's scent will always be on the other. Whatever reason they let me through, I'm grateful.

I follow the pull to Amelia and it's not long before I hear the savage sounds of wolves trying to rip each other to smithereens. I also hear the sound of projectiles cutting through the air. Must be the tranquillizers Amelia mentioned. Brilliant idea by the way.

The air is thick with tension and the smell of blood as wolf fights wolf, but I'm only interested in one wolf. I smell her before I see her. The delicious and inviting scent of mangoes and pineapples cuts through the blood with ease and engulfs me like a heady caress. My eyes find Zara's black and white form in the crowd, fur matted red and her poor body littered with injuries. But she doesn't seem to mind as she moves into an attack position, her eyes focused on something in the distance. I don't have time to look because as I'm approaching, I see a large brown and grey wolf barrelling towards her from the right, aiming for her heavily injured side.

Hell. To. The. Fucking. No.

"They're dead," Ace snarls.

Ace lets out a murderous growl that makes the very earth quake.

Well, this is new.

He picks up the pace and slams headfirst into the approaching wolf, colliding with its side to the sounds of bones shattering, sending it tumbling Gods know where. He quickly turns his attention to our animai. Our beautiful animai, who is looking back at us with those bright turquoise eyes.

Chapter Thirty-Six
Amelia

"**D**o you deliberately keep waiting until I'm gone to end up under attack? Is this your way of punishing me, by giving me a fucking heart attack?" Marcus huffs, his voice full of panic, frustration and concern. Ace whines as he looks over Zara who I'm sure looks pretty battered right now. He quickly trots over and licks her wounds, and she nudges his side affectionately.

"*Actually, yeah. I have an arrangement with Mykel to only attack when you make such a jerk of yourself, you have to leave.*"

"*Your sarcasm is noted,*" Marcus snorts.

"*You sure? Because I can take it up a notch,*" I offer.

"*We have missed you so much!*" Ace whines.

"*We missed you too, but if you don't mind, we have an 'Alpha' to kill, so if you could scoot to the side, my fury lover, we'd appreciate it,*" says Zara.

"*You're sexy when you're bossy,*" Ace growls lowly.

Zara quickly leaps on an approaching wolf coming up behind Ace, tossing them aside like a ragdoll. I catch a quick glance of Mykel who is looking a mixture of pissed off and amused; quite the dichotomy. Not sure how he's pulling that off.

"*Aww, you do care about us!*" Ace cheers.

"*Would you focus! We're in a war,*" Marcus scolds.

"Right. What can we do?" Ace says, turning serious.

"Mykel is mine, do your best to incapacitate enemy wolves instead of killing them. Keep as many as you can away from our fight," I tell him.

"I've got your back," says Marcus, a pang spreading through my chest as I remember the last time he said those words to me. *"I know we need to talk, and I promise we can talk all night, and I mean really talk, no fighting. So don't you dare fucking die."*

"Don't you dare die, either."

"Only one allowed to kill me is you, Ma Reine," he coos as Ace winks. Ace and Zara quickly nuzzle each other, the electricity from the contact giving us a boost of adrenaline. Ace then jumps into the fight with everyone else; it really is a warzone out here.

"You have to admit, he can be very charming when he wants to be," says Zara.

"Fight now, compliment animai later," I tell her.

We make our way over to Mykel as he pushes off the tree he's leaning on and starts toward us, exuding arrogance from every pore in his body.

"How long do you need me to give you?" I ask Zara.

"Ten minutes should do."

"Ten minutes it is," I say as we shift back into my human form. Once shifted I tap into the reserve in my human side and feel the healing of my injuries pick up speed. Zara needs to get her strength back before we can shift again. The asshole Alpha wannabe is raking his eyes over my body, his eyes dark with lust and it's making me want to puke up my breakfast.

"Finally getting to meet little Amelia Dolivo. Well, not so little, I guess," he smirks, licking his lips.

BARF!

"Sorry, this party was invite-only, and your name isn't on the list," I say regretfully.

He throws his head back in a laugh that sounds more like a bark, "Sense of humour. I like that in a woman. You know, I wondered what Elias did wrong for the Goddess to only bless him with a daughter and no sons, but she does work in mysterious ways. I'm starting to think she gave you to him so I would have a worthy Luna."

DOUBLE BARF!

"Wow, if you'd made that offer before I let my animai mark me…" I take a deep thoughtful breath, "Yeah, I'd still have told you to go fuck yourself."

For a second, his eyes flash with anger, but he quickly covers it up "If you won't be a good girl and be my Luna then I guess I'll just have to kill you. See, this pack will be mine. It was always supposed to be mine. Elias was a shit Alpha and now there's you. This pack needs to be saved and I'm just the man for the job." He stretches his arms wide.

"Is it just me, or do all the men in your family really love the sound of their own voice? But I guess someone has to, right? Sorry about your brother, by the way," I pout.

"I should thank you for that. He was useless anyway – you saved me having to kill him. But I'm definitely going to enjoy killing you," he says with a malevolent gleam in his eyes.

"So do it already," I roll my eyes, "Who stands around talking about killing someone instead of just killing them? Aww is this your first fight? Want me to go easy on you? Wouldn't want *little* Mykel getting hurt." I smirk, glancing at his dick to make my point. He lets out a vicious growl that shakes the earth beneath my feet. Good, I pissed him off. That was too easy.

He doesn't bother to shift; he runs right for me and I'm not stupid enough to think it won't hurt if he collides with me. I'm still healing and, while we are both Alphas, he's got a couple hundred pounds of muscle mass on me. He's got size and strength on his side, but I'm lither which means I'm faster and can manoeuvre better.

He feigns a punch from the right, but I can see his left on standby, so I duck and land a double punch to his gut and listen to the whoosh of air that leaves his lungs. I jump back, putting space between us. Now he looks even more pissed off. He's savagely swinging punches and throwing kicks, putting me on the defensive as I duck and dodge. At one point, I dodge a punch coming straight for my head and he hits the tree behind me instead. The tree splits in fucking half and I'm very grateful that wasn't my head. With the way his body is positioned, I use his knee as a step to leap up and wrap myself around him as I rain down blows on his head. He grabs me and throws my body into the ground with all his force and starts landing punches to my ribs.

One.

Two.

Three.

Three ribs broken in his onslaught and I'm struggling to breathe. I sacrifice my torso as I stop shielding myself and slam the heels of both palms into both his ears. He cries and rolls off me, allowing me to slowly move out of his way. My breathing is laboured and painful, the ribs on my left side are fucked and if he gets in one more punch, I'm likely to end up with a pierced lung. Just as I position myself to shield my left flank... SNAP. My knees nearly buckle as I feel my link to a pack member break.

My eyes are fiercely trained on Mykel.

I've lost another pack member and it's because of him. How many more people are going to suffer because of this son of a bitch? How many more lives is he going to ruin? Instead of pain or grief, all I feel is fury. The beast inside me isn't just stirring, it's erupting and I'm letting it out wholeheartedly. I want to watch this abomination weep at my feet. I want to watch the life leave his eyes the way he's done to so many others. I want his blood. A life for a life. With rage burning and bloodlust coursing through my veins and tingling on my tongue, I stalk towards my prey.

SNAP.

SNAP.

SNAP.

More pack-link's sever and that bastard uses my momentary distraction to punch me right in the fucking face. What is with these Mathers Betas breaking my Gods damn nose?! Unlike last time, I barely even feel it. All I can feel is the pain of the severed links morphing into strength as it feeds the bloodlust swirling around me.

"Zara..."

"NOW!" She cries.

I close my eyes as Zara's spirit and my own merge as one. I feel my nails extend into claws, my jaw reshape itself as canines distend, my broken nose turns into a broken snout, my ears forming points and light tufts of hair sprouting over my body.

A partial shift.

The human and the wolf, becoming as one.

A partial shift is one of the hardest things a mutolupus can do and requires being in perfect harmony with your wolf. But, when accomplished, the combined strength of both spirits unify into a whole new level of strength. A strength I'm about to use to kill this motherfucker.

As we merge, I can hear his fist breaking through the air, ready to collide with me, but I'm able to sense its direction – I guess all that sensory training paid off. With eyes still closed, I reach out and catch his hand. My eyes open and glow a fierce turquoise as I stare down the man responsible for the deaths of my people. Fear coats his features, his eyes blown wide open as he stares at the half-human, half-wolf form before him. His face begins to crumple in pain as I squeeze his fist, shattering the bones in his hand. I relish the scream he releases that pierces through the forest. A warning to all animals that there is a predator on the loose and that predator wants blood. My Alpha Spirit bursts from me like an atom bomb.

"What... are you?" He whispers, horrified as his body shakes before me.

"A fucking Alpha," I growl, my voice overlapping with Zara's.

I plunge one clawed hand through his chest, wrapping my hand around his heart, and the other into his neck, wrapping my fingers around his trachea. With one tug, I rip his heart from his chest holding it in my bare hand and with another tug, I rip his trachea from his neck. Blood coats my skin like a blanket as I watch the life leave this bastard's eyes. Blood gurgles through the hole in his throat as his body falls to the forest floor in a heap.

I crush the organs I'm holding in my hands and toss them aside like the worthless trash they are. Adrenaline is rushing through me, and my heart is pounding like a war drum. I hear the howls, I hear the carnage, but I also hear the snapping of twigs behind me. I quickly turn, my hand clasping around the throat of a familiar figure, but before I can crush their windpipe, I feel searing pain like acid, pierce my stomach.

A victorious smirk takes over their face, joy filling their amber eyes as I feel an agonising twisting sensation in my gut. "I told you he's mine," is the last thing I hear before my senses are overrun by pain and my screams are filling the air around me.

Chapter Thirty-Seven
Marcus

I t's hard to fight when you're worried about the person you love who – for Goddess knows what reason – has shifted into their human form to fight and is trading blows with some naked fucktard. Turns out I am not mentally equipped to handle that.

She's healing faster than I expected, but she's still pretty banged up, so this is an uneven fight in so many ways. The fucker clearly hung back, waiting for his army of wolves to wear her down so he can swoop in and take an easy win. What a weak fucking prick. Too scared to take her on at full strength so he waits till she's vulnerable. Even then she's terrific. She's effortlessly dodging his attacks, but she's not making any of her own, which I don't get.

"She's stalling. She's waiting for Zara to regain her energy," Ace informs me.

"Huh? How do you know that? Wait, that's a thing?" I ask confused.

"Zara and I have a very healthy relationship, thank you very much. Zara and Amelia work as a team. Everything they do is like a dance they've rehearsed a million times. We are so lucky to have them," he swoons as he grabs an enemy wolf by the tail and yanks them off an injured warrior. We see a wolf – who by scent I can tell is Chris – get cornered by three others, but he's not backing down. He looks like hell, though. He's bleeding heavily and he's keeping his weight off his front left paw.

One wolf goes in for the kill but before the other two can move, Ace and I have rammed into them, knocking them out of the way. Sometimes I wonder if Ace is secretly a goat rather than a wolf with the way he likes to headbutt things.

Chris is struggling with his opponent and we're about to help when six wolves come down on us. These are very, very bad odds. Ace moves into a crouch, not about to back down, but at speed faster than anything I've ever seen, there's a streak of black and gold and then something giant whipping through all six wolves like a bowling ball going for a strike. All six wolves go flying and land, crumpled in a heap. We're left with our jaw hanging slack.

Standing at eight feet tall is Mei, but not Mei as we're used to seeing her. Her eyes are those of a snake, full orbs of gold with a black slit down the centre. The top half of her body is human-like but black and gold scales move down the edges of her face, down her neck and coat her usually creamy skin. Her entire torso is littered in black and gold scales in fascinating geometric patterns. Her torso is shaped like that of a woman – a naked woman – but the scales prevent her from looking exposed. As you get to her waist her legs are replaced with the largest fucking snake's tail I have ever seen. It has to be at least ten metres long, also covered in geometric black and gold scales.. She's massive and intimidating, but at the same time she looks… majestic. Something about her makes Ace and I want to submit to her.

We've already seen how strong Mei is in human form, but it seems in this gargantuan form, she's even stronger and faster. I mean she just knocked six wolves away like she was swatting a fucking fly. Her eyes lock on the wolf attacking Chris and I can see fury cross her normally sweet face. She strikes at a speed faster than a cobra and yanks the wolf by the scruff of its neck, tossing it aside like nothing. Her face softens as she coils around Chris' wolf, protecting him and comforting him. I can't really see what she's doing because her tail is acting as a wall around them, shielding them, but I can see a soft yellow light shining from behind the wall of scales.

Suddenly, I see another wolf launch itself at Mei's tail, its teeth bared, ready to sink through the scales. But as it makes contact with her scaley flesh, the wolf's teeth shatter, causing the wolf to howl and whine in pain. Mei, on the other hand, hasn't even flinched. Fucking hell, how indestructible are nagatas? Thank the Gods she's on our side. Remind me to ask which God made her species.

This whole time I've felt the pain of Amelia's fight. I know that fucker is hurting her, but I haven't been able to get to her and it's killing me. When I feel that familiar bloodlust seep through our bond, I'm very certain this fucker is about to meet his end, but I am not prepared for what I see. Through the crowd I see Amelia fighting Mykel, but Amelia doesn't look like Amelia anymore, she looks….

"Beautiful," Ace sighs.

She's part human, part wolf. Amelia can do a partial shift? I thought those were myths. Only the strongest and most in sync wolves were said to be able to do those. I'm watching in stunned awe as she completely demolishes that motherfucker, ripping out his heart and throat until my sight becomes obscured by two wolves clawing at each other in front of me. I go to move around them when the scent of lilies wafts my way and instantly every hair is on end.

Davina.

Where the fuck is that psycho bitch?

Ace is whipping his head around furiously when agonising pain pierces through our stomach, knocking us to the ground. It feels like my link to Amelia just got set on fire. Ace lets out a devastated howl. He's up on his feet leaping over the wolves in front of us and my heart doesn't just stop, it gets pulverised as I see Davina standing in front of Amelia with a dagger plunged into her stomach. Suddenly all I can hear is the sound of Amelia's screams.

Why didn't I kill Davina when I had the chance? Why didn't I hunt the bitch down? I knew she was crazy; I knew she was violent and yet I was stupid enough to think Amelia's threats had been enough to make her back off. I should have known better.

I've never felt so much anger and fear in my entire life. It's like the earth is being ripped away and nothing is making sense. Ace and I are on the same page and he finally gets his wish as we charge at Davina in a blind rage, lunging at her, jaw open wide. She has the decency to look at us in fear, her life flashing before her eyes. Our jaws clasp around her head, tearing it right off her miserable body.

Davina's head rolls away, eyes still wide, blood spurting out of her neck, her arms twitching before the rest of her falls to the ground. I take over the shift and catch Amelia as she starts to drop. She's shifted back into her human form. I drop to the ground, cradling her in my arms, brushing the hair out of her face. I look her over and see the dagger sticking out of her stomach. I know this isn't a normal dagger, I can smell it and feel what it's doing to her, so in this case, it's better out than in. I swiftly pull the dagger out and before I can place my hand over the wound, she catches my hand, stopping me.

"Wolf... ram," she struggles to say.

I feel the blood drain from my face and my soul leave my body as I hear that word. I look down and I can see thick, black, poisonous veins quickly spreading across her stomach. Tears fall from my eyes, and I feel like lava has been poured into my stomach and is moving through my body. This is what Amelia is feeling.

"FUCK!" I scream as a sob breaks from my lips. I hold a hand to Amelia's cheek, keeping my eyes on hers while I keep her body close to mine. "Amelia, listen to me, you stay with me, alright? You are not fucking dying on me, you gave me your word. You're meant to be the reliable one, I'm the fuck up. I'm sorry, okay? I'm sorry for every fucking stupid thing I said, I was wrong, I was so fucking wrong. I love you, I want you, I want our pack, I want to be your Luna and I can't be your Luna if you're gone, so you can't die," I beg, pain and desperation coating my words like a glove.

Her body is writhing from the agony she feels, but Amelia being Amelia, instead of screaming from the pain the poison is causing, she smiles, placing her warm bloody hand against my tear-stained cheek. I don't care, I hold her hand in place like it's the most precious thing to ever exist. Tears slip down the sides of her face and she whimpers before silencing her pain.

"Your timing... is impeccable," she teases. "But I love you anyway."

I let out a strangled laugh as I rest my forehead on hers, "If you love me then stay with me. I'm not letting you go, not now, not ever."

"Luna, give her to me," I hear Mei's gentle voice.

I shake my head furiously, refusing to let Amelia go. They'll have to kill me first, and with the way my heart is shattering into pieces, I don't think I'd fucking mind death. If I lose Amelia, I'm following after her. Simple as that.

"I can save her," Mei says, her voice strong.

Something about her tone tells me to listen and not to question her. So with a shaky breath and more reluctance than I thought imaginable, I gently place Amelia on the ground and scoot back, keeping a tight grip on her hand.

Mei's massive body coils around us as she leans over Amelia. She places a hand over Amelia's chest and a warm yellow light quickly spreads from her hand through Amelia's body. I watch the light travel until it reaches the poison. It's like the light and the poison are living entities having a battle of their own, and the light is winning. It pushes forward and, as it does, the black veins begin to recede until they vanish completely. The wound in her stomach seals closed.

I feel as the agonising pain rippling through her disappears, and watch as she gasps and smiles, her face relaxed. I only just notice I can feel all her other wounds are gone too. I look her over and there's not a scratch or bruise to be seen, even her nose – which had been crooked – is now back to its normal, adorable shape.

Mei pulls back, smiling down at Amelia, "All good?"

"All good, go take care of the others," she smiles.

"On it!" Mei chirps, and in the blink of an eye, she's slithered off.

Amelia sits up, her eyes assessing me carefully, while I'm trying to process what just happened. "Did you mean what you said? Were you serious or was th–"

I silence her questions and her doubt by grabbing her face and capturing her lips in a consuming kiss that I want us to burn in for all eternity. Her fingers weave themselves into my hair as she kisses me back with the fire of a thousand suns.

My Amelia, my sweet, strong Amelia is okay.

"I meant every fucking word," I breathe as we break for air, resting our foreheads against each other. "I wanted to tell you in person. I choose you. I choose our pack. I'll proudly be your Luna, if you're willing to accept my dumb ass, that is."

She gives me a bright smile, tears twinkling in her eyes like crystals, "I would love nothing more than to guide and run this pack with you. No matter how many times you put your foot in your mouth."

"I'm going to start attending Foot-In-Mouth Anonymous meetings first thing tomorrow," I jokingly swear as I wrap her in my arms.

Her laughter vibrates through her chest and against mine while she wraps her arms around me, amplifying the electricity coursing through me. I don't get to enjoy it for too long before she's pulling back and looking around. I'd completely forgotten there was a war going on. I help her to her feet and survey the scene with her. All the enemy wolves are either unconscious or cowering in fear, looking confused and unsure what to do. It seems Mykel's command over them broke once he died and now they're just confused animals.

"We need to get Mykel's body to the medical staff. They need his blood so they can start curing everyone," Amelia says calmly.

"Let's get to work then. We've got a lot to do," I say, squeezing her hand.

We quickly fall into a rhythm, checking on the wounded and commanding a team to get Mykel's body to the triage unit. At least something good can come from this. I have no idea what happens once we turn these people back into themselves, but at least one part of their nightmare will be over. Then maybe Amelia and I can finally have some time with each other. At least I hope so.

Chapter Thirty-Eight
Marcus

During the battle, we lost four good warriors. It's never good or easy to lose anyone, but the fact this pack took on such a large scale attack and only suffered four casualties is a fucking miracle. But I won't say that out loud. It's pretty obvious we owe our victory on two main factors. Amelia's smart planning and the sniper team who were taking down enemy targets swiftly and effectively. And, of course, Mei.

Without our resident nagata, we would have all been spectacularly fucked up the ass with a branding iron. Just have it rammed up there good. She single-handedly was able to keep most of the enemy wolves back and healed so many warriors, preventing further casualties. She's being humble about it of course, but we know we owe a great deal to that woman.

I wasn't here when the pack said their goodbyes to Izac and Kylie, but at least I was able to be here for these fallen warriors. Jacob Ford. Jessica Platt. Shane Black. Robert McCarty. I never knew them, but I will forever remember their names. Their bravery and sacrifice saved their pack.

My pack.

The service for them was beautiful and hearing their friends and family share stories about them made me feel like I had known them all my life. Mourning their loss was genuine. Their service also meant stepping inside the pack temple. We didn't have a temple dedicated to our Goddess back at

Aurum Obscuro. Naturally, we believe in the deity who created us, we're just not very spiritual, nor do we believe that praying to her gets us anywhere. I guess we view her more as another supernatural being, one who just so happened to create us and could uncreate us if we pissed her off.

I have to admit though, being inside that temple, being close to her statue, was pretty surreal. It made me realise how small I am in the grand scheme of things and how stupid I had been over things like arguing and nearly ruining my relationship over a fucking title. But I'm finally starting to get my priorities in order.

Amelia and I haven't had a chance to sit down and have that talk. Neither of us are putting it off, we've just been busy. Cleaning up after the battle, seeing to the injured, ensuring the cure was handled and helping administer it to all the poor people Mykel had turned. Yildiz and Nuray had arranged for a makkari to erase the memories of what was done to them and replace them with different memories. Memories that would spare the humans trauma and sound plausible for why they'd been missing for so long. They have since been returned to their families fully healed.

Ryker Mathers – the turd stain who poisoned Amelia – was executed the day after the battle. I graciously volunteered for the task and can honestly say I took a great deal of pleasure killing that fucker. I nearly lost the love of my life because of him, and I despise anyone who would betray their Alpha or their pack. So killing him was the highlight of that day.

After the funeral service, Amelia and I return to the packhouse and up to the Alpha suite. Apparently, her parents had moved out while I was away. They have a cottage being built, but they decided to move into it while it's being finished. This was great news; means I don't have to worry about them interrupting anything, also Amelia said she never told them about our fight, which I am grateful for. I don't need her mum punching me again. Or worse, her dad.

"Drink?" Amelia asks as she walks over to the liquor cabinet in the corner.

"Please," I say while taking off my tie throwing it over the couch.

Amelia pours two glasses and walks over handing one to me. I take it while looking her over. The sight of her still takes my breath away. Her yellow sundress makes her hair look more golden, her skin glow and her eyes look like tranquil beach water. She's perfect. She sits down taking a sip of her drink and I sit down beside her feeling the nerves bubble up inside of me.

"Is now okay to talk?" I ask hesitantly.

"I appreciate you asking, but yeah, we can talk," she nods.

"What I said that day…"

"You meant every word, we both know that," she sighs.

"I did. I won't insult you by lying, but you were also right, about everything," I say with sincerity. She looks up at me assessing me as if she's trying to crack some ancient code. I guess women struggle to understand us men, just as much as we struggle to understand them.

"Marcus, I know you haven't been lying or pretending when you've said you wish to be Luna. I've seen the way you've cared for this pack as your own the last few days. I just am struggling to understand how your opinions could change so fast," she admits.

"I had an epiphany," I tell her. She looks at me dubiously and she looks so cute with that look on her face that it makes me chuckle. "I'm serious. It was because of Mei."

"Mei?" She says in surprise.

"She came to speak to me after our fight. She was being so sweet and not at all judgemental, her words came from the heart, and I realised a couple of things. First, I realised I had not a fucking thing to complain about. Seriously, what was my issue? I have a great family, amazing friends, the love of a terrific woman. Her family accepted me – even after I was an asshole – her friends are accepting me, and Gods think I'm worthy to run a pack. My life is full of so many blessings that I was taking for granted and still finding something to complain about and I was doing it in front of Mei. In front of a woman who lost everything that mattered at an early age and spent years being horrifically treated, yet she didn't hate the world or those around her. Instead, she appreciates everything because she knows what it means to have nothing, and there I was being an ungrateful asshole," I say regretfully.

Amelia's eyes soften as she reaches out squeezing my hand. "I don't even think I could be as sweet as she is if I'd lived her life," Amelia admits as I kiss the back of her hand, the contact making my lips tingle.

"The way she viewed Alphas and Lunas… it was like everything shifted. You were right, too much of my mum's values and beliefs were burned into my brain and they are wrong. Mei said an Alpha is the leader born into the pack and a Luna is the leader chosen by the Gods to assist them. I thought it was kind of beautiful, the way she said that."

"You know that's basically what I was trying to tell you," she snorts.

"I know. I was just being too stubborn to listen and that's on me. Amelia, I don't want to think the way my mum does. I love her to death, but it doesn't mean her views are right. I couldn't help but think what would happen if we had a little girl," I say causing Amelia's eyes to go wide, "Could I sit my daughter down and tell her she can't and shouldn't follow in the steps of her ancestors or pursue anything her heart desired because she's a girl? That instead she should be some fucker's baby maker? Not fucking happening. Also if we do have a girl, *IF* she has children that shit ain't happening until she's like thirty. And if her animai turns out to be some prick who just wants to knock her up and sees that as all she's good for… well, let's just say I know a lot of good places to bury a body."

Amelia chuckles as she wipes tears from her eyes.

Fuck, did I upset her?

Wait, no, she doesn't feel sad…

"You think about us having pups?" She asks with a sweet smile.

"Well, yeah. I mean, not right now, but someday," I say, rubbing the back of my head.

"Someday sounds nice," she sighs contentedly leaning against my shoulder.

I smile placing a kiss atop her head and breathe in her perfect tropical scent. Fuck how I love it.

"So, when do you want to have the ceremony?" I ask.

"We can have it whenever you want. If you want something casual then we can whip it up in a day or two. If you want something extravagant, going to need at least a week minimum," she says, sitting up.

"What did you do for your Alpha ceremony?"

"We had a big cookout," she shrugs.

Is she serious?

"You're kidding. You did not have a cookout to celebrate becoming Alpha," I chuckle.

"I'm serious. Traditionally it should have been on my twenty-first birthday, but we knew to expect challenges. So, for my birthday, we had a big party hosted on the training grounds, and then the next day we had my Alpha ceremony during a nice cookout. Which was smart since I ended up having to defend myself and title from two nutjobs," she scowls.

A growl rumbles in my chest thinking about the fuckers who tried to kill her at her Alpha ceremony. She couldn't even have the ceremony she deserved like so many Alphas before her all because of some fucking assholes.

"That settles it then. We're going to have the biggest, most lavish Luna ceremony the Invictus Pack has ever seen," I announce.

"What?" She asks with surprise, her eyebrows shooting up.

"You didn't get to have the Alpha ceremony you deserved, so let's make up for that with this ceremony. We're not just celebrating my title, we're celebrating us becoming a team, so let's go all out," I grin, thrilled with my idea.

"You'd do that for me?" She breathes, a tremble in her voice.

"I'd do that for us," I tell her firmly, holding my hand against her cheek. Her eyes close and her face leans into my hand that way I love oh so fucking much.

In a blink, our glasses are set aside and she's straddling me. Her lips find mine and proceed to dominate my own in a bruising kiss that has blood rushing south and need pumping through my veins. Her fingers tangle in my hair, and I taste the bourbon on her tongue as my sweet sexy Alpha drowns me in her kisses. I surrender to the force of them. I want to drown in them. I want to be consumed by them until I can't breathe and even then I don't want her to stop. My hands take their time exploring and memorising the curves and dips of her fantastic body, a body I haven't experienced in an entire fucking week.

My lips respond to hers, following their every command. The mouth-watering scent of her arousal fills my senses as she tugs on my hair forcefully and the tingle of pain in my scalp shoots pleasure right to my fucking dick. I growl into her hot mouth and grip her hips, forcing her to grind against the bulge straining in my pants. Her sweet moans enter my mouth and spread through my body as she finds her own rhythm, grinding herself against me, seeking friction and fuck does it feel good.

Her lips pull away and I almost whimper at the loss, but my whimper turns into a groan as she runs her hot tongue down my neck and teases my mark. Pleasure ignites like a fire inside me and all I can think about is being buried inside of her, feeling her wet walls clenching and quivering around me as she finds her release. She pulls my earlobe into her mouth sucking and biting on it, driving me fucking insane. My hands come up and cup her perfect tits, squeezing and massaging them in my palms, running the pads of my thumbs over her taut nipples through the fabric of her dress. Fuck, she's not wearing a bra.

"I want you inside me," she whispers seductively in my ear, and I nearly explode in my pants.

"Yes, Alpha," I smirk, giving her breasts a firm squeeze and making her yelp.

Grabbing her ass, I get up from the couch with her arms and legs wrapped around me. I carry my sexy woman to the bedroom as she continues to suck and kiss my neck, no doubt leaving her mark wherever she can. Having my woman claiming me is the fucking hottest shit in this universe.

I kick the door shut behind me, throwing us both onto the bed, her body trapped underneath me. I trace her Alpha's Mark on her heaving chest with my tongue to the sound of breathy moans as she bucks her hips against me, her needy pussy seeking what it knows can bring it unmatched pleasure. I press into her, grinding my hard bulge against her soaking wet panties.

"Is this what you want?" I ask as I slide my hand into her dress, massaging her breast while gliding my tongue up her neck.

"No," she breathes, and before I know it she's flipped us so she's on top. Fucking hell, this is a nice view. "This is what I want," she says, her eyes and voice full of lust.

"Show me," I tell her as I glide my hands up her inner thighs. She quickly pulls off her dressing, tossing it away, my eyes getting hypnotized by the way her tits bounce. She guides my hands to her panties, her eyes on me with so much dominance. You'd think I'd feel weird about it, but it's fucking turning me on. I want to see her dominate me, I want to see and feel her use my body for her pleasure. There is no one I would rather share control with or surrender to than this Goddess of a woman.

"Rip them," she commands.

"With pleasure," I smirk, and, as she commands, I tear her panties off her body, exposing her dripping wet pussy to my hungry eyes. I notice the traces of hair starting to grow on her mound and my dick twitches painfully at the sight. She's growing it out just like I asked her to. Fuck, I love this woman.

With sexy ferociousness, she rips open my shirt and claws her fingers down my chest, the sting of it making my dick ache. I'm not sure how much more I can take. She undoes my pants, pulling my dick out and, without any teasing or hesitation, she slowly, agonisingly, sinks down onto me. I throw my head back, letting out a throaty groan that is in sync with her own. It's so fucking hot knowing my woman craved my cock so badly she couldn't bother to undress me. She really is perfect for me.

She places her hands on my chest as she starts rocking her hips back and forth, her walls perfectly massaging my cock. My hands knead her thighs, her hips, her sides and finally her tits as she continues to ride my cock at an excruciatingly slow pace, which I fucking love. With her slow movements, I can feel every glorious inch of her, every little flutter of pleasure her pussy takes from my cock. It is pure heaven.

Gradually, she starts working herself up and down on my cock, lifting slowly up to the tip before plunging me balls deep inside her again. How did I end up with such a fucking pro? The room is filled with our groans of pleasure and my eyes are fixated on every movement she makes. The flush of her skin, the bounce of her breasts, the arch of her back, the way her mouth dips open in pleasure. My hands caress every inch of her soft skin and I feel like a man who is lost at sea, and she is my life preserver. I can't exist without her.

Her body is coated in a sheen of sweat as she works to take her time building us up to the height of pleasure. Coming isn't the goal right now. We're one in our wants and needs in this moment, all we care about is feeling each other, feeling connected and getting lost in the pleasure we give each other. If I could live in this moment forever, I fucking would.

Her hands grip onto my forearms as my hands travel into her sunshine hair. Her mouth latches around my thumb sucking and moaning around it making me twitch and thrust up into her pussy. A deviant smirk spreads across her face, and with her lust-filled eyes she thrusts those perfect fucking hips, picking up speed with each thrust and I watch as she loses herself to pleasure.

"I need to feel you come," she cries in ecstasy.

Fucking hell.

I keep one hand around the back of her neck, another gripping her hip, urging her on, forcing her to ride my cock with everything she has. I want all of her, I want to watch her give me every last piece of herself until she comes undone.

Sweat coats our skin and I'm grunting as my balls tighten, begging for release. Her breathing speeds up until she's holding her breath, her tell-tale sign she's on the brink of climax. Her hips are thrusting like her pussy is trying to demolish my cock and I want it to.

"Fuck… that's it… strangle my cock with your pussy," I say through gritted teeth as I watch her pussy in action.

"M-Mar-cus… fuck… I'm…. fuck…"

"Come for me baby, fucking come for me!" I shout, barely holding on.

"MARCUS!" she screams, thrusting uncontrollably as her eyes roll back and her pussy tightens around me and she finds her release. I finally let go, my orgasm erupting from me in explosive pleasure. Black spots swim across my vision as I empty myself deep into her channel.

"AMELIA!" I grunt as her walls quiver around me.

Amelia collapses on top of me and my arms wrap around her in a protective cocoon. We're panting, our hearts racing as we just bask in the aftermath of our release. My fingers trail up and down her back and I smile at the little shiver it elicits from her.

"You have brought me more despair than I ever thought I could feel in my life," she whispers, causing my breath to catch in my throat and my body to turn to stone. "But you've also forced me to feel more joy than I could ever imagine. The despair was only what it was because the joy and love I feel for you is so strong. I understand why Kylie did what she did because I don't think I'd be strong enough to live in this world if I lost you," she says lifting her head to look at me. So many emotions are swirling in her eyes, but the clearest emotion is love. "I need you, Marcus. I love you more than I ever thought I could love someone, and I can't see my life without you in it. I don't want to, because for all your faults, I know there's no one who will ever love me the way you do. There is no one who will love you like I do."

My throat feels clogged, and my heart feels ready to explode. Tears prick my eyes at this beautiful woman's confession. I've put her through so much, I've said things I can never take back and yet she still chooses to love me. Or maybe she never had a choice. Either way, I will make sure from this moment on she never regrets loving me. I pull her lips to mine, sharing with her all my love, all my need, and all my determination to be a better man. A man worthy of her and this pack. This is a new beginning, and I won't take anything for granted anymore. From now on I will treasure every moment I have and every day I have with this woman in my life.

Chapter Thirty-Nine
Marcus

Luna ceremonies are a lot of fucking work but, thank the Gods, I haven't had to lift a finger. I used to make jokes about how all Lunas did was plan parties and events. I never meant it, but it is a big part of running a pack and props to those Lunas. Amelia, Evalyn, and Eric have been working hard on planning this Luna ceremony, the only thing I've been asked to do was pick flowers, a colour scheme and whether I want it indoors or outdoors. I chose indoors; the pack colours – so green and black – and red roses. I did ask to be left to handle what I'll be wearing since I want to surprise Amelia.

What a blessing Grandma Sorrell had been. She is a feisty bite-sized woman. She is so delightful until she gets annoyed and then she's dropping the hammer. The moment someone around the pack makes a snide comment about me being Luna, Sorrell is whipping them into shape. She doesn't even have to do much. A strong smack to the head or a tug of the ears has them in tears and then she makes them do chores. Alden just watches her with amusement and pride. Clearly still madly in love. My grandparents passed away many years ago, so having Alden and Sorrell adopt me as their own has been really nice. I love those two.

Fleur has been incredibly supportive, teaching me the words I'll need to say during the ceremony while Elias has been teaching Amelia what she needs to do. We've gone over it enough times so I'm hoping I don't fuck it up tomorrow.

My parents should be here any minute and I'm nervous as fuck. Dad, I know, will adore Amelia. Mum… well this could get ugly, but I know my woman can handle herself. I take a deep breath as I see my parent's car pull into the long dirt path and park in one of the open spots in front of the packhouse.

Dad – chivalrous as ever – gets out and goes to open mum's door, helping her out before they walk over to greet me. My dad pulls me into a big burly hug. I look just like my dad. Same black hair, black beard, naturally tan-coloured skin, and brown-green eyes. The only difference is he keeps his hair short and I keep mine shoulder length.

"It's good to see you, kid," he says warmly, clapping me on the back.

"I've been gone like a week," I chuckle.

"Cut me some slack, it ain't easy going from having you around to having you far away."

"It's never too late to come home," my mum says hopefully as she comes over for a hug.

I pull mum into a strong one. I've never had to lean down with her because my mum is a respectable six-feet-tall. We look nothing alike, however. She is tall and slender, with wild curly blonde hair and pale blue eyes set in cream coloured skin. I don't get how I never inherited a single feature from my mum. I seem to have inherited her ignorance and prejudices, but that's not something I want to brag about.

"Mum, this is my home now," I say softly as I pull back.

She huffs indignantly, looking around, "I see your animai couldn't be bothered to come and grace us with her presence. As an *Alpha* she should be more courteous."

Fucking hell, is this what I was like to Amelia?

"Yes, this is exactly what you were like and it was painful to endure," Ace shudders.

"How am I still breathing?"

"Our animai is merciful," he says proudly.

"Ha! Amelia is not merciful. She's savage as fuck, and we love her that way."

"We sure do!" He cheers, wagging his tail with excitement.

"Jessica, you promised not to do this," scolds my dad disapprovingly.

"I said no such thing," she says sticking her nose up.

The scent of mangoes and pineapples floats into my nose and the tension quickly leaves my body.

"Beta Jerome and Beta Jessica, I am so sorry I wasn't here to greet you," I hear Amelia's respectful voice as she saddles up beside me and I wrap my arm around her waist. "I was finishing up an important phone call."

"Don't be silly, Alpha Amelia, you have nothing to apologise for," my dad says waving a hand dismissively.

"What could be so important you can't greet your guests?" Asks my mother saccharinely.

Gods, give me strength

"Mum…" I say in warning.

"I was always taught it was never good manners to put the Delegation on hold," says Amelia in a calm voice. The word 'Delegation' has my mother going still as a statue. Yeah, she realised she just implied they were more important than the Delegation. Even I'm not that crazy.

"Our son mentioned you had friends in high places and that he got to meet some of them. I've never had the honour of meeting one myself, so I'm a bit jealous," says my dad, trying to ease the tension.

"You're in luck, two of them will be joining us for the ceremony tomorrow. I would be more than happy to introduce you," Amelia offers with a sincere smile.

My dad's face lights up like a Christmas tree, "You… really? I would be honoured."

"Consider it done."

I smile at the two of them interacting. I knew dad would love her. He already approved before he even met her. Mum, however, is being cold as fuck. What the fuck is her problem?

"Not that it's needed but, Amelia this is my father, Jerome, former Beta of the Aurum Obscuro Pack, and this is my mother Jessica. Dad, mum, this is my animai and Alpha of the Invictus Pack, Amelia," I introduce proudly, while I notice my mother scowling.

"It's a pleasure to finally meet you, Beta Jerome," Amelia greets while offering her hand.

"None of that nonsense, young lady. Let me give my new daughter a hug," he says throwing his arms open wide. Amelia chuckles and happily steps into his arms giving him a warm hug. She nearly disappears into his monster arms when he hugs her.

"You're good for my son. Zarseti knows what she's doing," he says giving her a soft kiss on her temple.

Seeing my dad take to Amelia so fast has my heart feeling so full. I never realised how good this would feel. I can tell he loves her already and that means the world to know he sees her as family because she is my family now. She's my world.

Amelia steps back offering her hand to my mum, but my mum just looks at it as if it's going to burn her, "So you're the woman who turned my son into a Luna."

"For Goddess sake, woman, do not start," my dad warns.

"You seem to have me mistaken for a God. As flattered as I am, I don't choose who is fated to whom," Amelia calmly shrugs and I have to suppress a smirk.

Mum balks at the comment and dad coughs to hide his snigger though he's still looking at mum with annoyance.

"A smart mouth like that is unbecoming of a lady. Further proof why women shouldn't be Alphas," my mum scoffs.

"Mum or not, I'll fuck her up if she keeps disrespecting our animai like this, I'm warning you, Marcus," Ace growls.

"I got this, I promise," I assure him.

"I did not just hear some frizzy-haired bitch insult my granddaughter," I hear the seething voice of Sorrell.

Amelia and I both sigh at the hurricane that just stepped out of the packhouse.

"On second thought I'm just going to sit back and enjoy the show," Ace grins,

sitting back on his hind legs.

"What did you just call me?" My mum shrieks.

"You heard me," says Sorrell, coming over and stepping up to my mum.

Sorrell is almost a full foot shorter than my mum, yet my mum is cowering a little at the ferocity coming off of Sorrell. After all, this woman isn't just a former pack warrior, she's the former Luna. "Who are you to show such disrespect?" Sorrell spits.

"Jessica Hayda, former Beta of the Aurum Obscuro Pack," she says confidently.

"Is it a common practice in your pack to openly disrespect an allied Alpha and, in the process, disgrace your own pack? After all, as a former Beta, your actions reflect on your pack. Do they not?" Sorrell says with a confident smirk.

Fucking hell, shots fired!

"Fight! Fight! Fight! Fight!" Ace cheers.

"You're not fucking helping," I snap.

"Fuck that, your mum had it coming," he snorts.

Colour literally drains from my mum's face. Mum is a traditionalist, and she holds to that firmly. Realising she's going against everything she believes in – disgracing her pack and her animai – has her almost turning green. I think it might have even short-circuited her brain.

"Insult our Alpha again and I swear I'll – " Sorrell starts, but Alden appears out of nowhere, clamping his hand over her mouth.

"Come now, dear. They need our help in the dining hall," he says, though his eyes are shining with mirth.

He loves seeing his sassy Luna be sassy. He probably wanted her to keep going, but the look on Amelia's face tells me she may have called for her grandfather.

"Mmph mmph, mmph, mmph," mumbles Sorrell.

"I know, dear, but now is not the time," says Alden gently.

"Mmph, mmph, mmph, mmph mmph," she mumbles.

Alden's eyes glaze over a bit and then suddenly, the tops of Sorrell's cheeks peeking out through Alden's hand start to turn red. In a flash, she's grabbing his hand, pulling him into the packhouse while Amelia chuckles. No idea what he linked to her, but I imagine it was effective.

"I can see where your animai gets it from," my mum mutters.

Dad looks livid, about ready to pop off, and Amelia has her usual calm as a cucumber expression on. I can feel her irritation and how offended she is, but none of it shows on her face.

"ENOUGH!" I shout, causing my mum to jump back in surprise. "Mum, I love you to death, but you need to cut it out. I get it, you don't like the idea of a female Alpha and you hate that I'm going to be a Luna, but too fucking bad. This is my life, and this is how I'm going to live it. Now you can either get on board or go back to Aurum Obscuro, because I won't have you standing here disrespecting me and the woman I love, or this pack. Am I clear?"

My dad looks impressed and proud. Amelia may not show it, but I can feel her pride radiating through her and her desire.

"That was the sexiest thing I've ever seen," I hear her low sexy voice in my head.

"Oh, I'll show you sexy later," I promise.

"Marcus… I am your mother; how can you speak to me like that?" She says with tears in her eyes.

Oh, for crying out loud.

"How can you stand there and be so rude to the woman I love? You're not even trying to get to know her. Dad's being welcoming, why can't you? She's done nothing to you," I sigh, rubbing my face in frustration, "I don't want to fight with you, but I won't let you keep this up, mum. Enough already."

I feel Amelia thread her fingers through mine, her touch soothing my frazzled nerves.

"I think perhaps we could all cool off. When you're ready, a member of the staff will escort you up to the Alpha suite where you'll be staying as our guests," Amelia says diplomatically.

"That's very generous of you, thank you, Alpha Amelia," my dad nods, trying to be respectful to make up for mum's disrespect.

"Amelia, please. I won't have my father-in-law calling me 'Alpha'. Family doesn't do that," she says adamantly, but with a smile on her face.

My dad's face softens and there's a twinkle in his eyes. Hearing her call him family has touched him, I can tell. Mum, however, is still scowling like Amelia's kindness is the most egregious thing to ever happen to her.

"Thank you, Amelia. You lovebirds go on ahead, we'll catch up later," dad says while placing his hand around mum's elbow.

I can tell she's going to get it, and to be fair, Sorrell was right. She disgraced her animai and her pack with her actions. I slide my arm around Amelia and guide her back inside just as I hear my dad whisper-yell 'what the hell were you thinking, woman', so I'm glad we got away from that.

"I'm so sorry you had to go through that. At least my dad adores you," I say comfortingly.

"He seems very lovely. I like him already. And, he gives good hugs," she beams.

"I'll let him know," I chuckle, but it quickly trails off, "My mum had no right speaking to you or your grandmother like that. She's just stubborn."

"Now I know where you get it from," she teases, making me sigh. "Hey, I didn't mean that as a dig," she says with concern, taking my hands in hers.

"I know you didn't. It's just seeing her treat you that way showed me what I must have been like with you when I found out you were an Alpha. Seeing it first-hand... makes me feel shitty," I admit.

"I thought we agreed not to dwell on the past. You made mistakes and you worked to be better; I can't ask for more than that. I'm not going to keep holding the past against you, so don't you go doing it either," she says sternly.

"Yes, my Alpha," I say as I peck her nose.

"Stop that," she says swatting me.

"Why should I?" I ask with a wide grin.

"Because I'm not your superior."

"True, but want to know why I love saying it?" I ask, pulling her flush up against me.

"Do tell," she says curiously.

I lean down brushing my lips against the shell of her ear and smirk when I feel her body shiver against me. "Because I love knowing all the dirty things I get to do to this Alpha," I whisper huskily into her ear and savour the sound of her gulp.

"You're incorrigible," she breathes, clutching my shirt.

"I believe the word you're looking for is 'insatiable'. And for you, you're damn fucking right I am."

****

Inhale. Exhale. Repeat. If I just keep doing that I should be fine. Is this how women feel before their Luna ceremonies? How do they not puke?

I have been in fights, I've fought battles, I've fought for my life, but this is the first time I've felt petrified. Becoming the leader of a pack isn't scary. I've been left in charge of Aurum Obscuro plenty of times when Jasper had to travel for business, but this is different. I don't regret my decision. I will be the Luna of the Invictus Pack. I'm not backing out, but I can't stop wondering what people will think of me. I'm about to be the first fucking male Luna. News will spread faster than an STD at a frat house.

Will it lead to more attacks?

What if I blow up at Amelia again because of all this?

"For Goddess sake, stop spiralling, you're making me dizzy," says Ace.

"Sorry, I'm just nervous," I mumble.

"Really? I thought you were writing poetry," he says rolling his eyes.

"A little support wouldn't kill you every now and then."

"I am being supportive. Arguing with me distracted you," he says smugly.

Well, damn. He's right, I feel a bit calmer now. I guess that fleabag is good for something asides annoying the shit out of me.

"Dude, are you seriously not ready yet?" Vitali huffs walking into the bedroom.

Amelia is getting ready in the Alpha suite, and I've been getting ready in the Beta suite. We're meeting downstairs afterwards.

"Fuck off, I just have to put my jacket on," I grumble.

He crosses his arms and patiently waits, leaning against the wall. I take a deep breath, throw on my suit jacket and smooth it out. I decided to dress in the pack colours to show Amelia and the pack that I am embracing them as my own. I've gone with a three-piece suit that is entirely emerald-green with a black shirt, black tie, and shiny black Derby's. But if I'm going to get dolled up, I like to do it right, so I had to throw in a little bling. I have platinum chains linked at the collar and another, linked from my breast pocket to my lapel with a black pocket square. I've got my hair slicked back and I think I look pretty fucking suave.

"Be honest, how do I look?" I ask as I turn to face Vitali with my arms out.

"If I'd met you dressed like this before meeting Eric, I'd have come out of the bi-closet just to get on my knees for you," he says bluntly.

I burst out laughing. That is a major fucking compliment and I will take it.

"Aww, you'd come out of the closet for me? That's the sweetest thing you've ever said to me. Didn't know you were such a bottom though," I smirk.

"Hey! I'm versatile," he corrects.

"Lucky Eric," I muse. "Can I ask you something before we go downstairs?"

"Sure thing."

"How do you not worry so much about what other people think? I never used to give a shit and then fate threw me a curveball and now suddenly opinions matter to me and I'm not really a fan of the feeling," I say putting my hands in my pockets.

"I spent way too fucking long worrying about what everyone would think about me being bisexual. I was so scared of what my friends and family would think and what things in my life would change. Meeting Eric, I had two choices; live my truth and tell the voices in my head to fuck off or lose the best thing to ever happen to me. I was terrified when I met him, but I wouldn't trade a single moment I've had with him for anything. The pack could shun me, and I wouldn't care, because I have him. He accepts me as I am and loves me for it, and that shit is precious," he says clapping me on the shoulder. "You have Amelia now, so whenever those ugly thoughts start up, tell them to fuck off and remember that you have her and you'll be fine."

"No wonder Amelia made you her Beta," I say, clapping him back on his shoulder.

"Because I'm fantastic, duh," he says throwing his arm around me. "Now let's go make you a Luna."

I stand at the bottom of the staircase and patiently wait for my woman. Punctual as ever, I feel her before I see or scent her. I look up and my heart literally stops. Fuck me, she is the most exquisite thing I have ever laid eyes on… and she's all mine.

As she walks down the stairs, I drink in the sight of her. She's wearing a gown that has a black lace strapless corset and an emerald-green satin skirt starting at the waist and cascading down sweeping the floor. The skirt has a slit starting at mid-thigh, exposing her gorgeous fucking legs and her green, velvet, strappy high-heels. Her hair is done in waves hanging loosely around her breath-taking face and she's wearing more makeup than I've ever seen her in.

Amelia rarely wears makeup, and frankly, she doesn't need it – my woman is a Goddess in her own right – but tonight she's gone all out. Red glittery eyeshadow, black outlining the edges and bold red lipstick. She looks delicious. The eye makeup makes her turquoise eyes stand out and the red lips… well they have me thinking dirty fucking thoughts. She's wearing the earrings I got her for our first date and she somehow managed to find a necklace to match. It's a platinum Celtic design with an emerald jewel at the centre, hanging on a platinum chain.

I feel like the luckiest man in the world right now as I reach out my hand and she places hers in mine and I help her down the final step. A smile is on her face and her eyes are twinkling.

"You look… there are no words in any language that do you justice. I may have to contact the Delegation and have them reach out to a God to create me a new word describing how fucking beautiful you are," I breathe.

Her cheeks heat up in my favourite shade of pink, the way they do whenever I get romantic with her. I will never, ever get sick of that.

"This is your night, shouldn't I be charming you?" She says as she steps back to look me over, her eyes slowly raking over every inch of me, "You may want to order two words from the Gods because I'll be needing one too."

I laugh shaking my head and lean in kissing her cheek as I breathe in her sweet scent.

"I'll be the envy of everyone tonight," I tell her.

"As will I. I can't believe you're wearing the pack colours," she says in disbelief, but the emotions inside her tell me how touched she is by my choice.

"It's about to be my pack, too. How do they look on me?"

"Perfect. Absolutely perfect," she smiles up at me.

"And we coordinated," I wink. Her eyes widen in realisation, then her face softens as she shakes her head. "What is it?" I ask brushing my thumbs over her knuckles.

"My parents tend to dress in clothes that match and I was never sure if it was deliberate or accidental. Now here we are, doing the same thing," she says in amusement.

"To be fair, I'd rather us both naked, but that might be weird during the ceremony," I shrug.

"Speaking of; are you ready to go do this?" She asks nervously.

"Yeah," I breathe. "Ready as I'll ever be."

With that, I wrap her arm around my elbow, and we make our way to the double doors of the dining hall. I can hear the light conversation on the other side and, as nervous as I am, I'm also excited to see what they've done to the place.

The doors swing open and my jaw almost drops. Don't get me wrong, what Amelia did for the Vernal Ball was stunning, but this is magnificent. Or maybe it's because this was done for me that has me so in awe. I've never had anyone do anything like this for me in my life, but she did. I don't know how Zarseti thought I deserved this woman, but I'm glad she gave her to me.

The glass doors around the room have been opened, red rose garlands and green vines with fairy lights hang from the ceiling, framing every entrance. Gone are the full-length wooden tables and, instead, the room is filled with circular tables just like at the ball. This time they are covered in black satin tablecloths with gold cutlery and gold chairs. The centrepieces are made up of red roses and greenery for a pop of colour. At the far end of the room is a large arch made of vines and red roses that looks like nature forged it itself. In the centre of the arch is a small table with a gold chalice and a dagger placed on it.

The room settles into the soft sound of whispers as Amelia and I make our way to the arch, arm in arm. As we make our way through the room, I see my parents sitting with Amelia's parents and grandparents. Dad is beaming with pride and joy and mum... has a deep frown on her face. Wow, she couldn't even try to fake a smile.

On the bright side, on the table next to that one is a sight that has a big ass smile on my face. Sitting there is Jasper, Isabelle holding Blake, Calix, Darla, Aiden, Muse and their daughter Kiara. I can't believe they're all here! They all grin and wave at me, and little Kiara slides off her dad's lap and waddles over to me. I let go of Amelia and squat down, scooping her up into my arms.

"Hey there Ki-ki! Gosh, I've missed you," I say as I give her a big but gentle hug. She hugs me as best she can even though her little arms can barely span out to my shoulders

"Unky Mar!" She cheers in my ear.

"You look beautiful," I gush as I look at the little one-year-old in her gold party dress. "I want you to meet someone. Ki-ki, this is Amelia, Amelia, this is Kiara, better known as Ki-ki."

"I am honoured to meet such a beautiful young lady," Amelia says with a curtsy and Kiara giggles.

Kiara reaches out and taps her hand lightly against Amelia's cheek. "Pwetty," she says in her cute little voice, making my heart fucking melt.

I told you this kid has us all wrapped around her little finger and by the look on Amelia's face, I think Kiara just found a new victim. Poor Amelia. She never saw it coming.

"Thank you," says Amelia affectionately.

I place a kiss on Kiara's cheek and put her down so she can go back to her parents while I join Amelia under the arch.

"When did you..." I say in disbelief, looking at my friends.

"So maybe it wasn't the Delegation I was on the phone with when your parents arrived yesterday," she shrugs with a cheeky smile. "I wanted to surprise you and make sure they would all be here."

"I can't believe you did that for me. All of this. It's more than I ever could have asked for," I tell her, bringing her hands to my lips and planting kisses on her knuckles.

"Marcus, I'd do anything for you. I just want you to be happy," she confesses, her eyes shining with more love in them than should be possible. She gives my hands a squeeze and turns to face the pack, her chin held high as she exudes grace, strength, and beauty.

"Tonight we have gathered to not only initiate a new pack member but to declare our new Luna. Becoming the first female Alpha was a big change and I know some of you were against it. But to those who accepted me and trusted me, I thank you. Tonight we experience another change as we welcome our first male Luna. Times change and we must change with them. Through change, we can become stronger and grow not only as a pack but as people."

Amelia picks up the dagger and proceeds to cut her palm. I suppress a wince as I feel my palm sting in response to her wound. She picks up the chalice and lets her blood drip into it. Quickly, her palm heals closed and she cleans it with the napkin that was sitting on the table. She hands the chalice to me and I take it, bringing it to my lips, letting her blood run into my mouth and down my throat. I don't know if it's because it's Amelia or because of our bond but fuck her blood tastes good!

She takes the chalice from me and steadies me as I feel my pack-link form instantaneously. It's like someone shoving a giant ball of yarn into my head made up of hundreds of threads and each thread connects to a different person. I take a breath to combat the pressure in my head as I feel myself connect to every thread. After a beat, the pressure in my head subsides and is gone. That empty spot inside me that was left after Jasper released me from his pack has finally been filled again. I feel strong and at home again. I give Amelia a reassuring smile and she smiles back.

"Welcome to the pack," she says, and as if on cue the whole pack begins to clap with choruses of 'welcome',

One step down, one to go.

"Are you sure you want to do this?" Amelia asks through our link.

Her face doesn't show it, but she is a bundle of nerves, and I can't help but feel bad because I created those nerves. I created a situation where she doubts me and fears my reactions. That shit fucking stings.

"I'm sure about you and this is part of the deal. I won't pick and choose the parts of your life to be involved in and not be involved in. I choose all of you, I'm in this one hundred per cent," I say out loud so everyone can hear how much I mean this.

Pride and hope swell inside her and a smile blooms across her face as she takes my hand and places it over her Alpha Mark.

"Enough of her family, friends and pack warriors have seen your dick, so try not to get a stiffy right now or the entire pack will know what you're packin'," Ace sniggers.

"Fucking asshole," I retort, much to his amusement.

"Marcus Hayda, do you swear fealty to the Invictus Pack and each of its members, current and future?" She asks with a strong voice.

"I do," I declare loud and clear.

"Do you swear to always serve your pack and its needs to the best of your abilities?" She asks.

"I do." And I know it's true.

"And do you swear to always love your pack?" She asks, brushing her thumb against the back of my hand, sending delicious electricity through me.

"I swear to love and honour the Invictus Pack and will continue to do so until I take my last breath," I announce proudly

"I, Alpha Amelia Dolivo, in the eyes of the Goddess Morrtemis, declare you, Marcus Hayda, my Luna and Luna of the Invictus Pack," she pronounces as her turquoise eyes start to glow.

"I, Marcus Hayda, accept the title and power of Luna of the Invictus Pack."

As soon as the last word of the ceremony leaves my lips, a white glow moves from Amelia's mark under my palm, shooting up my arm directly to my heart. I feel the glow's warmth caress my heart and then travel further up my chest and wrap around the mark on my neck. I feel my mark tingle and sing with energy, causing me to suck in a breath as a burst of power both physical and mental spreads through me, settling into my bones. I don't have to look to know the mark on my neck has become raised like a brand more than a print, because I watched it happen to Isabelle.

A smile spreads across mine and Amelia's faces as she raises my hand high in the air, "Invictus Pack, I give you your new Luna!"

The room erupts into cheers and howls as people stand, applauding. I feel on top of the fucking world. I feel invigorated, powerful, and complete in a way I never expected. This feels right. Like this is how it was always meant to be. Like I have finally discovered my purpose in life and now everything makes sense. That leaves me with only one thing left to do.

I pull Amelia close, dipping her as I crash my lips down on hers. She squeaks in surprise but quickly her body is melting in my arms and our lips are moving together. I savour each brush of her lips against mine as her soft hands cup my face. I am faintly aware of people hooting and hollering, but I don't care. All the nerves, all the worry and the fighting was for nothing because this is one of the best moments of my life. My only regret is not doing it sooner.

"I love you, Amelia," I breathe as our kiss breaks and I rest my forehead against hers.

"I love you, Marcus," she smiles, pecking my lips.

Chapter Forty
Amelia

He did it. He really did it. I'm so elated that tears keep stinging my eyes, but I don't care if people see me cry. Growing up, I always figured I'd run this pack alone. That anyone the Goddess sent me wouldn't want to be with an Alpha and certainly wouldn't want to be a Luna. I tried to mentally prepare for it until the day Marcus blew into my life like a tornado.

We have had highs and lows and through them, I still never thought we would be here. Marcus is now a member of this pack and its rightful Luna. I know he will care for everyone around him and fight to protect them; it's who he is. I know that any fight or battle I face, he'll be right there beside me and vice versa. We are one now in all the ways that matter.

We've gone around chatting with pack members as he properly introduces himself to those he hasn't met yet and receives welcomes and congratulations from everyone. My family and friends are so happy for him and for us. Seeing them support Marcus means the world to me and more. A bright smile splits across my face as I watch Marcus exchange hugs with all of his friends from his birth pack. They are his family, so I knew the night wouldn't be complete without them and I'd been right. However, I never could have expected how amazing he is with kids! He's such a natural, and I swear he looks a hundred times sexier while he's holding little Kiara or

Blake. It's doing things to my libido.

"Congratulations on everything and thank you for making an honest man out of this idiot," Jasper cheers, pulling me into a hug.

"Not sure I can take the credit for that," I chuckle.

"And here I was hoping he'd made you less modest. I'm sure it'll happen eventually," he shrugs confidently.

"Don't hold your breath," I nudge him.

"We have a pool going to see how long until you regret your decision and send him packing," says Aiden.

"You are setting a terrible example for the pups," his animai, Muse, scolds while holding their daughter on her hip.

"I planned to split it with you when I win," Aiden says with a pout.

"Oh," she chirps, "In that case put me down for two weeks. We can double our chances of winning." She grins.

"That's my girl," he grins wrapping his arm around her.

"You know, since I'm now the Luna, I have the authority to kick your asses out, right? And right now, I am very tempted to do that," Marcus says, glaring at his friends as I chuckle into my champagne flute.

"Oh please, you'd be doing the exact same thing if you were in our shoes," Calix scoffs.

"I would at least have the decency to do it behind your back," Marcus points out.

"How much is in the pool so far?" Darla, Calix's animai, asks.

"Three hundred," says Jasper.

"Put me in for a month," says Darla.

"Geez woman, what did I ever do to you?" Marcus says in a wounded tone.

"What? That money can go to a future pup's education," she shrugs.

"I think you're all being mean. Aren't they, Blake?" Isabelle coos to her son who giggles.

"Throw me down for a hundred," I interject as shocked faces stare back at me.

"Amelia! What the fu… hell?" He says, a quick glance at the kids.

"A hundred bucks says his ass stays put. Do keep in mind I have access to silver cuffs and a prison cell so, me winning this bet is pretty much a slam dunk. I'm not against holding him against his will," I say matter-of-factly.

Everyone laughs and I see a twinkle in Marcus' eyes and feel the desire rising inside him. He pulls me close and leans down till his lips brush against my ear.

"Not sure about the silver, but you can cuff and tie me up anytime," he whispers nipping my earlobe as his thumb strokes my side.

I swallow thickly and feel my core flutter with anticipation as ideas swirl around in my head, ideas I would very much love to see be acted out. I love how sexual he makes me feel and I love how much he encourages me to try things out. I never worry or feel embarrassed because I know he's there for the ride along with me. There's security in that. I just know he'd never judge me in that department.

I'm thrown from my thoughts when I feel someone staring at me. A quick glance is all it takes to lock onto the light blue eyes who are indeed burning holes into my skull.

"What is this bitch's issue?" Zara hisses.

"I'm trying to be civil for Marcus' sake, but if she keeps testing me, I'm putting her in her place," I say confidently.

"We are an Alpha; how dare she look down on us. Ace agrees I should claw her eyes out," she preens.

"We are not clawing out our mother-in-law's eyes, Zara," I say, rolling my eyes.

"Oh, dragon lady at seven o'clock," Darla mutters into her drink.

Everyone glances in Jessica's direction,. Marcus's face immediately sets into a frown.

"She'll come around," Isabelle says optimistically.

"It's sweet that you think that, love," Jasper says sadly, pecking the top of her head.

Marcus downs his drink and places the glass down on the nearby table and picks up another glass as a waiter passes by.

"Babe, are you okay?" I ask through our link.

I hate how his mother's behaviour is affecting him. I don't care how she treats me, but this is her son, and he doesn't deserve this from his own mother.

"As long as she doesn't start anything, I'll be fine," he says, holding me a little closer. I stroke his hand on my side and kiss his cheek.

"Sounds like Darla isn't a fan of your mum…" I say with caution.

"Darla is a pack warrior. My mum used to lecture her on how she should be focused on giving Calix a pup like Muse and Izzy instead of playing warrior. Darla never told us, not until I was venting to them about how my mum reacted to my news about leaving the pack to be a Luna. Calix was fucking livid and I don't blame him. I wish Darla had said something. I would never have condoned that behaviour," he says firmly.

"You're a good man, Marcus, I hope you know that. You care about people, and you fight for them, and you want to grow and be a better person. There aren't many people like that," I say compassionately.

Marcus smiles, placing a light kiss on my forehead, but I can still feel that underlying guilt he holds for his past actions. It'll take time, but I hope to free him of that guilt.

We return to the conversation, and I can still feel that woman's eyes on me. I discreetly glance at her to find her nodding for me to follow her outside. I see we're going to have that talk, this should be fun.

"What if she's like Kathleen Turner in Serial Mom or the mum in Psycho?" Zara gasps.

"That was Norman in a dress and wig," I correct her.

"Oh yeah…"

"I'll be right back, I just have to check on something," I tell everyone.

"Don't be too long," Marcus pouts.

"I promise," I say giving him a chaste kiss that still has his face lighting up like a child seeing his birthday cake. I step away and discreetly make my way out the nearest open glass doors.

I don't have to walk too far before I'm standing in front of Jessica. I must admit she puts herself together very nicely. She's wearing a beautiful ivory gown that hugs her slender frame. It has a built-in choker with a triangular front and half-open back and it has a high slit at the front of her right leg. She has her hair wild and free and has kept to simple gold band earrings, a gold bangle, and nude strappy high-heels. Elegant and flattering.

"You wished to speak to me," I surmise.

"I had hoped you would do the right thing before it went this far, but you proved me wrong. You're his animai, you're supposed to show him respect. Instead, you are ruining my son. Everything he has worked for his whole life, gone in an instant. You've taken him away from his friends, his family, his home and turned him into..." she trails off with a spiteful look on her face.

"I'm going to stop you there," I interject. If she wants to insult me, she can do it until she turns blue, I really don't give two shits. But I won't stand here and listen to her insult Marcus. Abso-fucking-lutely not. "The only person disrespecting Marcus here is you. You're his mother and yet all you have done before even meeting me is put him down, insult him, me, his decision, and a path that was mapped out for him by a higher power. Your son had some very hurtful and demoralizing things to say to me the night we met, and the day after that and the day after that, to the point I was ready to reject him. But I see he didn't form those thoughts and opinions on his own. They were put there by you. Now if you wish to hate me or the fact that I'm an Alpha, go for it. I couldn't care less. But how dare you stand there and degrade your own son and the man I love?" I snarl pushing my Alpha Spirit forward, relishing the way she cowers under the force of it.

"What are you-"

"Doing? I'm making a point. Your son is now more powerful than a Beta and holds more authority. He now has a pack of his very own to run right beside me. He has been welcomed by my family and this pack and has earned their respect because he has fought at their side and mourned with them. The only person hurting and disrespecting him is you and I won't tolerate it, so either shape up or ship out because you don't want to get on my bad side," I say in a low threatening tone and enjoy watching her gulp.

"What the hell is going on here?" Comes Marcus' voice, the sound of it caressing my ears like silk.

541

"Marcus! Thank goodness," she cries rushing to his side and clinging to his arm, "Your animai was threatening me."

"You ever notice our animai attracts crazy women like a moth to one of those electric zapper things?" Zara quips.

"What does that say about us?"

"We don't count, we were chosen for him. Big difference," she says confidently.

"Don't insult me by lying, I heard everything," he says viciously as he detaches her from him. "Ruined me? She's ruined me? I'm lucky she's given me as many chances as she has. She's perfect for me and I wish you could see that. I don't know any person alive who could do what she's done, who could brave through all that she has. Being with her hasn't ruined me. It's made me a better person and opened my eyes." He slides an arm around my waist.

"You're choosing her over your own family," she hisses.

"She *is* my family," he says confidently.

Holy crap!

There is something so damn sexy about watching him stand up to his mother for me. That's love right there.

"I will not accept her as my daughter-in-law," she says curtly.

"Then you're the one choosing hatred over your family, mum," he sighs sadly. I hold him close, hoping my arms can bring him solace. I don't want him feuding with his family, but I'm not giving him up either. Not after all the shit we've been through.

"Marcus, I'm your mother, I know what's best for you," she cajoles.

"Jessica!" Booms Jerome. "Stop this madness!" He exclaims coming over, grabbing her by the shoulders and shaking her. "Why are you so hell-bent on destroying an animai bond? Have you completely lost your senses? This is not the woman I have known and loved for nearly thirty years." The despondency in his tone nearly breaks my heart.

"She's not good enough for him! I know these she-wolves. They care more about being the best. She'll neglect him. I doubt she'll even give him pups. We'll never have grandpups, we'll never see our boy again. Marcus should have taken Davina as his chosen animai, she would have been good to him," she says in a shrill voice.

My mask of calmness is fucking gone as soon as I hear that bitch's name. I'm officially done being polite, I'm done trying to be reasonable, but before I can snap, Marcus lets out a murderous growl beside me and his hands are replacing his father's on his mother's shoulders. His eyes are glowing and his entire body is shaking with rage. I've never seen him this angry. I move to his side, calmly grabbing his arm, worried he'll accidentally hurt his mum.

"Marcus, calm down," I say soothingly.

"How fucking dare you utter that cunt's name?" He growls in fury as his Luna Spirit pushes forward, making his mother shrink back in shock and fear.

"Marcus…" his father warns, but I shake my head for him to stay out of it.

"That girl loved you," his mother reasons, sweat forming on her brow.

"Loved me? Did she love me when she beat up Quinn when I tried to comfort her because her mother was sick? Did she love me when she started harassing me? Did she love me when she broke into my room and sexually assaulted me?" He grits and that causes his father to gasp and his mother's face to pale. "An assault that Amelia had to feel every bit of. Did she love me when she got herself banished and then joined the pack leading a war against Amelia? Did she love me the day I watched her plunge a wolfram dagger into Amelia's stomach?"

I don't know which hurts more, remembering the pain as the metal of the dagger poisoned my insides, or feeling Marcus' despair and heartbreak remembering that moment. He didn't just see it, he felt it all. Something I would never wish on him, ever.

"Amelia…" his father whispers my name in disbelief.

"I'm fortunate to be alive," I say simply.

"I nearly lost her mum. I held her in my arms and felt every ounce of her pain as if it were my own. Can you imagine what that feels like? Imagine someone doing that to dad and then having to watch and feel him dying a slow, agonising death," he chokes..

Tears fill his mother's eyes as she glances over at her soulmate, then me, then back to her son. I swallow the lump forming in my throat as hot tears start to spill from my cheeks. I can handle a lot but feeling Marcus' pain right now breaks me.

"And that's the woman you would choose for me? My own mother is so stuck in her ways she would rather see me with a violent psychopath than with a woman who loves, supports, and comforts me? Who accepts me in spite of all my flaws and raises me up?"

Tears fall from her eyes as Marcus releases his grip. She stares at him like a gaping fish. I take his hand in mine and pull him close, wrapping my arms around him and burying my face in his chest. I breath in his caramel scent. His arms surround me as he buries his nose in my hair and inhales.

"Son... why didn't you tell us?" His father asks sadly, putting a hand on Marcus' shoulder.

"I was taking your advice. You were right to call me an idiot when I told you about Amelia kicking me out and why. You told me to beg for forgiveness and fight to make it work and that's what I've been doing. I stumbled a bit, and I don't know if I'll ever forgive myself for it but feeling her slipping away from me like that..." he trails off in a whisper.

Jerome yanks his son into his arms, hugging him tight and clasping his hand on the back of his neck, with tears in the eyes he shares with his son.

"I understand. I can never know the pain you felt. Either of you," he says glancing at me solemnly. "But I know you, Marcus, and I see how much you love her. I see how much she loves you. You will look after each other."

"Thank you, dad," Marcus chokes, fully embracing his father.

I smile at the interaction wiping, the tears from my cheeks. I'm thrilled to know he has such a beautiful relationship with his dad and I'm sure before all this he had one with his mum too. She had to have done something right, after all, Marcus isn't a bad person, but I'm done with the woman until she sorts herself out.

"Please stay as long as you like, Jerome. I would never in a million years wish to separate you from your son. I am so glad you were able to be here, and I would love to get to know you better," I say warmly but turn a cold glare on Jessica. "As for you, I respect that you birthed and raised Marcus, and you clearly did some good because he is a wonderful man who I am honoured Goddess Zarseti chose for me. But let's get one thing straight. I do not answer to you, nor do I owe you anything. If you insult or hurt my animai one more time, consider our borders closed to you. You will never be welcome in our territory ever again," I threaten.

Jerome sighs but says nothing. Jessica opens her mouth to speak but Marcus cuts her off.

"Think over what has happened tonight, because I fully support Amelia's decision, and for the record, I took great pleasure in ripping Davina's head off," he says reaching out and taking my hands as his mother gulps. "Let's go, Ma Reine."

I let him guide me back inside, but instead of re-joining our guests he leads me through the dining hall and pulls me upstairs to our suite. He's got a barrier up so I can't read his feelings now and I'm a little worried. Maybe I crossed a line back there and he's upset with me.

We enter the main space, but he doesn't stop, he pulls me straight into the bedroom and I can hear his heart beating faster.

"Marcus, I– " My words are silenced as he presses me against the door, devouring my lips and sucking the air right out of my lungs. My body's reaction to him is automatic; instinctive; I fist the lapels of his jacket and pull him against me, needing to feel his body crush mine. Our lips are moving at a speed that screams hunger.

"Hearing you stand up for me like that was one of the sexiest things I've ever fucking heard," he growls seductively as he trails hot kisses down my neck and his hands explore my body.

"I couldn't stand her talking about you… like that," I breathe out, trying to remember how to speak as his kisses send tingles of pleasure right to my core.

"Fuck, I love you," he says as his mouth latches onto my mark and his hands knead my breasts through my corset. A cry of pleasure leaves me as his tongue lavishes my mark and wetness pools between my legs.

"I love you too," I pant as my fingers nestle into his black hair. In a move so fast it makes my head spin, he turns me around pressing my front against the door.

"You won't be needing this," he promises as he unzips the back of my dress, planting feather light kisses against my back. My hands are braced against the door, my breath uneven and my need for him is growing as he pushes my dress to the floor, leaving me in just my heels and panties. "Won't be needing these either," he says, his voice laced with lust, the sound of it making my insides coil. In one fluid motion, he rips my panties from my body, a cool breeze teasing my lower region as my wetness only increases. The sharp action has me pressing my thighs together and biting my lips but the smell of my arousal more than gives me away. "Is your pussy hungry for me?" He breathes against my ear as he palms my ass cheek. I gulp and nod, my head brushing against the wood panel of the door because I can't form a single word right now. Suddenly a feel a sting across my backside causing me to yelp in surprise. "Words, Amelia," he warns as his hand caresses the cheek he just spanked.

"Y-yes, my pussy is hungry for you," I pant, feeling my juices drip down the inside of my thighs.

"Good girl. But I'm hungry too and I want my meal now," he growls.

In another fast action, I'm thrown onto the bed, my body bouncing as I hit the surface. I look up and see his eyes dark with so much carnal lust it has me squirming under his gaze. I sit up on my elbows as I watch him stalk towards me like an animal coming upon its prey. His eyes never leave mine as he discards his clothes at a leisurely speed, driving me mad with anticipation.

He stands before me like a gift from the Gods, all olive skin and hard edges with his cock standing at attention. My eyes drink in every last detail, once again committing him to memory. I reach down to unstrap my heels…

"Leave them on," he instructs, and I oblige. "Now spread your legs."

I gulp but do as I'm told, bringing my knees up and spreading my thighs as far as they'll go. His eyes take their time to travel down my body before becoming laser-focused on my centre. Having him look at the most intimate part of me like a wild animal has me feeling hot all over.

"Now take your hand and spread that pussy for me," he says in a low husky voice that has my thighs quivering.

I guide my hand down to my folds and spread my lips apart, now completely exposing myself to him, my heart thudding away in my chest.

"So fucking perfect," he growls as he drops to his knees.

He kisses and gently bites the inside of each thigh, his beard tickling against my skin making me squirm. Slowly, he runs his tongue up the length of my pussy.

My head is thrown back in a moan as pleasure shoots through me. "Shit… Marcus."

"You're going to take all the pleasure I give you," he orders as his mouth latches onto my pussy and his tongue begins the most exquisite assault I have ever endured.

My hands are in his hair, gripping his locks like a vice as my body bucks and writhes, unable to stay still. His tongue teases my opening then comes up to flick my clit as my moans bounce off the walls. My thighs try to clamp around his head, but his hands press against them, holding them firmly apart. Keeping my pussy at his mercy. He's a man on a mission and I am that mission.

"M-Marcus… holy fuck…" I pant as his tongue works my clit like his very life depends on it. He alternates between tonguing my opening and swirling and flicking my clit; the combination sending me into a frenzy, craving a release that can't come soon enough.

He growls against my sensitive flesh, sending shockwaves through me. He picks up inhuman speed focusing his attention on my clit and my muscles lock up, my breathing stops, heat swells in my lower abdomen and, like a dam bursting, my orgasm erupts through me, turning my limbs to jelly. A moan is forced from my mouth that sounds unrecognisable to my own ears.

I pant and lick my now dry lips as I come down from my high, but there is no reprieve as instead of stopping, Marcus laps up my cum like a thirsty man desperate for water. When I think he's done, he proves me wrong. Instead, he thrusts two thick fingers inside me and begins pumping them in and out, making me throw my head back. He places quick kisses on each thigh before encasing my clit with his plump lips. My hips buck as I try to squirm away from the contact with my sensitive nub.

"I want another one," he demands as he starts sucking and flicking my clit with his tongue while his fingers massage my insides.

I thrash around, gripping his hair, trying to escape the overwhelming pain and pleasure caused by my sensitivity. "Marcus I can't… it's too much," I cry out.

"Yes, you fucking can," he growls.

He curls his fingers in a 'come here' motion and proceeds to fuck me with his fingers, hitting the perfect place inside me that has my toes curling and me crying to the Gods. His sucking and thrusting is merciless, causing pleasure to build quickly inside me. My body coils around him, my hands gripping his hair like it can keep me from shattering as a series of cusses fly out of my mouth with no filter to hold them back.

"Fuck… Marcus… I… FUCK!" I cry out while light bursts behind my eyelids and my back arches. My fingers dig into the bedsheets as my orgasm explodes from me like a bomb being detonated. My legs are quivering and my lungs are gasping for air as a sheen of sweat coats my body. At this moment I can't remember who or where I am, all I'm aware of is the aftershock ripples of pleasure that are radiating through my body. I feel like a damn live wire.

Marcus trails kisses up my body, his hands massaging my aching thighs. He places tender kisses on each nipple as his lips make their way to mine. His lips dominate mine and I let him. My lips follow his lead and I taste myself on him when his tongue traces the seam of my lips while my hands caress the planes of his muscular torso. Gods how I love this man.

"I'm not done with you. Turn over, and get on all fours," he gently orders as his lips graze along my jaw.

Feeling my strength coming back to me, I guide my hands to his firm ass giving it a strong squeeze as I wink at him before doing as he says.

"Is my Sexy Little Alpha trying to be playful?" He muses, landing a hard smack to my ass that jolts me forward.

I bite back a moan. "Is that a problem?" I ask innocently, looking back at him and batting my eyelashes.

"From you, baby, never," he coos, trailing kisses up my spine, his hand on my hip as he lines himself up with my entrance. I try to push back, to feel him sheathed inside me but he holds me still, making me whimper.

"Press your knees together," he instructs, kissing my shoulder blade.

I bring my knees together, eager to please him however I can. Slowly his cock enters me causing us both to groan as our bodies come together. He keeps pushing until he's completely buried inside me. I feel his length twitching and my walls flutter around him, still reeling from the orgasms he forced from me.

"So fucking tight," he breathes against my shoulder.

I'll never get tired of the way his cock makes me feel so stretched and so full at the same time and with my knees pressed together like this it makes me feel even fuller if that's possible. He slowly pulls back leaving just the tip before he plunges back into me with a hard, deep thrust that rocks my body forward, making me cry out. With one hand on my shoulder and another on my hip, he proceeds to ram into me mercilessly.

I brace myself as his cock pounds into me like it has a vendetta against my pussy. I want it. I want all of it. I don't know if I'm being punished or rewarded, and I don't fucking care. I want whatever his cock is willing to give me. I push back against his cock, needing to feel him so deep inside me I can feel him in my throat.

"Fuck you're so greedy for my cock aren't you, baby?" He says as he grunts with every mind-numbing thrust.

"I need it. Please, I need you to fuck me," I cry out.

My throat is hoarse from every moan he forces from me. The sounds of my moans, his grunts and our skin slapping against each other fill my ears like a sweet song only the two of us will ever know.

He yanks my back up against his front, one hand digging into my hip no doubt bruising my smooth flesh while his other hand comes up and wraps around my throat. There's nothing I can do but surrender and take what he gives me. My face scrunches up as he pounds my pussy so hard and fast, it has me seeing stars.

"Keep your eyes open, My Queen. I want you to watch yourself scream my name while you come on my cock," he grunts into my ear as the hand he had on my hip glides against my flesh, down to my folds finding my nub.

He begins rubbing it in a circle while his cock imprints itself in my pussy, branding it as his.

I force my eyes open and they connect with the mirror along the wall in front of us. My eyes are transfixed on the image of him fucking me while his fingers work my clit. Our bodies are dripping with sweat, hair stuck to our skin, my breasts are bouncing with every thrust, and I realise his eyes have been glued to the mirror this whole time. His gorgeous face showing all his pride and pleasure as he watches every reaction my body has to him as I take his cock.

The sight of it increases my pleasure to a level that can't possibly be of this world and with a couple more hard thrusts, he has my body and brain shattering into a million euphoric pieces as my orgasm completely consumes me.

"MARCUS!" I scream as my pussy clenches around him, every muscle in my body going taut as wave after wave hits, leaving me but a shell in their wake.

My arms flail around as my head disconnects from my body and I lose all sense of control over my limbs. His hand on my throat tightens, quietening my screams as he thrusts out my orgasm before emptying himself into me with a sated groan that echoes around the room, sending a shiver through my overwhelmed body.

He sits back on his knees holding me against him, still seated inside me as his cum coats my insides. My head lays back against his shoulder and we both pant, desperate for air. His arms wrap around me like I'm the most precious thing in the universe and I bask in the feeling, wrapping my arms around his.

"You are my everything, Amelia," he breathes as he peppers kisses up my neck.

I smile feeling more content than I have a right to and press my forehead to his cheek. "My world starts and ends with you," I tell him.

With a smile on his beautiful face, we lose ourselves in another kiss, but this time we take our time, letting ourselves enjoy each linger and stroke our lips make in this single perfect moment.

Chapter Forty-One
Amelia

It's been a month since the Luna ceremony and life has never been better. We've had a lot of new changes – mostly to hierarchy structure in the pack. Eric, as the second Beta of the pack, has taken on a lot of 'traditional' Luna roles. He oversees pack events and gatherings, and his pack support group continues to work wonders. He's basically the pack's resident therapist, which I'm realising many were in desperate need of. As superhuman beings, we tend to brush aside our mental health and wellbeing and it's definitely something that needed to change, so I'm thrilled it has.

Evalyn still holds the title of Gamma, but now she works alongside her brother Chris handling pack finances. She's not as skilled in that area as he is, but the woman knows how to budget and she's a good go-between for the pack and Chris. Evalyn was never going to be built for fighting and physical labour, but she wants to contribute as a ranked member. Nowhere does it say how those bonded to a ranked member need to contribute, so I'm doing what we do best in this pack, utilising strengths.

Mei has been the biggest surprise. While she's the rank of a Delta, she now assists Tyson with pack training and her own training has completely evolved. Yildiz sent her sister Setia to come to our pack and help Mei train a couple of weeks ago. Apparently she has a lot of experience with nagatas, so

As for Marcus… I swear I fall more in love with that man every day. We work so seamlessly together it's like we share a brain. We have become a well-oiled machine and we are dedicated to our pack and each other. We can't get enough of each other. Anytime we have a moment to ourselves it's filled with pleasure that quite literally rocks my world. My family absolutely adores him, and he has become closer to them than I ever expected. Things with his parents are not perfect, but they're improving. Jerome stayed with us for a week after the Luna ceremony and I can safely say I love the man and couldn't be happier to have him as another father figure. To my surprise, he and my dad have become the best of friends, and I think my dad was sad to see him leave. Clearly, they have entered a beautiful bromance, which is just adorable.

Marcus' mother is still not a huge fan of mine. and I still don't like her. Maybe I never will. Jerome sent her home after the Luna ceremony saying she needed to figure herself out and he needed to be there for their son. I think what Marcus had told her did knock a little sense into her but expecting her to change her entire way of being so quickly is unreasonable. However, she does call and have civilised conversations with Marcus and asks about the pack, how he's doing and what he's up to, so that's progress. I don't care if she never speaks to me again, as long as she's supporting him. That's all I care about.

Because we've all been working hard, we're treating ourselves to a night on the town. We all decided to hit one of the human clubs we love to go to and, while we may have had to sneak in a couple flasks of Tezus just so we can feel a buzz, we're still having an absolute blast.

"Have you ever hooked up with anyone here?" Eric innocently asks.

"Why, you offering?" Vitali smirks leaning in and placing a kiss on Eric's mark, making him shudder.

"That's not what I meant," he says in a shaky breath.

"Oh, I know exactly what you meant," he says, grabbing Eric's chin. "And if you don't get those thoughts out of your head, I'll be forced to drag you to the men's room and fuck them out of you," he threatens, but the glint in his eyes suggests he's hoping Eric takes him up on it. Eric has gone bright red, which is just adorable, so Vitali takes mercy on him and gives him a soft kiss. Those two are so damn cute.

"Amelia!" Evalyn nearly screams, rushing over to me and grabbing my arm. "Come dance with me! Tyson is being a stick in the mud and I want to dance."

"It's not my fault I can't keep up with you. You're a dancing machine," Tyson grumbles, flopping down on an available spot on the lounge we have claimed as our own.

"How can you spend majority of your time training, yet dancing is too much for you?" Evalyn asks through narrowed eyes.

"My sister raises a good point," Chris points out.

"Thank you," she chirps. "I can always rely on you."

"Nice try, but I'm not dancing with you," he chuckles.

"You know what? I don't need you!" She huffs, stomping her feet and returning to the dancefloor.

We all laugh, though my laugh is a bit strangled because of the way Marcus is drawing circles on my upper thigh, edging very close to my core. I squirm in his lap and can already feel the bulge starting to form beneath me.

"I'm sure she'll find herself a dance partner in no time," Marcus muses while taking a sip of his drink. I hide a smirk knowing exactly what my man is up to. He's a sly thing.

"Huh?" Tyson quirks up a brow.

"She's a beautiful young woman unattended at a club surrounded by single human men who don't know the mark on her neck means she's taken," he shrugs. "I'm sure someone will offer to dance with her soon enough."

Chris, Vitali, and Eric snigger as Tyson's eyes narrow into slits and a growl rumbles in his chest.

"Yo, Firecracker! Wait up!" Tyson shouts quickly, getting to his feet and stalking after Evalyn, much to our amusement. Marcus leans forward, his lips brushing against the shell of my ear making me shiver.

"Have I told you how fucking sexy you look tonight?" He whispers.

I gulp, "Once or twice."

I've come out tonight in a red sleeved bodycon dress that stops mid-thigh. It has a high neck with a cut-out midriff and chest. The fabric across my breasts is barely held together and I just know Marcus is dying to rip it. I plan on letting him. I've teamed it with gold and silver stilettos and accessorised with gold bangle hoop earrings, light makeup, and a high ponytail.

Did I dress to drive my man crazy? Yes, yes I did. But best believe he's doing the same, and to think he calls me the minx. He's in all black, as usual. A tight-fitted tee that shows off every bulge of this man's physique. The shirt can barely contain him and neither can his tight-black jeans, although I do love his ass in them. Everything about him exists to torment me in the best way. His scent caresses me, his body excites me, and his words have a direct line to my core.

"Have I told you how sexy *you* look tonight?" I ask as I lean in, planting a kiss on his. I smirk as I hear his sharp intake of breath.

"Not nearly enough," he says in a husky voice as his hands tighten on me.

"I'm going to get a refill; you guys want anything?" Chris offers as he stands up.

"I'll have another martini, thanks," says Eric.

"I'm good," says Vitali.

"I'm good too, man, but thanks," says Marcus.

"Amelia?" He asks.

"Sure, I'll have a long island iced tea," I smile.

"Coming right up," he says as he kisses Mei's temple and heads off to the bar.

"You sure you don't want a cocktail or something, Mei?" Marcus gently asks.

I'm surprised with how close those two have gotten, but I love it. He treats her like a little sister and it's the sweetest thing. Mei doesn't answer. I notice her eyes are focused on something across the room. I look in the direction she's focused on, but I can't see anything past the crowd of people.

"Mei? Is everything alright?" I ask. Marcus and I are both sitting up, more alert.

"Huh?" She says, finally bringing her attention back to us. "Oh. Yes, I am fine, I just..." she glances back where she was looking and furrows her brows. "There was a man over there looking at me."

Marcus and I are both on our feet looking for the man in question, but we don't see anyone suspicious.

"I swear he was there. He... there was something familiar about him," she whispers.

"It's okay, we believe you. If you see him again you let us know straight away, got it?" I tell her.

She nods adamantly.

Chris returns with our drinks and can sense something is wrong. We fill him in and he's instantly in bodyguard mode, tucking Mei under his arm and scanning the room for danger. Whoever was looking at her better not come over here, not if he wants to keep his limbs attached. Chris is a kind and level-headed man... unless you threaten his woman. Should have seen what he did to the pack members of the pack who enslaved Mei. Can't say they didn't deserve it.

"Care to dance?" Marcus asks as he takes my hand.

"You don't have to ask me twice," I grin and walk with him out to the dance floor just as the music shifts into a slow song. My arms slide around his neck as his snake around my waist and in this moment we are all there is. We're lost in each other's eyes as we gently sway to the music, our hearts completely in sync with each other. I never imagined I'd have this kind of happiness. I never thought we'd make it here, but I've never been so happy to be so wrong.

"Thank you," he says.

My eyebrows knit together with confusion. "For what?"

"For being everything I never knew I needed. For making me happier than I have a right to be, and most of all, for loving me as much as you do," he says with soft sincerity. Tears pool in my eyes and I swear I see the whole galaxy shining in his. Can someone this wonderful even be real?

"You never have to thank me for that. Thank you for wanting me, thank you for accepting me and thank you for making each day better than the last," I tell him, my voice thick with emotion.

"To quote the smartest woman I know; you never have to thank me for that," he grins cheekily, making me chuckle. Through my laughter, our lips find each other and the world melts away as we escape into our happy place. Each other.

SOME OF THESE CHARACTERS WILL
RETURN IN BOOK 2....

About The Author

Ashleigh Dana Burnell is based in Melbourne, Australia. After spending years as an aspiring film critic and YouTuber, she spent her free time working on screenplays. This soon birthed the realisation that her passion was in storytelling, and with many stories to tell, she finally took the plunge in putting them on paper and sharing them with the world.

You can learn more about Ashleigh and stay up to date on future projects by following her on Instagram: @adb_stories or Twitter: @ADB_Stories